THE AGONY &
THE ECSTASY

A COMPREHENSIVE HISTORY OF THE FOOTBALL LEAGUE PLAY-OFFS

RICHARD FOSTER

www.ockleybooks.co.uk

To Y

Thanks for your unswerving and invaluable support throughout.

THE AGONY & THE ECSTASY

CONTENTS

THE AGONY & THE ECSTASY

ACKNOWLEDGEMENTS

After my first book, *The A-Z of Football Hates*, which was clearly centred on the negative aspects of football, *The Agony & The Ecstasy* is much more balanced between dark and light. Exploring the history of the Play-Offs has been a project that has been with me for so, and quite possibly too, many years and I fear that many worthy people will slip through the net that is my failing memory. If that is the case please forgive me and let's have a pint to compensate.

As I have mentioned in the book I have been overwhelmed by the universally positive responses I have received from my many requests for interviews and I have only stumbled across one or two refuseniks along the way, so that is a testament to the enduring appeal and interest of the Play-Offs. Everyone has an opinion on their value and their standing and there was barely a whiff of dissension amongst those I interviewed. It has been a pleasure talking to so many advocates and I appreciate the time and effort of the following in giving freely of their time: Dan Abrahams, Phil Alexander, Gavin Barber, Bobby Barnes, Stephen Browett, Adam Bull, Alastair Campbell, Clarke Carlisle, Tony Cascarino, Steve Claridge, Mark Clemmit, Olly Dawes, Kevin Day, Terry Heilbron, Ian Holloway, Ritchie Humphreys, Laura Jones, Dave Lane, Martin Lange, Martin McFadden, Roger Maslin, Alan Marriott, Grant McCann, Pat Nevin, Ian Rands, Lee Richardson, David Sheepshanks, Gary Simpson, Daniel Storey, Neil Warnock, Mark Watson and Andy Williamson.

A couple of people deserve a separate mention for their continuing support over the last few years. One source of reference, which stands out from the others, is Simon Inglis's authoritative and comprehensive book, *A History of League Football and The Men Who Made It*. John Nagle at the Football League has been a rock throughout and he has always encouraged and assisted whenever asked. Mick Kinlan, who designed the book, has done a superb job in making it visually stunning and never over-complicating the process. No author can survive the lonely process of book writing without an enthusiastic publisher and Dave Hartrick of Ockley Books has always been there with words of encouragement and sage advice. Considering our respective allegiances to Crystal Palace and Brighton, it is even more extraordinary that we have such an excellent working relationship.

As ever, my family have had to suffer the obsessive nature of a writer, putting up with my endless wittering, and I owe them all masses of gratitude for their forbearance and good humour. My wife Yvonne has worked incredibly hard in allowing me to indulge myself, for which I am eternally grateful. And to my equally long-suffering children Jessica, Amelia and Tristram – thanks for your patience and I promise not to mention the Play-Offs again for a little while.

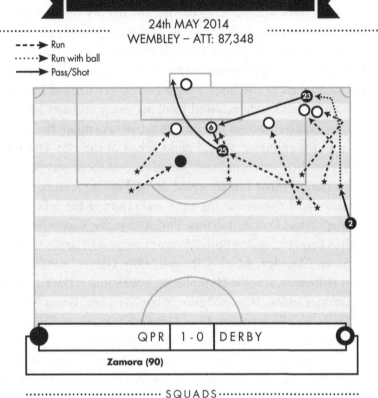

BOBBY ZAMORA 2013/14
CHAMPIONSHIP PLAY-OFFS FINAL

24th MAY 2014
WEMBLEY – ATT: 87,348

- - - ▶ Run
· · · · ▶ Run with ball
──── ▶ Pass/Shot

QPR 1 - 0 **DERBY**

Zamora (90)

········· SQUADS ·········

Green	**1**	**1**	Grant
Simpson	**2**	**33**	Wisdom
Onuoha	**15**	**6**	Keogh
Dunne	**5**	**25**	Buxton
Hill (67)	**6**	**3**	Forsyth
Doyle (57)	**14**	**8**	Hendrick
Barton	**17**	**34**	Thorne
O'Neil	**36**	**19**	Hughes (68)
Hoilett	**23**	**11**	Russell (67)
Austin	**9**	**9**	Martin
Kranjčar (33)	**19**	**10**	J. Ward (90+2)

Traoré (33) Henry (67)
Zamora (57) ⏣

Bryson (68) Dawkins (67)
Bamford (90+2)

Final League Position: 4th
SF 1st Leg: Wigan 0 - 0 QPR
SF 2nd Leg: QPR 2 - 1 Wigan

Final League Position: 3rd
SF 1st Leg: Brighton 1 - 2 Derby
SF 2nd Leg: Derby 4 - 1 Brighton

GOAL FACT: This 90th-minute strike was QPR's only shot on target.

FOREWORD

It is a rare and much-treasured luxury to go to a football match as a complete neutral. To be able to enjoy a game from an objective viewpoint, to not be overly concerned or exercised about the result, to be stress-free whilst all around are having kittens, is delicious and a moment to be savoured. It represents an opportunity not to be missed. And so when given the chance I jumped at the prospect of going to Wembley to watch QPR take on Derby County courtesy of my local youth football club which had kindly donated a ticket to the match as gratitude for me running a quiz night for them.

My pleasure was enhanced because this was the Championship Play-Offs Final and I am ever so slightly obsessed by the Play-Offs, as you will discover during the course of reading this book. For the ultimate in nerve-shredding, gut-wrenching tension this match is a must-see. When the stakes are so high that the difference between winning and losing is by far the widest of any sporting contest anywhere in the world, let alone in English football, this is an experience I recommend for anyone interested in sport at its most elemental.

Normally I would have been amongst the committed and the faithful, desperate for my team to win and even more desperate for them not to lose. I have been in that position of nauseous anticipation as the build-up drags on interminably and wishing the whole thing would just get started. Then to suffer the game's ebbs and flows with that uncertainty gnawing away at your chest and your head throbbing, one wonders why we go through it much of the time.

This was the seventh Play-Offs Final I have attended, having been to four with my club, Crystal Palace, stretching over four different decades and all the way back to 1989. The late 1980s seem so far removed from today's football that it feels like so much more than twenty-five years ago. Football has changed more dramatically over this period than any other corresponding twenty-five years and the Play-Offs exemplify this. They have become a totally different beast almost unrecognisable from its original incarnation and this book will reflect on all those seismic shifts and changes.

I feel extremely fortunate to have experienced a 75 per cent success rate over those four Palace Finals and have greatly enjoyed and been thrilled by my club's ultimately positive relationship with the Play-Offs. Mind you the one, solitary loss still burns and churns my inner self, but much more of that later. Success in this match is as sweet as it gets for many, but failure is correspondingly as deflating as any feeling in football. The massive chasm between winning and losing is what makes the Play-Offs such compelling viewing. Much of modern football is sanitised to the point of anaemia but the Play-Offs are characterised by the contrasting fortunes of the protagonists. The rawness of the emotions exposed harks back to a time pretty much forgotten and generally unloved. The mid-1980s was an awful period for English football when passion turned into violence but out of this nadir came the germ of the idea for the Play-Offs and the foundation blocks for the rebuilding of the national game emerged, tentatively at first, but subsequently with increasing confidence and even a hint of swagger.

So this was my third non-Palace Final and I was determined to enjoy it. As I made my way from Wembley Central along the grim, grey, soulless high street I watched the fans closely to see if I could detect the tell-tale signs of tension etched into their faces. Most were in a buoyant mood; after all they had reached Wembley, on the other hand, which was cause enough to celebrate and a day at the national stadium is not to be sniffed at. Considering QPR's last visit was over thirty years ago in the 1982 FA Cup Final against Tottenham, probably more than 50 per cent of their fans would not have been alive to witness that so this was a new, exciting experience for the majority of them. Derby's last appearance at Wembley was when they tasted success in the 2007 Championship Play-Offs Final after defeating West Brom, so they were furnished with a relatively fresh memory; their excitement was nonetheless also palpable.

But underneath the cheery disposition of those wending their merry way to the ground there was surely the undeniable trace of tension and potential trauma. Some seemed oblivious and that worried me. Did they not know the history? I became fatalistic and increasingly concerned for whoever was going to lose, as they were about to suffer, horribly. They needed to be made aware of the many desperate tales of utter dejection that lie strewn over the course of the last twenty-seven years; that this could potentially be one of the very bleakest days of their lives. But on they went with jaunty step, full of bravado and good cheer, reminiscent of the unknowing marching to battle with not a care in the world, blind to the catastrophe that lay in wait.

How many of this crowd would know that the very first Play-Offs took place in the 1986/87 season. Less than 1 per cent, if my instant straw poll was anything to go by, and this concerned me as most football fans lap up the history of the game, revel in the detail and are thirsty for more. So clearly there was a gap that needed to be filled and hence I was doubly determined to right this wrong and give everybody the chance to learn more by finally writing this book, which has been gestating for many years. Since 2006, I have been yearning to chart the various trials and tribulations, as well as the triumphs, of the Play-Offs. I was also determined to uncover the lessons that can be learned about how they prevailed despite their inauspicious and tentative beginning. And then there is the wider significance of the changing fortunes of English league football that warranted a thorough examination through the unique lens of the Play-Offs. The truth must come out.

In that inaugural Play-Offs season in 1986/87 Derby were actually crowned champions of the Second Division, achieving their second successive promotion under Arthur Cox's astute leadership. They would have hardly noticed what was going on beneath them as the Play-Offs were quietly, almost surreptitiously introduced. Charlton Athletic preserved their status as a First Division club; indeed they were the only one out of six clubs to avoid the ignominy of relegation via the Play-Offs in those first two years. Leeds United's failure in the Final meant that only one other club, Portsmouth, went up with Derby by dint of finishing second. Meanwhile QPR ended up sixteenth in the First Division and thus avoided being dragged into the Play-Offs from the other direction. One club that did suffer the drop that same year were Manchester City, who were relegated from Division One in 21st place. This set a precedent for the most troubled decade or so in the club's history, one which was ultimately rescued via one of the more extraordinary Play-Offs stories, which will be covered in full later in this book.

But back to the match of the day. Entering the stadium at the QPR end there was that special frisson of excitement which accompanies a match of stature and importance, and even though I was a neutral the nerves were still jangling. And, lest we forget, there were more people here to watch a second tier club match than have attended any of the last five World Cup Finals. English football is often accused of being parochial and myopic and quite often this accusation is fully justified but the sheer scale of this match provides clear and incontestable evidence of just how healthy the game is. Apart from Germany, it seems inconceivable that any other country could attract such a crowd to a match at this level. In truth, most leagues across the world would struggle to fill Wembley with a top division showdown so this does underline that England is still one of the pre-eminent football nations, despite some of its manifest faults.

The game itself was an anti-climax and will certainly not be challenging for a place in the Top 10 classic matches featured throughout this book. With the match entering its final minute everyone in the stadium was preparing themselves for the rigours of extra time. A close-fought struggle riddled with tension had not yielded a goal despite the sending-off midway through the second half. Derby County had been the dominant team even before the dismissal of Gary O'Neil and had been peppering Robert Green's goal for most of the second half but QPR were obdurate and their defence stood firm against all Derby's advances. Amongst the 87,348 present, I was in with the QPR fans, who were bracing themselves for another thirty minutes of one-way traffic. They had adopted that form of siege mentality that so often follows having a player dismissed and they were supporting their team more in hope than expectation.

As QPR managed to move the ball into the Derby half, the Rangers fans urged them to keep it, to eke out the last minutes of the match as far away from their own goal as possible. The thought of hanging on for extra time was tantalising, and if they could survive the additional thirty minutes it would have been time for the infamous Russian roulette that is the penalty shoot-out, in which, being a lottery, anything could happen. There was a deep sense of desperation in their urging, the sort of desperation that is peculiarly a property of the Play-Offs. The prize is so close but also so far away, it hurts. I could empathise with their predicament as all four of my Palace Finals went to the wire, with three going to extra time and the other being won in the 90th minute. None of those games were particularly pretty but what they lacked in aesthetics they certainly over-compensated for with massive slices of drama and excitement. This is true of so much of the history of the Play-Offs and gives them their own particular piquancy.

At the other end of a sun-drenched Wembley, the Derby fans' restlessness was understandable. They had dominated the match but had not made the expected breakthrough and were now readying themselves for extra time. It must have been a frustrating experience but the more optimistic would have been consoling themselves with the view that QPR would not be able to hold out for another thirty minutes and the undoubted superiority of their team, both numerically and qualitatively, must bear fruit. Those of a pessimistic nature would be chewing over the lost opportunities to wrap up the match and grinding their teeth over what still seemed the admittedly remote possibility of missing out on the biggest prize of them all.

Then, in front of our very eyes, a QPR attack developed down their right side and the ball was played into the box. Like most of their earlier efforts it looked as though this move would also peter out as the pass was slightly aimless and the untroubled Derby defence anticipated gobbling this up before launching another sortie into the QPR half. However, the captain, Keogh, had an aberration as he slipped, disastrously prodding the ball into Bobby Zamora's path instead of either clearing his lines or bringing it under control. That Zamora, who had hardly had a touch of the ball since coming on as a substitute some thirty minutes earlier, did not hesitate, curling a shot into the far corner with unerring accuracy, compounded the mistake. Derby's players sank to the ground in horror and most of those watching shared their sense of shock and amazement, as the goal had come out of nothing. I defy even the staunchest QPR fan to say they expected it.

Zamora had been here before, having notched the solitary goal for West Ham when they beat Preston in 2005 at the Millennium Stadium in Cardiff. A goal that was worth a mere £60 million, mere baubles compared to today's riches. Less than ten years later, Zamora's strike had more than doubled in value to at least £134 million. But on the flip side you can guarantee that poor old Richard Keogh will not have been through such hell before. There will be nights ahead when he will wake up screaming and sweating over the £134 million mistake, because that is how it now will be forever portrayed. The spectre of setting up Zamora for his sublime left-footed finish will haunt him for the rest of his life and he will be counting the cost of that again and again.

As with so many titanic tussles in Play-Offs' history there was to be a hero and a villain created in a trice. The syndrome of instantaneous hagiography and matching demonisation that was encapsulated in the space of those few decisive seconds is a continual theme of the Play-Offs. The saints and sinners will be highlighted throughout the book through the mini-profiles at the end of each chapter. It is very much in keeping with the tension and excitement that make the Play-Offs such an absorbing contest that the identification of light and dark are so clearly delineated. But the division is never as simple as black and white and quite often those heroes do not progress as they might have hoped; similarly the villains often gain some form of retribution and can claw their way back into a club's good books, which is reassuring for the likes of Richard Keogh.

The injustice of it all was cruel in the extreme. That goal was the only shot on target that QPR managed, compared to over ten of Derby's. Very rarely have I witnessed such a one-sided match go the way of the weaker side at the very death and the denouement was as surprising as it was unjust. In that moment the match was decided, encapsulating the drama, significance and excitement that marks out the Play-Offs. Stunning in more senses than one; the contrast in emotions between the two sets of fans is broader than any other experienced in football. Utterly delirious QPR fans and thoroughly dejected Derby fans were united only in disbelief. The euphoria is all the sweeter because of its unexpected nature, the despair so much worse. This is the nub, the sharp end of football when everything can be decided in one fell swoop, or even slip.

The emotional impact on the supporters was as intense as anything they have been through either before or since. Leaving the stadium where the Rangers' fans were still exulting in their victory and meeting the shell-shocked, disconsolate Derby supporters as they sloped away, still shaking their heads and muttering darkly, the contrast could not have been more striking. I felt as if I was invading on their grief in closely observing their despair. Some were angry and bitterly resentful of QPR's undeserved victory but the overwhelming sensation was one of numbness and incomprehension. Having that glory snatched away is difficult to take and there is a whole summer ahead to lick one's wounds and try to stop thinking of what might, and probably should, have been.

It was not the greatest match from a neutral's point of view but that fine, curling effort of Zamora's will remain in the minds of QPR fans for the rest of their lives. Derby fans will try to forget, as will the unfortunate Keogh, but such scars are not so easily healed nor hidden. But this is the way we want our football to be – tooth and claw, life and death – and that is exactly what the Play-Offs gave us that day and have delivered throughout their history. I for one cannot get enough of them. They have developed their own identity and have established a special place in the hearts and minds of so many by stirring, and often toying, with the emotions. They can be the cruellest of mistresses or the most generous of white knights, and in their capacity to move us so completely they have become the epitome of the very best of English football.

In that cherished neutral role that I had adopted for this match I recognised so much of why and what makes the Play-Offs particularly enticing. Once they have you gripped they will not relinquish their hold, so welcome to their history and strap yourself in, as it is going to be a bumpy, eventful but ultimately entertaining ride over the past thirty years. By standing outside and looking in we can all gain an invaluable insight into the core, the heart, the very essence of the Play-Offs and what has made them such an indispensable element of our football lives.

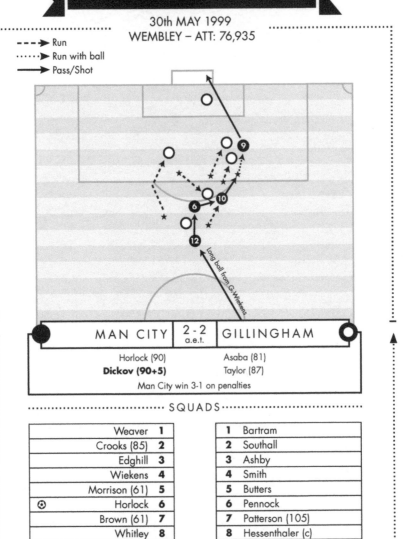

PAUL DICKOV 1998/99

SECOND DIVISION PLAY-OFFS FINAL

30th MAY 1999
WEMBLEY – ATT: 76,935

- - - ▶ Run
······▶ Run with ball
——▶ Pass/Shot

Long ball from G.Wiekens

MAN CITY	2 - 2 a.e.t.	GILLINGHAM

Horlock (90)	Asaba (81)
Dickov (90+5)	Taylor (87)

Man City win 3-1 on penalties

·········· SQUADS ··········

	Weaver	**1**	**1**	Bartram	
	Crooks (85)	**2**	**2**	Southall	
	Edghill	**3**	**3**	Ashby	
	Wiekens	**4**	**4**	Smith	
	Morrison (61)	**5**	**5**	Butters	
⚽	Horlock	**6**	**6**	Pennock	
	Brown (61)	**7**	**7**	Patterson (105)	
	Whitley	**8**	**8**	Hessenthaler (c)	
⚽	**Dickov**	**9**	**9**	Asaba (87)	⚽
	Goater	**10**	**10**	Galloway (56)	
	Cooke	**11**	**11**	Taylor	⚽

Vaughan (61) Bishop (61) Taylor (85)   Carr (87) Hodge (105) Saunders (56)

Final League Position: 3rd	Final League Position: 4th
SF 1st Leg: Wigan 1 - 1 Man City	SF 1st Leg: P.N.E 1 - 1 Gillingham
SF 2nd Leg: Man City 1 - 0 Wigan	SF 2nd Leg: Gillingham 1 - 0 P.N.E

GOAL FACT: Dickov's late goal was scored past Vince Bartram,
who had been best man at his wedding.

INTRODUCTION

As you will have realised from the Foreword, I have an obsession with the Play-Offs. Some might even venture that it borders on the unhealthy but I prefer to house it under the good practice of attention to detail. If you are embarking on writing a history, you have to spend endless hours thinking about the subject matter, delving into every nook and cranny to find the best nuggets. Those best nuggets are, almost by definition, not the easiest to find and therefore are all the more rewarding once you stumble across them, having travelled down a series of cul-de-sacs, a maze of blind alleys and hundreds of dead ends. But those frustrating seemingly futile journeys are the ones that bring the writer nearer to the ultimate prize.

In writing this book about the history of the Play-Offs, I have spent a great deal of time considering the best way to approach the subject. Initially I was going to do so with a strict chronology, detailing their development from their conception in the mid-1980s all the way through to the present day. But then I was struck by the idea of a more thematic style, drawing together the different strands and aspects of their evolution. Ultimately, I have plumped for a hybrid, part chronology and part thematic but guided by both the personalities and features that have been inextricably involved with the Play-Offs, hence the additional profiles at the end of most chapters. Those profiles allow some breathing space to look at those key aspects in a little more depth, and often provide the real crux of that particular theme or period.

I also felt it was essential to reflect the views of the fans, as they are the lifeblood of the game and they have as much, if not more, of a right to voice their opinions than any player, manager or chairman. It was as a fan that I was first attracted to the Play-Offs and I was always determined to reflect the views of supporters. Apart from the handful of clubs at the very top of the league pyramid who have not tasted any Play-Offs action and a smattering of smaller clubs towards the other end of the spectrum, the vast majority of current league clubs have participated. Those clubs' supporters will have experienced the cut and thrust of the Play-Offs and for the most part will retain strong and abiding memories of their involvement. For the majority of teams throughout the Football League, seasons can come and go with not much to differentiate between them, but the Play-Offs will invariably stand out for good or for bad. They leave a distinguishing mark on the fans, establishing a connection that goes beyond the realms of regular matches. The strength of this bond is almost unbreakable, as the Play-Offs get under the skin of fans more than any other aspect of football, and one of the key objectives of this book is to address exactly why and how this has happened.

It has been an absolute pleasure and a privilege talking to a whole range of people whilst researching and writing this book; indeed it is those conversations that keep us writers going as we plough our lonely furrow. The overriding sense of warmth and generosity I have come across in interviewing all the characters who bring this history to life show that, despite some evidence to the contrary, football has a good heart and that there is a genuine affection for the Play-Offs. It is already pretty clear that I am a strong advocate of the Play-Offs and although I have tried to remain objective, it would be disingenuous to suggest that I am not a huge supporter of my subject matter, especially as my club, Crystal Palace, have been very much a winner over the years. As a club, Palace do not hold many positive records, so to be the club with the most promotions to the top division via the Play-Offs is something to shout from the rooftops. To have done it four times is something that has gladdened the hearts and moistened the eyes of thousands of Eagles fans since the late 1980s. So please forgive me if I slip into partiality now and again; this reflects genuine enthusiasm rather than any desire to skew the argument.

The hallmark of the Play-Offs is their ability to stir emotions and encourage the strongest opinions on both sides of the divide. When a chairman from the losing side describes them as "the best invention ever", whilst a winning manager asks for them to "be scrapped immediately", you can appreciate that you are dealing with an unusual animal. No other football match has so successfully combined the significant with the spectacular, the crucial with the dramatic, the ecstasy with the agony, in quite the manner that the Play-Offs have over the last three decades. Love them or hate them you simply cannot ignore them. The Play-Offs may not have the cachet of the Champions League, the traditions of the FA Cup or the allure of the Premier League, but at times, they can rival, even overshadow, these more illustrious competitions and punch well above their weight.

Additionally, the Play-Offs have made the most positive and lasting impression on the landscape of English football over the last twenty-seven years. After their introduction as a system for deciding the last promotion slot for the three lower divisions of the Football League in the 1986/87 season, they have proved to be a key element in ensuring football's standing as the most popular spectator sport in the country. Without their influence, the football industry may have gone down a radically different path and its position could have been undermined to such an extent that it might have surrendered its status as the national game.

Despite their acknowledged importance, the Play-Offs still divide opinion into two distinct camps. The advocates view them as a suitably dramatic climax to the league season, a season that is considerably enlivened by the prospect of a handful of clubs battling to contest this eventful denouement to the bitter end. By providing teams, which might have previously been destined to mid-table mediocrity, with a real sense of purpose and an achievable aim, the Play-Offs have injected fresh impetus into many a club's season. The critics talk of 'a lottery' by pointing to the inequality of a team finishing a few places and many points above a rival after a full league season and yet potentially losing out on promotion to that team with an inferior league record. Whilst there are plenty of hard-luck stories and this argument does have some credence, surely the numerous benefits outweigh any sense of injustice.

A lottery is defined as something that 'is governed by chance' and whilst any game of football has an element of fortune, there is so much to be admired in the skills and aptitude of all those who perform under the most severe pressure. When everything is up for grabs is the time when the very best excel, so the Play-Offs can be seen as the ultimate test; less a lottery, more a high-grade laboratory providing the ultimate in litmus tests of performance under pressure. If you can thrive in this environment it augurs well for your career as a player or as a manager.

The Play-Offs are not only an integral part of English football but they have also become one of the most enjoyable and entertaining aspects of the domestic game. Nearly everyone recognises the way in which they have developed from their humble origins into one of the most attractive and vibrant features of the season. The manner in which they have transformed the flow of the season, with so many more clubs being in with a shout of promotion, has left an indelible mark on English football. There is a particular type of tension, a distinctive atmosphere that characterises the Play-Offs, and even though many fans have suffered at their hands, their popularity has grown consistently over the last twenty-five years or so.

Whatever role one may have, whether it be as a neutral observer, a historian or a fan, the vast majority of football people hold a deep and lasting affection for the Play-Offs. Through this book I want to show the reasons why they are so well liked and hope that others can appreciate the virtues that make them so attractive. Speaking to an array of fans, players, managers, chairmen and chief executives, the response was universally very positive. Ian Holloway can remember being an opponent of the system initially. He was dead against the concept and his comments are typical of the response of so many within the game. "At first I didn't like the Play-Offs as I felt the team that finished third deserved to go up," Holloway admits. "After forty-six games that's long enough. But I'm now the biggest fan ever because it not only keeps your season alive, but it also allows your club to develop." The initial scepticism that greeted their introduction has been largely swept away. Encouraged by the almost unanimous approval that the Play-Offs have received when researching this book, I do not believe I am alone in my fondness of them. Of those I have spoken to within the wider football family, 99 per cent have fully endorsed their existence and have been incredibly supportive.

Beneath the generally positive impression made by the Play-Offs there are some darker stories; stories of scheming skulduggery, of careers blighted and of lives adversely affected by their experiences. For some, the intense pressure of the Play-Offs sets the stage for incredible, spellbinding drama, but for others such a level of pressure can lead to their downfall. These undercurrents are also explored by the 'warts and all' approach to the subject, so those uncomfortable truths are also looked at in detail and provide a contrasting perspective against which to analyse the multiple benefits derived.

Irrespective of those arguing for and against, the Play-Offs are very much an established part of the Football League calendar, where dreams are fulfilled and hopes dashed in equal measure. In fact, so well established are the Play-Offs that very few of those interviewed could get within five years of the correct date, when asked to name the very first year that they took place. By looking closely at the origins of the system, its evolution, the history of dramatic matches and the strong relationship that has been established with the fans, players and managers, this book assesses the importance of the Play-Offs to the game. There is also a look at the psychology of the Play-Offs and the specific challenges in preparing a team for 'the game of their lives'. As the financial implications have risen inexorably there is also an examination of how the value of the Championship Final has developed to such an extent that it is now, by far and away, the most lucrative single match in world sport. Finally, I will consider if the Play-Offs should be rightfully regarded as one of the saviours of English league football in inspiring and leading its remarkable recovery over the last few decades from a point of the utmost weakness to a position of considerable strength and impressive status as the most attractive game in the world.

When attempting to evaluate the Play-Offs' overall significance and the positive contribution that they have made to English football, it is essential to provide some historical perspective. Many of the younger fans, who currently enjoy or endure the dramatic culmination to their clubs' league seasons, will have little understanding or concept of the state football was in when the Play-Offs were first mooted. In 2015, English club football is held in the highest regard throughout the world and consequently boasts the richest and most diverse league and the largest crowds bar none. The turnaround has been comprehensive and in light of the depths that were plumbed in the mid-1980s it has been a quite remarkable journey.

English football has held its current exalted position for many years, consistently attracting a galaxy of international talent playing in front of packed stadia. The Premier League has built a reputation for providing the most exciting, as opposed to the most technically gifted or skilful, football of any domestic league globally. There is an almost insatiable appetite for English football as people follow it on every continent and broadcasters duly vie to get in on the action. Watched by a global audience of nearly five billion people, including 300 million in China alone, and across 212 countries, the omnipresence of the Premier League shows no sign of relenting. It is hard to imagine, but important to appreciate, the contrast with the parlous state of the game three decades beforehand.

Another important consideration is the sheer range of clubs that have been involved and affected by the Play-Offs, from poorest to richest, from smallest to largest. One needs to look no further than the wealthiest club in Britain and the 2012 and 2014 Premier League Champions, Manchester City, to judge how far and wide this influence stretches. If two dramatically late goals rescuing Manchester City sounds distinctly familiar, their 2012 triumph against QPR has strong parallels with their 1999 Play-Offs victory against Gillingham. Although the climax to the 2011/12 Premiership season did mark a historic moment in the club's history, forty-four years after they last won the top division, maybe the more significant match for City took place thirteen years before.

Switch from 13th May 2012 at the Etihad Stadium to Wembley on 30th May 1999. As the Football League Second Division Play-Offs Final is about to enter the

THE AGONY & THE ECSTASY

final minute, Gillingham are getting ready to celebrate promotion to the second tier of English football for the first time in their history. After scoring two goals in the previous ten minutes, the Kent club seemed to have timed their surge to victory to perfection. Their illustrious opponents, Manchester City, look to be consigned to a further year in the Football League Second Division, having just spent their first, uncomfortable season in the third tier of league football, and obscurity beckons. Another year at such a lowly level could have been ruinous for a club of City's stature and their slide might have become irreversible. There are plenty of examples littered across the recent history of large clubs struggling to regain their former glory after slipping down the divisions and becoming mired in the lower leagues too long for their own good. If it had not been for the events of those last few, mad minutes then the Manchester City we know today may never have had the chance to rebuild.

Even when Kevin Horlock scored in the 89th minute it seemed a mere consolation as Gillingham's keeper Vince Bartram was announced as the man of the match and many City fans headed for the exits, resigned to their fate and not wishing to witness the dying embers of the match. It was not until the 5th minute of added time that Paul Dickov scored a second, a barely credible equaliser past Bartram. Not only was this recovery improbable but there was also a delicious sub-plot entwined within this match, as Bartram had been Dickov's best man at his wedding and vice versa, so this was a particularly and peculiarly poignant moment for both men. The balance of this Final had swung decisively to Man City and they duly won on penalties (although Dickov missed his spot kick) after a goalless extra time, to cap an amazing climax, and the club were back on the rise to the upper reaches of the league.

Arguably this amazing transformation of fortune in the dying minutes of the 1999 Play-Offs Final paved the way for the future success of the club, as the consequences of not getting promoted that year could have set City back for a while, if not terminally. There are many City fans who regard this victory as the one that turned everything around for the club and Dickov is still revered because of his goal. What made it all the sweeter for those fans was that another club from Manchester had scored two equally implausibly late goals to win the Champions League Final against Bayern Munich four days earlier in Barcelona and so this went some way to ensuring that there was at least some sharing of the glory. Although crawling out of the third tier of football may not have come close to winning the treble in terms of level of achievement or kudos, it was as important in the development of City in arresting the slide.

If those 120 minutes and the penalty shoot-out were not dramatic enough, there were further twists to this incredible match, which came to light after the

Final. Firstly, the perpetually controversial Gillingham chairman, Paul Scally, demanded a replay when the referee, Mark Halsey, was spotted enjoying a drink with City fans in a nearby hotel after the game. This desperate appeal was summarily rejected but was just the start of more off-the-field revelations surrounding the match. The crushing disappointment felt by the Gillingham camp after their first trip to Wembley had been somewhat mitigated by their chairman.

Scally was found guilty of placing bets on his own team by an FA commission in 2005 and fined the not inconsiderable sum of £10,000. One of those bets was on Gillingham to be beaten in that Play-Offs Final, so Scally had found a convenient, but illegal, way of cushioning the blow. To add fuel to the fire Scally also sacked his manager, Tony Pulis, for 'gross misconduct' in the aftermath of the Final, which initiated a long-running legal feud between Pulis and Scally with a series of claims and counter-claims. Eventually Pulis settled out of court for £75,000 but the rancour still rumbles on fifteen years later. Pulis and Scally had been on such bad terms in the build-up to the Final that they hardly spoke to each other and the lid was finally blown off the smouldering cauldron in the days after the Final.

Given all this kerfuffle it was quite an achievement for Gillingham to join the surprisingly large number of teams that have shaken off the disappointment of failure in the Play-Offs to gain success the following year. Displaying admirable bouncebackability (a concept which will be covered in more detail later) Gillingham triumphed against Wigan in 2000 in what was one of the last Finals to be played at the old Wembley stadium. Nobody could rightly expect the same level of excitement as the Man City match but it turned out to be another game with plenty of fluctuating fortunes that saw Gillingham yet again face extra time. Despite having a player sent off towards the end of normal time, Wigan took the lead in the first half of extra time and there seemed to be little response from Gillingham, maybe feeling that history was repeating itself. But just as in the previous year, they scored twice in the space of five minutes late in the game and there was no way back for Wigan. In a further parallel with 1999, Gillingham's manager, Peter Taylor, left the club in the summer, but in much less controversial circumstances than Pulis's departure, as he moved to Premier League Leicester City. Thus Gillingham made it to the second tier of the league for the first time in their history, and within the space of twelve months the Play-Offs probably squeezed in as much drama as they had done in the previous 107 years of the club's existence. For a club that had spent 106 years getting to Wembley, to do it twice in the space of a year was especially momentous for the men from Priestfield. And Gillingham are in good company, as plenty of clubs can point to their experience in the

Play-Offs as being amongst the most important and influential in recent times, if not their entire history.

If asked to nominate the single greatest innovation introduced by the football authorities in just over four decades since Manchester City last prevailed as the English Champions, there would be a few worthwhile candidates. Some might suggest that three points for a win, which was first tried in 1981, should take the accolade for its positive impact on teams' attitudes to winning matches. Others would point to banning the direct back pass to the goalkeeper in 1992, as it prevented teams wasting time and reduced the chance for the overly negative play that plagued the 1990 World Cup. However, the introduction of the Football League Play-Offs in the 1986/87 season has brought such a wealth of benefits, and successfully provided a much-needed boost to a game which was on its knees and at its lowest ebb in the mid-1980s, that this must surely far outweigh any other nominations. The Play-Offs have become the most significant and richly entertaining part of the football season; in the words of Andy Williamson, chief operating officer of The Football League, "the Play-Offs are the single most beneficial innovation to be introduced into football".

The Play-Offs have evolved into such an integral part of the Football League calendar that it is difficult to imagine modern football without them. In the space of just over twenty-five years, an idea that was conceived originally as an unobtrusive means of reducing the old First Division from twenty-two teams to twenty has steadily grown into the most important and positive change brought about in English league football. There has been a sea change in attitude and accomplishment amongst the three divisions of the Football League, and the Play-Offs have made a huge difference to the way clubs now approach their seasons, especially in terms of their heightened expectations and raised aspirations.

The breadth of their influence is summed up by the fact that of the current ninety-two clubs in the top four divisions, eighty, in other words the vast majority, have been involved in the Play-Offs. Add a further fifteen clubs that are no longer in the professional leagues and almost 100 clubs have had some experience of the Play-Offs. So from Manchester City to Maidstone United, from Chester to Chelsea, the full gamut of clubs have contributed to this rich and varied history. The Play-Offs have not only been symptomatic of the change in fortunes enjoyed by English league football over the last three decades, but they have also been instrumental in turning what was the sick man of Europe into the strongest league in the world. In his 2011 submission to the Culture, Media and Sport Select Committee on the state of football, Professor Stefan Syzmanski asserted that "English football now dominates its European rivals thanks to the large commercial income that it generates from ticket sales, broadcasting rights and merchandising". Since then the gap has grown ever wider to the point that in 2013/14 when Cardiff City were relegated from the Premier League they earned £58 million for coming twentieth. This figure was more than double the amount in domestic television revenue that Bayern Munich received. So having reached the point at which being rock bottom of the Premier League is now twice as lucrative as being Bundesliga champions, the race to get there has intensified beyond compare.

Whilst all the headlines and statistics point to the lofty pinnacle of the Premier League and the stratospheric rise in revenues, it should be noted that all these riches are founded on the healthy base that is the Football League. The top division cannot be treated in isolation (however much some might desire it) and the three lower divisions have shown a steely and long-lasting resilience over the last thirty years. Without that flourishing pyramid below, the top flight would never have had the opportunity to grow in such a way and much of the Premier League's financial success has relied on the roots of a strong Football League. Such strength emanates from the body of the league, from bottom to top, and the Play-Offs have played a huge part in reinvigorating and emboldening that structure.

The message from a whole host of people involved in football, from administrators to chairmen, from fans to players, has been an extremely positive one. Such an approval rating would be the envy of any politician, and even those who have suffered from heartbreaking failure have room for kind words. Comedian and author, Mark Watson, has had to swallow many a bitter Play-Off pill following the plight of Bristol City but is still an advocate. "Given my track record of zero promotions from five," Watson points out, "I'm in a pretty good position to criticise the system, but I have to say I'm still in favour of the Play-Offs and probably always will be, no matter how much they punish me." In a similar vein, Barry Hearn's reaction to Leyton Orient's defeat to Blackpool in the 2001 Third Division Final, makes up in hyperbole what it lacks in bitterness. He described the Play-Offs as "the best invention ever". It is surely the ultimate compliment to have such ringing endorsements not just from winners but also from losers.

It is fascinating to consider that when the Play-Offs were first brought in, there was a significant number of dissenters who argued against the inequities of the system. In their eyes it was unfair to allow a team lower in the league to be promoted ahead of one that had finished in a higher position after the completion of the regular season. Forty-six games should be sufficient to sort out the wheat from the chaff, it was argued, thus rendering any additional competition an unnecessary appendix. There is still the odd gripe along these lines but this viewpoint is restricted to a modicum of sore losers and killjoys.

Any such negativity is swept away by the strong tide of approbation that accompanies any discussion of the Play-Offs' worth. The testimony to their enduring success is the adoption of the system in nearly every major professional league globally (of which more later); there has even been talk of introducing them for the Premier League to decide qualification for European places. For so many, the only remaining debate around the Play-Offs now is whether they should be extended to widen their remit by incorporating more clubs in the post-season qualifiers. Having made such impressive strides in their infancy and matured so successfully over the following decades, this is an ideal time to assess their impact and legacy.

STOKE CITY 0 - 0 BURNLEY
1898 TEST MATCH

30th April 1898
VICTORIA GROUND

ACTION AREAS

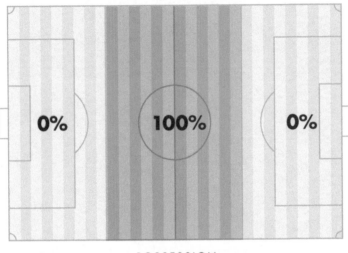

0%   100%   0%

POSSESSION

STOKE 50%   50% BURNLEY

SHOTS ON TARGET
0 - 0

SHOTS OFF TARGET
0 - 0

RESULTS

Newcastle	2 - 1	Stoke
Stoke	1 - 0	Newcastle
Burnley	2 - 0	Blackburn
Blackburn	1 - 3	Burnley
Blackburn	4 - 3	Newcastle
Newcastle	4 - 0	Blackburn
Burnley	0 - 2	Stoke
Stoke	**0 - 0**	**Burnley**

TABLE

		P	W	D	L	F	A	PTS
1	Stoke	4	2	1	1	4	2	5
2	Burnley	4	2	1	1	5	3	5
3	Newcastle	4	2	0	2	9	6	4
4	Blackburn	4	1	0	3	5	12	2

Stoke and Burnley knew that a draw in the final match guaranteed a top-two finish, meaning both sides would be playing in Division One the following year.

MATCH FACT: This match became known as 'the match with no shots' as both teams played out a dull goalless draw. Tom Wilkes, Stoke's bored keeper, ended up wearing an overcoat to keep himself warm.

ORIGINS

Although the modern Play-Offs were introduced in the mid-1980s, the concept's roots stretch back to the very beginnings of league football in England when a similar idea was used some ninety-odd years before. William McGregor, the Scottish founder of the Football League, was influenced by the model used by American sports such as baseball in which play-offs were employed to determine the Championship from the outset in the 1880s. The adaptation of the system was distinctively British in its execution as it concentrated on the movement between divisions rather than determining the champions.

The Football League was founded to provide some order and meaning to the stream of friendly matches that were being played, but had no ultimate purpose. Phil Shaw pointed out in his piece on McGregor for the Football League's 125th anniversary that "as a spectacle, the league was hamstrung by a chronic lack of organisation". There were far too many occasions when clubs pulled out of their fixtures at the last moment because either they had a better offer or they simply could not be bothered to turn up. It was a little like some of the more haphazard Sunday morning football experiences than a gathering of the leading clubs in the country. Such disorganisation adversely affected the revenues of the clubs and the spirits of the fans who had grown tired of watching one-sided friendlies or were frustrated by the number of 'no shows'. So McGregor's brainchild of "a regular and fixed programme" of matches was born, with the main aim of bringing order where there was previously chaos. In many ways this need for a new structure that would reinvigorate the moribund state of the game had close parallels with the issues faced in the mid-1980s. Both situations required strong action that could provide a sense of direction and purpose.

In 1892, four years after the Football League was formed, the league expanded into two divisions to accommodate a further dozen clubs. The powers that be, led by McGregor, wanted to encourage movement between the divisions and decided to give the teams from the lower division the opportunity of reaching the top division. The ethos of promotion was an important facet established at the very beginning of this extra division and this is where English football was different to those American leagues from which the concept of play-offs was originally copied. There was, though, to be no automatic promotion at first, but rather a series of one-off 'test matches' pitching the bottom three teams from the First Division against the top three teams from the newly formed Second Division to determine the final places in the respective leagues. The joint involvement of teams from both divisions was repeated in the first two years of the 20th century Play-Offs, and so it is possible to trace the lineage of the modern Play-Offs back to Victorian times and acknowledge the precedent set from more than a hundred years ago, albeit in a slightly different format.

Some themes that have come to characterise the modern Play-Offs were also prevalent back in the late 19th century, such as those clubs who were perennial failures, the yo-yo teams that spent their time criss-crossing between divisions, and even Iain Dowie's rather 21st-century concept of 'bouncebackability'. They all manifested themselves in the McGregor era only to reappear a century later, proving one of the sport's eternal truths: football is cyclical. One of the first of these test matches in 1893 featured Newton Heath, the team that spawned Manchester United, who preserved their First Division status by overcoming Second Division Champions, Small Heath (the team that would later become Birmingham City) over two legs. So even in these earliest of days of league football and well before the reign of Alex Ferguson, Manchester United had the edge on their rivals.

The following year, Newton Heath were not so fortunate and ended up losing to some upstarts from the lower division. Liverpool had just joined the league, won the tie and thus one of the great rivalries of English football was born. Although Liverpool's tenure in the top flight lasted just one season as they lost out to Bury in the 1895 test match, they came straight back up the following year via the new version of test matches, which had been turned into mini leagues involving four teams playing each other home and away. With these fluctuating fortunes over successive seasons, it could be argued that the Liverpool of the mid-1890s were the original exponents of a yo-yo club, exhibiting both resilience and a dash of 'bouncebackability'.

The close parallels with the modern era were never stronger than when there was even a whiff of match-fixing back on 28th April 1898, as Stoke and Burnley played out a blatantly pre-arranged goalless draw which ensured the latter's promotion and the former staving off relegation. As quoted in Simon Inglis's encyclopedic and exhaustive tome, *League Football and the Men Who Made It*, the Manchester-based *Athletic News* sports newspaper was corrosive in its report: "The teams could have done without their goalkeepers, so anxious were the forwards not to score." The crowd became increasingly exasperated by the 'action' in front of them and ended up amusing themselves, as the ball was constantly being cleared into the fans, by playing their own game alongside the supposed main attraction. Although this was nothing compared to the scale of some of the mass, sprawling Italian scandals over the years such as 'Calciopoli' of 2006, in which a handful of large clubs were embroiled rather than a pair of transgressors, this may qualify as the original match-fixing case, as the league was still in its infancy.

Newcastle United, who had finished below the miscreants, alongside Blackburn in the mini league, suspected some secret deal had been struck and urged action to be taken by the League. At the Management Committee meeting in May a compromise was finally reached. Inspired by Charles Sutcliffe, who represented Burnley, there was an increase in the number of clubs in each of the two divisions to eighteen, thus enabling all four clubs involved in the test matches to qualify for the conveniently expanded Division One. It is perhaps reassuring to know that the 'dark arts' are not just a recent phenomenon, and were being practised with some vigour back in the dim, distant past as well. No further action was taken against either Burnley or Stoke but after this scandal, automatic promotion and relegation were brought in to avoid any possibility of such dastardly collusion and nefarious machinations happening again. And so this prototype of the Play-Offs was quietly withdrawn under a cloud of scandal and it was not until the 1960s that the idea was seriously considered again.

The modern English Play-Offs have never been tainted with any such scandal and are generally above suspicion as their importance to a club's future is paramount and it would be a major shock if the integrity were to be compromised in any way. However, there have been incidents of 'arranged matches' in other countries and one of the most recent was amongst the most striking and blatant of all time. In stark contrast to the Burnley–Stoke stalemate when neither side was interested in venturing into opposition territory for fear of notching a goal, there was a pair of games that produced such a glut of goals that suspicions were understandably aroused.

In July 2013 there were a couple of high-scoring play-offs matches which raised eyebrows across the world and led to drastic action being taken by the Nigerian Football Federation. With Plateau United Feeders and Police Machine locked on the same points going into the last play-offs matches, the battle was on to outscore each other and settle promotion to the lowest tier of the Nationwide League Division on goal difference. There was no great subtlety in the cack-handed attempts by either side or their complicit opponents. If there was concern at the one-sided half-time scores, with Feeders 7-0 up on Akurba FC and Police Machine 6-0 to the good against Bubayaro FC, this was just the quiet prelude to the second half, which saw a rapid acceleration in the push to improve their respective goal differences. When Police Machine powered into a 67-0 lead, including scoring four goals in a minute, they must have been confident that this would have secured that play-offs place. This plan however was foiled as Feeders gorged themselves with seventy-two goals in the second half to end up as 79-0 victors, with one player notching fourteen times.

Unlike Stoke and Burnley, who escaped any real punishment, the football authorities in Nigeria were uncompromising in their response, banning all four teams for ten years. There was no hiding place for the wrongdoers as an official statement from the Nigerian Football Federation revealed that "we will publish all the names of players and officials with their photographs and details". One wonders if something similar had happened in England how the authorities might have responded; in particular, the man who was responsible for bringing the idea of the play-offs back after a gap of some seven decades.

The fearsome and highly opinionated Football League secretary, Alan Hardaker, who was unkindly dubbed "Lytham's answer to Idi Amin" (after the notorious Ugandan dictator of the 1960s), wanted to conduct a radical overhaul of the game as outlined in his 'Pattern of Football' manifesto in 1957. Hardaker toyed with some form of play-off system amidst a host of other ideas to rejuvenate football, including the successful introduction of the League Cup in 1960/61. He generally met stiff resistance to most of his ideas from the ultra-conservative members of the league but in 1972 he did gain agreement to increase the number of clubs promoted and relegated from two to three in each division. Hardaker's rationale resonates with how the Play-Offs have altered the regular football season: "[this change] has injected new interest into games that would otherwise mean nothing in the closing stages of the season; and so while there may be fear at the bottom, there is certainly less complacency in the middle". Hardaker had decisively proved that broadening the net to incorporate more teams in with a chance of promotion or relegation was of benefit to the game and this principle stood the Play-Offs in good stead.

So when that Football League working party met in 1985 to address the serious decline that football was suffering, part of the solution was a proposal to introduce the Play-Offs. There was sufficient precedent with the combination of the recent history of the Hardaker-inspired deliberations as well as McGregor's legacy from the Victorian era. Indeed there had been a multitude of proposals and initiatives generated by the League over the previous five years to effect changes, including an ominous-sounding charter from 1980 called 'Soccer: The Fight for Survival', which paved the way for "an experiment to encourage more attacking football, so that in 1981/2 three points instead of two points would be awarded for a win". The hope was that this would inspire a more positive attitude from teams and ultimately make the game more attractive to the public. However, the crowds did not return as hoped and in fact they were still steadily falling away in the early 1980s. So whilst there were several laudable attempts to improve the game, none had been successful in really halting the malaise that enveloped football during the first half of the 1980s.

The main driving force behind the idea of the Play-Offs was inspired, like McGregor, by the American model of a post-season series of matches, used by all of the big four sports leagues. The New York Pro Football League, which was a regional predecessor of the NFL, actually hosted a form of play-offs way back in 1919, three years before the NFL was formed. Baseball's world championship series, in which the American Association's champions played the National League's winners, started at the same time as the English Football League in the 1880s. So baseball can lay claim to having introduced the earliest play-offs system and even predates McGregor's 'test matches', as was explored earlier in this chapter. There have been many changes in the organisation of all the major American sports' play-offs since their introduction, with numerous expansions and the odd contraction along the way. In contrast, English football's version has pretty much stood the test of time, staying the same since 1987, just with the odd tweak here and there, such as Williamson's idea of a Wembley Weekend and the pre-planned phasing out of the involvement of the team from the top division after two years.

The crucial difference is that the American system has always been geared towards deciding the various divisional champions and then the overall league champions rather than promotion from the lower leagues, as US Sports do not engage in the messy business of promotion/relegation. Since it is anathema to the ethos of British sport to deny regular movement between the leagues, the concept had to be simply re-configured to attend to the pressing needs of football at that time. Just as McGregor's test matches were designed to facilitate the movement between lower and upper divisions, so the Play-Offs did the same across the entire league.

With extensive business interests in the United States, Martin Lange, then chairman of Brentford, had seen first-hand how the play-offs system could work to such good effect. "I'd seen it in America," Lange explains, " I liked the idea of it and I just thought how do we adapt it to our game?" Lange was one of the three representatives of the Associate Members, i.e. Third and Fourth Division clubs, during the fraught negotiations of 1985. He was a shrewd negotiator and enlisted the help of that notably tough enforcer, Ron Noades, then chairman of Crystal Palace, to rally the support of Second Division clubs and to help implement the new system. Lange and Noades championed the Play-Offs and duly persuaded their fellow chairmen and committee members that it was now time to bring them in, as part of a ten-point proposal to restructure league football, known as the Heathrow Agreement. The Heathrow Agreement also temporarily quelled the attempt by the Big Five (which in those days comprised Everton, Liverpool, Manchester United, Arsenal and Tottenham Hotspur) to form a breakaway top division by agreeing to reduce the number of clubs in the top division, as well as doubling the share of total revenues for Division One clubs from the existing 25 per cent to 50 per cent.

The Play-Offs were designed to facilitate the reduction of the top division down to twenty teams and were accepted as a practical solution, with little resistance and hardly any debate. Considering the bitter squabbling and rancour that had preceded their introduction, such a smooth passage was an achievement in itself. The schisms that had been rife in the various discussions and negotiations up to and surrounding the Heathrow Agreement, were swept away in the rush to conciliation. Maybe everyone had had enough and needed a well-deserved rest from the perpetually pugilistic activities. It was to be a brief spell of harmony before the feuding factions were back at it again, fighting tooth and nail. But by the time normal hostile service was resumed, the Play-Offs were up and running, although, as we will learn, they did not begin with universal approval.

It is surely a testament to the quality of the Play-Offs concept that they have survived and indeed prospered, having made their mark so long ago and then been restored a century later under a different guise. Those visionaries, William McGregor and Alan Hardaker, would undoubtedly have approved and been delighted to witness how an idea of such simplicity could make such a material difference to the league whilst showing itself in its very best colours. As most people appreciate, the football authorities are prone to the odd dither now and again and are not universally known for their progressive attitude, so it is reassuring to find that there are times when they do get it right and make an enlightened decision. It is also just as well that the Stoke and Burnley farrago of the 1890s was a mere blip rather than setting a precedent for any more nonsense that might have stained the reputation of the league and derailed the Play-Offs. As a form of pure, unadulterated entertainment, the Play-Offs have very few equals, many admirers and a century-old lineage that goes back to the very origins of English league football.

But the emergence of the Play-Offs was primarily a response to one of the bleakest periods the domestic game had encountered. Just as the Football League was nearing its centenary, it was faced with the most serious crisis of its long, illustrious history. Shaken to the core by a series of catastrophic incidents in the space of a few months, football's name was about to be dragged through the mud, its reputation tarnished and the game left floundering.

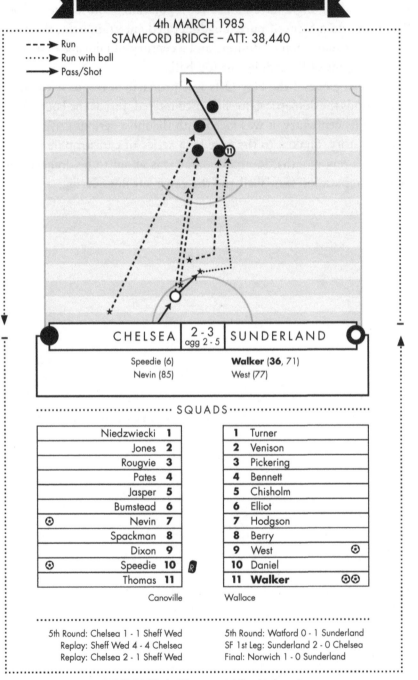

CLIVE WALKER 1984/85

MILK CUP SEMI-FINAL 2ND LEG

4th MARCH 1985
STAMFORD BRIDGE – ATT: 38,440

- - - ▶ Run
...... ▶ Run with ball
——▶ Pass/Shot

CHELSEA 2 - 3 SUNDERLAND
agg 2 - 5

Speedie (6)   **Walker (36**, 71)
Nevin (85)   West (77)

·········· S Q U A D S ··········

Niedzwiecki	1		1	Turner	
Jones	2		2	Venison	
Rougvie	3		3	Pickering	
Pates	4		4	Bennett	
Jasper	5		5	Chisholm	
Bumstead	6		6	Elliot	
Nevin	7	⊙	7	Hodgson	
Spackman	8		8	Berry	
Dixon	9		9	West	⊙
Speedie	10	⊙	10	Daniel	
Thomas	11		11	**Walker**	⊙⊙

Canoville   Wallace

5th Round: Chelsea 1 - 1 Sheff Wed   5th Round: Watford 0 - 1 Sunderland
Replay: Sheff Wed 4 - 4 Chelsea   SF 1st Leg: Sunderland 2 - 0 Chelsea
Replay: Chelsea 2 - 1 Sheff Wed   Final: Norwich 1 - 0 Sunderland

GOAL FACT: As West scored the third goal,
the police were on the pitch, chasing an invading fan.

MARCH–MAY 1985:
ENGLISH FOOTBALL'S DARKEST DAYS

By the middle of the 1980s football in England had sunk to such a low point that it was difficult to envisage how it might possibly recover and, to a certain extent, whether it would survive at all. It was in danger of facing if not quite extinction, then certainly an extended period in the wilderness. Bedevilled by problems since the sixties, the game had been ravaged by hooliganism, falling attendances, negative publicity and a government vehemently opposed to its irksome presence. Football had been brought to its knees and there seemed very little prospect of anyone being able to turn it around. There was a pervading sense of doom surrounding the game and this overriding atmosphere of gloom and despondency was smothering the life out of football as a major spectator sport.

The media's sensationalist reporting, especially by the tabloids, exacerbated the problems, increasing the notoriety of the hooligans with tales of a range of 'firms' and their tribal names such as The Headhunters, The Bushwackers and The Zulus, striking fear and loathing across the country every Saturday. A strong sense of moral panic gripped the nation, so that every incident drove a further nail in the coffin as the English game looked to be in danger of heading into oblivion. Lurid headlines and vociferous editorials followed each outbreak of trouble and piled the pressure on the powers that be.

The football authorities were in desperate straits as they battled against a growing sense of isolation and disillusionment that had not only engulfed this country but had spread across the world. English football was consequently treated as a pariah and shunned universally, in stark contrast to today's global popularity. Just as it seemed things could not get any worse, a series of terrible events came together in rapid succession towards the end of the 1984/85 season, which catapulted football into an even deeper trough, reaching its absolute nadir from where there really seemed very little chance of recovery. The task of finding a way back looked insurmountable.

In the 1984/85 season, fewer than 7.5 million people came through the turnstiles to watch the lower three divisions, an appreciable drop of many millions from the heyday of the 1950s. This figure has more than doubled over the following thirty years, reaching the levels of the 1960s again as football has recovered from its darkest days. By 2013/14 the average gate of just under 10,000 for lower-league teams would not have looked out of place in the top division of 1985/86, when Chelsea, who finished sixth in the old First Division, attracted a mere 12,000 hardy souls for their last home league game in May 1986. The rot had well and truly set in. Put off by fears of crowd violence, a government virulently opposed to the sport itself and a tabloid press campaign of vehement vilification, people turned their back on the beautiful game. Fans found better, and markedly safer, things to do on Saturday afternoons. Football had a fight on its hands, both metaphorically and literally.

To make matters worse this growing sense of disenchantment was given plenty of supporting evidence between March and May 1985. It was a period which marked a new low, alienating everyone apart from the game's staunchest supporters and even they grew tired of trying to defend the indefensible. Within the space of a couple of months there was a catalogue of damaging football-related incidents, with several major crowd disturbances, that ratcheted up the pressure on the authorities to get their house in order or risk the most punitive sanctions. Just when they needed something positive to alleviate the doom and gloom they were deluged by a string of negative incidents that pushed football closer to the abyss.

In March 1985 Chelsea met Sunderland in the second leg of a Milk Cup semi-final. The game was marred by violent scenes both inside and outside Stamford Bridge, including a series of pitch invasions, which even led to physical threats to players and a police horse being present on the pitch when Sunderland scored their decisive third goal which secured a 5-2 aggregate win. The result became an irrelevance as all the attention focused upon the pitch battles. The bare facts were that 104 people were arrested and over forty injured, including twenty policemen, but the heaviest toll was being levied on the game's deteriorating reputation and tarnished image. The anti-football brigade had been given plentiful ammunition and the mood of the nation was swinging decisively against the game.

The most depressing aspect of this sort of trouble was its predictability. Nearly any match, whether important or mundane, had the potential of being plagued by disorder and this became the norm and a familiarly bleak routine. Indeed it had reached the point where one man's solution to the situation was to erect electric fences to keep the spectators off the Stamford Bridge pitch. This was not the design of some maniac or oddball (although some would argue that such descriptions do hold true) but of the then chairman of Chelsea football club, Ken Bates. The very notion of keeping would-be pitch invaders at bay with something so crude and dangerous was, amazingly, not rejected immediately. Not only that but Bates's radical idea actually went as far as an application to the local authority, in this case the Greater London Council, where it was seriously considered before being turned down because of safety concerns. This is a clear illustration of the desperate straits football had reached and the ludicrous extent to which it had lost the plot.

Only nine days later came a second major incident, which Bert Millichip the chairman of the FA at the time witheringly described as "the most disgraceful I have ever seen – and I have seen a lot". Millwall fans invaded the pitch on numerous occasions at Luton Town's Kenilworth Road before, during and after an FA Cup tie, disrupting the match several times as fighting continued almost without check. In some of the worst scenes seen at an English ground even in those terrible times, Luton's keeper, Les Sealey, had a knife thrown at him, whilst a policeman trying to resuscitate a colleague, who had been knocked out, was punched and pummelled. At the height of the violence, the police were confronted by the Millwall fans and subjected to a barrage of bright orange seats that had been unceremoniously ripped out of the stands and used as weapons. The image of police being pelted by a hail of missiles was broadcast around the world and merely underlined the widely held opinion that English football had simply become a hollow pretence for civil disorder.

Luton's response was to introduce a ban on away fans, which the Conservative government under Margaret Thatcher fully endorsed, and she was determined to extend this idea to every English club. For a game that was already suffering from dramatically declining crowds, this was the stick that was going to be used to beat football into submission. When this was rebuffed as unworkable the next step saw Luton chairman and local MP David Evans asked to lead a taskforce to investigate introducing a national ID scheme for attending football matches. Football violence was now top of the political agenda and the exasperated government demanded severe action.

So standing alongside Evans there was his fellow chairman Bates, as dangerous a couple as Scylla and Charybdis. With English football being asked to chart a safe passage between the rock of a national ID scheme and the hard place of an electric fence, the likelihood was that it would end in a disastrous solution being foisted on to football, but in the absence of any other ideas this was a distinct possibility. With such draconian moves being considered, the future looked bleak and if either of them had been accepted, arguably they may well have signalled the death knell of football as a major spectator sport.

Just as these radical measures were being considered and only two months after the Stamford Bridge and Kenilworth Road disturbances, an altogether more horrific scene unfolded at an English football ground. On 11th May, Bradford City played the last match of their season at home to Lincoln City. This was supposed to be a day of celebration, as Bradford had already won the Third Division title and their fans were all set to enjoy their successful season. But it turned out be the worst day in Bradford's history as a fire swept through an old wooden stand at Valley Parade resulting in the deaths of fifty-six people, with another 265 injured in the inferno. This was not in any way a result of hooliganism but a tragic accident; however it meant that football was further associated with a decrepit and dangerous environment.

On the same day as the Valley Parade disaster, there was another football-related death, but this one was precipitated by an outbreak of violence that shook everyone to the core. Leeds United and Birmingham City fans rioted at Birmingham's St Andrews ground and a teenager died when crushed by a collapsed wall as a result of fighting outside the stadium. The scene was described by Lord Justice Popplewell in his report as being "more like Agincourt than a football match". It was a strange analogy to compare a battle between the French and the English from the fifteenth century with a football match 570 years later, but it served its purpose in shocking the British public.

Death and destruction were becoming the motifs of the game and there seemed to be little respite from the desperate litany that plagued English football. Looking back, this period did seem a little like the Dark Ages, so maybe Popplewell was right after all in his choice of simile. The difference is remarkable when you consider recently announced figures showing that the number of arrests of football supporters in 2013/14 was the lowest on record, with 2,273 arrests recorded out of 38 million people attending the top five leagues and all domestic cup competitions, European competitions and international matches. That equates to one arrest for every 16,800 fans attending matches, or 0.01 per cent, which is a far cry from the mayhem being caused just thirty years earlier when hooliganism was at its height.

With the domestic season ending in such desperate circumstances, there was a glimmer of hope that Liverpool's appearance in the European Cup Final against

Juventus might just remind everyone that there could be something uplifting to celebrate and show the world English football at its finest. Liverpool were admired as Europe's pre-eminent club, having enjoyed unparalleled success over the previous two decades. Under legendary managers Bill Shankly and Bob Paisley, Liverpool had been a powerhouse in European football, winning the European Cup four times since 1977. Along with Nottingham Forest and Aston Villa they had spearheaded English dominance to the extent that only one non-English club had won the biggest club prize in Europe in the previous eight years. It was the ideal time to provide a much-needed tonic to the beleaguered game.

This match could and should have been the pinnacle, a further reminder of English football's strength, but it turned into yet another catastrophe and in this instance the awful scenes were broadcast live across the world. The ensuing Heysel disaster where thirty-nine people, mainly Italians, died, and hundreds were injured after a wall collapsed under the weight of fans trying to escape from brawling fans spreading across the terraces, was the last straw. The inadequacy of the ground facilities at the dilapidated stadium had compounded the problems but this did not stop UEFA imposing a harsh, but justified, penalty, with English clubs banned from all European competition for five years. The Football Association had already decided to take pre-emptive action by withdrawing all clubs from Europe as Ted Croker, Secretary of the FA at the time, announced after being summoned to No. 10 "it is now up to English football to put its house in order".

But to many in the Conservative government Croker was too late and Thatcher was being encouraged and emboldened by a few of her colleagues, led by the Minister for Sport, Colin Moynihan, to push ahead with further measures, such as the football identity card scheme, that would have exerted further debilitating pressure on the game. That was eventually abandoned in the wake of the Taylor Report but Moynihan did push the Football Spectators Bill through Parliament. A compromise was reached by the Football League, led by President Philip Carter, with a partial membership scheme introduced and a voluntary target of 50 per cent agreed and met by almost half the clubs by September 1987. This was still not enough to placate some of the more hostile members of the government, who were now scenting blood and would not let go of their prey.

Football had become a 'law and order' issue akin to the miners' strike, and by antagonising the Prime Minister there was a danger of her response being to squeeze the life out of the game. That all the incidents described above, from the disorder at Stamford Bridge to the Heysel disaster, took place within less than three months, eighty-six days to be precise, shows how calamity followed calamity with very little respite. This confluence of events heaped more pressure on the football authorities and gave the government all the ammunition it needed to remove this blot from the landscape. As Dr Rogan Taylor, Director of the Football Industry Group at Liverpool University, commented on Sky News, "Mrs Thatcher saw football as a kind of working class industrial wasteland – one of those rust bucket industries that she wanted to kick into touch like the miners and the trade unions and shipbuilders. Like everything else she saw it as something she ought to suffocate, rather than give life too." English football was now well and truly cut adrift; having been ostracised, unloved and unwanted, both internationally and domestically, English clubs had become outcasts.

Hooliganism had tarred the game to such an extent that 'The English Disease' became the common term for any outbreak of trouble at football grounds in the latter half of the 1980s, wherever or whoever was involved. So strong was this link that even to this day this reputation still lingers, even though the hooliganism problem is far worse in other countries such as Poland and Russia. The Heysel disaster cast a shadow over the relationship between the domestic game and the rest of the football world and especially in Italy, as outlined in John Foot's excellent history of Italian football, *Calcio*, in relation to the transfer of Ian Rush to Juventus in 1987. Rush had been a member of the Liverpool side that day. "Juventus fans had certainly not forgotten that tragedy and Rush's transfer is sometimes seen as a way of building bridges between the two clubs after 1985. Rush claims that there were no problems with Heysel during his time in Turin, but some of the diffidence towards him may well have originated with the bitterness still there amongst many fans."

FOOTBALL LEAGUE'S RESCUE PLAN

Ten Key Points

1. First Division to be reduced from 22 to 20 clubs

2. Automatic promotion and relegation between the Gola League (now Conference) and Fourth Division

3. Majority required for changing League regulations reduced from ¾ to ⅔

4. First Division clubs' share of television and sponsorship revenue increased to 50% from 25%

5. The 4% League levy on match receipts to be reduced to 3%

6. Management Committee changed so First Division clubs have four representatives

7. All League Cup receipts changed from 20% to 10% for all clubs

8. All FA Cup receipts changed from 20% to 10% for all clubs

9. Pools revenue to be distributed equally between all clubs

10. Introduction of system of playoffs to make a fair and equitable transition for reduction of First Division

The introduction of the Play-Offs 'went under the radar', barely noticed and the most anonymous point of ten.

BACK FROM THE BRINK: 1985–87

Having reached rock bottom, the future looked unremittingly bleak, and with this doomsday scenario unfolding, the League needed to find a cure and respond positively. Unfortunately one of the first acts of this now beleaguered group was to reject the near £19 million deal being offered by the BBC and ITV for television rights. Jack Dunnett, president of the League, summed up the defiant stance. "It seems that football is prepared to have a year or two with no television if it comes to that. We know the huge financial losses that would be involved but, on the other hand, we might induce more people to come through the turnstiles."

Dunnett's notion that starving the public of televised football would encourage them back to the grounds was naïve, wrong-headed and potentially ruinous. With the entrenched positions held by both sides the result was that there was no live football on television during the first half of the 1985/86 season. So just when they needed both the coverage and the revenue most in order to start restoring the game's battered image, the chairmen, in their infinite wisdom, decided to embark on an act of brinkmanship which took league football off UK's television screens for over four months. In these days of wall-to-wall broadcasting coverage when rarely a day goes by without a range of live televised matches, it seems absurd that there could be such a long, protracted break. With its unerring capacity to shoot itself in the foot, the game in England had become a model of incompetence and inaction.

A compromise deal was eventually struck and live games were brought back in January 1986 but the damage had been done. Unsurprisingly with the key component of television coverage suffering from chronic uncertainty, there was very little enthusiasm for sponsorship of the league after Canon withdrew at the culmination of the 1985/86 season. One could hardly blame the corporate world for shunning a close association with a game that had such a predominantly negative image and one that was in seemingly terminal decline. As a result of this fundamental failure, Dunnett was removed at the League EGM in April 1986 and became the first President to be voted out of office. The much more pragmatic and dynamic Philip Carter engineered this coup d'état with characteristic skill and strength, sweeping into power, and one of his first tasks was to rescue the television deal and then address the wider problems.

With the league suffering from bitter internecine strife, understandably there was a hiatus in commercial backing and it was not until October 1986 that a sponsor was eventually confirmed as the *Today* newspaper agreed to pay £4 million over two years to become the league's sponsor. As a relative newcomer (having launched in March 1986), *Today* was struggling to establish itself within the fiercely competitive daily newspaper market and the deal was struck with an air of desperation as two weakened and flawed organisations were forced together in a last-ditch rescue attempt. Neither party entered the agreement with much confidence and the writing was firmly etched on the wall from the outset.

Suffice to say this ill-fated sponsorship lasted less than a year, as a new proprietor took over at the paper and once a hasty review had been conducted it was decided almost immediately that this arrangement was not working. The sponsorship was pulled just weeks before the start of the 1987/88 season. There was not too much debate as the cons outweighed the pros by a considerable margin, so this would have been a straightforward and pretty much uncontested decision. For the proprietor in question this was his first, rather short-lived involvement in football and he could have been forgiven for shunning the embattled sport for good, once bitten twice shy. But he did return and was to have an altogether more positive, far greater and longer-term impact within five years. He was none other than Rupert Murdoch.

English football was in a pickle and something had to be done. Fortunately Philip Carter proved up to the job and having cut his teeth on the Television Negotiating Committee, which had constructed the earlier four-year deal with the BBC/ ITV for £18.8 million only for the recalcitrant clubs to throw it out, Carter was aware of the endemic problems and was ready to tackle them head on.

More than ever before, the game needed a massive boost, as the likes of Murdoch would need to be convinced of the overall health and future of the

English game. The all-encompassing negativity surrounding the game at this time was not something with which any right-minded company or commercial entity would want to be associated. A dynamic and far-reaching programme of regeneration was required to turn the tide as without the necessary support and financial backing, there would be little chance of any meaningful renaissance.

Just before the Play-Offs started, attendances at English Football League matches had reached that nadir of fewer than 7.5 million watching the lower three divisions in the 1985/86 season. As was outlined previously, football's problems were deep-seated and would require more than just platitudes and the odd sticking plaster; far-reaching and radical remedial work was needed and fast. In the short term, things had to be turned around, but there was also the need for lasting solutions. There could be no simple panacea; a range of changes across all aspects of the game would have to be introduced. One of those agents of change was the introduction of the Play-Offs.

After decades of declining crowds, there was a significant and steady growth in attendances in the lower leagues from 1986/87 onwards just as the Play-Offs were introduced, with successive rises of over a million for the next four seasons. In sharp contrast, the top flight was still suffering a serious decline in spectators – with the leading clubs banned from Europe, much of the interest in the upper reaches had waned. The result was that between 1986 and 1990, Division One attendances dropped by more than one million, a fall of 13 per cent. During the same period Divisions Two, Three and Four enjoyed a total increase of over 4 million reaching a total of more than 11 million, up by an impressive 56 per cent.

This switch in fortunes led to a major shift in the balance of popularity between the top division and the others; during the 1985/86 season, 1.5 million more people attended Division One matches, but by 1989/90 the pendulum had swung decisively towards the three lower divisions, which were attracting 50 per cent more people through the turnstiles than the previously dominant Division One. This massive swing of five million people in the space of four years cannot have been a mere coincidence or statistical blip and pointed to the lower divisions proving to be more popular than the higher division. These first green shoots of recovery were principally down to the interest generated by the Play-Offs throughout the lower three divisions and the positive impact felt across a much broader range of clubs. This was surely one of the key differences in this period between Division One teams and their supposedly poorer cousins. So there was a sliver of irony mixed with a touch of arrogance in the fact that whilst the lower leagues were regularly outperforming the top division in attracting fans during the late eighties, this was just the time that the leading clubs were itching to distance themselves from the other three divisions, as they viewed them as holding the top clubs back.

By helping football recover its equilibrium, the Play-Offs effectively steadied the ship and managed to shift focus away from the negative connotations of the preceding years of toil and trouble and point towards a brighter future. The game's problems did not disappear overnight and there were still incidents of crowd disorder and hooliganism, as was clear at the Chelsea versus Middlesbrough Play-Offs Final second leg at Stamford Bridge in 1988, which echoed the Sunderland League Cup trouble of a few years earlier. Importantly, the concerted effort to control hooliganism was beginning to have some effect and serious outbreaks of violence were much reduced, if not eradicated. They became isolated incidents rather than regular occurrences and the overall atmosphere was changing for the better. At least the media had something else to report and were given a shining example of the attractions of football that reminded everyone that a stadium did not have to be a battleground but could again be host to some excellent sporting entertainment. The vicious circle of negative publicity feeding off a series of disastrous events was interrupted, as something more positive came to the fore.

There were several other contributory factors as to why English football attendances recovered over the following decade but hardly any of those can be attributed to this initial rise in the late 1980s. Some have argued that the main reason behind the turnaround of football's fortunes was the improvement in grounds and general facilities as a result of the Taylor Report. The Taylor Report was commissioned after the Hillsborough disaster of 1989 when ninety-six Liverpool fans died during the FA Cup semi-final against Nottingham Forest. Justice Taylor's main recommendation was the introduction of all seated stadia and the consequent removal of the terraces. Whilst the measures undertaken did improve safety in the grounds and crowd control, this does not explain the recovery across all three lower divisions in the late 1980s, as the recommendations only related to the top two divisions and they only came into effect much later, in the early 1990s.

The final Report was not published until 1990, so the positive impact was not truly felt for a few years after. Most clubs had to undertake considerable rebuilding of their grounds in order to comply with the new regulations and in the short term there were actually reduced capacities and consequently quite a few clubs had smaller crowds. Any uplift in attendances from improved facilities started from the early to mid-1990s and not before. Division One crowds did pick up from 1990, breaking through the 10 million threshold for the first time in over ten years in 1991/92, the year before the Premier League started, whilst the lower divisions were still attracting a healthy 10.4 million.

The significant renaissance in popularity enjoyed by the lower leagues from 1986 onwards points to the Play-Offs being the major influence in sparking this resurgence of interest. They provided the platform from which football beyond the top division managed to re-invigorate its tarnished image and begin to ensure that it retained the mantle of being the most popular spectator sport in England, a position that had been seriously under threat during those grim, depressing days. The tide was turned in the latter part of the 1980s well before the 'feel good' factor created by the 1990 World Cup or the advent of the Premier League in 1992, which to a certain extent relied on the health and strength of the Football League. It is extremely doubtful that Rupert Murdoch and Sky would have invested such an enormous amount of money if the game had stayed in its mid-eighties rut with its attendant poor image and negative connotations. So the steady growth of crowds from Division Two downwards showed there was still an appetite at the grass-roots level. It is worth remembering that Murdoch had already shied away from football a few years beforehand as the proprietor of the *Today* newspaper. As had been proved, given a positive environment, people would happily return to watching football in large numbers and so broadcasters along with sponsors could make the most of this growing audience. If Division One was naturally the primary focus for the new deal, the lower leagues formed the foundation block upon which the deal was built and the Play-Offs contributed to ensuring that this base was solid, healthy and robust.

The creation of the Premier League in 1992 brought about an enormous and permanent change to English football, as the oft-threatened breakaway of the top division finally materialised. The big clubs could no longer be denied their independence and resistance was now futile; the time for a seismic change was nigh. Sky's huge injection of money massively increased television revenues for the leading clubs overnight and, allied to the considerable boost to the game's profile, the crowds started returning to the upper echelons of league football, building on the base of 10 million that had been reached at the dawn of the Premier League. But despite the hype and hullabaloo surrounding the launch of the Premier League, "a whole new ball game" as the publicity proclaimed, Football League crowds continued to build over the following ten years, reaching just under 15 million in 2002/03 compared to 13.5 million for the Premier League.

The lower leagues have also proved the durability of their appeal in the twenty-odd years since the birth of the Premier League, as clearly illustrated by the fact that for eight consecutive seasons from 2003 onwards, over 16 million people attended Football League matches. Despite a slight dip in overall attendance in the last few years, Football League games still attract more spectators than the much-vaunted Premier League, albeit from many more matches. The seeds of this enduring popularity were sown with the introduction of the Play-Offs, which helped English football recover from its lowest point during the mid-1980s. In providing the necessary momentum to reverse the pattern of decline that had plagued the game for many years, the Play-Offs transformed its prospects and continue to provide a healthy, vigorous stimulus to its appeal today.

HEROES & VILLAINS

THE HEATHROW AGREEMENT

Prior to the commercial meltdown when the League and the television companies were at loggerheads and in the light of the catastrophic sequence of events between March and May 1985, a Football League working party was set up at the beginning of the 1985/86 season to try to rescue the sick and ailing game. The ten members of this committee included the strong triumvirate of Irving Scholar (Tottenham), Philip Carter (Everton) and Martin Edwards (Manchester United), representing the Big Five clubs who were pursuing their own agenda of wanting to control their own destiny. John Smith, chairman of Liverpool, starkly summed up their plight. "Surgery to the league of one kind or another is long overdue. The big clubs are very, very impatient for many reasons. We are suffering financial hardship because there is no television agreement, we are not in Europe, gates are declining and altogether the state of the national game is in disarray." As Smith pointed out, the harsh realities of life had finally struck home and it was time for something to be done.

Amongst those representing the cause of the smaller clubs was Martin Lange, chairman of Brentford, whose main task was to make sure that the interests of the lower two divisions were not trampled under the larger clubs' dash for cash. Lange's diplomatic skills were to be tested to the limit and one of the key instruments for protecting the well-being of the Division Three and Four clubs was the introduction of the Play-Offs. The main findings of the working party led to a ten-point plan known as the Heathrow Agreement, so named because the initial meeting on 18th December 1985 was held in the rather drab surroundings of the Post House Hotel near Heathrow.

English football faced a bleak future and desperately needed to take radical, remedial action. That the football authorities did manage to resuscitate the game and subsequently, over the next few decades, transform a basket case into the strong, flourishing industry that it is today was a considerable, and possibly unexpected, achievement. If the same situation occurred today, there would undoubtedly be a host of external consultants engaged to tackle the problem and the majority of suggested remedies would not have come from the football authorities themselves. However, in 1985 things were different and the solutions were indeed generated internally by the committee, which comprised the league chairmen representing the different divisions and Gordon Taylor, Secretary of the Professional Footballers' Association (PFA). Taylor played a crucial role in ensuring that this worked out, as he was fully aware that all his members' livelihoods were at stake. This group was assembled to conceive a way of helping football back on to its feet and there was a huge responsibility laid at the committee members' door.

The majority of the issues addressed by the committee were centred upon redressing the balance of power between the big clubs and their smaller brethren. Such an internal focus could be considered slightly myopic, as there was clearly a need to address the fundamental weakness of the game's popularity. Unless spectators could be attracted back to football, the share of revenues and voting rights would be largely irrelevant. What football really needed were some ideas that would bring people back to watching matches. As Ian Jones, Doncaster Rovers, chairman and a member of the Management Committee, commented at one stage of the negotiations, "We are disappointed that there has still been no suggestion on how to improve the game or bring people back through the turnstiles." Little did Jones realise that in amongst the proposals was the perfect antidote.

There were only two aspects of this ten-point rescue plan that made a material difference to the game as opposed to redistributing revenues and voting rights. Consequently these two ideas deserve consideration as being fundamental to the subsequent renaissance of English football. The first one was the introduction of automatic promotion and relegation between the old Fourth Division and the Conference. Automatic promotion and relegation replaced the archaic, inequitable and almost incestuous system of re-election, which involved league chairmen voting on whether teams should stay up or be confined to non-league football. As many of the chairmen entitled to vote represented clubs that could have been in danger of being relegated in the future, the notion of self-preservation prevailed. The fact that no team had failed to be re-elected since Southport's demise in 1978 emphasised the stasis that was symptomatic of this rather antiquated, tawdry and ultimately flawed process. Just as turkeys are not that keen on Christmas, neither were these chairmen willing to jeopardise their precious league status.

Carter's view was clear: "We wanted to complete the pyramid of football, so that any one of the 40,000 clubs in the country could, on merit, eventually make its way through the minor leagues up to the Football League itself." Few could argue against the rationale behind the idea of automatic promotion/relegation, as it freed up the movement between non-league and league football. Over the next twenty-five years only one major change to the system adopted in the Heathrow Agreement was undertaken. The addition of a second team to be promoted was brought in for 2002/03, and having seen the undoubted success of the first fifteen years of Football League Play-Offs, it was decided that the Conference would have its own series to determine the second promotion slot. Although introducing automatic promotion/relegation from the Conference was an excellent idea, its impact was relatively limited as it was only felt in the lowest division, whereas the Football League Play-Offs had a much broader significance across all three of its divisions.

The Play-Offs surely merit a special place as the key initiative of all those that were launched at this critical juncture in 1985, having grown and developed since into such a pivotal feature of league football. Furthermore, the fact that the Play-Offs are still pretty much in their original format almost thirty years later proves their intrinsic value. Although conceived as a short-term expedient measure, the system has more than stood the test of time and has flourished, exerting a positive influence on the league throughout its history. Like most successful innovations, it has been much copied across football and the wider sporting world. The Play-Offs are now generally accepted as the standard way of deciding final promotion slots or, in some cases, as was the case originally, even relegation.

The larger clubs agreed to the Heathrow Agreement proposals as they had successfully increased their share of the pie, both financially and in terms of power, so they were satisfied, although this compromise proved to be a stopgap measure that was never likely to last. Much of the impetus for this approval came from a different style of owner who had come into football in the early to mid-1980s, such as Irving Scholar at Tottenham Hotspur. According to Lange, the main driving force behind the Play-Offs, there was a distinct switch in approach from those now heading up the larger clubs. Scholar et al. were younger, more aggressive, entrepreneurial guys who were beginning to displace the old dynasties such as the Richardson and Wale families at Tottenham and the Cearns at West Ham.

This new breed of chairmen was far more hard-nosed in their approach and were focused on getting a better return on their financial investment in the clubs. Running a football club was no longer the preserve of patriarchs, and the Scholars of this world were certainly not as wedded as their predecessors were to the greater good of the league. They questioned the idea of 'commonality'; given that the larger clubs generated the vast majority of the revenues, they argued that the pooling arrangements (where the revenues were shared evenly between all clubs) were disproportionate and ultimately unfair as they were not getting their just rewards for being the main drivers of income. Lange knew that there would have to be a compromise and whilst he was keen to protect the interests of the lesser clubs, he was astute enough to know that some ground had to be conceded to the bigger clubs, otherwise any agreement would have collapsed before it got off the ground.

Understandably, most of the attention was focused on the share of overall revenues, voting rights and divisional representation, so the Play-Offs slipped through almost unnoticed. As Lange recalls, "We threw in the Play-Offs at the end and as all the guys were interested in was the money side, they were not too concerned about the Play-Offs." This was primarily seen as an expedient, temporary measure; a way of easing the transition to a twenty-team top division without too much of a sudden jolt to the system, and consequently it passed under the radar without too much debate.

As the financial landscape changed, the Play-Offs were established to principally compensate the Associate Members, namely the Third and Fourth Division clubs, which had lost out through the new revenue agreement, having had their share of league income halved at a stroke. One of the more significant components of the agreement was that half of the revenues generated by the Play-Offs would be pooled and shared between all the clubs rather than just those that competed in the Final. The split was arranged as 25 per cent for each of the finalists, then the remaining 50 per cent was to be divided equally amongst all the clubs in that division, apart from those clubs that had gained promotion. At a time when the chairmen from the top division were obsessed with negotiating a bigger share for themselves, this initiative showed a refreshing understanding of the need for a more even distribution of revenues to support the lesser clubs. Ensuring the overall health of the league above the needs of individual clubs is a worthy trait of the Play-Offs and one that crops up with pleasing regularity throughout their history. The lack of self-interest displayed is an endearing and unusual feature that in a way distinguishes the Play-Offs from the image of modern football as a haven for the greedy and the selfish.

After much huffing and puffing, some last-minute bravado and a fair bit of posturing from the so-called Super Leaguers and the Associate Members, the final vote proved to be a comfortable majority of 43 to 10 and the Heathrow Agreement had served its purpose in affecting change but not alienating the clubs on either side of the divide. Having said that, the League was extremely cautious in its assessment of the short-term prospects; the rather tentative wording of the proposal suggested "initially the Play-Offs would operate for two years, but if they proved popular with spectators they could become a permanent part of the calendar". The committee clearly had limited faith in the very idea of the Play-Offs and none of the League officials anticipated their overwhelming impact.

Indeed Lange himself did not foresee a future much beyond that initial trial period. "I couldn't see them lasting for twenty years, ten years, probably not even five years," he confided in an exclusive interview. But this rather downbeat prognosis for the Play-Offs was to be cast aside through the vibrant, electric manner in which they started life, setting a precedent for the sort of exhilarating action that is now one of their essential ingredients.

STEVE WHITE 1986/87

THIRD DIVISION PLAY-OFFS FINAL REPLAY

29th MAY 1987
SELHURST PARK – ATT: 18,491

- - - ➤ Run
······➤ Run with ball
——➤ Pass/Shot

GILLINGHAM 0 - 2 SWINDON

White (2, **65**)

···················· SQUADS ····················

Kite	**1**	**1**	Digby	
Haylock	**2**	**2**	Hockaday	
Pearce	**3**	**3**	King	
L. Berry	**4**	**4**	Coyne	
Quow	**5**	**5**	Parkin	
Greenall	**6**	**6**	Calderwood	
Pritchard	**7**	**7**	Bamber	
Shearer	**8**	**8**	S. Berry	
Robinson	**9**	**9**	Henry	
Elsey	**10**	**10**	White	⊗⊗
Cascarino	**11**	**11**	Bernard	

Smith   Jones

Final League Position: 5th
SF 1st Leg: Gillingham 3 - 2 Sunderland
SF 2nd Leg: Sunderland 4 - 3 Gillingham

Final League Position: 3rd
SF 1st Leg: Wigan 2 - 3 Swindon
SF 2nd Leg: Swindon 0 - 0 Wigan

Final 1st Leg: Gillingham 1 - 0 Swindon, Final 2nd Leg: Swindon 2 - 1 Gillingham

GOAL FACT: This win secured Swindon a second successive promotion,
they having been Division Four champions in 1986.

LIFE ON THE ROLLERCOASTER:
FANS AND THE PLAY-OFFS

Football had reached a point in the mid-1980s where clubs could no longer rely upon the slavish devotion of the general public to turn up week after week, come what may. The accompanying malevolence and real threat of violence made attending a match an unsettling and frankly disturbing experience for many. Such an atmosphere had dissuaded a lot of people from attending matches; it was imperative that they should be attracted back to a game which they had abandoned. It also needed to be done pretty quickly before these lost millions were gone for ever. In those days when television deals were counted in millions rather than billions, it was even more important to have that match-day income as this was the mainstay of club finances. The umbilical link that connected fans with their clubs needed to be restored as soon as possible. The search for a magic wand was on but it was found in a most unlikely guise, as it was the Play-Offs which provided the much sought-after impetus. As a positive stimulus to an ailing game, the restorative impact was thankfully both swift and significant.

One of the more reassuring aspects of the Play-Offs is the intensity and closeness of the relationship with the fans. By engaging so closely with supporters from the outset, the Play-Offs were accepted more readily than anyone could have imagined. Supporters thrive on the visceral, when emotions are laid bare, and the Play-Offs have delivered such moments in spades right from the off. Although we can be damaged by such experiences when our team loses in controversial or sensational fashion, that is all part and parcel of being a fan and deep down we would much rather have to go through the mill now and again than just meander aimlessly without anything to exercise us or test our resolve. The Play-Offs are renowned for providing those critical moments time and again and hence their popularity, even with those fans whose teams suffer regularly from their distinctive brand of traumas.

And there are not that many fans who have been through the mill and out the other side again as much as Ipswich Town's did in the late 1990s. So for a fan's perspective on what it feels like, Gavin Barber of Ipswich's blog *Turnstile Blues*, provided his own subjective, pained account of life at the rough end of the Play-Offs, which is featured in the mini profile at the end of this chapter. If you do not want to or find it uncomfortable to intrude into other people's misfortune it may be best to skip through this as it may be a little awkward, but for an illuminating look at how it feels when the odds are seemingly stacked against you this is essential reading.

On a more positive note, amongst the leading benefits of the Play-Offs has always been their inclusiveness, with more teams having something to play for during the latter stages of the season, thus extending supporters' interest. Where a fair slew of teams would have previously been marooned in mid-table with little prospect of going up or down, the Play-Offs provided the opportunity for most of these teams to still achieve promotion by reaching the top six (or seven in the case of the lowest division). Consequently, the crowds returned in increasingly healthy numbers to follow the machinations of the race for the Play-Offs. With fewer meaningless matches, the season was very much alive for the majority of clubs throughout the season and the Play-Off places remained an obtainable objective for so many more clubs than was previously the case. As Mark Watson, comedian and Bristol City devotee comments, "People have got to remember what it was like before the Play-Offs. If you were anywhere from fifth to about seventeenth, the final three months could be largely meaningless."

The Play-Offs became a key focal point for clubs, with supporters becoming more fully engaged and excited by the prospect of having their clubs' season kept alive, whereas before there was hardly a flicker of interest in the latter stages as clubs drifted towards a tame, flat conclusion and apathy was the over-riding emotion. The race has become a separate, discrete competition within the structure of each division, adding another dimension to the regular season. Furthermore the enticing prospect of a Wembley Final energised and enlivened the tail-end of the season. Burnley fan and former Director of Communications and Strategy to Tony Blair, Alastair Campbell, concurs: "The main advantage is that excitement it brings at the end of the season. In the pre Play-Off days, the season was more or less over for many of the clubs with weeks to go.

The Play-Offs can keep a dozen or more clubs involved and engaged to the last couple of matches. The two-leg knock-out format, and then a Wembley Final, keeps the season going long and hard. I wouldn't change a thing."

For Palace fan and comedian Kevin Day, his early memories of life before the Play-Offs is one of frustration and ennui. "For most of that exuberant, over-indulged, shoulder-padded and Ben Elton-ed decade we were losing to Shrewsbury and Notts County. If we were knocked out of the cup in the 3rd round; I say 'if'; then our season was pretty much over by February. Even when we reached the heady heights of fifth one season, we were so far behind the automatic spot that I may as well have eaten my season ticket at the same time as my Easter Eggs."

Day's relief at finding an escape route from this tedium is clear. "The Play-Offs then offered a way out. And as one of my mates said, it does seem unfair that this could reward a piss-poor team, but as we were that piss-poor team, why not make the most of it?!" He continues about his first brush with the Play-Offs: "As it happened, I got a glimpse of Play-Off fever early on. The first-ever Third Division Play-Offs between Swindon and Gillingham went to a replay at Selhurst Park. It was a cracking match played with a crackling atmosphere that was unlike any at Selhurst for quite a while. It was clear already that a Play-Offs win brought a different kind of joy. And the irony of my initial opposition is that, as a Palace fan, I have experienced that different kind of joy more times than any other club."

The Play-Offs certainly ensure that the season goes to the wire for a fair few clubs and it would be highly unusual for there not to be at least half a dozen clubs in the hunt for the Play-Offs places across all three divisions right up to the last games. So for example in the 2012/13 season, there were four Championship clubs – Bolton, Palace, Leicester and Forest – all vying for the last two berths going into the final weekend and during the course of their concluding league game each one of them had a spell when they were in the Play-Offs for a while. The last day of the season provides another one of those gut-churning, tension-laden afternoons, as the final permutations of the Play-Offs unfold. Most fans have had to endure the apprehension of watching their own team play – often with radio glued to the ear or, more likely nowadays, mobiles flickering with the scores from the key games – whilst keeping tabs on what is going on in other matches as the consequences rebound around the country.

These fans are at the end of a journey of widely contrasting emotions where a mixture of hope and expectation is encouraged by even a limited run of success, then tempered by a sudden loss of form. The belief that anyone can reach the Play-Offs has become almost a mantra stretching all the way from pre-season deliberations through to the early season adjustments, followed by the mid-season assessment and on to the very last knockings of the league campaign and beyond. Such a depth of engagement is one of the reasons why people started to return to following football in significant numbers just as the game had reached its nadir. Fans became hooked once again as the slow burn of a forty-six-match league campaign was suddenly ignited. There was a quickening of the pulse as teams were thrust into the febrile, intoxicating atmosphere of a semi-final against familiar foe. The whole season was now on the line and that inevitably racked up the tension to an almost unbearable degree.

There is a palpable strengthening of the bond between the club and the fans during a Play-Offs campaign. Having been through the rigours of a long season, this is the sharp end when hero status can be achieved by players who make a vital contribution. Clarke Carlisle, former PFA chairman, quotes the example of Graham Alexander, who had been a Preston stalwart for many years but then became a firm Burnley favourite almost overnight after their Play-Offs victory in 2009. Alexander is just one of many long-serving players who have cemented their reputation with the fans following Play-Offs exploits. The likes of Steve Walsh, Dion Dublin and Dean Windass are all vastly experienced but are most likely to be remembered for scoring winning goals in the Play-Offs rather than anything else in their extensive careers. Saša Ilić will always be revered by Charlton fans for that penalty save from Michael Gray in the 1998 Final rather than the club record ten consecutive clean sheets he kept prior to that. It is in such a decisive moment that reputations are forged or destroyed, as Gray will also testify.

Despite these players making numerous appearances and scoring many goals or making crucial saves in their careers, the one thing that fans often associate them with is their Play-Offs contribution. Given that the fans have endured the tension, it is not surprising that the outpouring of relief manifests itself in the odd spot of idolatry. There is an additional sense of unity forged within the club that surrounds and engulfs all those who have been on this journey, underpinned by fans and players having been through this cathartic experience together.

Considering the stakes are so high, the quality of the Finals has generally been of a very good standard, with plenty of high-scoring, dramatic games. A host of memorable matches have delighted neutrals, captivated the media and enraptured the protagonists. As the importance of the outcome is so great it would have been expected that a series of taut, tense affairs would follow, providing little in terms of excitement. But there has been much to admire in the generally positive approach that clubs have adopted when facing matches of such significance. For example, the Championship Final has featured nearly ninety goals over twenty-seven years averaging over three goals a game, and on five occasions there have been six or more goals. Compare that to the FA Cup Final, which over the same period averages less than 2½ goals per match, with only the 2006 Final amassing six goals. Such a comparison suggests there is, surprisingly, a little more freedom and sense of adventure in the approach from the Play-Offs finalists, which adds considerably to the levels of excitement and entertainment on offer. I suspect that on the evidence of recent matches, most objective fans looking for a good game would opt to watch one of the Play-Offs rather than an FA Cup Final.

As a fan who has experienced both Play-Off and FA Cup Finals I can relate to the difference in moods between the two. For the FA Cup Final of 1990 there was a general feeling of elation mixed with pride as Palace were about to make their first appearance, and although ultimately we lost in a replay, the overriding sense was still one of euphoria. We had enjoyed the journey and even in defeat we celebrated the achievement of just being there. For the Play-Offs Finals, the build-up is racked with tension as the whole season hinges on that one game, the pressure huge as being runners-up ultimately represents nothing. Unlike the honour of being an FA Cup finalist (and quite often enjoying the benefit of securing a place in Europe) there is nothing to console the loser of a Play-Offs Final. There is the frustration of having come all that way, after forty-nine games and been so close to promotion but now facing the prospect of remaining in the same division and having to start all over again next season. There is a distinctly hollow feeling, an emptiness that lingers and quite often spills into the next season unless the negativity is contained.

The depth of this frustration has been acknowledged by the Championship Play-Offs winners, as tradition now dictates that they magnanimously agree to waive their half of the 50 per cent share of gate receipts from the Final. Whilst the rules stipulate that this 50 per cent should be shared between the two finalists, this revenue is actually given solely to the defeated team, cushioning the financial blow of losing out. Of course the winners can afford to be generous as they have secured the bigger prize of promotion but it does show that there is room for sympathy for their opponents. It is a gesture, and a relatively small gesture at that, but at least it is an example of the more egalitarian attitude of football at the lower level. This healthy approach, whereby the winner does not necessarily take all, is seldom exhibited elsewhere in football, so is all the more refreshing because of its rarity.

For fans of lower-league clubs the Play-Offs have become such an important and intriguing part of their season that they now occupy a place amidst the pre-season discussions and debate over a club's prospects. Talk of securing a

Play-Offs spot becomes part of that nascent optimism which is such a perennial feature of being a fan. Before the start of the season, many supporters who are realistic enough to know that their team are not automatic promotion candidates console themselves with the aspiration of being in contention for that much-sought-after Play-Offs place. It is as if the Play-Offs have become part of the supporters' DNA, a crucial element that provides a clear sense of purpose and meaning to the coming season. The resilience of supporters in making a virtue of clinging on to even the slightest of straws is an admirable trait and provides an essential security blanket that wards off feelings of inadequacy.

The benefit of this approach is that it combines realism with a sense of fantasy, allowing the fans to dream, which is an essential ingredient of supporting a team of limited means. Additionally, this is not a crazy, unattainable dream but it allows the fan to be rooted in the often grim acceptance that their team is not good enough to make the grade whilst anyone can still imagine scraping into the Play-Offs. After all, a top six finish is eminently attainable even by the weaker-looking sides. A strong run at the right time can make all the difference so even the most pessimistic of fans can envisage this small step being within their club's grasp. Failing that, the sum of their ambition must be steering clear of relegation trouble, as mid-table anonymity is pretty much a thing of the past.

The further advantage for the fan is that this tantalising glimpse of promotion is not blown away by a poor start to the season. The faith can be justified by past experience that being in the bottom six at Christmas is not a bar to getting into the Play-Offs. The dream can remain alive based on the examples of clubs making remarkable recoveries from seemingly hopeless positions halfway through the season and bounding up the table to then suddenly appear in the Play-Off positions at the last moment.

Alas, the reality is slightly different; research shows that the vast majority of clubs who compete in the Play-Offs occupy the upper reaches of the league for much of the season. In twenty-seven years, the average position for the Play-Off winners at the halfway stage of the league season is as shown in the chart below.

So under normal circumstances, at the midpoint of the season, the clubs destined for the four available slots are either already occupying a Play-Offs position or are just on the fringes of contention. Taking the Championship (or its equivalent) as an example, only twice out of twenty-seven seasons have clubs gained promotion through the Play-Offs having been outside

The Championship	**6th**
League One	**5th**
League Two	**9th***

*Unlike the other two divisions League Two includes those finishing 4th–7th in Play-Off places.

the top ten at the mid-point, a ratio of less than 7.5 per cent so not particularly encouraging. Crystal Palace's 2003/04 run from 21st after twenty-three games to breaking into the Play-Off places for the first time after the penultimate game is the outstanding example of a team completing such a dramatic transformation, seemingly proving Iain Dowie's concept of 'bouncebackability', but this is very much the exception that proves the rule.

There is a distinctly wishful element behind the notion that teams can catapult themselves into the Play-Offs from nowhere, but the feeling is still strong enough amongst fans that it can happen, allowing them to keep the faith. Fan's logic dictates that if something is within the realms of the possible, then there is sufficient reason to imagine that the fortunes of the club will turn around. The flame of hope and expectation is not extinguished by fact, but fuelled by belief. Fans can live off myths and misconceptions, so why let the truth get in the way? Getting into the Play-Offs is now so ingrained into everyone's expectations at the outset of the season that a fan survey undertaken by the Football League for 2012/13 season had 'Securing a Play-Off place' as one of the stated objectives for the season ahead. Indeed in an interview before the start of the 2013/14 season, Mick McCarthy, Ipswich's experienced and wily manager, openly admitted when discussing prospects of the season that lay ahead that his ambition was limited to a Play-Offs berth. "We've got to be aiming at that," said McCarthy ahead of tricky games against relegated Reading and Queens Park Rangers in Ipswich's first two away outings. "It's a tough start, but I don't think anybody will be rubbing their hands thinking, 'Happy days, Ipswich are coming here and they're going to be a soft touch,' because they know we're not – we'll aim for as high as we can possibly finish." McCarthy may have been unaware of the less than successful record of Ipswich; otherwise he may have adjusted his sights somewhat.

McCarthy's pragmatic attitude is summed up as a grudging acceptance that the club are not quite good enough for automatic promotion but there's always the escape route offered by the Play-Offs. So no longer do we have to wait for the first manager to comment "we can still make the Play-Offs" after a shaky start to the league campaign. Such a call to arms is football's equivalent to hearing the first cuckoo, which traditionally heralded the onset of spring, and is usually issued as early as September following a handful of games without a victory and with the team being cast adrift at the foot of the table. This gives the fans a glimmer of positivity that the season can be rescued and all is not lost. McCarthy trumped that by making his statement before a ball had been kicked. Some would accuse him of limited ambition but others would acknowledge the practical approach to the season ahead.

The Play-Offs have become the default position for many fans of middle-ranking clubs who, without them, would be facing a long grim nine months slog, leaving the only aim as merely avoiding relegation. Such a prospect does not leave much to excite or entice the punters; hanging on to an escape route from such drudgery has proved an important crutch for a whole host of fans across the country, enlivening and invigorating their approach to the forthcoming season and during its formative stages. In a way the Play-Offs have developed into the fans' equivalent of the Holy Grail; an ideal to strive for but primarily an illusion.

However, there is some solace for those still dreaming of a dramatic rescue, there having been a couple of recent examples of clubs breaking out of the mid-table morass and achieving promotion from inauspicious beginnings. In the 2011/12 League Two season, Crewe Alexandra managed to recover from losing their first four games and a generally poor start which left them fifteenth at the halfway stage. A strong unbeaten thirteen-match run up to the end of the season saw them climb into the last Play-Off slot from where they beat Southend United in the semi-final and Cheltenham in the Final to secure what would have seemed the unlikeliest of promotions throughout the early part of their campaign.

Crewe's notable achievement follows a similar story to Stevenage the year before, who steadily climbed the table to reach the Play-Offs from being seemingly marooned in mid-table at the midpoint of the season. They were eighteenth in January but recovered well, eventually beating Torquay in the Final at Old Trafford to achieve back-to-back promotions and a first tilt at League One. More recently, Bradford's impressive push from an unpromising mid-table slot to seventh, and eventually Play-Offs glory, after their League Cup exploits had ended, gives us all hope.

So at least there is some precedent from these three clubs to keep those idealistic Play-Off fires burning, even if history is not littered with a massive body of evidence. It is clear that fans do not need much to get them going, many believing that their club will be able to shrug off a poor start to the season and catapult themselves into the Play-Offs, to ultimately savour success from the most unpromising of situations and in general to live the dream. There is an infinite capacity, inherent in every fan, to believe that miracles do happen and to be stubbornly oblivious to facts and figures. Unshakeable belief, backed up by an all-consuming blind spot, form the bedrock of many supporters' attitudes whose clubs do not provide them with much recent glory to feed off. They will not budge until harsh reality hits home, and, even then, there is always next season's push for the Play-Offs to console them.

Qualifying for the Play-Offs can often be an achievement in itself, but it can conversely also be a dangerous time for the fans as it is at this stage that those idle fantasies of promotion begin to crystallise, with the elusive objective suddenly becoming a plausible aim. As that well-worn cliché (attributed rightly or wrongly to Adrian Chiles) testifies, "it's the hope that kills you". Driven by the impetus of being one of the semi-finalists, the fans can sense that this could well be their moment and it all comes frighteningly close to fruition. If the semis are successfully navigated then the Final looms ever larger and its one-off nature lends itself to contemplation of the possible turning into the probable. The fans are now agog with anticipation and the rush is on to secure a ticket for the biggest game in years.

Even those people with only a loose association with the club are suddenly energised. Clubs with average attendances barely in five figures will have 30,000-plus heading for Wembley. For clubs unaccustomed to such clamour these can be heady times and this is one of the beauties of the Play-Offs as clubs revel in this unlikely and intoxicating atmosphere. It would have been highly doubtful that these additional supporters would have made the trip in such numbers back in the troubled times of the mid-1980s, which underlines how far football has moved away from the negative image that had enveloped the game.

The total audience for the Play-Offs Finals over the last six seasons has reached over 1 million with an average attendance of just under 60,000 for each Final. Crucially, the vast majority of those 60,000 people are fans of the finalists. Whether they are diehards, lapsed or occasional, they will have a connection of some sort. In comparison to the FA Cup, where the protagonists only receive just over 50 per cent of tickets between them with the remainder going to the likes of local Football Associations, other league clubs and Club Wembley Members, the allocation of Play-Offs Finals tickets is closer to 90 per cent for the competing clubs. So even though there were 4,000 fewer people at the Championship Final of 2013 than the 86,000 attending the FA Cup Final between Manchester City and Wigan, Crystal Palace and Watford each received initial allocations of around 35,000 tickets compared to 25,000 for City and Wigan. Even a fair number of the 18,000 Club Wembley tickets somehow make their way to supporters, thereby reducing the proportion of 'neutrals', aka the disinterested. By glimpsing at the multitude of fan sites for each competing club it is clear how totally immersed the fans are in what is the biggest day of their supporting lives. The frisson of excitement is almost tangible, carrying tens of thousands on a tide of emotion and undiluted passion. As this game can determine the direction of each club in the short and long term, no other game quite matches the thrill and expectations of a Play-Offs Final.

The impressive attendance levels for the Play-Offs show that the fans are very much engaged and attracted by the spectacle and drama that so often unfolds, and, no doubt, they will continue to be so. Indeed of the seventy-four clubs that have reached the Finals since the one-off Final was introduced in 1990, a staggering sixty-three have surpassed their home attendance record at the Final. As the vast majority of those record attendances date back to the 1960s or before, the Finals have become crucial landmarks in the recent history of numerous clubs, typically being watched by more of their fans than any other match had been in the last five decades.

To a certain extent appearing in the Play-Offs has replaced the increasingly remote dream of an FA Cup Final appearance, which (as has been explored elsewhere in this book) is generally becoming the preserve of the bigger fish. The Play-Offs Final may not have the tradition going back over 140 years but it is ultimately more significant to the future of the clubs involved. More often than not it is the biggest match that the supporters, players and managers will share with that club. For example, any Blackpool fans under the age of sixty would not have been alive when they last reached an FA Cup Final in 1953, so the four Play-Offs promotions culminating in the 2010 Championship victory hold much more resonance for those supporters. This sense of creating history is illustrated by the fact that in the 2012 Final Ian Evatt equalled the record number of three Wembley appearances for Blackpool, sharing this honour with club greats Stanley Matthews and Stan Mortensen.

Even for the fans of West Ham, a bigger club that has spent most of the last four decades in the top division, the 2012 Final was their first visit to Wembley since 1981. Over those thirty-one years, they had contested two Play-Off Finals and an FA Cup Final but all three took place at the Millennium Stadium, so a large proportion of Hammers fans had the chance to walk up Wembley Way to see their club for the very first time. Even though the magic of a trip to Wembley has been slightly undermined by the hosting of FA Cup semi-finals there, the integrity and distinctive pleasure of appearing in the Play-Offs Finals is still intact and cherished by those involved.

Roger Maslin, Managing Director of Wembley Stadium, is in no doubt about the special nature of the day; he recalls that many of his most memorable moments in his fourteen years at Wembley are drawn from watching the sheer, unadulterated joy of the fans arriving for the Play-Offs, drawn to Wembley "as if they were iron filings with that wonderful magnetic pull for what is the epitome for these fans". Maslin also points to the dichotomy between winning and losing, as within a few minutes of the final whistle one half of the stadium is in raptures whilst the other half has emptied. In no other match throughout the country and especially at the national stadium, Maslin asserts, is the contrast so striking as that in the wake of the Play-Offs. The winners revel in their glory whilst the losers beat a hasty retreat from the scene of the crime.

A new generation of fans will now have that opportunity to enjoy the big occasion, adding their own colourful, contemporary stories to the folklore of their club rather than relying on tales of yesteryear and distant memories passed down from the older fans. The whole experience of entering the Play-Offs and reaching the Finals binds those fans closer to the club, almost irrespective of the result. For once there is no other domestic football to compete with, the clubs are at the centre of the media's and football world's attention. In complete contrast to the early years when there was barely any recognition of their existence, you can see how far the Play-Offs have come. There is a stronger sense of attachment and belonging derived from that sense of importance, especially as the spotlight is so rarely trained on the lower levels of the football pyramid. Thus the Play-Offs genuinely offer the current crop of fans a rich seam of strong, vivid memories, establishing and embellishing their affinity with their club.

Back to Kevin Day, who sums up that Play-Offs feeling, after being fortunate enough to be allowed to take the trophy to stage at a Palace Comedy night shortly after the win against Watford. "It struck me how grand and heavy the trophy is. And we got that for finishing fifth in the league. The Champions' trophy was smaller than ours! And there really is no way better to get promoted. If you could guarantee a Wembley win you'd be nagging your players to take it easy in the league from around Easter (which is almost where we came in isn't it?)." Day touches on the heart of the matter: the Play-Offs do offer a gloriously convoluted path to promotion, riddled with tension and imponderables compared to the straightforward, rather more prosaic demands of going up automatically.

The restoration of pride in the club is a key factor and that affinity is well established in his mind as Day continues. "We now have a unique relationship with the Championship Play-Offs. We've won it a record four times and only lost one. We've won it in every decade since it was introduced. We're the only team to have won it the old two-legged way, at Cardiff and at Wembley (both old and new). In fact, for all we moan about under-achieving, Palace are in the Play-Offs Final just about every five years. And each visit seems to get better. I still think a league system is fairer, but the excitement of that mini-league and Final is incredible almost to the point of being unbearable. It was impossible for me to watch the game at Brighton (2nd leg of the 2013 semi-final); I had to walk the streets of Streatham until an explosion of texts brought good news." Day's story concludes with the 2013 Final. "The last thirteen minutes at Wembley were exquisite agony but the hours before and after – filled with colour, noise, friends, family, alcohol, disbelief and, of course, tears – were special. God bless the Play-Offs!"

Given the choice between reaching an FA Cup Final or Play-Offs Final, I believe that most fans would opt for the latter. There is so much more to be gained in terms of the future of the club, and whilst prestige and heritage is potentially nice to have, gaining promotion is nearly always a more pressing requirement. Next season's status easily outweighs the addition to the trophy cabinet and has far greater long-term benefits.

Fans may be hopelessly romantic and idealistic on the surface but underneath it all there is a kernel of practicability, which yearns for the opportunity to move up the football ladder. Plying your trade in the lower divisions may be good for the soul but ultimately nearly all fans want to get the chance for their club to test themselves at a higher level.

Throughout the history of the Play-Offs the fans' enthusiastic endorsement has been the cornerstone upon which their success has flourished. The whole-hearted support from the outset has grown and developed to the very pinnacle of fandom, as summed up by Roger Stubbs, a lifelong West Bromwich Albion fan. When it reaches all members of the family, as it did for the Stubbs's in the Division Three Final of 1993 when they overcame Port Vale 3-0, the impact is lasting. "It was the first time all three of my children had been to Wembley, the last big occasion my mum and dad would go. We had been in the wilderness since leaving the top division in 1973." Stubbs adds, "I remember saying that many of the top clubs' supporters would not get as much enjoyment from winning the Champions League as we did that day." Stubbs's point is a very good one as the vast majority of fans will not get within a sniff of the Champions League, which is now effectively a closed shop, rotated between the five biggest clubs. That experience is too distant, too far removed, but many will have followed their club in the Play-Offs.

By coincidence I went to the West Brom versus Port Vale match and can still remember vividly the sensational atmosphere. It was the first time I had heard the recently launched Baggies' 'Boing-Boing' chant and it will always remain one of the most electrifying matches I have ever watched as a neutral. The remarkable environment of that day encapsulated the spirit of what the Play-Offs mean to the fans, which goes way beyond the normal match-day experience. The special bond that unites clubs and fans makes the Play-Offs both distinctive and desirable. If anybody has any doubt over this point they should attend one of the Finals and sample the unique, all-consuming atmosphere that prevails. Underpinned by tension and riddled with nerves this makes for a day with a highly wrought emotional charge that is almost tangible and fizzes in the air. No other game feels quite like a Play-Offs Final or means as much. There is something verging on the cathartic for the supporters, as this is the point to which everything has built up.

Never have so many fans been so deeply involved and enjoyed so much excitement across the domestic football scene, and when trying to assess the depth of feeling, it is always instructive to get the viewpoint of a loser, so again we turn to beleaguered Bristol City fan, Mark Watson, who sums up the sense of loss. "People who support huge clubs don't always understand how this feels: worse even than losing an FA Cup Final. This isn't just about a trophy – it's about the whole status of your club. It's about either playing Torquay next season, or Leeds. And especially if you've blown your chance of automatic promotion, it's a massive blow." As Watson underlines, by getting to that showpiece Final and tasting the exalted, elevated life albeit briefly, the downside is so much harder to bear. It is as if a malevolent spirit has dangled the prize in front of your very eyes, only to snatch it away just as you are about to grab it, and it is all the more tantalising and soul-destroying when it happens.

And for a postscript of misery here is Gavin Barber, of Ipswich blog *Turnstile Blues,* on Ipswich's travails in the late 1990s:

HEROES & VILLAINS

PORTMAN ROAD SEMI-FINAL FAILURES 1997-99

The stormy late-1990s relationship between Ipswich Town and the Play-Offs was as unexpected as it was traumatic. Town had featured in the first-ever Play-Offs tournament, in 1987 (in which, inevitably, they lost in the semi-final), but spent the following decade giving them a wide berth, either by loitering in mid-table like surly teenagers at a family wedding, or by racing straight up to the inaugural Premier League as champions in 1992, only to return three years later.

By 1996, life back in the second tier wasn't going that well. George Burley was still striving to impose himself on a squad that lacked discipline and cohesion. In November 1996, following a run of one win in ten games, just 7,086 people turned up for a Tuesday evening game against Swindon. At that time, the idea that Burley's team would be inches away from a Wembley place by the end of the season seemed, to say the least, remote. But an inspired second half to the season, including a run of five consecutive wins in April, saw Town finish fourth in the table. Suddenly we were in the grip of the Play-Offs, and who was to know that it would be four more long years before they'd let us go?

The 1996-97 semi-final was against Sheffield United and a bad-tempered affair. In fact, many Town fans still regard Sheffield United as 'the Norwich of the North' as a direct result of this. The Blades went through on away goals after a 2-2 draw in the second leg at Portman Road. Steve Sedgeley hit the post with a free-kick in extra time, and a game of nasty, niggly fouls ended with some less-than-sporting words being exchanged between Jan-Åage Fjørtoft and home fans' favourite Mauricio Taricco. We were only beginning to find out how cruel the Play-Offs could be.

Twelve months later, and after another impressive late-season run, Town went into a Play-Offs semi-final against Charlton with renewed confidence. Portman Road was packed for a ridiculously sunny afternoon in the first leg. There were blue and white balloons everywhere, and an air of fevered anticipation. It didn't last. Once again it was a snarly sort of a game. Jamie Clapham put through his own net and the second half descended into a tense and tedious scrap. Danny Mills was sent off but Town couldn't capitalise. The atmosphere at the end was so flat, it was as if a giant cartoon anvil had been dropped on Portman Road. Things didn't get any better in the second leg, and it was Charlton who progressed.

Fast-forward twelve months to 1999, and Ipswich were starting to look like a different proposition. Burley had assembled an exciting side, typified by the pace and trickery of Kieron Dyer and the sharp finishing of David Johnson. Town had narrowly failed to go up automatically, but surely that didn't matter? Bolton were the opponents this time. We lost 1-0 in the first leg at the Reebok. Could've been worse. Surely we could finish off Colin Todd's lumpy Lancastrians at Portman Road?

Here's a thing we were learning about the Play-Offs: they're not nice. They're all hyped up as the pinnacle of excitement and drama, but they're not the place to go if you want to see any actual football. Bolton came to Portman Road for the second leg with a game plan that should have been familiar by then – they kicked everything that moved. We were learning (failing to learn, perhaps) that other teams tactical preparation for Play-Off semi-finals appeared to consist of an intensive course in sly trips, flailing elbows, and kickboxing on the blind-side of the referee. And they were better at it than us.

Even so, that second leg at Portman Road in 1999. The . . . Sheer . . . Pain . . . Of . . . It. Matt Holland levelled the tie in the first half. Yay us! We're definitely going to Wembley this time. The law of averages says so. The law of averages, as it turned out, said so what? Bolton equalised, putting them back ahead on aggregate. Dyer scored for us – we just need one more goal now! Of course not. It was Bolton – whose forward line consisted of future Barcelona star, Eidur

Gudjohnsen, and big bloke who kicked people, Bob Taylor – who got another one. We were heading out again. No! Dyer's cross-shot took the tie into extra time. When's the last train? Who cares. This is the Play-Offs. This is OUR YEAR.

It wasn't our year, 1999. Taylor scored again in extra time. Holland levelled the scores on aggregate but we were still behind on away goals, and never really looked like making the decisive breakthrough. I remember us getting a corner in injury time of extra time. The crowd urged goalkeeper Richard Wright to go up for it. He hesitated, looking nervously at the bench. Burley seemed to shrug, as if to say "go up if you want, what does it matter now?" For some reason he held back. One more goal needed to redeem nine months of slog, and he held back. I've always imagined that if he had made that forward run, he'd have powered a header into the corner and passed into Play-Offs folklore. But he didn't, and it was all over once again, and we spent another summer hating football and Life.

But I'm glad Wrighty didn't go up for that corner, because if he had, and he'd scored, we might never have ended up at Wembley in 2000, and thousands of Town fans wouldn't have the cherished memories of that 4-2 win against Barnsley that we now have. I can quite categorically say, with extensive experience of the latter, and glorious if limited experience of the former, that the Play-Offs are the best way to win and the worst way to lose.

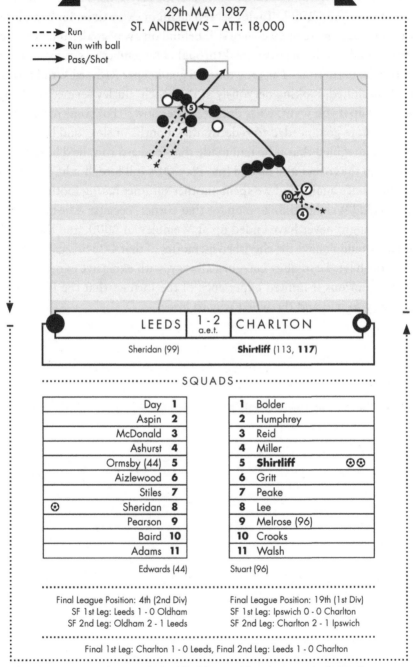

29th MAY 1987
ST. ANDREW'S – ATT: 18,000

- - -▶ Run
· · · · ·▶ Run with ball
——▶ Pass/Shot

LEEDS	1 - 2 a.e.t.	CHARLTON

Sheridan (99)　　　　**Shirtliff** (113, **117**)

···················· SQUADS ····················

	Day	**1**	**1**	Bolder
	Aspin	**2**	**2**	Humphrey
	McDonald	**3**	**3**	Reid
	Ashurst	**4**	**4**	Miller
	Ormsby (44)	**5**	**5**	**Shirtliff** ⚽⚽
	Aizlewood	**6**	**6**	Gritt
	Stiles	**7**	**7**	Peake
⚽	Sheridan	**8**	**8**	Lee
	Pearson	**9**	**9**	Melrose (96)
	Baird	**10**	**10**	Crooks
	Adams	**11**	**11**	Walsh

Edwards (44)　　　　　　　　Stuart (96)

Final League Position: 4th (2nd Div)　　Final League Position: 19th (1st Div)
SF 1st Leg: Leeds 1 - 0 Oldham　　　　SF 1st Leg: Ipswich 0 - 0 Charlton
SF 2nd Leg: Oldham 2 - 1 Leeds　　　　SF 2nd Leg: Charlton 2 - 1 Ipswich

Final 1st Leg: Charlton 1 - 0 Leeds, Final 2nd Leg: Leeds 1 - 0 Charlton

GOAL FACT: In his career Shirtliff's fifteen goals came at an average of one
every thirty-four matches; in this match he scored two in the space of four minutes.

LIFT-OFF

The 1986/87 football season was memorable for many reasons. The Merseyside clubs occupied the top two positions in the First Division, with Everton pipping Liverpool to the title. Ron Atkinson was dismissed by Manchester United in November and replaced by the Aberdeen manager, a relatively low-key appointment in the shape of one Alex Ferguson. Lincoln City became the first club relegated automatically to the Football Conference. And just in case anyone may have overlooked it, the Play-Offs were launched. It would have been entirely possible to miss the Play-Offs given the way the media shunned their arrival and the League's timid, almost apologetic, approach to their introduction.

The very first Play-Offs took place in May 1987, when there happened to be one of the finest FA Cup Finals of recent times. I remember vividly meeting up with a group of friends to watch the game and it feeling like a massive event. The weekend revolved around the FA Cup Final; it was the centerpiece even though none of us supported either finalist. We gathered together because there was a sense of occasion and that is what you did in those halcyon days. Very few of this group would have noticed that the Play-Offs were already underway, even though there were plenty of fans of lower-league teams. One of the main reasons why they slipped by unnoticed was because the media coverage was so minimal.

Looking at *The Times* newspaper coverage from May 1987, there was barely a mention of the first legs of the semi-finals that took place a couple of days before the Cup Final on 14th May. The sports pages were dedicated to the run-up to the FA Cup Final, with endless player profiles, and nothing was going to be allowed to distract attention from that all-important match at Wembley. As an illustration, here is the full report of Aldershot's first-leg semi-final against Bolton Wanderers:

"Gary Johnson raised Aldershot's hopes of third division football next season with a goal 13 minutes from the end."

Not the most descriptive or detailed coverage, with less than twenty words expended in total. Even though it was a Fourth Division match, the scant exposure is telling as the the Play-Offs struggled to win the attention of the media and gain public approval.

Other Play-Offs matches did warrant slightly more in-depth coverage, which was not difficult, with the Leeds vs Oldham Division Two game running to a full seven paragraphs. The relative lack of importance of football in general and the Play-Offs in particular was striking. To put this into perspective there was considerably more space devoted to a couple of cricket matches than to all six of the Play-Offs semi-final first legs. Those cricket matches were not Test Matches, One Day Internationals or even high-profile county games, but Pakistan's tour match with Somerset and a Minor Counties game against Glamorgan. Such an imbalance in favour of cricket, and pretty inconsequential cricket at that, would be difficult to imagine now.

By the second leg of the semi-finals there was a little more space devoted to the Play-Offs but this was nothing on a par with what happens today, as can be judged by the Wolves–Colchester report: "A goalless draw yesterday was enough to secure Wolverhampton Wanderers, 2-0 leaders from the first leg, a place in the Fourth Division Play-Off Final at the expense of Colchester United." Again this is not exactly the level of detail one would see now. By the time Wolves reached the Finals there were a few more column inches and even the odd photograph but exposure was still partial at best. Within the coverage itself, minimal though it was, it is interesting to note the relatively negative attitude portrayed towards the Play-Offs, such as the following words bemoaning the situation of Oldham, "who could feel hard done by at having to justify themselves all over again after finishing eight [actually seven] points in front of Leeds".

Understandably Joe Royle, the Oldham manager, was not so keen on the new system either, as he faced up to the consequences of his side's gut-wrenching defeat. "We finished seven points clear of Leeds," he said. "And so to go out on away goals to them means there is something unjust. I welcomed the Play-Offs but possibly hadn't considered the long-term ramifications."

Ultimately those "long-term ramifications" were all for the good but Royle's disappointment was still raw and his comments were subjective. Royle had to wait a while for his next experience of the Play-Offs but that was to be a much happier occasion and considerably more dramatic, when he was in charge of Manchester City's extraordinary 1999 success.

Less understandable was the reaction of Lou Macari, who oversaw Swindon's triumph in the Division Three Final but in that moment of victory, decided to call for an end to the Play-Offs system. "I never want to go through a night like that again," he said. "The Play-Offs are unfair and should be scrapped." Goodness knows what sort of tirade might have followed if Macari's team had lost. As *The Times* pointed out, "The 18,491 supporters who travelled to South London [for the replay at Selhurst Park] may disagree with Macari's view. The home and away legs produced a level of entertainment which should not have been expected considering so much was at stake, yet the teams managed to raise the tempo, even higher on neutral ground." And in this comment lies a central conundrum: the fluctuating fortunes of the teams can seem incredibly unjust but the Play-Offs do provide gripping delectation for neutral onlookers and observers.

What could not be denied was the level of excitement and drama that this first series of games generated, as acknowledged by *The Times* report on the Swindon versus Gillingham Third Division Final. "Yet another exhilarating match last night added further weight to the argument supporting the controversial Play-Off system; Swindon Town and Gillingham gave their all in an epic encounter." Macari's words of condemnation ring a little hollow considering what happened three years later when Swindon were denied the promotion they had secured through the Play-Offs because of a series of illegal payments made to players by chairman Brian Hillier and other club officials. I am not sure this outcome was what Macari had in mind when he called for them to be abolished.

There were taut, titanic tussles across all three divisional Play-Offs in 1987 with one semi-final in each division going to extra time and two being decided on that thinnest and cruellest of margins; the away goals rule. Added to which, two of the Finals went to a replay, so stretching the fans' nerves even further and prolonging the drama to such an extent that it would have been difficult to write the script without straining credulity. Looking at the games of 1987 in more detail shows just how extraordinary they were, a true cornucopia of pulsating action. The irony was that all of this passed under the radar for most, apart from those whose teams were involved.

It was not just the press that ignored the Play-Offs; there was barely any television coverage either. Trawling through the schedules of the main channels available there was not even a highlights package at a time when there was live coverage of an England vs Scotland match; not a full international as you might expect, but a schoolboys' fixture. There was even sufficient room in the schedule to accommodate a full hour's worth of highlights of The Dry Black-thorn London Pool Championship from that cauldron of international sport, the Orchard Theatre in Dartford. Compare the situation now where all fifteen matches are shown live, a minimum of twenty-two hours of action and usually a great deal more with the demands of extra time and penalty shoot-outs. The contrast could hardly be more striking.

So not much could distract us from the FA Cup Final, in which a plucky Coventry City overcame the firm favourites Tottenham, who had finished a free-scoring third in the old First Division. Although Coventry had been a respectable tenth in the top division, not many would have given City a prayer after the prolific Allen put Spurs ahead in the second minute. Most of the pre-match build-up had focused on the free-scoring team that David Pleat had assembled. But Coventry eventually prevailed 3-2 in an exciting tussle, which is remembered as much for a Gary Mabbutt own goal as for Keith Houchen's spectacular diving header. Very few FA Cup Finals have matched that 1987 game in the subsequent twenty-seven years; indeed the widely respected John Motson considers it to be the best Final he has commentated on in his vast experience of over forty years.

One of the most appealing aspects of this Final is that it was a victory for the underdog, as it was the following year when Wimbledon beat Liverpool 1-0, a match that was remembered for the result and Dave Beasant's penalty save rather than for the quality of the game itself. A couple more decent years ensued with Liverpool's emotionally charged post-Hillsborough 3-2 victory over Everton and Palace's valiant 3-3 tussle with Man United, which was then followed by the direst of replays. The FA Cup Final was generally enjoying a purple patch and was certainly the pre-eminent match domestically with media and public alike in its thrall. So just as the FA Cup Final reached its apogee, the little-heralded Play-Offs were launched, with the semi-finals straddled almost incognito either side of the FA Cup Final in May 1987.

In one of those intriguing coincidences that crop up every now and again, Coventry and Tottenham are amongst the dozen existing league clubs to have never competed in the Play-Offs. The Cup Final match between them seems to have been very much a watershed moment as the fortunes of the two competitions then started to head off in completely different directions. Whilst the venerable FA Cup began to lose its lustre, the unheralded Play-Offs made huge strides in creating a reputation for the most enticing and thrilling action. Tradition counts for a great deal in the football world and nobody would deny the fabulous history of 140 years that the FA Cup offers. With such longevity there is inevitably a sense of fatigue and as attitudes and priorities have changed so has the relative standing of each competition. The FA Cup is no longer the hallowed institution it once was, having lost some of its kudos compared to the more vigorous and upbeat perspective of the Play-Offs' progress over the last two decades. Shortly after their inauguration the FA Cup was to be given a good run for its money as the supreme end-of-season domestic competition.

Almost unnoticed by the football community as a whole, the Play-Offs burst into life in suitably exhilarating fashion during the close of the 1986/87 season. In this very first season there were plenty of twists and turns engulfing clubs, both large and small alike, testing the fortitude of even the most resolute fans. In May 1987 three clubs, former giants of the game that had been struggling in the previous few years, were thrust into the maelstrom of the Play-Offs. Wolverhampton Wanderers, Sunderland and Leeds United were embroiled in the first season and all three suffered at the hands of much smaller clubs. Their respective capitulations were symptomatic of the Play-Offs' endless capacity to surprise and shock, and merit closer inspection.

During the 1950s and 60s, Wolves, founder members of the league, had become one of England's top teams, making their mark at the vanguard of European club competition in its formative years. By the 1970s they were no longer such a force but were still solidly established in the top division, winning a couple of League Cups on the way. However, by 1986 they had dropped so far from grace, enduring three successive relegations, that they were languishing in the bottom tier, the old Fourth Division, for the first time in their history. The club was in imminent danger of going out of business as Simon Inglis pointed out in his book *League Football and the Men Who Made it*. "Wolves, who in the summer of 1986 were £2.5 million in debt and yet again tottering on the brink. The new Management Committee adopted the same line as its predecessors by stating that if Wolves dropped out they would not be replaced."

The club was at an all-time low and faced the bleak prospect of liquidation after their disastrous slide down the league. Any sliver of upwards trajectory was not to be sniffed at and so the glimpse of a small chance of salvation was offered when, having missed out on the top three and automatic promotion by a single point, they faced the minnows of Aldershot in the Division Four Play-Offs Final. Aldershot had already disposed of Bolton Wanderers – yet another league founder floundering in the bottom tier – in the semi-finals. Any expectation of beginning the ascent back up the league was decisively dashed as they surprisingly capitulated 3-0 over two legs to a team that had never risen higher than Division Three in their history, and never would. The attitude of Bobby Barnes, the scorer of an impressive twenty-six goals in this, his only season with the Shots (including two out of the three goals in the Final), is a clear illustration of the inferiority complex Aldershot carried into this match. The players were slightly in awe of their opponents, "who were such a great name and we were just thinking to ourselves how great it was to be playing at a large stadium like Molineux". The glaring disparity in size and stature between the two clubs was highlighted by the respective crowds for each leg of the Final. For the first leg, the Recreation Ground was bursting at the seams with a 5,000 capacity crowd whereas the return leg attracted just under 20,000 in a half-full Molineux. But it was Aldershot who prevailed and plunged Wolves back into crisis mode.

A few years later in March 1992, the tables had turned and it was ironic that Aldershot were to be the club that went bankrupt, were consequently expelled from the league and ultimately ceased to exist altogether. Wolves did survive and started to climb back up the league soon afterwards, gaining promotion as champions in the following season, with Bolton also getting promoted, both clubs responding well to the disappointment of their first-year failures. But it would be hard to imagine a nadir of darker proportions for this once-mighty club than the low point of that surprising Play-Offs defeat of 1987.

So Wolves were one of the first clubs to experience the raw and harsh realities of the new system, a glimmer of hope was being brutally extinguished, but they were not alone. Sunderland – another club that had fallen from its peak, having been one of the earlier members of the league – had a proud history but had been on a similar slide to Wolves, which culminated in them finishing one place above automatic relegation from Division Two at the end of the 1986/87 season. They were pitched into the Play-Offs with the three sides aiming for promotion from Division Three. A two-legged semi-final against lowly Gillingham offered Sunderland the chance of avoiding the indignity of playing third-tier football for the first time in their history. The intense drama and fluctuating fortunes of the two legs were a further portent of the Play-Offs' capacity to toy with the emotions. Any tie that ends 6-6 on aggregate is bound to have been a thrilling encounter and this was no exception. The man who scored five of Gillingham's goals, Tony Cascarino, has a unique perspective and insight into the impact of the match *(see Heroes & Villains feature at the end of this chapter)*.

This game set a powerful precedent for a host of spectacular Play-Offs matches but for Sunderland, just like Oldham, the climax ended in heartache as they lost by that most slender of margins, away goals. This loss not only beckoned in their only season in the third tier but also was the start of a series of eventful adventures in the Play-Offs for both Sunderland and Gillingham. Like so many of the ninety-five clubs which have played in them, both teams have experienced a mixture of highs and lows, stories which, together, comprise the rich and entertaining history of the Play-Offs. Sunderland's inglorious record is littered with lows and is covered in more, gory detail later in the book.

The combination of thrilling success and heartbreaking defeats was already established in the two lower-league Play-Offs of 1987. This pattern was continued and even extended in the third Play-Offs Final of that first year when Leeds met Charlton Athletic for the right to play in the top division. Leeds had beaten Oldham in the semi-finals by dint of substitute Keith Edwards' penchant for late goals. In the first leg, Edwards finally broke Oldham's stubborn resistance in the 89th minute; only to follow that in the second leg with a 90th-minute effort just as it seemed Oldham would prevail. "Athletic, who would have been promoted in any other season, were just sixty seconds away from moving forward into a two-legged Final vs Charlton Athletic to contest the last vacant place in the top flight", *The Times* reported. However, their nemesis Edwards popped up again to deny them and Leeds made it through on away goals. Considering Edwards only scored six goals in his whole career at Leeds this was clearly his stage, much to Oldham's chagrin.

Leeds had been the team to beat for a period in the 1970s and had reached a European Cup Final in 1975, but had dropped down to the Second Division in 1981. This Final offered a return to the top tier following a six-year absence. After both sides won their respective home legs 1-0, a replay was required and, as befits the drama of this first season of Play-Offs, the match went into extra time. When John Sheridan of Leeds finally broke the deadlock in the 9th minute of extra time United must have felt they were home and hosed. But they did not account for the unlikeliest intervention of Peter Shirtliff, Charlton's journeyman central defender. Shirtliff averaged less than one goal a season throughout a career that spanned over eighteen years, five hundred games and just fifteen goals overall. Against all the odds, Shirtliff broke the habit of a lifetime as he suddenly popped up to score two goals in the space of four minutes to cap another extraordinary climax. The fact that Shirtliff was a Yorkshireman, born and bred in Barnsley, and had previously played for Leeds' rivals Sheffield Wednesday, rubbed salt into the most painful of wounds.

Charlton survived, admittedly by the skin of their teeth, and became the only team out of six to earn a reprieve and avoid being relegated through the Play-Offs in those first two years. Chelsea, Sunderland, Sheffield United, Bolton and Rotherham were not so lucky, suffering the ignominy of failing to take the chance to redeem themselves against a team from a lower division. In a way this was more painful than just straight relegation; as these teams passed up the opportunity to stay in the division afforded by the Play-Offs it amounted to a double failure, leaving the club disappointed and demoralised as well as being relegated. Conversely, those teams that were promoted, namely Middlesbrough, Swindon, Walsall, Aldershot and Swansea, were on the crest of a wave, having battled through both semi-finals and Final to secure the newly available promotion place. It was fascinating to watch and gripped the previously disillusioned and disenchanted fans, encouraging them to return to the game they had pretty much abandoned. More than anything it showed there was some life and vibrancy in amongst the rubble that league football had become.

HEROES & VILLAINS

TONY CASCARINO, GILLINGHAM 1987

Tony Cascarino made over six hundred senior appearances, including playing in an FA Cup Final for Chelsea, and in France with Marseille and Nancy, scoring almost 250 goals in the process. He also represented Ireland eighty-eight times over a fourteen-year international career. So, as his excellent autobiography *Full Time*, revealed, he has a myriad of memories from his colourful and chequered career. But one of his clearest, and fondest, recollections is of his experience of the Play-Offs when he played for Gillingham. Given he was one of the players who took part, and quite a decisive part at that, in the Play-Offs' very first year, it is instructive to hear of the importance he attached to this newly launched competition.

Cascarino remembers very distinctly the impact that the Play-Offs had on him and the club at the time. "At first we didn't quite know what to expect but from day dot they were a huge success. It was like a big smack in the face." The Play-Offs clearly hit the ground running; there was no such thing as a 'soft launch' in those days. Cascarino was plunged so fully into the idea that there was no time to weigh up the merits, simply a burning desire to make the most of it. It was something of a personal epiphany as he began to appreciate the sheer significance of it all. What struck Cascarino most markedly was seeing the fans queuing up for tickets as the players arrived at the ground for training, which was such a novelty for the Gillingham players that it really brought it home that this was a taste of the big time. "We just didn't see that," Cascarino says. "It was quite surreal and bear in mind, this was happening at every club involved in the Play-Offs."

He explains how the feeling grew rapidly amongst the players, the fans, indeed everyone involved at the club that this was their moment and one that had to be seized with gusto. The players were enjoying the sensation of what it was like to play in front of big crowds, and the idea of being in a Cup Final made them all feel special. Indeed Cascarino was so taken by it that he wanted more and when Gillingham failed in their Final bid he was determined to move on to bigger and better things. "There was a big change in me and having experienced this higher life it proved to be the turning point in my career. For the first time I realised what football could do, the power it had, and it gave me an appetite for more and I wanted to be a part of it."

The result was that as soon as the Play-Offs were over, negotiations for Cascarino to join another club started; in fact they had already begun during the semi-final against Sunderland. It would have been unsettling enough and a major distraction to be courted by another club in the middle of the most important two matches of his lifetime. But it was even more of an issue when Cascarino discovered which club was pursuing him with some vigour.

"Before the second leg of the semi-final at Roker Park I was in a room with a bunch of journalists who were asking me about the chances of an imminent move to Sunderland, of all clubs. It was really weird as Bob Stokoe (the Sunderland manager) was in there whilst I was being interviewed." That Cascarino managed to focus on playing for his current club rather than possibly his future one is shown by the fact he added two more goals to his first-leg hat-trick, so there was no indecision there. Ultimately Cascarino rebuffed Sunderland's interest, as they were heading towards Division Three, courtesy of his five goals in the semi-final, and he went on to play at the top level for both club, domestically and abroad, and country. Those five semi-final goals are the ones about which he still remembers every single detail as if they were yesterday, whereas he can barely recall the majority of his league goals.

Cascarino started a trend that continues to this day, whereby players make their mark through the increased focus of the Play-Offs, which and provide the springboard for the next stage in their playing careers. Almost every year since 1987 a clutch of players has emerged and blossomed via the Play-Offs before moving on to a higher level, having proved themselves when the pressure is on. Without the stimulus of the Play-Offs, Cascarino admits that he may have never thought about getting further ahead in his playing career and could have stayed in the lower leagues for the remainder of his days rather than moving on to represent the likes of Chelsea, Celtic and Marseille.

On the negative side, when it came to the Final there is one thing that really rankles with Cascarino to this day. Gillingham would have beaten Swindon if the dreaded away goals rule had counted, having lost 2-1 away after winning the first leg 1-0 at home. The rule was not enforced for the Final and therefore it went to a replay that Swindon won. It pains him to think that this was the only time that a team suffered a Final defeat because of the *absence* of the away goals rule. The fact that twenty-eight years later this still irks Cascarino is an indication of how much it mattered to him at the time and is a strong example of how the powerful piquancy of the Play-Offs stays with the players.

But overall Cascarino retains "fantastic memories" of the Play-Offs, which undoubtedly rank in his mind alongside his two World Cups in 1990 and 1994 and the 1988 European Championship for Ireland as the outstanding achievements of his long, impressive career. He was, after all, the first player to score a Play-Offs hat-trick and that is a source of considerable pride and satisfaction for him to this day. In conclusion, he sums up his opinion of the Play-Offs: "Flip it round the other way and how would it feel if we removed them? There would be an outcry; that shows how valuable they have become."

Cascarino is right in that there would be a massive hullabaloo if anyone tried to turn the clock back and had the temerity to suggest the Play-Offs' removal. And he proves in the strength of his feelings and clarity of his memories that from the very start of their existence, the Play-Offs made a deep and lasting impression in changing the face of football. There was now a motivational force pushing forwards so that, where there had been apprehension and apathy before, there was now a clear sense of anticipation and excitement. Without such a positive influence, the future of Cascarino specifically, and of hundreds of players and league football in this country in general, could have been all so very different to what we know today. The Play-Offs may have sneaked in through the back door of the Heathrow Agreement but, as Cascarino discovered in that first year, they came to affect and improved the profile of a whole raft of people who should be eternally grateful for their introduction. Anyone underestimating the Play-Offs' almost instantaneous but long-lasting impact should spend some time talking to Tony Cascarino.

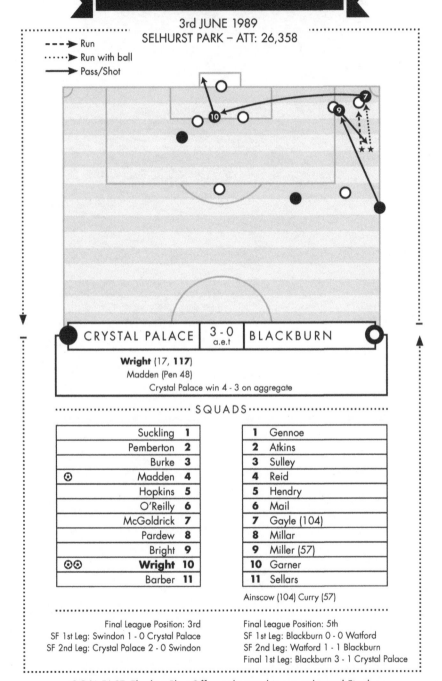

IAN WRIGHT 1988/89

SECOND DIVISION PLAY-OFFS FINAL 2ND LEG

3rd JUNE 1989
SELHURST PARK – ATT: 26,358

- - -► Run
······► Run with ball
——► Pass/Shot

CRYSTAL PALACE | 3 - 0 a.e.t | **BLACKBURN**

Wright (17, **117**)
Madden (Pen 48)
Crystal Palace win 4 - 3 on aggregate

········· S Q U A D S ·········

Suckling	**1**	
Pemberton	**2**	
Burke	**3**	
⚽ Madden	**4**	
Hopkins	**5**	
O'Reilly	**6**	
McGoldrick	**7**	
Pardew	**8**	
Bright	**9**	
⚽⚽ **Wright**	**10**	
Barber	**11**	

1	Gennoe
2	Atkins
3	Sulley
4	Reid
5	Hendry
6	Mail
7	Gayle (104)
8	Millar
9	Miller (57)
10	Garner
11	Sellars

Ainscow (104) Curry (57)

Final League Position: 3rd
SF 1st Leg: Swindon 1 - 0 Crystal Palace
SF 2nd Leg: Crystal Palace 2 - 0 Swindon

Final League Position: 5th
SF 1st Leg: Blackburn 0 - 0 Watford
SF 2nd Leg: Watford 1 - 1 Blackburn
Final 1st Leg: Blackburn 3 - 1 Crystal Palace

GOAL FACT: The last Play-Offs goal scored in a two-legged Final.

THE EARLY YEARS: 1988–90

The Play-Offs had well and truly arrived. It would be hard to envisage how to improve on the manner in which this first series of matches panned out. As an introduction, the matches grabbed the lapels of the watching public and shook them until they begged for mercy. They were very much in your face and everyone was thrust full pelt on to the breathless helter-skelter with which the Play-Offs are now associated. There is no other facet of English football that has sparked into life in quite this way; most new competitions take a little time to settle down before finding their feet. This was palpably not the case with the Play-Offs, as they began with a most audible bang. Maybe partly because there was no great fanfare about their arrival or any fuss made at their introduction, the Play-Offs generated their own momentum.

Through the far-reaching implications and their overall impact on English football, the Play-Offs deserve consideration as one of the key aspects of the modern game. Together the fans, players and clubs were instrumental in building a colourful, action-packed history over this critical period. They have encapsulated more drama and entertainment than many other longer-established, more traditional competitions. The early years of the Play-Offs were a period of rapid change, of seismic shifts in the landscape of English football to the point at which it could be argued that even the venerable FA Cup, which is now over 140 years old and pre-dates the league by more than ten years, was replaced as the true climax to the season. This may seem like heresy to traditionalists but the modern game has moved on so quickly that it has unpicked the tapestry that had lasted for so long and has changed people's perception of what is important. Consider that for most clubs a run in the FA Cup is now often treated as a lower priority than securing promotion, to the extent that shadow teams are often fielded in order to rest the club's leading players for the league campaign. A berth in the Play-Offs is regarded as a more valuable and ultimately more realistic prize than FA Cup glory by a swathe of clubs outside the top tier.

From the outset the Play-Offs were on a different level to other matches. They have risen in prominence and their star shines as brightly as ever today, which is a notable achievement considering the darkness in which they were launched. English football had heaped calumny and shame on itself for the best part of a decade and for a nation that had long been considered to be the founder of the modern game there was a serious threat of its progeny moving on elsewhere to find a more suitable home. In charting the Play-Offs' development from a low-key, understated component of a practical solution into a platform for some of the highest-profile and most keenly anticipated matches in the football calendar, this is a fascinating journey of long-lasting transformation.

Amidst the prevailing doom and gloom, at last there was something positive on which to focus and this had a galvanising effect on the game. There was a raw intensity about this first series of matches that immediately grabbed the attention of the football fraternity, and the ensuing excitement has continued pretty much unabated throughout the next twenty-seven years. There is hardly a year that goes by without some outstanding Play-Offs moment, where the sharp vicissitudes of the clubs involved make for an ever-entertaining canvas against which the key issues of the last promotion slots are decided. Crowds bounced back as hundreds of thousands returned to the national game, their faith and appetite restored. No other aspect of the domestic calendar can match the Play-Offs for their inherent sense of theatre combined with the weighty significance of the outcome. The ever-quotable Iain Dowie once described them as having "something of the circus about them" and indeed there are plenty of parallels with the world of high wires, juggling, lion taming and even the odd act of clowning thrown in for good measure.

The second year of the Play-Offs had to go some to live up to the heady momentum built up in the first year. There was little to fear though as, just as in 1987, a mixture of teams were thrown into the deep end, reflecting different pedigrees and contrasting fortunes, leading to as many dramatic games and as much heady excitement as had been enjoyed in the inaugural season. Again all three divisions generated their own intriguing stories, matching each other for the spectacular and the surprising, the weird and the wonderful, the sublime and the ridiculous. The Play-Offs etched their place in football's map at every turn.

Starting with the basement battle, Swansea City and Torquay United served up a high-scoring, entertaining Fourth Division Final that belied their troubled backgrounds. Both clubs were thankful to be contesting promotion after their recent traumas. Torquay had survived in the previous year when, in injury time on the last day of the season, they scored the goal that saved them from being the first club to be automatically relegated to the Conference. Famously, that additional time was necessary after Jim McNichol, the Torquay defender, required treatment having being bitten by a police dog. A quirky fact that still rankles with those of a Lincoln persuasion who harbour various conspiracy theories.

Swansea City were also in the doghouse, but mainly through their own failings both on the pitch and off it. Having hurtled down the divisions as quickly as they had risen up in the late 1970s, Swansea were struggling to cope and were another club whose very existence hung in the balance. They faced a winding-up order four years after reaching the top level in 1981 and were only rescued from liquidation when Doug Sharpe, a local businessman, stepped in with some much-needed funds in December 1985. With Swansea still languishing in the Fourth Division, the Play-Offs represented a make or break time for the Swans.

So the fact that these two teams were vying for promotion was a blessed relief from their recent travails and maybe this provided the impetus for a classic encounter. After Swansea's 2-1 victory in the first leg, the Final came alive for the second leg at Plainmoor with Swansea racing into a 3-1 lead and seemingly wrapping up promotion. A determined fightback from the Gulls pulled the game back to 3-3 with McNichol adding to his 90th-minute goal in the first leg with two in the second, setting up a tense last fifteen minutes with only a single aggregate goal now separating them. Swansea's hero was Sean McCarthy, who achieved the considerable feat of scoring in all four matches of that Play-Offs campaign. He was not the only player to make the goal-scoring headlines that year.

Division Three's Final featuring Walsall and Bristol City was equally pulsating and also had one goalscorer who blazed an impressive trail by notching seven goals throughout those Play-Offs games, including a hat-trick in the Final Replay. Step forward David Kelly. Despite City taking the lead in the first leg at Ashton Gate, three second-half goals saw Walsall assume control with a 3-1 away win, only for Bristol City to win the return away from home 2-0, thus leaving the teams all square and a replay required. One of the curious traits of the Play-Offs is the number of times teams win their away legs comfortably only to then blow it at home. This was the first in a surprisingly long line of jit-ters suffered by clubs and is explored in more detail later. Possibly unluckily for Walsall considering what happened in the previous two legs, they won a hastily arranged penalty shoot-out to decide the venue and the replay was to be held at Fellows Park. But the topsy-turvy nature of this Final continued and rather than a close encounter between two evenly matched sides, Walsall were three goals to the good within the first twenty minutes and eventually ran out as convincing 4-0 winners. City's implosion in the replay set a precedent for Bristolian failure that has rarely been interrupted.

And so to the Second Division, which saw Chelsea's only appearance in the Play-Offs. Having disposed of Blackburn 6-1 in the semi-finals, Middlesbrough were expected to provide little resistance to Chelsea preserving their First Division status. But a 2-0 reverse at Ayresome Park proved too much to overcome, even in front of over 40,000 at Stamford Bridge, and a side which counted a host of internationals such as Kerry Dixon, Pat Nevin and Gordon Durie amongst its line-up were consigned to relegation. So yet another so-called English giant fluffed their Play-Offs lines and Chelsea have the dubious honour of being the only side to be relegated from the First Division via the format. Their fans also heaped disgrace upon dishonour as violence erupted in and around the ground, the dark shadow of hooliganism still lurking dangerously over the game.

By the end of the 1987/88 season one of the prime objectives of the Play-Offs had been achieved, with the top division reduced to twenty teams and the lower leagues each having twenty-four each. The trial was over and that could have been the end of the Play-Offs: mission accomplished, transition achieved and job done. As a mechanism of reorganisation, the main issue had been resolved and there was no compulsion to continue beyond the initial period. But having been such a resounding success in the first two years, there was clearly a strong case for keeping them as a permanent feature of the season. In the words of the original agreement, they had indeed "proved popular with spectators [so] they could become a permanent part of the calendar". And there was a bit more to the Play-Offs than just being popular with the supporters, as countless managers, players, chairmen and, eventually, broadcasters would testify. In a small but specific way the Play-Offs had broken the mould of football being in decline, providing some positive momentum to replace the atrophy that had been smothering the game for the previous ten years or so. This was no mean feat considering how low in the public's standing football had fallen.

The next year's Play-Offs, those for the 1988/89 season, saw the end of the system that included one team from the division above being involved. The four Play-Offs teams were those highest placed who had missed out on automatic promotion, just as it stands today. Chelsea's West London neighbours, Fulham, had their chance to gain promotion to the Second Division and must have fancied their chances in the semi-final after only losing 1-0 away to Bristol Rovers. However, the second leg at Craven Cottage did not quite go according to plan and after a goalless first half, Rovers trotted out comfortable 4-0 winners with a young Ian Holloway amongst the scorers. Alas for Rovers they then lost to Port Vale in the Final, continuing the poor record of both Bristol clubs.

The two other London clubs fared better than Fulham, with Orient overcoming Scarborough and Wrexham to win the Fourth Division Final, whilst in the Second Division Crystal Palace managed to recover from first-leg deficits in both the semi against Swindon and the Final against Blackburn to give me that first taste of Play-Offs success. The first leg of that Final had plenty of late drama, as Eddie McGoldrick scored what seemed to be a priceless goal in the 86th minute at Ewood Park to make it 2-1, only for Simon Garner to restore Blackburn's two-goal advantage in the last minute.

Selhurst Park was a cauldron for the second leg and a broiling hot June day added to the frenetic atmosphere in front of over 26,000 fans who saw Ian Wright score twice, the second with three minutes remaining of extra time to secure the 3-0 victory, and consequently Wright's legendary status with the fans was confirmed, as was the Eagles' promotion. That third goal was the last to be scored in the two-legged Final format and personally I could not think of a more fitting way to mark the end of those early years. Very rarely have I felt so heady leaving a football ground; it was sheer, unadulterated joy, and as for the Play-Offs themselves, I was well and truly hooked. It would be nigh-on impossible to beat that feeling of elation, but a new era was on the horizon and little did I know how much more I and millions of others would come to experience as Wembley became the home of the Finals.

26th MAY 1990
WEMBLEY – ATT: 26,404

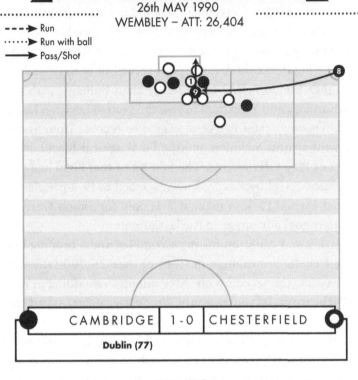

- - -► Run
·······► Run with ball
———► Pass/Shot

| CAMBRIDGE | 1 - 0 | CHESTERFIELD |

Dublin (77)

········· SQUADS ·········

	Vaughan	**1**	**1**	Leonard
	Fensome	**2**	**2**	Francis
	Kimble	**3**	**3**	Ryan
	Bailie	**4**	**4**	Dyche
	Chapple	**5**	**5**	Brien
	O'Shea	**6**	**6**	Gunn
	Cheetham	**7**	**7**	Plummer
	Leadbitter	**8**	**8**	Hewitt
⊙	**Dublin**	**9**	**9**	Chiedozie (78)
	Taylor (62)	**10**	**10**	Rogers
	Philpott	**11**	**11**	Maris

Claridge (62)   Waller (78)

Final League Position: 6th   Final League Position: 7th
SF 1st Leg: Cambridge 1 - 1 Maidstone   SF 1st Leg: Chesterfield 4 - 0 Stockport
SF 2nd Leg: Maidstone 0 - 2 Cambridge   SF 2nd Leg: Stockport 0 - 2 Chesterfield

GOAL FACT: The first Play-Offs goal scored at Wembley.

WEMBLEY WAY 1990

The Football League's Andy Williamson set about continuing this positive momentum that had been created. Williamson realised the potential for making the Final for each division more of a showpiece event, even though the two-legged format had provided more than its fair share of drama and tension already. He proposed that the 1989/90 Finals, across all three divisions, would no longer be played as home and away matches but as one-off matches at a neutral venue. Not only would these be single games to decide promotion but also, significantly, they would take place at Wembley, the national stadium, ideally over a bank holiday weekend in late May, providing a suitably imposing setting for a series of matches which were of such importance. Increasingly over the next twenty-odd years, the Play-Offs built on the impetus generated in those early years with some extraordinary matches, which captivated both protagonists and neutrals alike, creating a lasting, positive legacy for English football. The climax of the Football League season was justifiably to be held at the spiritual home of the English game. It was a natural fit that was mutually beneficial to both parties.

This was the point at which the profile of the Play-Offs took off to reach another level, when they sat up and demanded the attention of the football public. It was a watershed moment and it worked a treat in immediately elevating the Final to a new dimension. However exciting two-legged Finals can be and had been, they do distil the drama somewhat by being played out over a pair of games.

The change meant this was no longer a promotion scrap conducted between the two clubs at each other's grounds (and a replica of the league encounters) but the focus was now very much concentrated on the showpiece Final where all was up for grabs. Williamson had advocated the classic format of 'winner takes all' which is so beloved of fans and the media. And so were established the seeds of the biggest game in world sport, and we will follow that journey all the way to its current status as the £134 million match.

Williamson's notion of a Wembley Weekend created a sense of occasion, especially for the smaller clubs whose hopes of reaching Wembley were generally confined to lower-division competitions such as the Associate Members Cup in its various sponsored guises. In 1989/90 it was known as the Leyland DAF Trophy which, with all due respect to the former truck manufacturer, symbolised the lack of glamour and prestige normally associated with a visit to the old Twin Towers (or what is now the new Arch). It would tax most fans outside the finalists to name the winners of the previous year's Football League Trophy; the significance of these visits rarely lingered in the collective memory. Just switching matches to Wembley did not guarantee success; there had to be an integrity and a true value to proceedings, which the Play-Offs provided from the outset.

The healthy crowds for the first-ever Wembley Play-Offs Finals across all three divisions in 1990, drawing an aggregate of almost 130,000 people, underlined their immediate popularity. Attracting an average crowd of over 43,000, the Play-Offs stood in good comparison with Division One attendances, where for example Manchester United averaged just shy of 39,000 that season whilst the champions Liverpool's highest league attendance was below 40,000 and their average was just under 37,000. Swindon's ill-fated win over Sunderland in the Division Two Final attracted a gate of 72,873, which dwarfed the highest attendance of the top division, a relatively paltry 47,000 at Old Trafford for their opening-day match with Arsenal. Within the context of domestic football support at this time, these were impressive numbers and a strong indicator of the increasing popularity of the Play-Offs.

Indeed the crowd for what was the biggest match of the English league season matched that of the World Cup Final in Rome two months later (there was a minimal difference of less than a thousand between the two). This not only provided instant vindication for Williamson's idea but most importantly, as a result of the Final being played at Wembley, it gave many smaller clubs a golden and increasingly rare opportunity to enjoy being in the limelight and sample a taste of the big time. Of the six clubs that competed in those 1990 Finals only Sunderland have reached an FA Cup Final in the twenty-five years since, whilst Swindon (1993), Notts County (1991), Tranmere (1991) and Chesterfield (1995) returned as Play-Offs finalists within the next five years. Cambridge United did so in the Conference Play-Offs Final of 2014, and with Sunderland themselves returning in 1998 for their classic encounter with Charlton, all these clubs have renewed their fond acquaintance with Wembley through the Play-Offs. Providing lower-league clubs with these opportunities of glimpsing glory is an essential ingredient of why the Play-Offs are so deeply appreciated and cherished.

The Play-Offs Finals were clearly already an altogether different type of occasion to Football League Trophy Finals, as they were imbued with far-reaching importance for all those involved in deciding the final promotion slot. The 'make or break' element ensured that there were some truly memorable moments, with the prize of promotion a suitably enticing proposition that made victory so deliciously sweet and defeat so achingly bitter. For the fans who turned up in such large numbers there was the reward of a series of games that fitted the bill, were a credit to the clubs and added to Wembley's rich and famous history. In these early years there were a whole host of Finals that involved a mixture of thrills, spills and late drama which forged the reputation of the Play-Offs. This succession of frenetic games led to a heightened sense of expectancy amongst fans and players alike, cementing their prestige and establishing an essential and dynamic part of the very essence of the football season. Over the same period there were very few FA Cup Finals that got the pulses racing by matching the intensity or level of excitement. Many of the FA Cup Finals of the 1990s and 2000s were turgid and predictable, whereas the opposite was true of the Play-Offs. It could be argued that the advent of the Play-Offs has eclipsed the FA Cup Final as the pinnacle of the season and the so-called 'Magic of the Cup' has been to some extent supplanted by their tension and thrills (see below).

After the 1990 World Cup Finals, in which, by hook or by crook, the England team, for once, fulfilled a nation's ambitions and reached the semi-finals, English football was on the rise again. There is no doubt that Paul Gascoigne's combination of talent and tears re-engaged fans who had abandoned the game and also encouraged a new generation of supporters. In the two years after Italia '90 Division One crowds rose from 7.9 million to 10 million or by just over a quarter. Interestingly, at the same time the other divisions levelled off slightly, losing a million fans in the process, so it could be argued that some of those fans were attracted to the bigger names in the top division as highlighted at the World Cup. The previous resurgence in the lower leagues, inspired by the Play-Offs, was somewhat stalled by football's higher and improved profile. This new generation of supporters was undoubtedly enticed by the prospect of watching England's heroes, the likes of Gascoigne, Lineker and Platt, perform on a domestic stage and at the highest level.

But before Gazza's inspiration had made its impact there had been a more important and lasting catalyst in the rebirth of the game – the Play-Offs. Having encouraged people to return to the grounds in significant numbers prior to 1990, they provided the platform from which English football started to regain the ground it had lost so dismally up to the mid-1980s. The Play-Offs were here to stay, having made such an immediate and extremely beneficial impression. Despite the growing popularity of top-level football, the success of the Play-Offs was to continue over the next few years of their evolution, as crowds continued to rise across all four divisions.

By providing such thrilling and dramatic climaxes, the Play-Offs have added an extra element to being promoted. Furthermore, numerous clubs have been afforded the opportunity to play on the big stage and have savoured the atmosphere of playing in front of large crowds in iconic stadia for the first time. For example, the first Wembley Play-Offs Final was held on 26th May 1990 where both Cambridge United and Chesterfield, whilst contesting the right to be promoted to Division Three, enjoyed the novel experience of playing in a Wembley Final. For a club such as Cambridge, whose record home crowd stands at 14,000, this gave the club an opportunity to be at the centre of the action in front of a crowd almost double this figure. Both sets of fans understandably revelled in their clubs appearing at Wembley and for many this match would have represented the zenith of their support.

The players, particularly those from the lower levels, could make the most of their big day, and for many it would be one of, if not the only chance to strut their stuff at Wembley. To illustrate the rarity, only one player from either team in 1990 had played at Wembley beforehand. Colin Bailie of Cambridge had been there with Reading a few years earlier for the Full Members Cup. With such limited experience on the pitch, the unique thrill of appearing at the national stadium made this a special occasion for the players as well as the fans, and even though players such as Steve Claridge and Sean Dyche would return many times, the Wembley debut would be a special moment in their careers and one to be remembered and treasured for ever. This is not a view merely restricted to journeymen who spend nearly all their time in the lower leagues. Claridge appreciated that this was the moment at which he and many of the other players could raise their profile and effectively be a launch pad for their futures. By winning that match many Cambridge players' lives were changed for the better. Claridge himself would return with Leicester City six years later to make his own indelible mark on the history of the Play-Offs and a permanent spot in my soul.

Bolton's Keith Branagan saves Steve Lovell's penalty to avoid going 3-0 down to Reading in 1995. Bolton won 4-3.

Neil Warnock leads out his Notts County side for their record-breaking second successive Play-Offs victory in 1991.

Ossie Ardiles and Alan McLoughlin celebrate Swindon's short-lived triumph in 1990.

Charlton players celebrate their epic victory over Sunderland in 1998.

David Hopkin curls his shot towards the top corner for the Palace winner against Sheffield United in 1997.

Dion Dublin lapping up the adulation of scoring the first Play-Offs goal at Wembley for Cambridge in 1990.

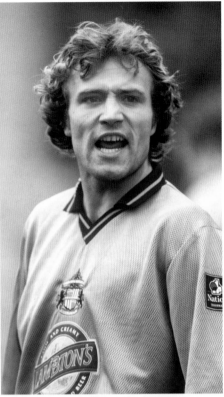

Michael Gray, who is still plagued by "that bloody penalty" from the 1998 Final.

Manchester City's Paul Dickov shoots over Mark Patterson against Gillingham in the Second Division Final in 1999.

Whilst Vince Bartram, Gillingham's keeper, reflects on their dramatic loss to Manchester City in 1999, Nicky Weaver celebrates.

Graham Alexander consoles his Preston team mate Sean Gregan after their loss to Bolton in 2001.

Wade Elliott wheels away in delight having struck Burnley's winner against Sheffield United in 2009.

Hull City's Dean Windass, scorer of the only goal of the game, gleefully lifts the Championship Play-Offs trophy in 2008.

© Offside Sports Photography

© Danny Last

Scarves on display for the League One Final – Rotherham versus Leyton Orient – in 2014.

A young Millwall fan at the League One Final against Swindon in 2010.

© Danny Last

Old Trafford decked in blue and white for the League One Final between Peterborough and Huddersfield in 2011.

Blackpool fans revelling in the Championship Final of 2010 and looking forward to the future.

Burnley fans celebrate their 2009 triumph.

Burnley fans 'living the dream' in 2009.

A Rotherham United fan bares all for the League Two Final against Dagenham & Redbridge in 2010.

Chairman David Sheepshanks and manager George Burley finally enjoying Ipswich's success in 2000.

Kevin Phillips heralds his winning goal for Palace against Watford in the Championship Final in 2013.

Steve Simonsen's horror at missing the penalty in the shoot-out for Sheffield United against Huddersfield in 2012.

Damien Delaney soaking up the champagne after Palace's win in 2013.

Ian Holloway directing operations for Blackpool in the Championship Final against Cardiff in 2010.

Crestfallen Torquay striker Billy Kee after losing to Stevenage in the League Two Final in 2011.

Brendan Rodgers thrown aloft by his victorious Swansea players in 2011.

Huddersfield players watch the penalty shoot-out in the 2012 League One Final.

Manuel Almunia, Watford's goalkeeper, shows his frustration at
failing to keep out Palace's Kevin Phillips' decisive penalty in 2013.

Huddersfield's Jack Hunt enjoys the moment of triumph over Sheffield United in the League One Final of 2012.

Bobby Zamora strikes the last-minute winner for QPR past the stricken Richard Keogh of Derby in 2014.

Even a successful Premiership player and England international such as Dion Dublin was clear about the importance of the Play-Offs when asked to nominate the outstanding highlight of his career. That career encapsulated some impressive landmarks, including the honour of gaining the first of his four England caps, winning both the English and Scottish Premier Leagues with Manchester United and Celtic respectively and being the Premier League's joint top scorer in the 1997/98 season. Above all those considerable achievements, Dublin is certain about the scene of his greatest personal triumph. "At Wembley in 1990. The match finished Cambridge 1 Chesterfield 0, and I scored the only goal, which was also the first in a (Wembley) Play-Offs Final. It ensured that we went up from the fourth tier." He might have scored over eighty Premier League goals and played for some of Britain's biggest clubs, but this was the goal that he ranks above all others as his most valued and valuable.

Alongside Dublin's moment of glory there was even the added spice of some off-the-field shenanigans to enliven proceedings in 1990. As Ossie Ardiles's Swindon Town celebrated their 1-0 victory over Sunderland (who for a second time in four years were suffering Play-Offs disappointment) and the West Country club started to contemplate life in the top tier for the first time in their 110-year history, there were darker forces underway behind the scenes which were to derail these celebrations and jettison them from their hard-fought elevation to the big time.

Unfortunately, the club was about to be engulfed in a scandal involving illegal payments to players under former boss Lou Macari and chairman Brian Hillier. Once the club had admitted to a variety of charges against them, their promotion was rescinded by the Football League and Sunderland ultimately gained promotion despite their final defeat, a particularly cruel twist of fate for the Robins. Whilst there was limited sympathy for Swindon's plight, as there had been a clear transgression of the rules by the board and management, the Football League were heavily, and justifiably, criticised for delaying the decision until after the Final.

For Swindon to go through the experience of winning a Play-Offs Final only to then have their promotion snatched away was unnecessarily heartbreaking. It was a curious and somewhat surreal way for the launch of the Play-Offs at Wembley to be initiated, with promotion not being decided on the pitch but in the offices of the Football League. At one stage even Division Three Play-Offs losers Tranmere Rovers were promoted, as Swindon were originally not just denied promotion but faced the further punishment of relegation. That decision was overturned on appeal and Swindon did stay in Division Two. So even the seemingly most straightforward of Play-Off promotions was thrown into disarray by events off the football field, leaving one club bereft whilst the other enjoyed a reprieve that nobody connected with Sunderland could have dared to anticipate. It was as though there was a confluence of the best and worst of the League, as a modern innovative approach collided with old-style bureaucracy. There was no hiding that this was a messy and unsatisfactory conclusion that slightly tarnished the concept of the Wembley Weekend. Such was the bitter irony in this one-off match, this decisive Final being undermined by affairs unconnected with football.

To suffer such a body blow would have floored many clubs but Swindon recovered and, as is so often the case, the Play-Offs provided them with a chance of redemption. So it was that a few years later, under Glenn Hoddle, who replaced a disillusioned and disheartened Ardiles in 1991, they contested one of the classic Play-Off Finals, which eventually paved the way to their only season in the top flight. Crucially, by this time that top tier was no longer called the First Division, but the recently formed Premier League, which would change the finances and the face of English football permanently. The arrival of the Premier League had a profound impact on the significance of promotion, rendering victory in the Play-Offs as increasingly important financially. Reaching the 'promised land' of the Premiership became an obsession for certain clubs – to the detriment of a fair few – which lost any sense of perspective in chasing that goal. The Championship Play-Off Final has since become the match the largest financial consequences throughout world sport, of which we will go into more detail in a subsequent chapter.

In 1993, three years on from Swindon's ill-fated first foray, the Final against Leicester City was the sort of match that Williamson could only have dreamed of when he originally envisaged his Wembley Weekend. Leicester themselves were returning to the Final, having been beaten by a contentious Blackburn penalty the previous year. So both sides had Play-Off scores to settle and a frenetic struggle ensued. A quiet first half was enlivened by Swindon taking the lead through their elegant player-manager just before the break when he curled a delicious shot into the corner of the net with the precision of a surgeon. Within ten minutes of the restart they were three goals to the good and coasting towards that promotion they had been denied three years before.

Leicester had other ideas, turning the match around by matching Swindon's three goals in the space of eleven minutes and the game was evenly poised at 3-3 with over twenty minutes remaining. It looked as though Swindon were going to be denied for a second time but somehow they bounced back from losing that three-goal cushion, showing a commendable resilience in restoring their lead through a late, and yet again, disputed penalty. As with so many of the most dramatic moments in Play-Offs history, the good fortune of one club is inextricably linked to the misfortune of the other. But as this was Swindon, there was bound to be a twist in the tail and despite Hoddle later saying that winning the Play-Offs was one of his greatest managerial achievements, which did after all take in managing England in a World Cup, he did not stick around to revel in the glory. Hoddle's heroics in his pivotal role as player-manager were coloured by the rumours that had been circulating about his future, echoing the background noise to Swindon's previous 1990 experience. Chelsea had failed a few years earlier to entice a successful Play-Offs manager, Neil Warnock, to join them but this time they were not to be denied. So just a few weeks after their Wembley success, Hoddle was lured to Chelsea and Swindon's world was yet again rocked on its axis. Although Hoddle's assistant, John Gorman, was persuaded to stay at the County Ground to steer the club in their moment of glory he proved to be no match for the higher echelons of the Premier League and with five wins and a paltry thirty points, Swindon became the first top-division team in thirty years to concede 100 goals. Having fought so resolutely to achieve top-flight status, their only season at this level was a bitter one and there will be many Swindon fans who feel that they deserved better after such a convoluted and complex route. But such is the often cruel and mischievous way that the Play-Offs toy with the emotions, where success can be and so often is of a fleeting nature.

As Swindon enjoyed their brief taste of success, which few could begrudge them, there was also Leicester's misery and the feeling that fate had dealt them a rotten hand once again. Undaunted, Leicester then qualified for a third successive Play-Offs Final in 1994, when they finally laid their hoodoo to rest with victory over Derby, even though they conceded the first goal to Tommy Johnson, the doyen of Finals goals in the early 1990s. Steve Walsh attained legendary status amongst Leicester fans by scoring twice to turn the game around for the Foxes at the third time of asking. Walsh's brace that day undoubtedly helped him to secure the Leicester fans' choice as their greatest-ever cult hero in a poll a few years later. Leicester showed their liking for this first taste of Play-Offs success by immediately getting relegated from the Premiership to try their hand again the following year, reaching their fourth Final in five years against Crystal Palace in 1996 *(see Heroes & Villains at the end of this chapter)*.

Over their first decade, the Play-Offs had left their indelible mark on dozens of clubs, hundreds of players and thousands of fans. In a period of uncertainty and doubt for football the Play-Offs were a shining example of the best aspects of the game and offered a chance of redemption. Although there was no simple panacea to the entrenched problems being faced by the authorities, at least there was something positive to build on. Not only had the Play-Offs become a vibrant, vital cog within the structure of English league football but they were instrumental in getting football back on its feet after the dark days of the 1980s. There was now an opportunity to look towards a brighter future and, buoyed by this rejuvenation, the Play-Offs continued to build on their reputation for involving the wider football community in some of the most intense, enthralling drama.

Pride had been restored and the knee-jerk response of outsiders that the sport was riddled with violence and fear was being replaced by perceptions of a much more attractive environment. Readdressing the equilibrium and gaining a more balanced perspective was no mean feat. A hard-fought match was now more likely to relate to what happened on the pitch rather than on the terraces. Media coverage no longer dwelt on the negative but could focus on stories of clubs that had rescued their season and provided their fans with a cause for celebration rather than condemnation.

HEROES & VILLAINS
STEVE CLARIDGE 1996 & DAVID HOPKIN 1997

I will be suspending any sense of objectivity at this juncture as a Palace fan; the 1996 Final is not a memory which I wish to dredge up as it has proved to be amongst the most painful in my forty-odd years of support. Indeed I still find it difficult to listen to Steve Claridge in his role as pundit/commentator without a shiver running through my body because of what happened in the 121st minute of that match. Fellow Palace fan and comedian, Kevin Day, agrees. "Probably the worst single moment was the 1996 Final when by an odd coincidence we lost to a last-minute 20-yard shot [see the following year's Final, below], only Steve Claridge didn't mean his! He still gets cross that the first thing I mention when I see him is his fluky shinned shot looping over our keeper."

"I've shinned it in, to be frank I'm not sure what happened," is a quote that will haunt Palace fans for the rest of our lives. Such a brutally honest acceptance of the luck that enabled Claridge to somehow loop the ball into the corner of the net from the edge of the penalty area is not much succour to the feeling of despair and dismay I, and all Palace fans experienced, in that Claridge 'shinning' moment. Not only was it a fluke, but the fact that Claridge did not wear shin pads, which the match officials seemed to have conveniently forgotten had been made compulsory in the run-up to the 1990 World Cup, rubbed further salt into the wounds. Being robbed by a combination of ill fortune and poor officialdom left a deep scar which has been difficult, nay impossible, to shake off.

So with Claridge's socks rolled down to his ankles, the ball spun off his bare leg in a weird parabola that left our keeper, Nigel Martyn, frozen to the spot. I am still convinced that this goal would not have been possible if Claridge had been properly stocking-ed and padded up. The tabloid headlines wrote themselves "Steve SHINS it for the Foxes", "SHIN when you're winning" etc. I have never felt so deflated after a football match; inconsolable doesn't really cover the desolation I endured, and, to a certain extent, still do every time Claridge makes his frequent media appearances, providing a flashback to that moment. When interviewed about the goal, Claridge recalled that he'd been on the edge of the penalty area when the ball dropped to him by accident rather than design. A free-kick had been taken too quickly for his liking, and he was so tired it took him a long time to rejoin the action, meaning that instead of being in the heart of the area he was outside it. So it was a case of wrong place, right time, and he duly delivered the barb to our hearts.

Just like former team mate Dion Dublin, Claridge told me that he views his Play-Offs strike as his most important goal, placing it above the one he scored the following year to secure Leicester's League Cup victory. Weighing up the significance of both, Claridge confirmed, "The goal in the Play-Offs, the one that secures promotion, is always going to be bigger. One hundred times out of a hundred." And such is the clear dividing line that distinguishes the Play-Offs – twinned with his moment of joy, the apogee of his playing days is my bleakest experience as a fan – which encapsulates the yin and yang.

Fortunately this miserable experience of the Play-Offs was in some way expunged by another last-minute goal in the following year's Final, when it was Palace's turn to come back with a vengeance. This was altogether more glorious, a pure strike of such beauty that nobody could deny the intentions behind this particular effort (bias now in full swing). David Hopkin was not known for his cracking goals but the one he unleashed against Sheffield United from outside the penalty area in the 90th minute of the most dour and stodgy affair would rank in my personal top-five Palace goals. This was one of a handful of moments when the celebration was so intense that giddiness took over accompanied by the football equivalent of a primal scream; uncontrollable, cathartic and raw. The ball was destined for the top corner, into which it duly arrowed to bring some sort of closure on Shin-gate. I've seen replays of the goal countless times, but still get goose-pimples watching it. As Hopkin collects the ball I cannot quite believe that it is really going in, half expecting his shot to sail harmlessly over the bar. Such is the iconic status of this goal that there is an excellent Palace blog entitled *Hopkin Looking To Curl One* to commemorate it. Kevin Day adds that he knew it was going in as he was directly in line with it. He also remembers the celebrations, which featured the odd and unnerving sight of goalkeeper Carlo Nash stripped down to just his jockstrap as the team cavorted in front of the fans.

Within the space of twelve months, I had experienced the sharp vicissitudes of the Play-Offs, from the painful, heartbreaking agony of cruel Claridge in 1996 to the most uplifting, unadulterated joy of heroic Hopkin in 1997. Of course, being Palace, there was a bitter twist in the tale as at the point at which Hopkin was reaching deification, he decided to up sticks in the summer and move on. What a time to move. Just as Hopkin had helped us to reach the top, to live the dream, he punctured it with his departure to Leeds. Here was the sharpest dig imaginable to the solar plexus and a resounding bump on our return to earth. Betrayal is a strong, emotive word but it is entirely apposite in these circumstances. Abandoned by the man who had made it all possible, one could already sense that the unadulterated joy we'd felt was a mirage and the following season duly ended in our ritual relegation after a single season in the top flight and with our player of the year plying his trade elsewhere.

This was a trait that became a familiar one throughout the Play-Offs whereby the hero of the Final more often than not moves on to pastures new. Hopkin's ignominious exit is not unusual and there is a curious sub-plot in Play-Off Finals' history, whereby the winning goalscorer regularly leaves the club he has just helped promote. This curious phenomenon is explored in more detail later on in the book as we take a closer look at those that jump ship or get sidelined in the wake of their moment of glory. To score the winning goal in a Play-Offs Final provides a decent epitaph for so many players it appears to be almost by design that this is how they sign off their careers with that particular club.

So just as success followed failure, inevitably failure reared its ugly head as we were savouring success. This microcosm of ups and downs reflects the power of emotions wrapped up in the Play-Offs and a multitude of fans of lower-league clubs will have similarly memorable episodes firmly etched into their collective football consciousness. These experiences will almost certainly be amongst the most vivid in a lifetime of supporting their clubs through thick and thin. The fact that my zenith followed my nadir within the space of a year made things all the sweeter when the Play-Offs gods finally smiled on us. Such is the strength of feeling coursing through the veins that one senses some higher force is at work, pulling the strings and toying with our fragile emotions. Football can be a cruel mistress and as fans we have to endure those sharp twists and turns, which are exemplified by the Play-Offs in their capacity to torment and delight.

GRANT McCANN 2010/11

LEAGUE ONE PLAY-OFFS FINAL

29th MAY 2011
OLD TRAFFORD – ATT: 48,410

- - → Run
····· → Run with ball
— → Pass/Shot

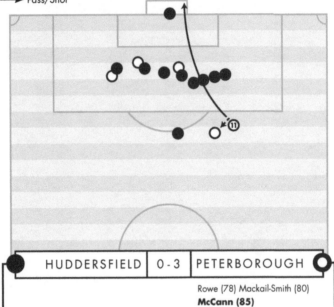

HUDDERSFIELD	0 - 3	PETERBOROUGH

Rowe (78) Mackail-Smith (80)
McCann (85)

···· SQUADS ····

	Bennett	**13**	**28**	Jones	
	Hunt	**32**	**2**	Little	
	Kay	**8**	**5**	Zakuani	
⚽	Clarke	**5**	**16**	Bennett	
	Naysmith	**3**	**27**	Basey (64)	
	Kilbane	**20**	**7**	Wesolowski	
	Ward (79)	**10**	**11**	McCann	⚽
	Peltier	**2**	**14**	Rowe (84)	⚽
	Arfield (81)	**16**	**10**	Boyd	
⚽	Roberts	**7**	**24**	Tomlin (90+2)	
	Afobe (81)	**24**	**11**	Mackail-Smith	⚽

Cadamarteri (79) Rhodes (81) Lee (81)   Lee (64) Whelpdale (84) Ball (90+2)

Final League Position: 3rd   Final League Position: 4th
SF 1st Leg: Bournemouth 1 - 1 Huddersfield   SF 1st Leg: MK Dons 3 - 2 Peterborough
SF 2nd Leg: Huddersfield 3 - 3 Bournemouth   SF 2nd Leg: Peterborough 2 - 0 MK Dons

GOAL FACT: McCann has won three Finals
with different clubs at different grounds.

THE PLAYERS

So it is clear that the fans did not just accept the Play-Offs but they embraced them with a gusto that had been sorely lacking over the previous decades. And such was the overwhelming enthusiasm and energy that greeted their arrival that their success with those who watched the game, and ultimately who generated the additional revenues, was pretty much guaranteed from the off. However, what of the players who had to play out the drama: how would they respond to the added, concentrated pressure and the burden of extra games at the end of the season? There is a general assumption that players should be just 'carrying out orders' and not be thinking too much about the wider implications of the structure or format of the league. Players are seldom asked for their opinions on broader football issues and this leaves a yawning gap in the overall picture as it assumes they do not have opinions, which is both patronising and erroneous.

As proved by the success of *The Secret Footballer* columns and books, there is the odd player with an interesting angle on the game, so it is important to gain some insight into their point of view. One of the major advantages of the growth of social media outlets such as Twitter is that players' views are now expressed and although these can have negative connotations, it does provide a closer link between the players and the fans. Most players do care deeply about their clubs and it is too stereotypical to band them all together as mere mercenaries or preening prima donnas on the lookout for the next big deal. If their attitude towards the Play-Offs had been at all negative then this might have limited the success in establishing them as an integral element of the football calendar.

As has been pointed out in an earlier chapter, there was a massive benefit for lower-league players, who after 1990 were offered a passport to playing at Wembley (or for six years from 2001, the Millennium Stadium). With chances few and far between at this level, the Play-Offs were a clearly defined path to a taste, at least, of glory, but surely there would need to be more to convince players that this was the best way to resolve the issue of promotion. After all, they are the ones who have to slog their way through an entire season of forty-six matches, only to face the possibility of all their efforts being decided by a moment of madness or brilliance in the full glare of the Play-Offs. These are the sorts of matches in which players really earn their corn, coping with highly pressurised situations where the weight of expectations is as heavy as the implications of failure.

There is a continuous and mainly valid carping over footballers' wages but when they perform under the sort of pressure they will face in the Play-Offs, then there is less justification in such complaints. A tiny minority of us have to carry out our duties under such circumstances, with the hopes and dreams of thousands resting on how well we do. During such high-profile matches every act is analysed and pored over, so mistakes are highlighted and magnified to an often excruciating degree. Being able to handle such scrutiny is part and parcel of a footballer's life but it is worth reminding ourselves that coping with this is not straightforward and these young men need to show a resilience and strength of character that most of us would struggle to achieve in similar circumstances.

In any other walk of life there would be a fair amount of sympathy and under-standing for someone who has to cope with the greater workload and added pressures whereby any weakness is leapt upon with such alacrity. Footballers are not afforded much room for manoeuvre; indeed they are allowed very little leeway as the image of pampered, overpaid high-maintenance stars is prevalent throughout the media. Whilst such prima donnas do exist, the vast majority of players, particularly those from the lower leagues, have worked extremely hard to make the grade as professional footballers and have the same doubts and vulnerability as most of us face in our careers and our lives.

Some glibly assume that the stresses and strains should be easy to handle as the players are well paid but this misses the point. Decent levels of remuneration come partly from the ability to handle the pressures but they do not inoculate the players from these burdens. It is often overlooked how vulnerable footballers can be and the assumption that high rewards can cushion any blow is as common as it is misguided. Erstwhile Aston Villa manager John Gregory once expressed a shocking lack of awareness when questioning how Stan Collymore could be suffering from depression when he was earning £20,000 per week. There are increasingly more stories emerging of how players have been unable to cope with the burden of living their lives in the public eye, aka 'the goldfish bowl', and the additional spotlight and higher intensity of the Play-Offs creates even greater tensions and pressure for those not accustomed to such scrutiny.

They also have to cope with the period after the spotlight has moved on and there is a long line of players who scored crucial, often match-winning, Play-Offs goals but who have not been able to make the grade and were jettisoned soon afterwards. Having been instrumental in securing promotion, their newly elevated status sadly marks the end of the road for them at that particular club. So the likes of Neil Shipperley in 2004 and Kevin Phillips in 2013 scored the only goals of the Final for Palace but hardly got another kick for the club before moving on. Dean Windass is another prime example of someone who reached the heights by scoring the winning goal for his hometown club, Hull City, in the 2008 Play-Offs Final. Despite achieving iconic status for that goal which promoted Hull to the Premier League for the first time, he then became a bit-part player for the Tigers, starting just one match in the following season before being released in January 2009, less than a year after the Wembley triumph. So in his moment of glory Windass had unwittingly made a rod for his own back and his career was effectively derailed and never reached those heights again. Having been sidelined, he struggled to cope with the realisation that this was as good as it was likely to get and subsequently suffered from bouts of depression and a battle with alcoholism which led to two suicide attempts in early 2012 after he had retired. Windass's rapid descent from the very pinnacle of his career to the lowest point of his life is a cautionary tale that shows just how quickly things can unravel, and provides an insight into the darker side of Play-Offs glory.

Alongside contemporary stories of players not being able to adjust to life after Play-Offs glory it is illuminating to discover how those involved in the first years of the Play-Offs in the late 1980s coped. These were the players who had to adjust to the new ways, to make the transition from automatic promotion to the new system, and so their response to this brave new world is worth seeking out as it goes beyond just the sheer joy of winning or the deflation in defeat. It is instructive to hear how they reacted to the newly created pressures of having the season up for grabs in this type of format. As revealed earlier, Bobby Barnes remembers the sense of awe and slight trepidation that the Aldershot players felt when they were facing the prospect of overcoming Wolves over two legs in the first year of the Play-Offs. For the vast majority of that team this was to be their first and, quite possibly, only Final and a daunting one at that. That they so successfully managed to cope with this rather novel, additional pressure was admirable and their decisive 3-0 victory deserves recognition as possibly Aldershot's finest moment.

If those Aldershot players were 'living the dream' then there were others who were thrust into a world of nightmares. Pat Nevin, the former Scottish international winger, had the dubious pleasure of being dragged into the Play-Offs in the early days. When Chelsea finished just above the automatic relegation spots in 1988 the London club tried and failed to ensure their First Division status. After a disappointing season, finishing one place above the automatic relegation slots, the players had to regroup and were expected to raise their game. Any anxieties seemed unfounded as they thumped their semi-final opponents, Blackburn, 6-1 on aggregate and there was an assumption that Middlesbrough would hardly provide more resistance in the Final.

Nevin recalls that he was in the unusual position of knowing he was leaving the club, having been told he was surplus to requirements halfway through the season. Nevin's ball-playing skills were not suited to Chelsea's newly adopted rumbustious style and he reveals that an assistant manager at the time informed him that if he took more than two touches he would be substituted. But despite this he was still bitterly disappointed at how his Chelsea career ended, when "the last moment was the worst moment".

The prospect of relegation seemed like the end of the world for many of the exalted Chelsea squad. Indeed, how could a club such as theirs be involved in this sort of unseemly dog fight; it was surely beneath them? But they were about to discover, like so many others did, just what a great leveller the Play-Offs were to be and just how the mighty can and often did fall, especially in those early days.

Even when Middlesbrough won the first leg 2-0 at Ayresome Park the expectations were that the match was going to be turned round at Stamford Bridge in front of over 40,000 and order would be duly restored. Little did Nevin and his team mates know that this was to be their swansong and that Middlesbrough would make it through despite the hostile atmosphere and seeming gulf in class between the two clubs. Nevin remembers the second leg against Middlesbrough as being predominantly one-way traffic – "we absolutely battered them" – but they could not add to Durie's 18th-minute opening goal. Nevin makes no bones about what a shock it was to the system for these players to be involved in this damaging relegation. He duly left the club to join Everton in the close season but he still distinctly recalls the overriding feeling of unease and embarrassment at Chelsea's demise; the sort of feeling he never experienced throughout the rest of his career. Even the pain of three successive semi-final failures with Tranmere between 1993 and 1995 did not even come close to the desolation he felt in that Chelsea dressing room. "It was bad, but not that bad, as we were striving to get up, so it was a great deal more positive," Nevin admitted.

Switch to the present day and the size of the prize is now well documented both further on in this book and elsewhere in the media. If a match can truly be worth £134 million then that equates to more than £1.5 million per minute, which is a frightening amount of money. But then consider how a key moment from a match might be valued: we could have the likes of the £70 million own goal or the £100 million penalty miss. If this seems to be taking things to ridiculous extremes, one just has to consider the size of the Sky/BT television three-year deal that began in 2013. At £1.5 billion for just the domestic rights, it is by far the largest deal of its kind in the world. If you add the value of overseas rights, which have been rising faster in recent years than the domestic, one can easily justify the huge amounts attached to individual moments within a match. With such weighty financial significance comes a huge sense of responsibility and the players have to take this in their stride.

So it seems important that the players are not omitted from voicing their opinion but are treated instead with some respect as their views are amongst the most important, providing they are asked the right questions. I maintain that the image of footballers as dull and unimaginative stems mainly from the fact that they are asked a series of dull and unimaginative questions much of the time. Given the opportunity to respond to a range of more interesting and varied lines of enquiry they show themselves to be far more intelligent and capable of independent thinking than is traditionally portrayed. By giving them a chance to make comments beyond the normal line of questioning, they can add positively to the debate.

As a former chairman of the PFA, Clarke Carlisle has a unique perspective on how players react and respond to a whole range of situations, including dealing with the pressure of the Play-Offs. Carlisle also has experience as a player himself, appearing in a couple of Finals with QPR in 2003 and Burnley in 2009. Dubbed "Britain's most intelligent footballer" after winning a couple of episodes of *Countdown* and appearing on *Question Time*, Carlisle has also suffered from the darker side of football fame, just like Windass, in battling with alcoholism which saw him admitted to a programme of rehabilitation with the Sporting Chance clinic in 2003. Most footballers have to deal with certain peaks and troughs but Carlisle has been to both extremes of the spectrum and is therefore well qualified to comment on, as well as help, players who are dealing with the particular stresses and strains of competing in the Play-Offs.

Carlisle confirmed that "the players do feel huge, huge pressure as they know there is a massive difference to bonuses, wages etc. all combined with playing at a different level". These are potentially life-changing moments. He admits to feeling the most tension prior to any football match in the lead-up to the Play-Offs Finals. He explained that there is this transition from thinking about the other twenty-three teams in the league to these being whittled down to just the two of you, head-to-head. Suddenly the heat is on and the players are facing what Carlisle describes as being a "Monte Carlo or bust" situation; a gladiatorial encounter with huge consequences for themselves, their team mates and all connected with the club.

He openly admits that the defeat he suffered when playing for QPR in the 2003 Final "was the lowest point in my career". More than ten years on he still vividly recalls the chance that he had to score in normal time. "I exchanged passes with Mark Bircham and then spread it to Kevin Gallen who crossed and I headed it just wide when I should have scored." The way he talks about this passage of play in such vivid detail makes it feel as though it happened only a few days ago, not over ten years, and is indicative of the impression it made on Carlisle. Cardiff went on to win the match in extra time and Carlisle, who slipped in the build-up to the winning goal, was inconsolable and ended up in tears on the pitch as the loss sunk in. Not only was the pain felt in the immediate aftermath of the Final, but also over the ensuing months. Carlisle was struggling to cope and he has identified the anguish of losing the Play-Offs as one of the contributory factors that sparked off his first fight with alcoholism and even led to suicidal thoughts.

In the darkest moments of Carlisle's alcoholism he was drinking heavily every day but still managed to turn up for training and play matches without anyone noticing. However, in October 2003 he was finally exposed when he tried to hide the fact that he was still drunk on the team coach whilst en route to an away match at Colchester. Ian Holloway, his manager at the time, quickly cottoned on to Carlisle's condition and he was withdrawn from the team. Holloway recommended that Carlisle go to Tony Adams' Sporting Chance clinic to begin his rehabilitation. Carlisle spent a month at Sporting Chance as he attempted to recover from his personal nadir, returning to the team in November, and he considers himself to be very fortunate to have been given that opportunity to rebuild and recover after his Play-Offs-induced meltdown.

Such is the depth of emotions that runs through the players when faced by the enormity of the Play-Offs that other competitions pale into insignificance by comparison. Carlisle endured losing in both FA Cup and League Cup semi-finals but "neither of those came close to the devastation I felt after the defeat in Cardiff", Carlisle admits. "Even the disappointment of relegation is not on the same page, in fact it's not even in the same book." Carlisle is not someone prone to exaggeration and his views are those of a mature, intelligent spokesman who commands respect. Bear in mind these comments were not made in the heat of battle or by a headstrong teenager, but with the cool perspective of a thirty-three-year-old, ten years on. Of course such a deep level of emotion also has an impact on the happier side of the coin when success is highly treasured and Carlisle's selection of his personal zenith is as telling as that of Dion Dublin from 1990.

Carlisle unequivocally chooses the Play-Offs promotion he gained with Burnley in 2009 as the highlight of his career, which spanned sixteen years up to his retirement at the end of the 2012/13 season. "That Final was by far and away," Carlisle confirms, "my best experience as a footballer. The combination of the chance to play in the Premier League, the purse at stake and the whole occasion of playing at the new Wembley. Added to this the fact I was made Man of the Match. It was the end of a long road." For a player who he himself self-effacingly admits was of "moderate ability" and played most of his career outside the top division, it was clearly a moment of enormous personal pride. Carlisle warmly reflects on the experience. "To play such a pivotal role meant that this without doubt was my personal highlight. Even though it was domestic club football, it far outweighed winning my first international cap at under-21 level which was, at the time, huge for me and my family." Perhaps more than anyone else in the game today, Carlisle understands how the pressures of football can affect players, and he can articulate their feelings, so his insight into the Play-Offs is invaluable.

Alongside the pressures of performing for your club at the Finals there is also the opportunity for players to showcase their talents and catch the eyes of larger clubs. So, for example, in the 2012 League Two Final Nick Powell enhanced his reputation immeasurably with a fabulous left-footed strike from the edge of the penalty area for Crewe's first goal, which was subsequently voted the fourth-best goal in a Play-Off Final. With that one sublime moment of skill, Powell sparked considerable interest in his future. However, he had already been spotted by Sir Alex Ferguson as a potential target and Manchester United had been monitoring the eighteen-year-old for some time. With his customary astuteness, Ferguson was keen to secure his signature before the Final and pre-empt any competition, as he explained on the official Manchester United website: "We thought that if we waited until the Play-Offs the secret would be out, so to speak. All the TV cameras would be focused on him and it might alert a few other clubs." So by lining up the deal in advance, there was no chance of

Powell moving to any other club apart from Manchester United, which he duly did in June 2012 straight after the Play-Offs, despite the added interest arising out of his much-enhanced profile.

But for the vast majority of players who are not picked out so early, an appearance in the Play-Offs is their golden chance to impress and take advantage of the unusually large and influential audience. There are dozens of current Premiership stars and England internationals, including the likes of Michael Carrick, Ashley Young, Phil Jagielka and Joleon Lescott, who all made their mark via the Play-Offs. Such players have made the step up to the elite level having proved themselves in the heat and light of the Play-Offs. As a barometer of talent there are few better indicators than being able to perform within that highly pressurised atmosphere, and leading managers will cast an eye over the future stars to see how they respond.

Grant McCann could be said to have established his reputation via the Play-Offs in that he holds a unique treble in their history. Not only is he one of the few players to have gained promotion with three different teams, namely Cheltenham Town, Scunthorpe United and Peterborough United, over a period of ten years, but he has also done so in three different stadiums, the Millennium, Wembley and Old Trafford respectively. With such extensive and unique experience, McCann is therefore in an excellent position to be able to talk about the different approaches to success and the determining factors. McCann has fond but slightly different memories of each of his hat-trick of triumphs, in which each of his clubs was considered to be the underdogs but ultimately emerged victorious. The biggest change was that with each successive Final he was increasingly aware of the significance to the club and all those involved.

In 2006 he played for John Ward at Cheltenham Town, whose vast experience included an unsuccessful stab at the Play-Offs with Bristol Rovers, and whose calmness stood out, helping to ease the pressure on the players. Although McCann missed a penalty in that match he is still considered one of Cheltenham's most influential players ever and much of that reputation is based on his part in their Play-Offs triumph. His second successful Final was achieved under Nigel Adkins of Scunthorpe in 2009. A relative novice compared to Ward, having only taken over The Iron as caretaker when previous manager Brian Laws was sacked, Adkins had famously been the club physiotherapist up to the time of his appointment. McCann was the playmaker for Adkins' team and he remembers the manager's main attribute being his ability to remain positive. Sure enough, having just squeaked into the Play-Offs in the last minute of the league campaign, Scunthorpe defied the odds by beating Millwall in the Final.

McCann's crowning glory was Peterborough's League One Play-Offs victory in

2011. He was captain of the team and very much led from the front throughout the Play-Offs as not only did he score in both legs of the semi-finals against MK Dons but he also scored the third and last goal of the Final, a wonderful free-kick, which extinguished any lingering hopes of a Huddersfield revival. He was awarded the Man of the Match for the second time in three Finals. McCann joins a select group of players who have scored in all three Play-Offs matches of a single campaign, notching up another notable treble. Yet again the format provided a player with the zenith of his working life, as McCann is happy to confirm. McCann has represented Northern Ireland but his Play-Offs experiences are amongst the sweetest of his career. Although still playing, at thirty-four years of age McCann made the move to Northern Irish side Linfield in January 2015 and is not expecting to reach the heights again, so one can safely assume that those Play-Offs games will remain as the lasting achievement of his time as a footballer.

Clearly there are larger, more glamorous competitions than the Play-Offs but for 80 per cent of professional footballers who play outside the Premier League, this is their chance to shine and grab the limelight. But because that moment is so precious it can also adversely affect some of those involved and can be a destructive force that adds to the strains of their lives. That some players, such as Windass and Carlisle, have clearly not been able to cope in their aftermath is a cautionary tale of the effects that such matches can have on their lives and livelihoods. Amidst all the hype and the ever-escalating price tag it is worth sparing a thought for those who suffer from the very same intensity and drama that we lap up as essential ingredients of the Play-Offs mix, especially as players do not attract a great deal of sympathy or compassion. By showing us their fragility and weaknesses these players indicate just how much is at stake and what it means to them when they are contesting the Play-Offs, which can often represent the pivotal moments of their careers for better and for worse.

HEROES & VILLAINS

RITCHIE HUMPHREYS, CHESTERFIELD & PFA CHAIRMAN

Ritchie Humphreys, the current chairman of the PFA, had an unusual career path that was the reverse of most footballers'. Rather than working his way to the top from humble beginnings, he started off being flung into the heat of the Premier League as a teenager, appearing and scoring for Sheffield Wednesday at the tender age of eighteen. His goals helped Wednesday to a brief spell as the leading club in the country as they topped the Premier League for a couple of weeks. After such a whirlwind start to his career there was bound to be a tailing off and sure enough Humphreys was soon being sidelined by the arrival of the likes of Paolo Di Canio and consequently went out on loan to Scunthorpe and Cardiff.

Humphreys ended up at Hartlepool United in 2001 and stayed for twelve years, notching up over 500 appearances for the club and becoming a club legend marked by being named, amongst other accolades, as their Player of the Century. A major element of his formidable reputation was based on his Play-Offs adventures. Not that they started that well. In his first season the club had a dismal opening in early October and were rock bottom of the Football League. Humphreys remembers this low point vividly as it coincided with someone whose star was very much in the ascendant. "It was the same weekend when Beckham scored that extraordinary free-kick against Greece in the World Cup Qualifier whilst we slumped to the bottom of the league." The divide could not have been broader.

But then Hartlepool and Humphreys set off on a brilliant run which saw them shoot up the table, reaching seventh on the last day of the season when they pipped Scunthorpe to the Final Play-Offs spot on goal difference. This was the third successive season they had reached the Play-Offs and with the team on the up, having won their last five league matches, they faced Cheltenham in the semi-finals with confidence and a feeling that this was to be their year. After both games ended 1-1, the tie went to a penalty shoot-out. Humphreys took the first of the sudden-death kicks to keep them in it and he hit the bar, the ball rebounded off the keeper and then rolled agonisingly off the post. Crucially, the ball did not cross the line and that was that. *The Guardian* report simply described Humphreys as being "the most distraught player".

Humphreys recalls that moment with the pain still very much evident. "It's fine when it is somebody else and you can console them but when it's you and the responsibility for the whole season rests on that one kick. I just felt that everyone had done their job, only for me to let them all down." That sense of desolation is reflected in Humphreys' diary of this period *From Tears to Cheers* and for those who want to understand how much it meant to him it is required reading. Humphreys explains how united that group of players were and in his darkest moment he felt the strength of his colleagues' togetherness – as he describes it "there was an emotional bond" – which they then used to inspire them the following season to automatic promotion.

Humphreys was relieved at going up as he still felt something of the onus of that miss against Cheltenham, but his Play-Offs penalty story had one twist remaining. In the 2004/05 season Hartlepool qualified for the Play-Offs and the chance to get into the Championship, a level that had never been achieved by the club before. Tranmere were the opponents in the semi-finals and after both clubs won their home legs 2-0 it was down to the penalty shoot-out. With the failure of 2002 still fresh in the mind Humphreys did not volunteer for duty. His team mates rallied around, conscious of Humphreys' reluctance to take a penalty. Humphreys recalled how two players in particular were keen to protect him. "Both Chris Westwood and Antony Sweeney realised and volunteered to take a penalty, so they both stepped up when they would not have normally expected to." But when they were both successful with the fifth and sixth penalties it came down to the seventh penalty and Humphreys knew he was next in line. He couldn't leave it to the goalkeeper to take one before him, so he duly stepped forward and gained his redemption as he stroked the ball home to win the tie and a trip to Cardiff.

"That was a truly special moment," Humphreys confirmed and an experience that he still cherishes with abundant relish. Not only because it went some way to erasing the mortification of a few years earlier but also because it set up that Final in Cardiff against, of all teams, Sheffield Wednesday. It was as if the wheel had turned full circle for Humphreys, back facing the club with whom he exploded on to the scene almost ten years before.

He had been instrumental in ending the run of four previous semi-final defeats and they then came so close to winning their first-ever Play-Offs Final. With Hartlepool leading 2-1 after eighty-one minutes they were within a sniff of the promised land, less than ten minutes away from making it to the Championship, when they conceded a penalty, Wednesday equalised and, with Westwood sent off as well, they went on to lose 4-2 in extra time. But despite that disappointment of being so close to making Hartlepool history, Humphreys still talks of that amazing day as the pinnacle of his time as a player.

Now in his position as PFA chairman he happily shares those moments, both good and bad, with the younger players and advises them to make the most of the opportunity should it arise. "I just simply would not have enjoyed many of my best (and worst) moments without the Play-Offs. That platform creates an extra level of pressure and that's why, after all, we're in competitive sport, to play in the bigger games with the highest stakes." Coming from someone who started at the very top of the tree and was pretty much an instant hit and then has spent a further twenty years in the game, this is a further ringing endorsement of how much the Play-Offs mean to even the most seasoned professional.

TOMMY JOHNSON 1990/91

SECOND DIVISION PLAY-OFFS FINAL

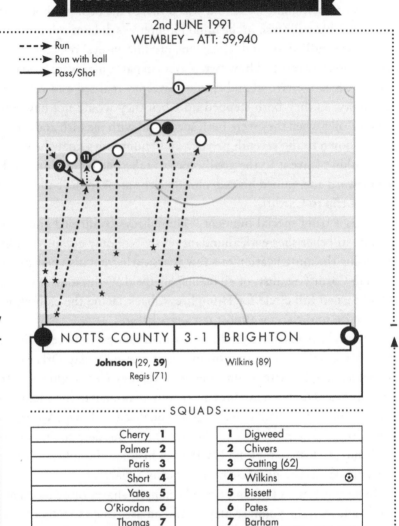

2nd JUNE 1991
WEMBLEY – ATT: 59,940

- - - ► Run
······► Run with ball
——► Pass/Shot

| NOTTS COUNTY | 3 - 1 | BRIGHTON |

Johnson (29, **59**)   Wilkins (89)
Regis (71)

···· SQUADS ····

	Notts County			Brighton	
	Cherry	**1**	**1**	Digweed	
	Palmer	**2**	**2**	Chivers	
	Paris	**3**	**3**	Gatting (62)	
	Short	**4**	**4**	Wilkins	⊙
	Yates	**5**	**5**	Bissett	
	O'Riordan	**6**	**6**	Pates	
	Thomas	**7**	**7**	Barham	
	Turner	**8**	**8**	Iovan (62)	
⊙	Regis (90)	**9**	**9**	Small	
	Draper (81)	**10**	**10**	Codner	
⊙⊙	**Johnson**	**11**	**11**	Walker	

Bartlett (90) Harding (81)   Byrne (62) Chapman (62)

Final League Position: 4th
SF 1st Leg: Middlesbrough 1 - 2 Notts County
SF 2nd Leg: Notts County 1 - 0 Middlesbrough

Final League Position: 6th
SF 1st Leg: Brighton 4 - 1 Millwall
SF 2nd Leg: Millwall 1 - 2 Brighton

GOAL FACT: Johnson scored in every Final he played in,
four goals in three matches for Notts County and Derby.

MANAGERS AND THE PLAY-OFFS

There are numerous times when managers have to show their mettle, providing strong leadership and clear direction when under the most severe pressure. As the Play-Offs are amongst the most pressurised and high-profile matches any team will face, this is often when the best managers come to the fore. In interviewing a selection of managers who have experienced the highs and lows of Play-Offs matches, a fascinating insight emerges into the different approaches and styles of the individuals as well as the need for a collective, unified spirit above and beyond the norm. The distinctive nature of the Play-Offs provides each manager with the prospect of a strange hybrid of success and failure, where reaching them is often considered an achievement but unless promotion is secured the whole season can be dismissed ultimately as a failure. Because of this thinnest of margins there is a particular type of stress that requires a different approach and attitude to the demands of a regular season match. Everyone understands this delicate balance but it is down to the managers to make the most of the intensity of this situation and turn it to their team's advantage.

In talking to a couple of the more seasoned and, let's face it, more charismatic managers in football, an interesting perspective was likely to emerge. Both Neil Warnock and Ian Holloway have been through the Play-Offs mill with a broad range of different experiences across the years, enjoying a fair amount of success and enduring the occasional failure. Having garnered the collective wisdom of these two wily Play-Offs protagonists, it is clear that there can be no magic silver bullet as to what determines the winners and the losers, but there are common principles that can improve the chances of success. Whilst each manager has their own individual style and methods, one can discern a couple of threads that bind these very different characters together.

But first it is time for a family affair and how a son stepped into the limelight, usually monopolised by his father, and how for once he was the triumphant one, the cock of the north (west). Family rivalries are usually the most intense and internecine wars the bitterest, so spare a thought for Darren Ferguson. His feats at Peterborough United in getting the team promoted three times pale into insignificance and are inevitably completely overshadowed by his father's record of incomparable achievement at Manchester United. It is nigh-on impossible for Darren to emulate Sir Alex and he will always suffer in any comparison with English football's most successful manager.

In May 2011 Darren did achieve the impossible by putting his father into the shade, albeit briefly, when Peterborough succeeded as Manchester United failed. Ferguson had taken over at London Road in January 2011 replacing Gary Johnson who had been embroiled in an irreconcilable disagreement with Darragh MacAnthony, the chairman. Fortunately for Ferguson he joined with the club in a healthy position, handily placed in fifth, and they stayed in the top six for the remainder of the season but never quite broke through to the automatic places. According to Grant McCann, Ferguson changed the style of play and the formation of the side, which he could do safe in the knowledge that they were heading for the Play-Offs. By the start of April, with seven games remaining, they were ten points ahead of the seventh-placed team so could be relatively certain that they would be contesting the Play-Offs and Ferguson could start planning ahead accordingly for the anticipated climax to the season. It is unusual to be afforded the luxury of taking over a club in such a healthy position, on the brink of success, and being able to make preparations for this series of vital matches. Ferguson took full advantage of this rare opportunity.

The victory he achieved over Huddersfield in the League One Play-Offs 2011 Final, which almost inevitably and with a heightened sense of irony just had to take place at Old Trafford, was clearly the highlight of his career. The fact that it came the day after United had been given the runaround by Barcelona in the Champions League at Wembley, when Ferguson Senior was forced to accept that his team had met a vastly superior opposition and been duly beaten fair and square, just added an extra dimension of satisfaction.

McCann, Ferguson's captain, felt the added weight of importance in the build-up to the match. On the eve of the Final the players gathered to watch the Champions League Final with Ferguson, who nailed his colours firmly to the mast by proudly wearing his United top. Ferguson's disappointment turned into a steely resolve to win his own Final the following day and there was an added intensity about the manager's attitude that made a positive difference to the mood of the Peterborough camp. McCann recalled feeling an overriding sense of fate that Peterborough were going to win, and as the pressure built in the hours before the match, he was filled with complete confidence even though they were facing a Huddersfield team that were on a twenty-seven-match unbeaten run stretching back to the previous year. Three unanswered late second-half goals wrapped up the victory and provided Ferguson with his big moment back at the ground where he had played for his father.

Ferguson's pleasure was self-evident. "It's a big day because after my dad losing at Wembley, I really wanted to get this one right." So for once Ferguson Junior outshone his dad and could revel in his own glory, describing it in the aftermath as "easily the best moment, either playing or managing". Darren could relish his moment of victory in light of his father's failure and it must have felt all the sweeter because of it.

What Ferguson may not have realised in his hour of triumph was that this victory confirmed Peterborough's status as the most successful team in Play-Offs history. The Posh became the only team to have a 100 per cent record having appeared in the Play-Offs more than once, this being their third successful campaign. But that proud run did end in the 2013/14 semi-finals when they were knocked out by Leyton Orient; their first and, to date, only failure. It is indicative of how tough the Play-Offs are that none of the ninety-five teams have managed to maintain a 100 per cent record aside from the handful of clubs who have won it in their only year of participation. Such a tough environment shows that there is a certain resilience and mental toughness required to be a regularly successful Play-Offs club. It is an uncompromising arena that separates the wheat from the chaff and casts a light on the effectiveness of the managers when the pressure is on.

At the start of the 2014/15 season there were eight managers in the Premier League with experience of the Play-Offs. Indeed of the 40 per cent of top-flight bosses a fair few of them had established their reputation with impressive Play-Offs feathers in their caps and owe a debt of gratitude to their Play-Offs success for their enhanced status. The qualities exhibited in getting their teams through the ultimate of acid tests does enhance the profile no end and accelerates them up the pecking order, placing them in demand. Brendan Rodgers, for example, shot to the attention of the football world when he took Swansea up in 2011 and within a year he decamped to the hot seat at Anfield after taking Swansea to a comfortable eleventh. Both Steve Bruce and Alan Pardew suffered

Play-Offs defeats before becoming winners in 2002 with Birmingham and in 2005 with West Ham respectively. Neil Warnock's position as the Play-Offs king is probably the key feature of his CV which has undoubtedly helped him secure some plum jobs including becoming Palace manager again at the grand old age of sixty-five at the beginning of the 2014/15 season.

After his Blackpool debacle in 1996 Sam Allardyce could be forgiven for harbouring a grudge against the Play-Offs but he shook off such bitter disappointment to secure two promotions this way. With Bolton in 2001 he set up the longest spell survived in the Premier League by a Play-Offs winner to date, overseeing the first half of that eleven-year stint. Then, perhaps even more crucially, he took West Ham up in 2012; anything less could have triggered a financial collapse for the Hammers.

Many scoffed at Allardyce's style but considering the undue pressure he was under to be promoted, his success would have brought immense relief and satisfaction to the West Ham board. His own sense of achievement was abundantly clear in his post-match comments. "This is a memory for life and we'll enjoy it. You want to go up automatically but if you don't and you win the Final then it's a memory for everyone for years and years to come," Allardyce said. "The delight you get out of winning at a venue like this, the trophy, the medals, the celebrations, it's an outstanding achievement. It's bigger than anything else; other games played here are cup competitions but this is everything, it's what's happened over ten months, not six or seven games."

Allardyce is one of those managers who firmly believes in seeking outside help when gaining an advantage. He is well known for his faith in and use of sports psychology, having come across the concept when he played in the US at the end of his playing career. He has been an enthusiastic advocate of such techniques since his early managerial days at Bolton. Hence one of Allardyce's earliest appointments at West Ham, when he took over in 2011 as he aimed to get the club promoted at the first time of asking, was sports psychology consultant Lee Richardson. Richardson is one of a kind, being the only former professional player in this country to have trained as a psychologist and also been a manager. Bringing his own experience of success in the 1992 Play-Offs Final with Blackburn, Richardson helped focus the players' minds on winning rather than regretting not going up automatically, something which had just eluded them as Southampton pipped them by three points.

So rather than letting them feel sorry for themselves, Richardson worked on inspiring the players to think positively about what lay ahead and to be in the right frame of mind to cope with playing "not just another game but a massive Wembley Final in front of 80,000 people". Having just read *The Chimp*

Paradox by Dr Steve Peters, Richardson was keen to impress upon the players the need to manage their minds as well as setting achievable targets in order to reach their true potential. As part of the preparation for the Final, Richardson offered to take the players to look around Wembley a few days beforehand so that they could get a feel for what it was going to be like. Interestingly, when he asked the squad, only one player put his hand up – Carlton Cole. So the trip did not happen, but Richardson felt it was significant that Cole had one of his most influential games in a West Ham shirt in the Final, scoring one and setting up the second. By being the player who more readily accepted the idea of visualisation and being more task-orientated than the others it could be argued that Cole set himself apart from his team mates, some of whom refused point blank to get involved. Richardson maintains that this led to some confused and below-par performances compared to Cole's effectiveness

As for Allardyce he was calm and authoritative even though under severe pressure, which could not be said of the rest of his staff. There were several non-playing personnel who needed calming down and Richardson's pre-match focus was as much on them as it was on the players. When he most needed to show it, Allardyce exhibited calm assurance. His two crucial substitutions before the hour mark, and just after Blackpool had equalised and were threatening to take control, changed the game. Those changes were aimed at nullifying the threat Blackpool were increasingly posing down the flanks and were evidence of his clear, rational decision-making. Not many managers would have taken such radical action but in the end it helped West Ham to secure that much-needed victory. As we are about to discover, other managers can suffer from indecision.

Dan Abrahams is one of this country's leading sports psychologists and has plenty of experience in advising a wide range of British football clubs, players (including Carlton Cole) and managers, as well as specifically advising during the Play-Offs. With an excellent working knowledge of what is required at the highest level when the pressure is on, Abrahams acknowledges that the Play-Offs are a special case akin to the qualifying tour for the European PGA, with which he draws some close analogies. Having been a professional golfer himself he understands how that pressure can build to the detriment of performance. It's the same do-or-die moment when the difference between success and failure is slender but the consequences are massive. This is the sharp end of sports psychology where strength of mind and resolute self-confidence are essential. The importance of self-efficacy, as championed by renowned psychologist Albert Bandura, is paramount. The ability of the individual to build a robust belief system in successfully achieving goals is crucial at these moments of intense pressure. So having a strong sense of self-efficacy will lead to a player reminding themselves of the good experiences, their own successes, which will build belief that they can perform well and foster an approach that will be in challenge mode as opposed to seeing this situation as a threat. By conditioning the mind to succeed, the theory of self-efficacy proposes that the chances of success are increased.

On the reverse side, negative thinking prepares for failure and there are plenty of examples of people freezing, or 'choking' at the crucial moment. Abrahams relates a story of a manager, who will remain nameless, who was so intimidated by the pressure of a Play-Offs Final that his decision-making became paralysed. This self-inflicted inactivity reached such a stage that he could not make a substitution, even though it was badly needed by the team. The fact that this manager, who was certainly no spring chicken having been in the game for many years, was struggling to cope and act decisively highlighted the intensity of the psychological burden to which even the most experienced can be subjected.

Abrahams confirms that players certainly feel the pressure, having become increasingly aware of the magnitude of the Play-Offs and especially the Championship Final, given that the gap between Premier League and the rest grows ever wider. How this pressure impacts on individuals depends upon their own coping mechanisms, and this is where support can make the difference. Whereas some will be cool to the point of diffidence, others will become hyped up, reflecting the different ends of the spectrum. For Abrahams it is pretty much a case of each to their own and what psychologists will do is to ensure that each player is in challenge mode and not feeling threatened. If there is any strong feeling of threat, this will probably lead to a state of anxiety that fosters an attitude of not letting anyone down rather than doing one's very best. During the lead-up to the Final, the players will be asked to concentrate on what they can tangibly control, such as their match-day mindset where the focus will be on a couple of achievement goals, such as 'be strong in my headers' or 'be vocal at all times' or even 'portray great body language'. Being properly prepared, Abrahams insists, gets the right chemicals flowing through the body and the mind, leading to a state where the player can perform to the best of their ability, which is the ultimate aim of all sports psychologists.

Naturally, most pre-match messages and pep talks are delivered directly by the managers rather than a third party. Whether the managers are of the harsh, cajoling type or the gentle, coaxing variety, the response needs to be delivered in the most appropriate manner depending on the situation. A manager cannot be expected to change his style or demeanour but he will have to adapt as befits the circumstances of this most important of matches. Singling out individuals can be problematic, Abrahams points out, as those players may feel they are being picked on, creating a negative and potentially hostile reaction. This can also be divisive within the team as others could view this treatment as preferential and feel excluded.

Football management is a balance of many elements of which psychology is but one and the very best managers will probably never over-think solutions or make too much of one particular aspect. To succeed in the Play-Offs the ability to relax seems to be a common trait, as encouraged by the likes of Warnock and Holloway, and one that is as influential as any technical improvements. As such, this is no mean feat when the financial and personal implications have reached such a dizzying level.

Ian Holloway was on the other end of West Ham's success in 2012 and he has over twenty years' experience of the Play-Offs as manager, player and player-manager – the full set. There have been as many failures as successes so he can see both sides of the coin. His chequered record, which stretches all the way back to 1989, did not start very well when as a Bristol Rovers player he lost out to Port Vale in the Final. By 1998 he was player-manager at Rovers and he does not hold very fond memories of the wild celebrations, led by the club's tannoy announcer who was crowing about going to Wembley, after beating Northampton 3-1 in the first leg of the semi-final. It struck Holloway at the time that it was all rather premature and he was to be proved right as Rovers duly threw away that two-goal lead against Northampton. A bitter lesson was learned.

He suffered more disappointment as QPR's manager in 2003 when losing to Cardiff in the Final but he did acknowledge the part played in that defeat by his opposite number. He cites Lennie Lawrence as "probably the bravest manager I have ever faced, when he took off his main striker Robbie Earnshaw, the fans' favourite" during the Final, for substitute Andy Campbell, who then went on to score the only goal of the game at Holloway's expense. He acknowledged that such decisive, affirmative action was the sign of good management. So by the time of Blackpool's famous triumph in 2010, when his team realised the dreams of so many Tangerines fans in reaching the Premier League, he was more than ready for some glory. Indeed that Blackpool success was Holloway's only successful campaign out of the five he had waged up to that point. So one could imagine that he would not have been overtly keen on the Play-Offs, but this is far from the truth. As his comment after the more recent disappointment of the defeat to West Ham in the 2012 Final shows.

"Good luck to Sam and his team," Holloway magnanimously reflected. "If you are going to go up this is the way to do it. You get the Wembley buzz all through summer and you get another medal." With his natural ebullience and gift for an outstanding quote he is a massive advocate. "Initially I was against them as I felt the team that finishes third after a forty-six-match season deserves to go up, but I have changed my tune." Holloway's conversion has been comprehensive and complete, to the extent that he has likened contesting a Play-Offs Final to a child's excitement and pleasure over Christmas.

In weighing up whether he would exchange a victory in the FA Cup Final for one in the Play-Offs he was loath to make a clear choice. Holloway considers the FA Cup to be a special competition even though he has never come close to winning it either as a player or manager. "It's just one of the most tremendous tournaments in the world. For any club to have a chance to play a big or better club is tremendous." But ultimately the primary focus of managers is not about cup glory. "What you're trying to do is to get to the top of the tree, week in week out, and that's the Premier League." And as the final route available to achieve that leap, the Play-Offs have to be selected ahead of the FA Cup, Holloway reluctantly admitted.

According to Holloway, the key aspect of the manager's role in approaching the Play-Offs is to be masterful, to exude confidence and create an aura of assured self-belief. As a keen student of military history, he has always taken a special interest in the leaders' role during battle and equates that to the managerial persona required to succeed. As he puts it, "If your fella sat on the big white horse is looking nervous, that'll come on to you, so you have to be the fella that believes the most." Holloway distinctly remembers that for both of Blackpool's Finals in 2010 and 2012 he was calmer than he had ever been and he is convinced that this feeling of self-assurance helped his players perform on the day.

He emphasises the need to, as much as possible, remove the emotion from what is as taut an occasion imaginable, otherwise this can play on the nerves, leading to below-par performances. As Holloway confirms, the sheer magnitude of the match hangs over all the playing staff. "There's an awful lot more at stake. It's your whole season, your whole livelihood." Holloway continues, "One minute it's there, all your dreams and all your aspirations and all that hard work. Every step you took in every single game has been wasted because you haven't got what you wanted." So if that sense of responsibility weighs down too heavily on your players' shoulders the likelihood is that this will burden them and not be conducive to them being at their best.

Despite all the previous failures, Holloway is grateful for the beneficial effects the Play-Offs have had on his own career and admits that his move to Selhurst Park in 2012 would not have come about if he had not secured promotion in 2010. "That was a life-changing moment. I wouldn't be sat here today (as Crystal Palace manager in November 2012) if I had lost that Final. It's on my CV that I got a team promoted to the Premier League." People take notice of, and are impressed by, the achievement of winning the Play-Offs because it clearly shows the calibre required when this intense level of pressure is exerted. Holloway can now add Palace's promotion in 2013 to his list of achievements and with his reputation enhanced he had given himself another chance to take on the challenge of competing in the Premier League. But that did not last as he departed in October 2013 with the Play-Offs victory shining like a beacon from a generally disappointing managerial spell.

As for the impact a manager can have on his team in the build-up to the Final, Holloway is not so sure. Managers and coaches do not have too long to get their troops ready, with just over a week normally in between the conclusion of the semi-finals and the Final. Ten days or so does not allow a great deal of special care and attention, especially as this will be the forty-ninth league match of the league season. So in dealing with tired minds and bodies, the focus is more on refreshing and re-invigorating than relaying complex strategies. Holloway relishes this period when the sense of anticipation is at its height. "That's the best week of your life, that is," Holloway enthuses. "Because you know you've done it, you're going to get a new suit, the season's over, there's a good atmosphere going as you're in a good, confident mood. It is just brilliant. It's like Christmas Eve over and over again for a whole week."

And of course Holloway enjoyed another string of Christmas Eves when he took Palace to triumph in the 2013 Final. This was a victory secured against the odds as Palace stuttered towards the end of the season and just limped over the line to secure a Play-Offs spot on the last day of the season when narrowly defeated former Play-Offs kings Peterborough, who were fighting to avoid relegation. So weak had their form been that many were questioning their chances of making it through the semi-finals against arch-rivals Brighton, especially after a goalless draw in the first leg at Selhurst Park, which also saw the team robbed of leading goal scorer Glenn Murray through injury. Holloway pulled the proverbial rabbit out of the hat in the second leg at the Amex with a fully deserved 2-0 win after Wilfried Zaha's brace. This showed Holloway in a much more favourable light, but not so for his adversary Gus Poyet, who suffered one of the more memorable meltdowns in Play-Offs history (see Heroes &Villains, Chapter 10). The victory in the Final over Watford was much more straightforward and a lot less messy.

If the build-up to a Final is feverish with anticipation and expectation, then the repercussions can be like a string of the worst New Year's Day hangovers – full of regrets, broken resolutions and shattered dreams. One manager who certainly would not share Holloway's almost childlike enthusiasm for the Play-Offs would be Danny Wilson. Wilson would be justified in feeling cursed, as he has been bruised and battered into submission by his singular lack of success. He started his managerial career at Barnsley and in his first season, 1994-95, led the Tykes to sixth in the old First Division, but they were denied the usual Play-Offs spot as the Premier League was being reduced to twenty clubs, so for this year only the last slot was fifth. Little did Wilson know how the Play-Offs were going to haunt him and blight his career.

This was only the start of his Play-Offs misery and hinted towards successive disappointments that lay ahead. His next port of call was Bristol City where after four years in charge he took the Robins to the Final against Brighton in 2004. Being City, they inevitably lost 1-0. Wilson was dismissed afterwards. Then he led another team of Robins from the West Country, Swindon Town, to the League One Final against Millwall in 2010 but again his team lost out 1-0. For his third crack at the whip, Wilson was in charge of Sheffield United and with their customary penchant for weak capitulation they failed to score against Huddersfield in the 2012 League One Final, subsequently losing in that unique, all-encompassing twenty-two-man penalty shoot-out. Then the following season, having taken the Blades into the Play-Offs frame yet again, he was sacked with only five games remaining. This, at least, ultimately saved him from further Play-Offs heartache as United fell to Yeovil at the semi-final stage a month later.

Wilson can lament over his three Finals with different clubs, not one goal scored and no promotion. Maybe it was his misfortune to have two of the least successful Play-Offs sides in Bristol City and Sheffield United to try and turn the tide. He may not have called on the services of a psychologist to sort out the endemic problems of both clubs but he probably could have done with one for himself. It is probably more galling that the manager who is still probably more closely associated with Sheffield United, and certainly more loved, is one whose managerial record in the Play-Offs is second to none.

Neil Warnock has experienced unparalleled success, winning the Play-Offs with three different clubs, as well as being the only manager to secure back-to-back promotions with Notts County in 1990 and 1991. But he has also been exposed to enough failure of his own and so, like Holloway, his views come with a sense of balance – an attribute which is not normally associated with Warnock. Opinionated, antagonistic and one-eyed are some of the politer epithets he has attracted in over forty years of football, spent mainly at the lower end of the leagues. Indeed he and Holloway are widely regarded as managers who have the credentials to get their clubs promoted but are limited in their ability to survive at the very top, and without their Play-Offs successes they would be deemed to be less successful. That may be an unduly harsh judgement but there is certainly some element of truth that the Play-Offs have enhanced, possibly even redeemed, their reputations, which are tarnished by their lack of success in surviving the rigours of the Premier League.

Warnock's first job as a Football League manager was with Scarborough, whom he led to being the first club to gain automatic promotion from the Conference in 1987, the first year of the Play-Offs. This innovation replaced the re-election system and was part of the same broad-ranging proposal which also brought about the introduction of the Play-Offs *(see the Heathrow Agreement)*. Warnock remembers the period prior to the Play-Offs as the doldrums when the vast majority of teams were cast adrift by the middle of the season with little to play for apart from pride and a paltry win bonus. Numerous games would be played out which meant nothing and the last few months of the league were filled with mundane and meaningless matches in front of dwindling and disinterested crowds. It was almost as if the clubs were treading water for a couple of months and Warnock hated this part of the season, condemning it as "a waste of time and effort".

So he was delighted by the introduction of the Play-Offs and their stimulating effect on the latter stages of the season. However, Warnock's first taste was not a particularly pleasant one and he clearly remembers the sense of injustice burning inside him as his Notts County team were playing Bolton Wanderers in the semi-final having finished a full eighteen points ahead of the Burnden Park outfit. His disconsolate mood was not improved by "an iffy penalty in the pouring rain, and being 1-0 down, and so I was cursing the Play-Offs". Warnock and Notts County recovered to overcome Bolton in the second leg and progressed to the Final and since then, unsurprisingly, Warnock's attitude has been extremely positive and he has "nothing but praise for them".

Warnock also has a vivid recollection of how the players coped with the pressure and of a surprising dichotomy between the younger players and their older counterparts. Before the 1990 Final against Tranmere he recalls people advising him that "the younger boys will freeze at Wembley", but in the end it was the eighteen-year-old Tommy Johnson who revelled in the occasion. He not only scored three goals in the 1990 and 1991 Finals, but also went on to do so for his next club Derby, so he was clearly not fazed as some thought he might have been. In fact it was the older team members, such as Craig Short, "who felt a bit nervous and edgy" according to Warnock. Lee Richardson agreed that in his experience the older players are focused on the outcome, being more aware of what is at stake and how this may be the last-chance saloon for those reaching the end of their playing days. By contrast, the younger ones naturally pay far more attention to the process, the game itself, with hardly any thought of the consequences.

As part of their preparations for the 1990 Final, Warnock arranged a practice run, taking the whole team to watch their opponents Tranmere beat Bristol Rovers in the Leyland DAF Cup Final at Wembley in the week prior to their encounter. The squad ended up amongst the Tranmere fans watching the team that they would be facing the following week. This was not the last time that Neil would end up amongst the crowd whilst watching a Play-Offs match, as will be revealed later on. The rationale behind this was to relax the players and make them feel as comfortable as possible in their surroundings. The only thing that can be achieved at this point of the season is "to work on their minds". Warnock insists that "there is no more fitness to work on, nothing physically to give, so aim at relaxing them by showing them highlights of all the good things from the season". Warnock's views chime with those of Holloway's in trying to create the right atmosphere for mental health rather than pushing any physical boundaries.

In fact Warnock was so keen an advocate of creating a relaxed atmosphere that when the players were assembled and expecting a video analysing Tranmere's strengths and weaknesses, they found he had instructed the kit man to put on a comedy video featuring "Jasper Carrott or maybe it was Chubby Brown". Whatever the principles behind this approach, it worked a treat as County beat Tranmere and then followed it up the next year, overcoming Brighton to reach the top division for the fourth time in just under seventy years. This remains the only time a club has achieved successive promotions via the Play-Offs and is a badge of honour for Warnock.

This notable achievement did not go unnoticed by the larger clubs, as both Chelsea and Sunderland, who had perhaps significantly both failed and been relegated through the Play-Offs in the years beforehand, showed interest in luring Warnock away. But he shunned their advances and stayed loyal to the team that he had developed at Meadow Lane and led them for their solitary season in the top flight before they failed to preserve their place in what was then to become the Premier League. Of course this was not to be the last time a Warnock team was relegated following promotion, as happened with his Sheffield United team in 2007. Within six months of the next season, Warnock had left County, but not of his own volition as he was sacked in January 1993.

However, it was Warnock's success with Plymouth which remains his fondest memory. Having been promoted via the Play-Offs with Huddersfield in the meantime, Warnock took Plymouth for the club's first appearance at Wembley in their history; his own fourth visit in seven years. The semi-final against Colchester was a taut, tetchy affair and when Colchester scored midway through the second half in the second leg to make the aggregate 2-2, nudging them ahead on away goals, the die seemed to have been cast. That goal was scored by Mark Kinsella and this incensed an already riled Warnock, who felt he "should have been given a red card previously". The blue touchpaper was well and truly lit and in the end it was Warnock who was sent off, not for the last time in his turbulent Play-Offs career, after berating the officials with his customary enthusiasm. Unusually he decided not to retire to the back of the stands but "jumped out of the dug-out and stood in with the crowd for the rest of the game", which was finally won by a Paul Williams goal five minutes from time. Plymouth then went on to beat Darlington, and Warnock recollects the journey back home to Devon as a very special day, as the green and white army celebrated all the way back to Warnock's beloved West Country.

Warnock also has strong and opposing memories of his experience in 2003 with Sheffield United which brought him one of his most cherished victories in his Play-Offs career. United recovered from being 2-0 down to Forest in the second leg to win 3-2 and it was made all the better for Warnock after "Forest's coaching staff had been showboating, led by Ian Bowyer". But, as so often is the case, immediately after the best moment came the most harrowing when United lost lamely to Wolves 3-0 in the Final in Cardiff, including another Warnock dismissal as he was sent to the stands after remonstrating with the referee at half time. The day ended on an unusual note for the ever-loquacious Warnock. He described it as "pretty horrific, I didn't want to socialise. Then when the chairman asked me to say a few words to the team, I had nowt to say." It may have been in part his shame at having been sent off but when Neil Warnock is lost for words, you know it is serious.

The fact that both Warnock and Holloway put a fair amount of emphasis on the importance of creating a relaxed environment for the players is a tad ironic as it would be difficult to find two more excitable managers in the entire league. Their touchline tantrums and post-match rants are legendary and it must make the players think long and hard when either of them is exhorting his team to be calm and collected. So as they are so insistent on the need to relax, this is surely a lesson that nobody can ignore, coming as it does from a pair of the most passionate, fiercest firebrands in the game.

WILFRIED ZAHA 2013/14

CHAMPIONSHIP PLAY-OFFS SEMI-FINAL 2ND LEG

13th MAY 2013
AMEX STADIUM – ATT: 29,518

- - -► Run
······► Run with ball
———► Pass/Shot

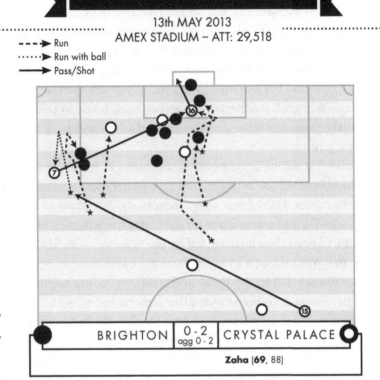

BRIGHTON	0 - 2 agg 0 - 2	CRYSTAL PALACE

Zaha (69, 88)

·········· S Q U A D S ··········

Kuszczak	**29**		**1**	Speroni	
Calderon (72)	**14**		**2**	Ward	
Greer	**3**		**27**	Delaney	
Upson	**20**		**33**	Gabbidon	
Bridge	**28**		**21**	Moxey	
Bridcutt	**26**		**8**	Dikgacoi	
Lopez	**21**		**10**	Garvan (61)	
Hammond	**4**		**15**	Jedinak	
Buckley	**30**		**16**	Zaha (90)	⊕⊕
Ulloa	**19**		**20**	Williams (62)	
Orlandi (64)	**11**		**18**	Wilbraham	

Barnes (64) LuaLua (72)

Bolasie (62) O'Keefe (90) Mortiz (61)

Final League Position: 4th

Final League Position: 5th

Final: Crystal Palace 1 – 0 Watford

GOAL FACT: Manchester United loanee Zaha's brace helped guide
his first club to the Final and ultimately promotion to the Premier League.

CHAMPIONING THE UNDERDOG

Supporting the underdog is a common facet of most British sports fans who love nothing better than seeing a team coming from a seemingly hopeless position to succeed. We also take a curious pleasure in tackling disappointment head on so supporting the outsiders of the sporting world gives us the chance to potentially enjoy an upset, but also readies us for accepting defeat. It is almost what defines how we follow our sports teams, with as much of an eye on the possible downsides as the positives. Unlike overt triumphalism, which generally only acknowledges winning and pays scant attention to the losers, the British appreciate a gallant loser almost as much as, if not more, than a crowing winner.

The Play-Offs are ideally suited to the championing of the outsider, as there is ample opportunity to revel in an unexpected victory and also wallow in the bitterness of a surprising defeat. Every team that enters the Play-Offs has, almost by definition, failed. By not securing an automatic promotion slot there is an implicit admission that each team has not quite made the grade. There is, though, that hugely enjoyable element of being in with a second chance which appeals to our love of seeing the underdog come out on top; a victory against the odds is all the sweeter. As soon as the Play-Offs are decided, the talk of survival at the upper level starts and barely relents. How could this team that has crept in through the back door possibly have the quality to survive in a higher league? Almost regardless of who wins the Play-Offs, their fate as they start the next season is to be on the back foot, marked as near-certainties for relegation by the bookies.

Operationally the club will always be at a disadvantage, as preparations for the next season, by necessity, will be a fair distance behind the other clubs. The majority of clubs will know in which division they are going to be plying their trade at least a few months ahead of the end of the season. Even the automatically promoted clubs can steal a march on the Play-Offs winners as they have a minimum of three or four extra weeks to start assembling a squad, line up transfer targets etc. and generally prepare themselves for their new surroundings. The Play-Offs winners, on the other hand, cannot be sure of their fate until the Final is decided, which is normally in late May, by which time the other clubs will most probably have their plans in place and be in an advanced state of readiness.

As the champagne is sprayed liberally around the changing room, thoughts have to turn quickly to how the next campaign will be navigated. Most of the best players will have been snapped up long before the Play-Offs have even started and there is quite often a reluctance on behalf of players (and agents) to move to the Play-Offs winners, as there is still this belief that they will be struggling to avoid relegation from day one of the next season. Thus the winners are viewed as being a few steps behind their rivals and they really have to start a season formidably if there is not to be further questioning of their ability to last the pace in the rarefied atmosphere of the higher division. They will almost undoubtedly be amongst everyone's favourites to be immediately relegated and this makes survival that much harder as they have to face up to psychological, as well as practical barriers.

Balanced against these obstructions is the boost that all Play-Offs winners invariably enjoy. It may be the most tortuous, and at times tortured, of routes to promotion but the impetus gained from winning the Final can provide a massive stimulus to the club. In the right environment this dramatic conclusion to the season can be used as a platform for the following season. Having proved themselves in the highly pressurised and demanding atmosphere that engulfs teams during the Play-Offs, competing in a higher division should be a challenge they can face with some degree of confidence. Any technical failings can be compensated for by strength of purpose and steely determination. In a way the Play-Offs winners enjoy a higher profile than those teams automatically promoted. The attention of the football public is drawn towards the Finals at Wembley as everyone's season is over, allowing fans of other clubs from different divisions to watch the frenetically dramatic climax. So fans of Premier League clubs who have paid little heed to matters in the Championship may be drawn to the Final, which offers the chance to watch a team that will be competing directly against them, even if the prevailing attitude will be that they have identified one of the easier opponents for the coming campaign.

Harnessing the attention and interest shown could prove to be a vital weapon for the coming season. It is interesting to note that in the last three seasons the teams that have been promoted to the Premier League have all secured their status, whilst the teams automatically promoted have not fared so well. So at the start of the 2014/15 season, whilst Swansea, West Ham and Palace were established in the Premier League, their respective champions QPR, Reading and Cardiff were all relegated back to the Championship within two years. Only QPR have regained their Premier League spot, via the 2014 Play-Offs naturally, but they were to lose it again the following year.

There is a special appeal to the Play-Offs that plays particularly well to the common trait of gunning for the underdog. One of the enduring qualities of the FA Cup used to be the giant-killing escapades of the lesser teams. Hereford's humbling of Newcastle in 1972 or Sutton United's unexpected victory over recent Cup winners Coventry City in 1989 stirred the emotions and remain vivid memories. But those type of shocks are very much less prevalent nowadays as the polarisation of football continues apace. As the top Premier League teams can easily field two teams of full internationals, the chances of a lower league team overcoming illustrious opponents are diminished, even when they do not play their strongest team. In recent years, even the lower-division clubs have started to play weakened sides in the knowledge that the FA Cup is no longer a priority and that league success is of greater importance. The minnows hardly ever reach the latter stages anymore and so Wimbledon's defeat of Liverpool in 1988 is really the last time a much smaller club upset the odds in a FA Cup Final, although Wigan's victory over Man City in 2013 may just qualify. It should be noted, however, that Wigan had become an established club in the Premier League over eight years prior to their Cup Final win so they cannot be truly classified as classic giant killers. With fewer shocks in the Cup there is an unfulfilled appetite for those yearning for a classic surprise and quite often these can crop up during the Play-Offs as some teams turn the tables on bigger, supposedly superior clubs and pip them to promotion.

As has already been mentioned, the very first season of the Play-Offs provided plenty of surprising results, with Aldershot overcoming both Bolton and Wolves, whilst Gillingham beat Sunderland just for starters. This pattern has continued over the subsequent twenty-seven years where so-called less fancied clubs have come out on top, providing us with a fair dollop of spice, giving some sustenance for all those who thirst for the victory of the underdog. Looking at the winners of the Championship Play-Offs since 2008, four of those clubs – Swansea, Blackpool, Burnley and Hull City – reached the Premier League for the first time. This quartet were returning to the top division after a combined absence of over two hundred years between them. Added to which they had all spent time in the lowest division of the Football League in the last twenty-odd years. All of them beat arguably bigger clubs in their Finals and brought a fresh, invigorating look and approach to the established nature of the Premier League.

Swansea, as was pointed out earlier, are the only one out of the quartet that have lasted beyond the second season so far. This does underline the notion that our much-favoured underdogs have their day in the sunshine but not much more; however, all four clubs made a positive contribution during their short tenure at the top, providing a breath of fresh air. And with Burnley and Hull having bounced back up to the Premier League since, albeit to be relegated again subsequently, the medium-term benefit of that season in the sun and the added financial comfort provided by the parachute payments are clear to see. Alongside our innate fondness for less-fancied clubs, maybe it is the fact that success for them has been relatively rare which makes their appearances in the limelight all the more endearing. Breaking the hegemony of the larger clubs, albeit possibly only for a limited time, is an attribute we can all appreciate and applaud wholeheartedly. Football in the upper echelons would become homogeneous without the arrival of a few outsiders and many of those get there courtesy of the Play-Offs.

Swansea's first taste of Premier League football proved to be something of a baptism of fire as they faced big-spending Manchester City at the Etihad in the opening fixture. Like so many since, Swansea were to suffer at the hands of deadly debutant Sergio Agüero, who came off the bench and inspired a 4-0 win with two goals, including a last-minute goal that set a precedent for his rescue act when securing the title in the last game of the season. Swansea were not disgraced but they looked as though they were going to be paired with the epithet plucky for the rest of the season.

When their next two matches yielded frustrating goalless draws against Wigan and Sunderland at the Liberty Stadium, followed by a 1-0 defeat at the Emirates to a freak Arshavin goal, the obituaries were being drafted as to their brief but noble shot at the top division. No goals scored after four games did not augur well and the plight of the plucky Play-Offs protagonists was seemingly sealed; it would be just a question of when, not if. But to their eternal credit, Swansea dusted themselves down and stuck with the idea of playing football. They escaped, not even by the skin of their teeth but with a healthy eleven-point cushion over the relegation zone and above QPR and Norwich, who had been promoted automatically.

Here was proof that the Play-Offs club could survive despite all the early portents pointing downwards and Swansea have certainly not looked back since. Indeed West Ham and Crystal Palace the following seasons repeated the trick of not only surviving but also finishing above the teams that had come up with them. Palace's unlikely revival under Tony Pulis came after a disastrous start following which there was talk of a lowest-ever points total (they'd amassed a paltry three points after ten matches) with the bookies at one point making them 9-1 on to be relegated. But against all the odds, turn it around they did and then some.

HEROES & VILLAINS

GUS POYET AND "POOGATE"

Following Brighton's painful loss to Palace at home in the 2013 Play-Offs semi-final there was a mass fallout between the club and their manager, Gus Poyet. Poyet's post-match comments were unusually frank about his own prospects. "I have always said that during the time we keep improving I am going to be at this football club and the day we hit the roof I'm not," he said. "So tomorrow morning I am going to ask if we've hit the roof and to know that I need answers and then we'll see." Later it was revealed that something else had hit the roof and the walls and floor of the Palace dressing room prior to the match. Taking up the story, here is the full transcript of Gus Poyet's email to all Brighton employees.

Hi All,

1) ... when Crystal Palace players and staff arrived to the Amex and went into their dressing room, they found themselves in a very uncomfortable situation, for some reason that still not clear to me, someone during the day had access to the away dressing room and done something terrible, trying to upset everyone related to Palace. To say it in clear English, someone had a 'poo' all outside the toilets, over and around the toilets.

Now, after careful consideration, and even after a meeting with the Chairman who assured me that MY REPUTATION IS INTACT, I feel that I must express my anger that anyone inside this organisation thought they could interfere with it.

I am angry that someone within this club could endanger our good reputation and stoop so low – did they imagine that this would affect the Crystal Palace players – well it possibly did – it may just have fired them up even more.

Well someone made a very bad decision and I think it is time to stand up and take responsibility – not just the culprit but those employees who are supposed to make our stadium safe and secure. Surely changing rooms are high up on securities check lists???

Surely someone should lose their job to allow such a breach of security -they do not deserve to be part of this club! ...

2) ... would someone like to admit it was their idea to hand out stupid pieces of noise-making paper -can I tell you it was an extremely silly idea and the result was an annoying noise -I am not for one minute blaming the result of the game on this, but it added only negative vibes to the proceedings along with the rubbish filled balloons that littered the pitch.

My team of players and staff have worked hard this season and I do not appreciate negative actions from others within the club ... whoever you are, you let the club down very badly.

Gus Poyet

Pandora's box was not merely prised ajar, but was wrenched open with such force that the hinges were tested to the limits when, to compound a miserable week for Poyet, he also came under fire from the former Spain midfielder Vicente, who was released by Brighton after the match. Vicente told the *Brighton Argus*, "He is the worst person I've come across in football. For me he is a selfish person, very egocentric. I say that because it's how I feel. I won't talk badly about my teammates, because they have been fantastic with me. What I think is unacceptable is that the manager makes fun of his players. I've seen things here that I have never seen in my career."

Then three days after that semi-final loss it was announced that Poyet, first-team coach Charlie Oatway and assistant Mauricio Taricco, were all suspended over an unrelated alleged breach of contract. There was a period of frosty silence of a few weeks until the club arranged a disciplinary hearing which Poyet failed to attend. Amazingly, the club had prepared a 500-page document detailing their case, so there was clearly some serious disgruntlement going on behind the scenes and more.

In a further twist to the extraordinary machinations of this fallout, and possibly even more unbelievably, Poyet was informed that he had been dismissed by the club whilst he was working on the BBC's coverage of The Confederations Cup in June and became the first manager to be sacked live on air, although in keeping with the atmosphere of acrimony, Brighton refuted the claims. Once the dust had settled on this bombshell, the club then released a statement on their website confirming their intention to dismiss Poyet for gross misconduct.

"Following a suspension, investigation, disciplinary meeting, and separate appeal hearing, which was conducted by three members of the club's board in London on 11 July and 12 July 2013, Brighton & Hove Albion today confirmed that after further consideration, Gus Poyet's dismissal for gross misconduct has been upheld."

So just as Brighton reached their best position in three decades they self-imploded and the manager who was largely responsible for taking them to the verge of the Premier League was blown away by the consequences of that Play-Offs defeat. The club's terse statement, grudgingly accepting Poyet's contribution, continued:

"The panel's decision was delivered to Gus Poyet and his advisers a short time ago. The club's internal disciplinary process is now complete. In line with the club's policy to ensure and maintain confidentiality and dignity throughout this process no further details of the disciplinary or appeal hearings will be released at this time.

"Despite the extremely disappointing end to Mr Poyet's career with Brighton & Hove Albion, the club would like to acknowledge Mr Poyet's service to the club, which included leading the club to the Football League League One championship in 2011 and to its highest league finish for more than 30 years in 2013."

But the saga did not finish there as a supportive League Managers Association advised Poyet that there could be legal recourse; he could now pursue the matter through the courts. In a statement on the LMA website the chief executive,

Richard Bevan, said, "I am really very surprised that the club has made the decision to dispense with the services of such an outstanding football manager as Gus Poyet.

"Gus has an excellent record of success with the club. We have every faith in Gus's integrity and have been impressed with the manner in which he has conducted himself during what, for him, has been an extremely difficult period.

"We have supported Gus throughout the disciplinary process and will continue to do so as required. We do not consider that the charges against him amounted to gross misconduct.

"Gus will now reflect on the outcome and discuss options with the legal team. It would, therefore, not be appropriate to make any further comment at this time."

Clearly, there had been tension within the club, with many observers noting the increasingly scratchy, uneasy relationship between chairman Tony Bloom and Poyet, which was finally exposed by what has been coined the Poogate affair. With Poyet gone, Brighton then qualified for the following year's Play-Offs in 2014, only to be denied by Derby in the semi-finals, but this defeat did not spark anything like the controversy of the previous escapade. Then again, very little could have done so.

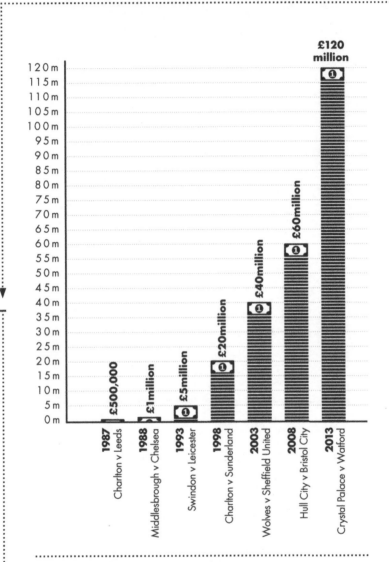

THE RISE IN VALUE OF PLAY-OFFS
1987-2013

£120 million

120m
115m
110m
105m
100m
95m
90m
85m
80m
75m
70m
65m
60m
55m
50m
45m
40m
35m
30m
25m
20m
15m
10m
5m
0m

£500,000 — 1987 Charlton v Leeds
£1million — 1988 Middlesbrough v Chelsea
£5million — 1993 Swindon v Leicester
£20million — 1998 Charlton v Sunderland
£40million — 2003 Wolves v Sheffield United
£60million — 2008 Hull City v Bristol City
£120 million — 2013 Crystal Palace v Watford

The Championship Play-Offs Final is worth more to the winners than the World Cup, Champions League and FA Cup combined.

Figures based on the difference in main revenue streams between the top division and second tier, comprising matchday, commercial and broadcasting income. As verified by Adam Bull, Senior Consultant at Deloitte Sports Business Group.

MIND THE GAP

The inextricable link between television revenues and football finance has been covered at great length elsewhere and the connection is immutable. As football has become such a massive industry and the sums of money involved have grown at such a dizzying pace, the focus quite often falls on the figures. From the average price of pies at the grounds, through the weekly income of the highest-paid players to the huge amounts that agents rake off, it is rare not to be assailed on a regular basis by the money that is swirling through the game. With the vast majority of the leading clubs' income now derived from broadcasting rights and with such a dependence on this revenue, it is flabbergasting to contemplate that for the season before the Play-Offs started there was no televised football whatsoever during the first half of that campaign. So between August 1985 and January 1986 there was no income from television for any club for a full six months. The relationship between the league and TV companies had reached such an impasse that Jonathan Martin, who was then Head of BBC Sport, felt that football had lost its pre-eminence as the No 1 televised sport. "Soccer is no longer at the heart of television schedules," Martin declared, "and it's not likely to be again." So low had the sport's star fallen in terms of popularity, and with its image having suffered seemingly irreparable damage during the tragic events of those fateful months in 1985, its value to broadcasters was now drastically reduced.

Contrast this with today's blanket coverage of football. In the 2011/12 season, between Sky and ESPN, 138 Premier League matches were broadcast live, in

addition to sixty-five games from the Football League on Sky. Add in the ter-
restrial players – ITV, BBC and Channel 5 – who also had their fair share of live
games for various domestic and international competitions, and the armchair fan
was spoilt for choice. The current television deal, which began at the start of the
2013/14 season, upped the stakes even further by increasing the number of live
matches between the two main broadcasters (with BT now Sky's main challenger)
to 154 Premier League matches. The result was that over 40 per cent of the total
380 Premier fixtures would be televised live. In comparison, the seventy-two
Football League clubs will have around 90 matches on TV, representing a mere
5 per cent of the 1,656 scheduled fixtures. Just as the regular season winds down,
the Play-Offs spark into action and every match, semi-finals and Finals from all
three divisions are covered live and exclusively by Sky. When the new television
deal starts for the 2016/17 season the number of live Premier League matches
will rise to 168, an increase of fourteen, meaning that 44 per cent of all Premier
League fixtures will be televised live.

Those who assume that the widespread television coverage we have today has
always been available would be gobsmacked to find that even after the impasse
with broadcasters was resolved in 1986, there was no great rush to televise matches.
In the late 1980s there was no live coverage whatsoever of the Play-Offs and any
broadcast coverage of the early years was restricted to a snippet on the local news
or, if you were lucky, you might have been able to unearth a late-night highlights
show. The importance of television's role has grown to such an extent that it is
now the single most important factor in any analysis of football's finances, but
that was not always the case. In the 1991/92 season, the year before the Premier
League started, the top division's share of broadcasting revenue was £15 million
per year, less than 10 per cent of the clubs' overall figure. Match-day income was
in the region of £85 million and other commercial sources such as the various
sponsorship deals pulled in £73 million. By 2009/10 broadcast revenues comprised
over 50 per cent of overall income for the first time and by 2010/11 when this
figure had reached £1,178 million, the proportion of club revenues derived from
TV rights had grown to 52 per cent. According to Deloitte's Annual Review
of Football Finances 2015, broadcast revenues for the 2013/14 season reached
accounting for 54 per cent of the league's total revenue – the highest proportion
from any revenue stream in the history of the division. With commercial revenue
reaching £884 million comprising 27 per cent and match-day revenues responsible
for the remaining 19 per cent so that for the first time in the history of the league,
match-day revenues were making up less than a fifth of total revenue.

More than ever before football is reliant on those broadcasting riches, just
as Sky's subscriber base is dependent on their coverage of football. As Rupert

Murdoch rightly predicted in 1996, premium sport, specifically the Premier League, would be the "battering ram" to drive pay-TV subscriptions. Such symbiosis between television and football has grown in leaps and bounds since the late 1980s and the relationship with Sky has caused a seismic shift. In the 1980s television used to be regarded by the football authorities as an adjunct, and a slightly irritating one at that. Such a negative attitude seems incredible now when broadcasting revenue is the central pillar of top club's finances. The fact that football risked killing the goose that was capable of laying the golden egg, beggars belief.

As an illustration of how little attention was paid to the Play-Offs, the following official Notts County report on the 1990 Final seems to come from a bygone age, not just a few decades ago. "Video cameras were at Wembley but only a brief goal report was shown on television that night on an ITN news bulletin ... Notts released a home VHS video of the whole match but this had an irritatingly poor commentary dubbed on after the event by Radio Nottingham's Mansfield Town correspondent Simon Mapletoft (who couldn't get Kevin Bartlett's name right either)." And so County's historic debut at Wembley was only just captured for posterity and the lack of any proper coverage makes for rather strange reading. Such amateurism would not be tolerated nowadays, but at the time there was no choice as there was such little interest shown by broadcasters towards what they regarded as a tawdry, tarnished product.

With such a minimal appetite for football from broadcasters there was hardly any competition between them to secure television rights back in the 1980s, so the level of revenues was nowhere near the astronomical figures being secured today. The current three year Premier League deal that started in 2013/14 was a shade under £3.1 billion for purely domestic rights shared between Sky and BT Sport, representing an astounding leap of £1.2 billion over the previous deal. With overseas rights coming in at the very least at £2 billion (some estimate much more) and BBC highlights worth £180 million, the total for 2013-16 is a minimum of £5.2 billion. The next domestic broadcast deal, which was agreed in February 2015, has seen the ante raised yet higher with Sky and BT Sport's combined spend of £5.136 billion to secure all seven packages available. When the overseas rights and BBC highlights packages are added, the overall figure is expected to be well over £7.5 billion for the next three-year cycle.

In contrast, back in 1988, ITV secured rights to show top division football exclusively for £44 million over four years, which in itself was a massive increase over the two-year deal struck in 1983 which was worth a mere

£5.2 million. That is a staggering increase of hundredfold over twenty-five years. To put this into perspective the total revenue for the two year ITV deal between 1983 and 1984 inclusively is around half the revenue generated by a single Premier League match in the current environment which, according to *Sporting Intelligence*, will be worth around £10.19 million on average from 2016 onwards. With BSkyB and BT's joint turnover amounting to £25.6 billion and profits in excess of £3 billion, the bidding war was always likely to be fierce and football has made the most of this increased competition. With other players such as ESPN, Al-Jazeera and new entrants such as Apple and Google expressing interest, there is only one direction this is heading.

This massive leap in terms of revenues has led to a polarisation within football whereby the gap in incomes between the Premier League and the three divisions of the Football League has developed into an almost unbridgeable chasm. Whilst the Premier League revenues have been escalating rapidly, the Football League deal has declined in the last cycle so the disparity grows ever wider. For ambitious Championship clubs, the rush to get into the Premier League has become a stampede as the fear of missing out on the riches on offer becomes more intense and increasingly desperate. Attaining the holy grail of a place at the top table has turned into an obsession for so many clubs and has been the downfall of quite a few, such as Portsmouth and Leeds, as they have struggled to cope with failing to maintain their status in the Premier League. The relative importance of the Play-Offs as a route to this nirvana has risen accordingly, but it should be noted how historically the success of each club promoted through the Play-Offs in staying in the Premier League has been limited. The survival of Swansea, West Ham and Palace over recent years is the exception that proves the rule and as they all avoided relegation in 2014/15 this was the first time in twenty-eight years that a trio of consecutive Play-Offs winners have stayed up for more than two seasons.

Over the first twenty-five years of the Play-Offs the team reaching the top tier had failed to survive the first season fifteen times, which is an alarming 60 per cent failure rate and proves just how difficult it is to acclimatise. Contrast this with the clubs promoted automatically over the same period and only a third of these have been relegated. The harsh reality is that Play-Offs clubs reaching the Premier League are generally twice as likely to suffer immediate relegation than the teams finishing in first or second. This is not a statistical blip, but a worrying trend and one that has to be taken into consideration when planning the future viability of the clubs involved. The commonly expressed view is that the Play-Offs winners have to overcome the handicap of being at least a month behind the other teams in terms of planning. The more realistic chairmen will factor in the possibility of an immediate return to the Championship and make the necessary contingency plans if that is indeed their fate. As has been discussed earlier in this book, with nothing resolved until late May, there is very little time to get prepared for the massive leap up, and with many of the likely transfer targets already gobbled up by clubs certain of their future position well in advance, the most practical approach is to anticipate relegation and its consequences.

Another challenge which Championship Play-Offs winners face the second they are promoted is the imbalance between rising expenditure and income following promotion. Costs start spiralling in preparation for entry to the Premier League. As Steve Browett, co-owner of Crystal Palace, highlighted immediately following promotion in May 2013, the club had to spend upwards of £1million in upgrading media facilities at Selhurst Park, which included a new television gantry, interview studios, laying cables etc. Add to this further monies for improving the stadium itself, a greater infrastructure, and more back-room personnel, alongside the increased demands of existing players and costly new transfers, and there is a lot of red ink covering the accounts from the outset and hardly any corresponding income at this early stage. Sponsorship deals and match-day income do increase but not at sufficient levels to cover those incremental costs, thus putting the club on the back foot financially for the time being.

The oft-quoted value of winning the Championship Play-Offs Final reached £134 million in 2014 prior to QPR's victory over Derby, comprising £62 million in prize money even for finishing bottom of the Premier League, plus £72 million in parachute payments. In fact the actual figure was less because QPR still had three years' worth of parachute payments outstanding from their relegation in 2013. The issue was also clouded by the impending Financial Fair Play fine that loomed large over QPR's heads after their previous loss-making season in the Championship. These were exceptional circumstances but the fact remains that the figure of £134 million is clear evidence of the gap that has developed. In contrast the majority of Championship clubs receive a base figure of around £4 million in solidarity payments and broadcasting revenue. Such parachute payments have created a clutch of clubs that have far more financial firepower than any of their rivals. Steve Browett pointed out that Palace moved from being a loss-making business into one with healthy profits of £20 million in just one season and as a business their turnover shot up eightfold. There are not many businesses in any walk of life that undergo such a dramatic transformation in the space of a year and it is a tough ask to make the transition a smooth one.

The bulk of this impressive figure is not made available straight away, with approximately £18 million paid in July and roughly £25 million spread over the ten months at £2.5 million a month, with another £12 million in January and a balance of £6.5 million, depending upon finishing position, final facilities fees etc. at the end of the season. The fact that only a sixth of the expected revenue is made available at the beginning of the season is something which Ian Holloway has bemoaned. Holloway argued that as a promoted club "you don't get the money quick enough and they should give you the money the second you go up".

He compares the wealth gap to "the difference between a Shetland pony and a racehorse", and it was little wonder that Palace were made odds on to return to the Championship within an hour of their Wembley triumph in 2013, indeed it would be highly unusual for the winners of the Play-Offs to be anything but firm favourites for the drop. Holloway had an interesting and, as ever, slightly quirky suggestion that "they should invert the pyramid, turn the whole thing on its head and give the lesser clubs more money". Such an idea is more akin to what happens in the much more democratic world of American sports where the weakest team gets the first pick of the player draft to even things out. "The way this is going, it's an unfair playing field with the rich getting richer, so Champions League money goes to the top four, concentrating even more power to those elite clubs." In light of Palace's 2013 Play-Offs success Holloway was clear about the task ahead. "We've got a lot of building to do. I know what it's like to be a club that come up late and we are not in the same echelons as the top half of this table we are now in. It's like starting a marathon and they are 20 miles away. Are we going to catch them? That's the target." Ultimately Holloway did not overcome that massive handicap and he left Palace in October of that year a dispirited figure and with the club well behind the pace, marooned at the foot of the table.

With the odds stacked so heavily against the Play-Offs winners it is no great surprise that the longest continuous stay in the Premier League is the eleven seasons achieved by Bolton Wanderers, after promotion via the 2000/01 Play-Offs, which ended in their relegation in 2011/12. Apart from Bolton, no other Play-Offs club has lasted longer than seven seasons and the average shelf life is worryingly short at just over two seasons, which does not help in building a sustainable football club. In comparison, the promoted Play-Offs clubs in the lower two divisions have a relatively healthy history of staying up initially. For new entrants to the Championship, or its equivalent, twenty-four of the twenty-seven clubs (89 per cent) have survived their first season, whilst of those reaching League One via the Play-Offs twenty-two of the twenty-seven clubs (81 per cent) avoided dropping straight back down. This suggests that there is a specific problem for clubs trying to bridge that ever-increasing gap between the Football League and the Premier League rather that Play-Off clubs per se are disadvantaged.

Play-Offs clubs rarely trouble the other end of the table, with Blackburn being the only club to have reached the Premier League via the Play-Offs and then gone on to win the title. Having won the Play-Offs in 1992 under Kenny Dalglish they finished a creditable fourth in their first Premier League season, the highest position achieved by any Play-Offs club straight after promotion. Buoyed by the extraordinary benefaction of Jack Walker and the strike power of Shearer and Sutton, Rovers made it to the very summit three years later as Premier League champions. But it is difficult to envisage this being achieved again by a Play-Offs winner, as the handful of clubs occupying the top spots have rarely changed over the last decade; only Everton and Tottenham have broken the stranglehold that both Manchester clubs, Arsenal, Chelsea and Liverpool have had on the top four.

There have been four other top ten placings achieved by Play-Offs winners in their first season following promotion, namely fifth achieved by Ipswich in 2001, Leicester's ninth in 1997, and West Ham's ninth in 2006 and tenth in 2013, but these are pretty tiny crumbs of comfort for Play-Offs winners' chances in the Premier League. The key focus has always been on survival and even though that has proved to be somewhat elusive, staying out of the bottom three will remain the principal target for any club promoted in this way.

There is a wide range of arguments as to why the Play-Offs winners have such a poor record, including less time to prepare, limited transfer window and overall uncertainty. But if this were the case then there would be a more consistent pattern throughout the three leagues. Promotion to the Premier League is clearly and conclusively a separate case. Irrespective of the reasons, the prognosis for promotion via this route opening up the opportunity for an extended spell in the Premier League is not good and should not be counted on by the clubs themselves. Indeed some yo-yo clubs have made a virtue of building a more solid foundation, refusing to radically alter their approach after being promoted.

According to David Sheepshanks, current chairman of St George's Park (the Football Association's national football centre), West Bromwich Albion have found the right formula in not overspending after promotion. As erstwhile chairman of Ipswich and an experienced Play-Offs practitioner, he cites Jeremy Peace, The Baggies' chairman, as someone who has proved "very skilful, nay brilliant, at running the club on modest means and avoiding the pitfalls if things go awry". West Brom's steady progress over the last few years has been based on a combination of prudence and not over-reacting to their frequent toing and froing between divisions. This consistency and level-headedness which they have displayed has culminated in a comfortable eighth position in 2013 and a slightly less convincing seventeenth in 2014, but they have the look of an established Premier League club and signs suggest that they have avoided the boom/bust cycle of the majority of clubs who oscillate between the top two divisions and fail in attempting to straddle the two. It may be significant that West Brom were promoted to the Premier League four times between 2002 and 2010 and it was always automatically rather than through the Play-Offs.

Swansea City are the latest club to be lauded as the prime exponents of financial composure following their Play-Offs triumph of 2011 and three solid seasons of mid-table respectability since. Added to this is their successful fan ownership scheme, described by Premier League chief executive Richard Scudamore as "probably ideal", which was based around the Supporters Trust holding a 20 per cent stake and a guaranteed place on the board for an elected supporter, currently filled by lifelong fan Huw Cooze. Allied to this innovative scheme the Swans have played flowing, attractive football and have justifiably become the darlings of the media, as David Conn of *The Guardian* extolled in April 2012: "Purred over for the triangles of Brendan Rodgers's passing game, midfield strings pulled by Leon Britton, who was with the club in the old Third Division, the Liberty Stadium hugging itself in glee, the Swans's is one of modern football's most remarkable rises." The fact that they came up via the Play-Offs makes it all the more noteworthy that they have achieved such stability.

However, we have been here before with the likes of Leicester City, Bolton Wanderers and even Sheepshanks's old club Ipswich Town all being held up as paragons of financial virtue, only to falter and face financial meltdown. In recognition of this financial gulf between the top two divisions, the idea of 'parachute payments' was introduced to cushion the blow of relegation from the Premier League. The level of parachute payments is worked out using a formula which is relatively transparent. According to *Sporting Intelligence*'s editor Nick Harris, who has studied this in depth, the parachute payments are based on a percentage of one equal share of the Premier League's domestic and overseas TV money less the 'solidarity payment' that Championship clubs receive each season from the Premier League.

In the very first Premiership season these payments amounted to an average of £1 million over two seasons for each club but, as with most football finances, the level has escalated dramatically over the twenty-odd years, reaching the current level of £64 million spread over four years as agreed between the Premier League and the Football League in June 2015, however, in future the payments will be paid over three years and if a club goes back down after a single year in the Premier League will get only the first two years of payments. Such an increase has now led to complaints that this gives those relegated clubs too much of an advantage over the other clubs who are currently receiving just over £2.3 million in solidarity payments, itself slightly more than they receive from the basic television deal. So the argument goes that this is creating a further rift between 'parachute clubs' and their immediate rivals in the lower leagues, almost creating another tier of wealth amongst those clubs battling it out in the Championship. This may also go some way to explaining why the likes of Burnley and Hull regained their Premier League status within a few years of both being relegated in 2010. Although both were relegated again at the end of the 2014/15 season and so are seeking to bounce back once more, bankrolled by parachute payments.

However, the evidence of the 2012/13 season challenges this notion, as for only the fifth time since the Play-Offs were introduced, not one of the relegated Premier League clubs got as far as even the Play-Offs, with Bolton, the highest-placed of the three, being pipped at the post to finish seventh and consequently just missing out on qualification. Blackburn's topsy-turvy season went into free-fall after their Indian owners Venky's forced the resignation of manager Steve Kean when Rovers were handily placed in third and just two points off the top. Kean's departure set off a managerial merry-go-round of four different managers in the space of a few months and the club went plummeting down the table, at one stage finding themselves in the relegation zone with only a handful of games remaining. In the end they managed to scrape into seventeenth place only four points above relegated Peterborough. This was a far cry from those heady days of Jack Walker's benevolent ownership and the team challenging for the title.

Poor old Wolves also found themselves struggling against the drop but unlike Blackburn they failed to survive and sunk to twenty-third place, facing the dreaded drop down to League One. So Wolves suffered back-to-back relegations in a worrying echo of their disastrous slide down the divisions in the early 1980s. They also became the first club to be relegated in the season after losing their Premier League status. But they did manage to stop the rot as, still bolstered by the parachute payments, they stormed back up to the Championship in 2013/14 with their revenues far outweighing the remaining twenty-three League One clubs.

Such a disastrous showing by the relegated Premier League clubs was in complete contrast to the previous season when all three clubs relegated from the Premier League featured in the Play-Offs. These included West Ham, who made an instant return after overcoming Blackpool in the Final and apparently saving themselves from a desperate financial situation. As West Ham chief executive Karren Brady pointed out at the time, the club's owners, David Sullivan and David Gold, had bankrolled the wage bill of £32 million and this would not have been sustainable through another season of Championship football.

The growth in the financial value of promotion has accordingly been stratospheric and led to the Championship Play-Offs Final becoming the first single sports match to be worth £100 million back in 2012. With the 2014 figure at around £134 million and with this raging inflation showing no sign of any discernible slowdown, the £200 million mark will surely be reached within the next few years as the impact of the next television deal is felt. Having already attained the status as the most lucrative single sports match in the world, the Championship Final is bound to be breaking more records in the coming years. Additionally, however much one might argue that parachute payments are skewing the playing field, they look set to remain part of league finances for the foreseeable future. Imagine the gnashing of teeth and wailing that would ensue if the payments were stopped, leaving relegated clubs without that way of softening the blow. In all probability they are here to stay and will be responsible for maintaining and extending the value of the world's most valuable match.

None of the people behind the original concept, neither Lange, Noades nor Carter, could have possibly anticipated the Play-Offs reaching such an incredible level of financial importance. The Play-Offs were originally designed to compensate clubs for lost revenue share, but now they serve to highlight the enormity of that loss and underline the gulf that has built up and is still growing. It is worth charting the progress of its significance in a little more detail, noting the key trigger points along the way and discovering how this epoch-making match has developed financially into such a leviathan from such humble origins.

When Charlton beat Leeds in the first year of the Play-Offs Finals to retain their top-flight status, winning that match was probably worth less than £500,000. The size of the television deal was so small that it hardly had any impact on the overall value. In 1986/87 the deal was around £18 million for three years, averaging out at £6 million p.a. for all ninety-two clubs, of which half went to Division One clubs and a quarter to Division Two. The difference equated to approximately £72,500, so when added to match-day income and commercial revenues, which at this stage far outweighed those of broadcasting, the figure could have possibly quadrupled but would still not have been much more than £500,000. There were no scheduled parachute payments either, so this was not even a consideration. The board at Charlton no doubt viewed their Play-Offs triumph as more of a face-saving exercise, a matter of pride, than a financial imperative.

There was little change over the following few years as football began the long, laborious climb to rebuild its tattered image. Whilst television revenues grew steadily in line with other revenues, and parachute payments were introduced, the relative importance of each income strand stayed roughly in the same proportions. The first radical step occurred with the onset of the Premier League and the impact was as sudden as it was significant. The Premier League clubs' collective broadcasting revenues shot up from £15 million, or less than £1 million per club in 1991/92, to £97 million, c. £5 million per club by the end of the 1996/97 season. At this stage parachute payments also began to increase by 50 per cent to £1.5 million p.a. and the value of the Play-Offs Final and qualifying for the Premier League suddenly moved into the region of £20 million. This figure was still not much on the grand scale of sporting contests, but it had started to creep on to the radar.

Four years further on and the television revenues really started to accelerate, reaching £360 million. At this point they had overtaken other sources of income, becoming the leading revenue generator for the clubs by 2000/01 for the first time. Parachute payments of £3.75 million pushed the value of the Second Division Final to over £30 million when Bolton began their record-breaking eleven-year spell at the top. There was a steady increase of revenues for the next couple of years, although the momentum was rather stalled by the recessionary pressures of the early 2000s. Between 2003/04 and 2006/07 the increases in broadcasting revenues ground to a halt whilst the other main streams rose steadily. Just as this evened out the contribution of the three main drivers of income, there was to be a sea change in 2007/08 when broadcasting revenues almost doubled from £543 million to £925 million, leaving match-day and commercial income in their wake. This was the tipping point for the Championship Play-Off Final; now worth at least £60 million, it was at this moment that it started to be considered the largest single match by value throughout sport.

Since then there has been an ever-widening gap between broadcasting revenues and the others so that by 2009/10 the level was reached whereby broadcasting was worth more than the other two principal revenue streams put together. This is now likely to be the case for the foreseeable future and certainly up to the end of the next deal in 2019 and beyond as there is the likelihood of the broadcasters' bidding war intensifying. The balance has swung dramatically over the last twenty years – with the overall figure for 2014/15 standing at £1,760 million, broadcasting revenues were worth 54 per cent of the clubs' total income. Compare that to 1991/92 when at £15 million they were worth slightly less than 9 per cent. The figures speak for themselves and give the background as to how the £200 million match may well be reached in the near future. If there is no slowdown in broadcasting revenues the £200 million level could be surpassed by the end of this decade. To put that into perspective the value of this one match is already greater than the annual turnover of every club apart from the Big Five – both Manchester clubs, Liverpool, Arsenal and Chelsea.

The figures go up in leaps and bounds and this has been the pattern for a while now. For each £5 million or £10 million added to the value, the difference between the riches of the Premier League and the relative impecuniousness of the rest of the league is laid bare. The price of failure is spelt out louder and clearer than it was beforehand; mind the gap. Therefore the pressure on all those involved is exacerbated and it is to the eternal credit of the players that, despite this financial backdrop hovering menacingly over every pass, shot or tackle, they still manage to create such spectacular football at the end of a gruelling and arduous season. They could be forgiven for taking a safe and cautious path with no risks taken, but the football is often as exciting as anything that has been seen during the regular season and the attitude is one of abandon, bordering on recklessness at times, and is all the better for that.

The accolade of being the world's most lucrative sporting contest is also worth a closer look. In footballing terms the figures for other major titles provide a telling and stark comparison. The combined total prize money for winning the World Cup, the Champions League and the FA Cup is just over £31 million, whilst the runners-up receive in excess of £21 million – the difference between winning and losing a relatively paltry £10 million. Such a figure is dwarfed by the stakes for that Championship Final and puts the financial status of the Play-Offs into context. The direct contrast between The Champions League Final between German giants Bayern Munich and Borussia Dortmund and the 2013 Championship Play-Offs Final, which took place two days apart at Wembley, is telling. The difference between winning and losing the leading European club competition was worth around 4 million Euros, some £117 million shy of the intrinsic value of the match to decide third place in the second tier of the English league. Not many people could have envisaged or anticipated this extraordinary, exponential growth.

Outside of football, there are plenty of high-profile and moneyed matches, so it is worth digging a little deeper into their individual values to see how they stack up. For example there has been much made of the riches on offer through cricket's Indian Premier League which is now in its sixth season. The 2014 tournament was won by the Kolkata Knight Riders who received 150 million rupees, and the runners-up, Kings XI Punjab, took home 100 million rupees. That difference is the equivalent of £517,000, so close to that original Play-Offs Final back in 1987.

Golf and boxing are sports that are commonly associated with big purses but again the winners do not get anywhere near the top Play-Offs prize. The Players Championship, considered to be golf's 'fifth major', carries a top prize of $1.7 million compared to the runner-up's $1 million, so a differential of $700,000 or about £470,000. As the prize money for the Players Championship has stayed pretty much the same since 2008, the value of the Play-Offs has more than doubled. Strangely, boxing's biggest purse up until recently was just under £36 million for a fighter who lost his bout. In May 2007 Oscar De La Hoya received twice the amount that his conqueror Floyd Mayweather did. Mayweather (aka Money May) then broke that long-standing record with a deal which brought him just under £48 million for his fight with Canelo Alvarez in 2013, regardless of the result. That was the sort of level that the Championship Play-Offs Final reached back in 2006.

Surely, though, one would expect that the big four American sports are going to be the main challenger for this title. The Super Bowl is the pinnacle of the commercialisation of sport and in 2014 CBS charged an average of $4 million for a thirty-second television advertisement. Despite the overall broadcast deal being worth in the region of $4.5 billion for the season, hardly any of these monies go to the team that wins the match. With over 164 million people in the US tuning in for at least six minutes to watch the Seattle Seahawks overcome the Denver Broncos in January 2014, one would have expected the Seahawks to be in line for a considerable payday. However, the truth is that despite the vast sums generated by the Super Bowl, in the words of David Tossell, PR Director for the NFL in the UK, "for a franchise there is no difference between winning and losing". Tossell continues, "The value would be in whatever winning the Super Bowl might add to the notional value of a franchise were it to be sold, but even that would be only a small and indirect factor in the overall value of a franchise." The players do gain some financial reward but the difference between winning and losing was $44,000 per man, plus the Super Bowl Ring, which is worth around $5,000, so the net gain is under $50,000, or less than £32,000. Those figures are mere peanuts compared to the financial uplift that a footballer will enjoy after promotion. According to a *Daily Mail* survey in November 2014, a Championship player's average income was £500,000 compared to the average Premier League wage which has now reached £2.3 million and climbing.

In conclusion, the value of the Championship Play-Offs Final has rocketed over the last twenty years, whereas other sporting contests have failed to keep pace. At current rates of increase the position as the biggest financial prize will be unchallenged for many years. Although this stands out as the biggest prize in sport by some distance, as has been identified earlier the actual phasing of the payment is a bone of contention for some. The Play-Offs winners may get an impressive trophy and the accolades of a huge and appreciative audience, but they do not receive a cheque for £134 million, indeed the actual money that is available upfront is relatively limited. As Ian Holloway argued earlier, it would be more equitable if the promoted clubs received the monies before the season commences rather than later, as this is when it is most useful in preparations for joining the Premier League.

Clubs promoted to the Premier League receive a share of the riches promised to them, with only a fraction of the headline figure made available at the outset. Balancing the books is a tricky challenge and a fair few clubs have made a pretty poor job of handling promotion in an astute and well-considered fashion, with the catalogue of failures much greater than the odd, sporadic success. Any commercial organisation which has its turnover multiplied several times overnight has to be wary of not getting carried away and tipping over into excess. It is hard enough trying to keep pace with the moneyed ranks of the wealthiest league in the world, but with the added burdens of this dramatic uplift placed in their path the Play-Offs teams need to be resilient, resolute and above all else realistic if they are to succeed on this most ridiculous of roller-coasters.

Steve Browett neatly summed up the difference between winning and losing the Play-Offs Final in 2013 for the co-owners of a club. "It is almost impossible to break even outside the Premier League. After beating Watford it dawned on me that rather than having to dip into our pockets again to keep the club afloat as we had done since taking over (in 2010), we could look forward to making a healthy profit. That was a massive change." So with that one successful penalty, Kevin Phillips transformed the fortunes of so many people; such is the massive financial impact of the Play-Offs.

Nobody can deny that the vast sums now talked about in relation to the value of the Championship Play-Offs are nothing short of staggering. By highlighting both the extraordinary increases in financial worth since their introduction in the late 1980s and the massive gap that has developed between the Premier League and the Football League, this serves as a timely reminder of both the progress and the inherent problems of English football. But in the end, the fans are not primarily concerned with such figures; all they are concerned with is watching their club performing at the highest level whilst not risking the financial future on getting there. The intense pleasure of winning the most lucrative match in world sport is derived from gaining that step up to the top division rather than in counting the considerable riches on offer. If the time spent at the top level, however brief that may turn out to be, and the accompanying monies go to sustaining the club over the medium term, then that is a success worth savouring and celebrating. Added to the flush of victory and ensuing promotion is the underlying reassurance of that huge financial boost to the club's coffers. It is what some would term to be very much a win-win situation. Just ask Stephen Browett for confirmation of how much it means at the sharp end of running a club.

There are thirty regular matches before the sixteen team division splits into three play-off groups.

CHAMPIONSHIP PLAY-OFFS

Teams play each other twice. Season points halved.

1 Anderlecht 🏆	Champions League Group Stage
2 Standard Liège	Champions League 3rd Qualifying
3 Club Brugge	Europa League 3rd Qualifying
4 Zulte Waregem	Play winner of Europa League play-offs
5 Lokeren	Europa League play-off round
6 Genk	

1 Standard Liège
2 Club Brugge
3 Anderlecht
4 Zulte Waregem
5 Lokeren
6 Genk
7 Gent
8 Kortrijk
9 Oostende
10 Charleroi
11 Cercle Brugge
12 Lierse
13 Mechelen
14 Waasland-Beveren
15 OH Leuven
16 Mons

EUROPA LEAGUE PLAY-OFFS

Two groups of four. Teams play each other twice. Group winners play-off. Winners play the 4th placed team from Championship play-off.

1 Oostende
2 Gent
3 Lierse
4 Waasland-Beveren

1 Kortrijk
2 Charleroi
3 Mechelen
4 Cercle Brugge

Oostende
v
Zulte Waregem

Winner enters Europa League 2nd Qualifying Round.

RELEGATION PLAY-OFFS

Teams play each other three times. Fifteenth-placed team gets a Three point advantage. Loser is relegated. Winner enters 2nd Division play-off with three 2nd Division teams.

RELEGATION PLAY-OFF TABLE		2ND DIVISION PLAY-OFFS	
1 OH Leuven	→	1 Mouscron-Péruwelz	↑
2 Mons	↓	2 Eupen	
		3 Sint-Truiden	
		4 OH Leuven	↓

ABROAD AND BEYOND

One of the most endearing, and indeed most enduring, features of English football is the breadth of its appeal throughout all four divisions. The popularity of the lower tiers was bolstered and maintained by the introduction of the Play-Offs as middle-ranking clubs were rescued from mid-table mediocrity to become possible promotion challengers. This trend continued well after the arrival of the Premier League and the resilience of the lower leagues has been equally impressive over the twenty-odd years since. There was considerable apprehension that with the concentration of attention, and power, on the Premier League the Football League would wither and die. This has proved to be far from the truth as illustrated by its inherent strength in continuing to attract crowds of which many top leagues would be proud. The English Championship, for example, has regularly been the fourth-best-attended league in Europe for over a decade. After the German Bundesliga (13.8 million), the Premier League and Spanish Primera Liga (11.5million) no other league has pulled in more spectators than the second tier of English football. Even Italy's Serie A, which used to be the doyen of European football, has slipped down to 8.9 million, still some 200,000 below the Championship.

Additionally, at the third tier of English football, League One's aggregate attendance of four million proves at least as popular as any other second tier league in the world apart from 2. Bundesliga. For example, Italy's second division, Serie B, produced an average crowd for 2013/14 of 5,577, well below League One's 7,488, which was on a par with Spain's Segunda Division figure of 7,778. Whilst the Premier League will always be the headline act, the other divisions serve as a key support and fully justify their existence in their enduring resilience.

The lasting strength and attraction of football outside the more glamourous, moneyed top tier is a distinctive feature of the English game. In its strength of depth, English football knows no parallel. No other country can get close to emulating England in sustaining ninety-two full-time clubs across four divisions. The Play-Offs have played a critical part in underpinning this success by stimulating more widespread interest than was previously there and sustaining interest in a season right through to the final day. Undoubtedly, there are some cracks in the system as illustrated by a whole string of clubs that have entered administration in the last five years or so through poor financial management and have fallen foul of the league such as Portsmouth, Palace, Leeds and Southampton. The most recent club to go into administration were Coventry City which put paid to their chances of making their Play-Offs debut in 2013/14. But despite their various trials and tribulations, a couple of these clubs have survived financial meltdown and have arguably come out stronger for the experience. Even taking into consideration some of the casualties, the principle of a fully functioning, dynamic league of four divisions is still very much alive; which is an impressive and unique achievement. Even the much-vaunted German league only boasts fifty-six professional clubs across three divisions.

In 2015, English football is in relatively fine fettle judging by the generally healthy crowds and ever-rising broadcasting revenues which have continued to prosper even amidst a generally difficult economic background. The regrettable demise of the likes of Hereford United is mostly down more to issues with ownership rather than a failure of the league structure. Some argue that the bubble is about to burst but although spiralling wage costs and a string of heavily indebted clubs have threatened to derail financial sustainability, levels of income and worldwide media interest have never been higher. Through their positive, lasting influence and the propensity for vibrant, memorable matches, the Play-Offs have been one of the major catalysts in transforming the league from being the sick man of Europe in the mid-1980s into its current position of being the most sought-after in the world. They encapsulate everything that is admirable in English football and hardly any of the people responsible for their introduction could have possibly imagined how the football landscape would change over the ensuing years. None of them could have dared to hope how crucial a role the Play-Offs would have played in those changes.

There is something about Play-Offs Finals that sets the pulses racing. The heady combination of the significance, the pressure, the tension and the sheer drama all wrapped up in a single game is distinctive. As a bloodied but unbowed Bristol City fan, Mark Watson sums it up. "There is no atmosphere in football quite as tense as a game which will potentially decide the next few years for the clubs involved. Nobody could have anticipated the unequivocal success of the Play-Offs at the outset, and nobody could now imagine football without them. And yet despite the tension, the games often give rise to some of the most adventurous, almost out-of-control football you will ever see. I'm a fan. I just hope it'll be sixth bloody time lucky." Having followed his team's five unsuccessful attempts to go up via the Play-Offs, Watson's endorsement is bordering on the magnanimous. He could be forgiven for feeling some bitter resentment towards a system that has denied City any joy and given him and his fellow fans every reason to gnash their teeth and rail against the whole idea, against the very concept itself. So Watson's lack of parochialism is laudable and the fact that a Bristol City fan can be so positive markedly underlines the impressive stature of the Play-Offs and the affection in which they are held.

As has been raised before, the FA Cup used to have an element of surprise, even romance, where the underdog had their chance and occasionally cocked a snook at the favourites, but in recent times this trait has pretty much disappeared as the bigger clubs have all but monopolised the Finals. Since the Play-Offs began and up to 2015, there have only been three Finals which have not featured either Arsenal, Chelsea, Liverpool, Manchester City or Manchester United. Between them these five clubs have won twenty-two out of the last twenty-nine Finals. Such dominance does not create sufficient variety or drama to attract non-partisan fans and even its most ardent advocates would admit that the FA Cup Final has lost much of its cachet over the last twenty years or so.

By contrast, when Norwich City triumphed in May 2015 they became the twenty-first club to do so over the last twenty-nine years with only six clubs – Palace (a record four times), Charlton, West Ham, Bolton, Watford and Leicester – winning it more than once. Such fluctuations bring a much more varied tale of success and a distinctly fresher feel to these Finals. The inclusive nature of the Play-Offs, which spreads its net far and wide, naturally leads to a broad range of teams chasing that cherished promotion place. Over 700 teams enter the FA Cup from across many levels of league and non-league but by the time the competition reaches the Final, the usual suspects will be lining up to take their customary place. From the year when Manchester United, the FA Cup holders, opted out of the competition so that they could play in the World Club Championship in Brazil in January, much of the prestige of the FA Cup was irreparably eroded. For many observers and fans, that decision in 1999 proved to be a watershed moment, undermining the value of the competition from which there was no return.

At the same time as the FA Cup became the sacrificial lamb in football politics, the Play-Offs were entering a purple patch, with the Finals at their most sensational. Charlton's epic win over Sunderland in 1998, which can lay claim to being one of Wembley's greatest-ever matches, was followed by Man City's ridiculously late show against Gillingham. Then, to follow these two incredible games, in 2000 Ipswich eventually reached the Final that they had been yearning and striving for over the previous three years and they triumphed in a suitably thrillingly manner with a 4-2 victory over Barnsley. Here was a triumvirate of matches in successive years which graced the hallowed turf of Wembley and put Manchester United's withdrawal from the FA Cup into perspective. But just as this series of Finals further embellished the reputation of Williamson's Wembley Weekend there were changes in the offing which could have had a detrimental effect. Plans to redevelop Wembley, which were long overdue, were agreed and the subsequent closure of the stadium forced a change of venue.

Like the FA Cup Final, the Play-Offs Finals had to make the transition to the Millennium Stadium in Cardiff from 2001 because of the redevelopment at Wembley, but this switch did not mean that there was any less drama, just that a new phase had started. Over the six years spent in Cardiff there was the by now customary mix of goals and entertainment. A healthy fifty-two goals over eighteen matches, including Bournemouth's 5-2 victory over Lincoln, which at the time of writing remains the highest-scoring Final over ninety minutes. And there was plenty of penalty drama as well, with three matches going down to the wire in that cruel but most captivating of ways to decide the winners.

With their integrity and credibility suitably enhanced, the Play-Offs are set to continue and flourish as an important cog in English league football – a shining beacon to be appreciated, even treasured. Apart from the planned change after the first two years in removing the relegation element and the significant introduction of Williamson's Wembley Weekend, the structure of the Play-Offs has remained pretty much intact since their introduction in 1987. There is hardly any need to adjust a feature that has brought so many benefits and so much pleasure (as well as a requisite amount of angst). It would be difficult to imagine a better way of rounding off the season although other sports and leagues have tried, making small tweaks and minor adaptations, none of them making much of an impression. Across South American football there are a whole variety of different play-offs systems, which are all geared towards providing the most dramatic ending to the regular season. Indeed in Brazil when they recently resorted to a pure league system having previously used the play-offs there was some disgruntled, rumbling discontent over the flatness of the finish and a demand for a return to some form of play-offs.

Most countries like to have their own version. In Italy, for example, they are perpetually tweaking the system in an attempt to find the perfect one. In the latest incarnation they have limited the criteria for inclusion in the play-offs so that if a side is fourteen points or more behind their potential opponent they do not qualify and are denied even the opportunity to enter the play-offs. This method leads to a variable number of teams qualifying, ranging from two up to a maximum of six. This has a cold logic to it in stopping the unfairness of a team overcoming too big a points' discrepancy, but this rather goes against the very ethos that enjoys seeing a team appear from nowhere to secure promotion. Another slight adjustment is that for ties that finish level after two legs, there is no away goals rule or penalty shoot-out – the team that finishes higher in the league from the regular season goes through and so is granted an advantage from the off. As from 2013, if the maximum of six teams qualified, the lower-placed teams, i.e. fifth to eighth, played out one-leg opening rounds before deciding who was to contest with third- and fourth-placed clubs in the semi-finals. There are also relegation slots from Serie B downwards, aka play-outs, with two teams trying to avoid the drop.

If this Italian version adds a layer of complication, then the Belgian system has taken things to an altogether different dimension. Since 2009/10 the top division, known as the Jupiler Pro League, has split into three groups in March and then the mayhem ensues. Every single team of the sixteen is involved in some form of Play-Offs across the three different groups. Surely this is a case of stretching a good idea too thinly without thinking of the consequences. The top six play each other twice to decide the Champions, Runners-up and Europa League place, with previous points accumulated in the so-called regular season halved and then carried forward to the Play-Offs. This system can see a team that finishes top after playing each team twice still lose out on the title, as happened to Standard Liège in 2014 who despite finishing first were overtaken by third-placed Anderlecht in the Play-Offs. Most people object to this idea as it reduces the importance of the regular season by placing too much emphasis on the results of the Play-Offs.

Next up are the teams finishing between seventh and fourteenth, who are divided into two groups of Europa League play-offs, allowing the winner a chance to enter the Europa League play-offs Final against the team finishing fourth from the first group of play-offs. However, this match was stymied because the winners of the Europa League Final in 2014, Oostende, did not receive a licence to play European football so the game was annulled. Zulte Waregem, who had finished fourth in the Champions League group, were awarded the spot. So after all these shenanigans and to add to the absurdity of the play-offs Belgian-style, the key match never took place. No wonder so many Belgian players head to England if this is how things are resolved domestically.

Then the bottom two, fifteenth and sixteenth enter a separate relegation play-offs (aka the Play Downs) over a lengthy series of five matches with three points allocated to team 15 for starters. This, as I'm sure you've already guessed, is all aiming to avoid entering another group of play-offs with three teams from the lower division. In 2013/14 OH Leuven managed to beat Mons twice and draw once which meant that Mons could not catch their rivals even though there were two games remaining, and they were duly relegated. OH Leuven were then joined by the three teams from the second division but their luck ran out as they lost out after six more group matches to Mouscron-Péruwelz, who had qualified alongside Sint-Truiden as highest-placed finishers who had not already qualified, as champions Westerlo won both second and third periods of the second division.

If like me you feel giddy and exhausted just running through the basic rules, goodness knows how the Belgian fans take to it. The fact that there have been serious protests and threats of boycotts maybe hints at the level of dissatisfaction generated by this excessive tinkering. When Belgian fans start to cast envious glances at the Dutch Eredivise league, where just ten teams enter the play-offs to secure two promotion spots, then one knows that experimentation has gone too far and the depths of unpopularity have been reached. Excessive tinkering can lead to a dilution of all the merits of a simple and effective system. So woe betide those who argue for any radical change because that is where the road to hell lies as so clearly illustrated by the Belgian waffle you have just had the misfortune to learn about.

Other sports apart from football have also experimented with different types of play-offs and perhaps the most interesting of them all is Rugby League's Play-Off Series. This introduces the concept of 'Club Call' whereby the highest-placed team that wins its initial match in the Qualifying semi-finals gets to choose their opponents for the right to be in the Grand Final. This system also allows the qualifying losers of the higher-placed teams a second chance by competing with the lower-placed teams in a second round of matches. But the increased complexity and additional games required do not lend themselves to straightforward adoption by football. The hoary old adage of 'if it ain't broke, don't fix it' has never been quite so apposite. It is often argued that simplicity and practicality are two of the key virtues of successful innovation and this argument certainly gains considerable credence from the example set by the Play-Offs. With no great pretensions or massive expectations, they have ploughed a quiet and steady furrow in establishing themselves as a main component of football's fabric.

With a status embellished by each successive year of twisting, tantalising action, the Play-Offs have attracted ever-increasing attention from the media. The contrast between the general indifference of the media over their launch and today's blanket coverage on Sky could hardly be more striking. As the widely acknowledged climax to the season, they continue to flourish and grow, fully justifying this additional focus. Having attained such a level of recognition and acclaim, the Play-Offs can be said to have reached maturity and now face a bright future as a fundamental element of English football. Such is the development achieved that the Play-Offs can now be viewed almost as a separate entity, effectively becoming a brand in their own right, and an extremely powerful brand at that. In the big four American sports that spawned the idea, the play-offs are branded separately and discretely, even with their own taglines, websites etc. The Football League have already taken the first tentative steps towards the creation of their very own Play-Offs brand, which are now presented as the Sky Bet Football League Play-Offs; it will surely not be too long before there is the complete evolution of a fully-fledged Play-Offs identity.

Since 1990 there have been a series of proposals put forward to The Football League aimed at improving the Play-Offs but none have really got close to being approved. Such changes have, on the whole, been focused on increasing the number of teams involved but there has been little appetite for such an expansion, especially as it creates a further burden of squeezing additional matches into an already jam-packed fixture list. Phil Alexander, Chief Executive of Crystal Palace, had a proposal provisionally accepted in 2003 for an extra two teams to be included. The proposal entailed giving the advantage of hosting a single Play-Offs semi-final to the higher-placed teams rather than battling it out over two legs, both home and away. Alexander's view was that the first legs are often cagey, cautious affairs with both teams being wary of not ruining their chances for the decisive second leg. The matches only really ignite during the second leg so Alexander's argument was to go straight to the crux of the matter by having single matches rather than two-legged ties, which would ensure that every match is akin to a Cup Final.

The League Management Committee did approve the idea "with a resounding number of clubs voting in favour", according to Alexander, so it was agreed that the proposal should go to the League AGM. The idea seemed to be a satisfactory compromise to those who argue against having the possibility of eighth-placed team overcoming third as there was an inherent advantage for the higher-placed clubs. But when Brian Mawhinney, then chairman of Football League, discussed the idea with Richard Scudamore, his counterpart at the Premier League, Scudamore raised some serious objections to the possible decline in quality of the promoted club. There was concern that a team finishing eighth and qualifying via the Play-Offs would find life a real struggle in the exalted company of a higher division and demean the competition, so it was taken off the agenda and the plans were consequently shelved. Since that proposal was quashed there have been very few changes mooted and the status quo has been retained, which clearly indicates the virtues of the original plan.

Alexander was appointed to the Football League Board in 2011 so there was a fair chance that the notion of expanding the Play-Offs to six teams would come back on to the agenda. It has remained a regular topic of debate within League circles, but any proposal will have to summon up a great deal more support from the Premier League than previous incarnations to succeed. Alexander was realistic about the prospects of his proposed expansion and acknowledges that there are more important issues to be addressed. Naturally, Palace's victory in the 2013 Play-Offs meant that the main person trying to push through the expansion idea was forced to resign, as his club was no longer part of the Football League, and the impetus for any expansion petered out. Ultimately there will have to be some additional benefits identified and a slightly more radical approach to win over the doubters. As my own straw poll amongst those who were interviewed for this book revealed, there was hardly a single voice raised when asked if there were any suggestions for improvements to the current system compared with a chorus of disapproval that met the idea of expansion, so the status quo looks likely to be maintained for a while yet.

Having noted the success of the Play-Offs in invigorating the Football League, the Premier League had been casting some covetous glances at how they might be used for the top division. In both 2010 and 2011 there had been serious consideration of the introduction of a play-offs system being brought in to decide the last Champions League slot. So rather than fourth place guaranteeing this slot, there would be a four-team play-off involving fourth down to seventh to decide qualification. It is reported that the main objectors to this idea were Manchester United as they saw this as a potential devaluation of the Champions League. Not unlike the situation in 2000 when the FA Cup took a hit from none other than United's withdrawal. But Sir Alex Ferguson was characteristically adamant that this would not be in the best interests of the Premier League. "There's always someone coming up with hare-brained schemes from time to time," Ferguson said. "I don't know why people would want to change the format of the Premier

League – it's very good." Ferguson added, "OK, all teams in the Premier League would like to be in Europe but there's a way of doing that and it's to finish in the right position." With such a dominant figure being so implacably opposed, that effectively put the kibosh on the idea, but now Ferguson has departed the stage maybe it will resurface in some form.

Although the debate has not gone much beyond initial sparring, there could be something in the offing and if this were to be adopted there would surely be a wry smile amongst the Football League grandees as they witness the big boys imitating their supposed inferiors. With a nod of recognition to the Football League, the Premier League would be in danger of choking on a large serving of humble pie were they to implement their own form of play-offs. Indeed this might spark further debate about the idea of re-introducing the relegation element as used in the inaugural two seasons of 1986/87 and 1987/88 to spice up the lower half of the table. Aside from the clubs from the self-preservation camp, who would undoubtedly object to the net being widened, there is an argument to be raised that this would add excitement and intrigue to the Premier League's rather stodgy and bloated mid-table.

But for the time being the Play-Offs remain the preserve of the Football League and they may truly warrant serious consideration as the most successful innovation in post-war football. This book illustrates their steady evolution into one of the most treasured and widely admired aspects of the English football season. Many leagues and indeed other sports have tried to emulate the system but none have come close to replicating the essential drama and pure simplicity of the original. I would confidently predict that in twenty-five years' time little will have changed and people will still be paying tribute to those Play-Offs pioneers whose vision made everything possible. Witnessing such a successful innovation motivates those at the head of the League to try more ideas and tweaks as to how football is administered, so ultimately encourages an environment conducive to positive change. Though the Football League is more naturally associated with tradition and conservatism than with innovation and change, the Play-Offs stand out as a shining example of the organisation's ability to adapt, and not only survive but thrive.

Without doubt the Play-Offs are here to stay and there can be very few who would seriously contend that they do not deserve to be a permanent part of the league schedule. One can only imagine what the next few decades might bring but if they provide a fraction of the entertainment that the first twenty-eight years have done then all football lovers are in for a treat.

As the Play-Offs have become much more than just an adjunct to the season, they have actually come to define the season for a whole host of clubs. As well as their huge importance, they have been responsible for some of the most outstanding events in those clubs' recent histories. The only threat to the future seems to come from the idea of 'a closed league', going back to the American sports model where promotion and relegation are treated with disdain and are consequently excluded. As more and more teams fall into the hands of US-based owners, the danger is that the league becomes more Americanised, leading to the endgame whereby the concept of promotion and relegation is removed. In the major US sports the only form of entry to the top leagues is by taking over an existing team or admitting a new franchise; there is no provision for promotion and relegation.

The idea of a closed league in English football was mooted back in 2008 by Phil Gartside, the Bolton Wanderers chairman. Gartside put forward a proposal to establish two Premier Leagues of eighteen clubs each, which would then be effectively separated from the other clubs, who would not be able to gain entry to this elite group. Ironically, one of Gartside's main motivations was a desire to quell the power of the increasing band of foreign owners, many of whom would be in favour of a closed league since this would shore up their clubs' finances by ridding the league of any pesky threat of relegation. So the very people who he theoretically opposed would probably be the most willing supporters of his idea. Since the original proposal was put forward, Gartside has tried to bring it back on to the agenda, albeit with some limited scope for promotion but under strict criteria for those clubs vying for it. At the end of the 2011/12 season he was confronted by the even deeper irony of Bolton's relegation to the Championship after eleven successive seasons in the Premier League – the record stay of a Play-Offs team. Of course such a damaging relegation was what he was desperately trying to remove as an option and as a result he has lost his influence amongst the Premier League chairmen. Tellingly, there has been little noise since Gartside left the stage, so maybe this idea has been thankfully buried.

In truth, the prospect of following the US model and removing promotion is still an unlikely scenario as the relative positions of the lower leagues are so different. The major US sports tend not to have strong enough leagues beneath the main championships to support promotion as they are in the most part run as amateur organisations and are not geared up to make the transition. Certainly for basketball and American Football the gap is too large to facilitate movement of teams, as *Sports Illustrated* pointed out in an article in 2011. In that piece the conclusion was reached that the only US sport that could possibly accommodate relegation/promotion would be baseball, as its Triple A League, the equivalent of their second division, is of sufficient strength and professional-ism. Significantly, *Sports Illustrated* concluded that Major League Soccer was the least likely sport to accommodate promotion/relegation as the owners were too protective of their revenue streams. Maybe Mr Gartside should move his Bolton team Stateside as his ideas would attract a better response and be more welcome on the other side of the Atlantic.

By contrast, English football has a robust league structure with plenty of ambitious clubs aiming to climb higher and maintaining the dream of making it to the very top. If English football were to ever go down the 'closed league' route then surely the whole ethos, the very *raison d'être* of the game would be lost. Unlike its distant American cousins, football is a pure meritocracy where big clubs can fall just as small clubs can rise and any system that facilitates fluidity between the divisions will remain core to the future health of the league. US sports fans shudder at the thought of their biggest clubs such as baseball's Boston Red Sox (owned by John Henry's Fenway Sports Group, Liverpool's current owner) or American Football's New York Giants losing their top-flight status, so it is simply not allowed to happen. The Red Sox or the Giants can have bad seasons but they never end in humiliating relegation, they just start again the following year. It is therefore somewhat quirky to consider that the Play-Offs are based on a system straight out of US sport. Without the prospect of promotion or the threat of relegation, league football would fade away and be consumed with atrophy and apathy – a return to the bad old days of the 1980s. As the Play-Offs have admirably proved, even the slenderest chance of getting into the promotion frame gives clubs added energy and sparks interest for a broad spectrum of fans, players, managers and owners.

Football is often a divisive and confrontational world and a united front on any issue is as common as England performing creditably at a major championship. So the widespread approval accorded to the Play-Offs is a ringing endorsement of their value and the esteem in which they are held. It has been an amazing journey as they have evolved from being a small, barely noticed part of a desperate rescue plan into one of the most formidable and attractive features of the game today. In the process the Play-Offs were instrumental in turning round a beleaguered, blighted sport into the flourishing multi-billion-pound industry it has now become. There is a great deal to be grateful for throughout the whole history; from the outset the Play-Offs have generated their own momentum which has carried them through the years to their current pre-eminent position.

****

As has been explored during this book, fans, commentators, pundits and chairmen stand together in rare harmony in approving of the Play-Offs. Similarly, the vast majority of the players and the managers are all in favour and would not change a thing. And so as fans we can look forward to being enthralled once again and we welcome their continuing existence, which can only be good for the future of the game. Players will see their chance to shine on a much grander, higher-profile stage than that which they normally occupy and enjoy potentially the highlight of their career and/or a passport to the next level. Managers can prove themselves in one of the toughest, most pressurised challenges they are likely to face. This is the litmus test that can make or break the combatants.

Over the entire history of English league football, twenty-seven years is a relatively brief period. However, since 1987 the game in this country has undergone the most radical shift since William McGregor formed the League. The Play-Offs have been a crucial factor throughout this transformation. Within that space of time, the Play-Offs have made their mark, creating their own rich tradition and to a large extent changing the fortunes of the game for the better. Both as a short-term palliative for football's ills and as a provider of long-term sustenance, their contribution has been hugely significant. By bringing so many benefits and from being such a positive influence, the Play-Offs can justifiably be considered to be one of the best things to have happened to the game in living memory.

There are still a few naysayers remaining who question their place in the grand scheme of things but they are very much in the minority. Indeed the Play-Offs have become indispensable; the season would appear strangely empty and rather flat without them. As Tony Cascarino suggested, earlier there would be an almighty commotion if the Play-Offs were removed. Hardly anyone would question whether the Play-Offs should continue, and so it is probably more pertinent to discuss how their undoubted success can be emulated. Over the next few years there will be plenty of other changes and far-reaching solutions suggested to improve football. For example, the use of goal-line technology has finally been introduced to the Premier League after years of tests and false starts and has helped the accuracy of key decisions made by match officials. Furthermore, UEFA's Financial Fair Play is being phased in to introduce more discipline and rationality in club football finances, thus evening out the imbalances of wealth amongst the leading European clubs and encouraging them to operate within their revenues. The suspicion is that there are bound to be loopholes that will be exploited by those under threat. But most of these proposals have been focused on some tinkering here, tweaking there, and surely none of them are likely to come near to matching the clear, immediate and lasting success of the Play-Offs, which have embodied the spirit of football.

One can be fairly certain that in the coming years there will be further polarisation of power and wealth towards the top end of the league. Alongside such a glass ceiling, one of the safer bets would be that the Play-Offs will be very much part of the landscape. Provided that the dreaded spectre of 'closed leagues' does not become a reality and that promotion and relegation remain part and parcel of the league structure, then the Play-Offs will be there to add vibrancy and intrigue throughout the length of the season.

The immense success of the Play-Offs was initially down to striking a chord with a disillusioned and disenchanted public. By energising this group, the reawakened enthusiasm for the game spread throughout it and gave everyone the sort of fillip that was undoubtedly required at that time. It was not a lone battle and the Play-Offs should not be viewed in isolation, but they should be held in the highest regard when assessing their invaluable role in bringing about the renaissance of football in this country. Due to their restorative powers, football was able to rebuild itself and regain its pre-eminent position as the people's game prior to the explosive advent of the Premier League in 1992. The far-reaching impact of the Premier League would not have been so dramatic if there had not been such sound foundations laid. Ultimately Sky's role as the paymaster was vital but the Play-Offs provided the essential building blocks upon which the resulting transformation relied. As more and more attention and money is siphoned towards the top of the league, it is worth remembering the importance of the solid core underneath. The Play-Offs were one of the key drivers in regenerating this core and the part they played should not be underestimated. Clarke Carlisle sums it up succinctly: "The Play-Offs system has been one of the greatest innovations in football over the last twenty-five years." Carlisle continues: "Their influence has been fantastic as they have spiced up the season, so that now from February onwards there is still so much to play for with teams all the way from first to fifteenth involved, culminating in that showpiece Final. An unforgettable experience for all the players and wonderful for the long-suffering fans."

Carlisle's enthusiastic endorsement is mirrored across the entire football land-scape, so long live the greatest innovation to be introduced into English football in the last six decades (if not of all time) and let us appreciate its unparalleled contribution to the modern game. English football does not have that much to look back on with any sense of satisfaction from the 1980s, but in the Play-Offs there is a lasting legacy of which to be extremely proud, a history that has cap-tivated a new generation of the football family. Through the Play-Offs so many people have had a positive impact on the game as well as gaining massively from their own experiences; there is a huge reservoir of notable, exceptional memo-ries. From fans to chairmen, from players to managers, there are a whole host of wonderful moments to share as well as some excruciating episodes to recall.

By triggering the gamut of emotions, from the depths of despair to giddying transports of delight, the Play-Offs have inspired as deep a level of engagement as any aspect of football.

Considering the dire circumstances in which the very idea for the Play-Offs was first established in 1985, and the low-key nature of their introduction, the progress made has been truly extraordinary. The evolution of the Play-Offs is a salutary lesson in excellent innovation and its ability to transform. Having brought about fundamental and lasting change, the Play-Offs stand out as a phenomenal achievement not just within football, but throughout the world of modern sport. Having become an institution to be cherished and savoured by the vast majority in the game, they will continue to be an important component of league football and that can only be for the benefit of all involved. It is just as well that Lou Macari's immediate plea to have them scrapped back in 1987 was ignored and maybe Barry Hearn was right after all that they are simply "the best invention ever".

PLAY-OFFS RANKING:

1987–2015

The following ranking is an attempt to put all the clubs who have competed in the Play-Offs into some sort of order. It was not a simple task and it may seem a little suspicious that Palace are top of the pile but I can assure you that this table was devised along with my publisher, who supports Brighton and would certainly not be doing us any favours. For an explanation of how the points are calculated please see the notes.

		TP	TW	%	↑	PO pts			TP	TW	%	↑	PO pts
①	**Crystal Palace**	12	9	75	4	**45**	21	**Middlesbrough**	5	3	60	1	**14.4**
2	**Swindon Town**	13	8	62	3*	**32.2**	22	**Walsall**	5	4	80	2	**14**
3	**Blackpool**	13	10	77	4	**32**	23	**Brighton**	6	3	50	1	**14**
4	**Leicester City**	10	6	60	2	**28.8**	24	**Millwall**	8	3	38	1	**13.7**
5	**Huddersfield**	12	7	58	3	**25.5**	25	**Tranmere**	8	3	38	1	**13.7**
6	**Bolton**	11	6	55	2	**25.3**	26	**Norwich City**	4	3	75	1	**13.5**
7	**Watford**	8	5	62	2	**24.8**	27	**West Brom**	5	3	60	1	**13.2**
8	**Peterborough**	7	6	86	3	**24**	28	**Scunthorpe**	10	5	50	2	**13**
9	**West Ham**	6	5	83	2	**23**	29	**Wolves**	8	3	38	1	**12.9**
10	**Notts County**	7	5	71	2	**20**	30	**Cardiff**	8	3	38	1	**12.9**
11	**Charlton**	6	4	66	2	**19.8**	31	**Cheltenham**	7	5	71	2	**12.8**
12	**Gillingham**	8	6	75	2	**19.5**	32	**Bristol Rovers**	7	4	57	1	**12.5**
13	**Preston NE**	14	5	36	1	**19.4**	33	**Leyton Orient**	8	5	62	1	**12.4**
14	**Swansea City**	10	6	60	2	**19.2**	34	**QPR**	4	3	75	1	**12**
15	**Derby County**	8	4	50	1	**19**	35	**Barnsley**	4	3	75	1	**12**
16	**Blackburn**	6	3	50	1	**18**	36	**Stockport**	8	4	50	1	**12**
17	**Burnley**	5	4	80	2	**16**	37	**Ipswich Town**	9	2	22	1	**11.5**
18	**Bradford City**	5	4	80	2	**16**	38	**Southend**	7	4	57	2	**11.4**
19	**Sheffield Utd**	12	4	33	0	**15.8**	39	**Reading**	8	3	38	0	**11.4**
20	**Crewe**	9	5	56	2	**15.7**	40	**Birmingham**	6	2	33	1	**11.2**

* Swindon accredited with promotion in 1990 as they did win Play-Offs but were punished for financial wrongdoing and beaten finalists Sunderland went up instead but we go with the result on the pitch.

KEY TO COLUMNS

TP	Ties Played
TW	Ties Won
%	Win percentage of Play-Offs ties (not individual games)
↑	Promotions
PO pts	Play-Offs Points (See 'How Are Play-Off Points Calculated' on opposite page)

		TP	TW	%	↑	PO pts
41	**Leeds Utd**	7	3	43	0	**11.2**
42	**Torquay Utd**	10	5	50	1	**11**
43	**Bristol City**	8	3	38	0	**10.6**
44	**Port Vale**	4	3	75	1	**10.5**
45	**Yeovil**	4	3	75	1	**10.5**
46	**Northampton**	8	4	50	1	**10**
47	**Sunderland**	6	2	33	0*	**9.9**
48	**Grimsby Town**	4	3	75	1	**9**
49	**Brentford**	11	3	27	0	**8.9**
50	**Stoke City**	6	2	33	1	**8.6**
51	**Chesterfield**	5	3	60	1	**8.4**
52	**Rotherham**	6	3	50	1	**8**
53	**Doncaster**	2	2	100	1	**8**
54	**Man City**	2	2	100	1	**8**
55	**Sheffield Wed**	2	2	100	1	**8**
56	**Hull City**	3	2	66	1	**7.9**
57	**Cambridge Utd**	3	2	66	1	**7.9**
58	**Wycombe**	6	3	50	1	**7**
59	**Plymouth**	4	2	50	1	**7**
60	**Bournemouth**	3	2	66	1	**6.6**

		TP	TW	%	↑	PO pts
61	**Dagenham**	4	2	100	1	**6**
62	**Fleetwood**	4	2	100	1	**6**
63	**Stevenage**	4	2	50	1	**6**
64	**York City**	4	2	50	1	**6**
65	**Aldershot**	3	2	66	1	**5.3**
66	**Colchester**	4	2	50	1	**5**
67	**Lincoln City**	7	2	29	0	**4.9**
68	**Wigan Athletic**	6	1	17	0	**4.1**
69	**Chelsea**	2	1	50	0	**4**
70	**Darlington**	5	2	40	0	**4**
71	**Shrewsbury**	5	2	40	0	**4**
72	**Hartlepool**	6	1	17	0	**2.7**
73	**Bury**	7	1	14	0	**2.5**
74	**Wrexham**	2	1	50	0	**2**
75	**Rushden**	2	1	50	0	**2**
76	**Burton Albion**	3	1	33	0	**2**
77	**Mansfield**	3	1	33	0	**2**
78	**Rochdale**	4	1	25	0	**2**

THE REST

Of the 95 clubs that have competed there are 17 clubs who have not won a tie so cannot be given a score as their win percentage is 0. Below is the list of the clubs with how many times they have appeared in brackets :

Nottingham Forest (4)   Hereford (1)
MK Dons (4)   Luton (1)
Barnet (3)   Macclesfield (1)
Oldham (3)   Maidstone (1)
Carlisle (2)   Morecambe (1)
Fulham (2)   Newcastle (1)
Scarborough (2)   Portsmouth (1)
Accrington Stanley (1)   Southampton (1)
Chester (1)

HOW ARE PLAY-OFFS POINTS CALCULATED?

The Play-Offs points are calculated by awarding points for appearances in the Play-Offs which are graduated across the three divisions ie promotion from Championship is worth 10 points, Finalist 8 points, semi-finalist 6; League One promotion 8 pts, Final 6, semi 4; League Two promotion 6, Final 4, semi 2. The total for each club is then divided by the win percentage of Play-Offs ties (not individual games) to give Play-Offs points in last column.

CLIVE MENDONCA 1997/98
FIRST DIVISION PLAY-OFFS FINAL

25th MAY 1998
WEMBLEY – ATT: 77,739

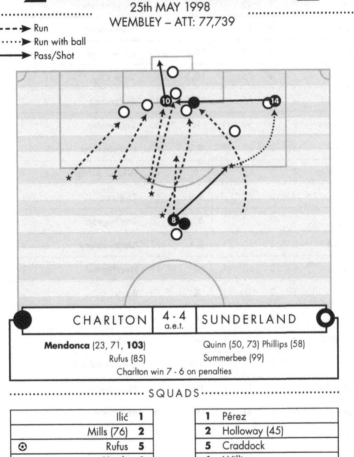

- – – ▶ Run
- · · · · ▶ Run with ball
- ———▶ Pass/Shot

CHARLTON	4 - 4 a.e.t.	SUNDERLAND

Mendonca (23, 71, **103**) Quinn (50, 73) Phillips (58)
Rufus (85) Summerbee (99)

Charlton win 7 - 6 on penalties

········· SQUADS ·········

	Ilić	**1**	**1**	Pérez	
	Mills (76)	**2**	**2**	Holloway (45)	
⊙	Rufus	**5**	**5**	Craddock	
	Youds	**6**	**6**	Williams	
	Bowen	**3**	**3**	Gray	
	Jones	**4**	**7**	Summerbee	⊙
	Newton	**7**	**4**	Clarke (100)	
	Kinsella	**8**	**8**	Ball	
	Heaney (65)	**9**	**11**	Johnston	
⊙⊙⊙	**Mendonca**	**10**	**9**	Quinn	⊙⊙
	Bright (93)	**17**	**10**	Phillips (73)	⊙

Robinson (76) Brown (93) Jones (65)   Makin (45) Rae (100) Dichio (73)

Final League Position: 4th   Final League Position: 3rd
SF 1st Leg: Ipswich 0 - 1 Charlton   SF 1st Leg: Sheff Utd 2 - 1 Sunderland
SF 2nd Leg: Charlton 1 - 0 Ipswich   SF 2nd Leg: Sunderland 2 - 0 Sheff Utd

GOAL FACT: The first hat-trick in a Wembley Play-Offs Final.

THE CLUBS: THE CURSED, THE BLESSED,
THE UNFORTUNATE AND THE BLIGHTED

In football, as with every sport, there are winners and losers, but in the Play-Offs the losers really carry an enormous burden, and as there are always three of them to one winner, the misery is spread far and wide. All four teams enter the Play-Offs semi-finals believing they have a realistic chance of progressing. There is very rarely any sense of inferiority amongst these four, as league form or position is not necessarily an accurate barometer of what will pan out. The lack of clear favourites and the tense uncertainty that is the prelude renders them all the more exciting; the extremes between winning and losing are laid bare and the accompanying consequences serve to ratchet up the tension a notch or two beyond the norm.

With the ratio skewed towards tales of despair rather than delight, the Play-Offs' landscape is of a darker complexion. So for each uplifting victory against the odds there will be a couple of tormented defeats and there are plentiful examples of pain and anguish outnumbering those of joy and elation for a variety of clubs over the last twenty-eight years. This section looks in more detail at the fortunes of a selection of those clubs, the few who have scaled the pinnacle of emotional highs or the majority who have reached desperate nadirs and plumbed new depths at the hands of the Play-Offs. For a system that was originally designed as a practical way of reducing the size of the top division it has become much more than a means to an end. Out of plain necessity come the thrills and spills associated with the Play-Offs. Each year seems to yield a new series of twists and turns, adding another dimension to the stories of those who succeed or fail at the final hurdle.

Throughout their history the Play-Offs have become the bane of particular clubs. Being offered the chance for salvation only to have that ripped unceremoniously out of one's grasp sometimes borders on the masochistic, as certain teams seem destined to failure, and failure of the most vindictive kind. Those associated with such perennial losers will bemoan the whole system and its perpetual injustice. The more superstitious amongst them probably believe that there is some external, malevolent force that is at hand to twist the knife perpetually into their very hearts. Those that love conspiracy theories will have plenty of material to work with and will construct a plausible reason why their club is so cursed.

Such thinking may well be used as a sop to guard against poor performance and too much harsh introspection or brutally honest self-awareness. After all, it is a lot easier to blame some nebulous being rather than looking too hard at yourself and your faults. Having said this, there is a trait amongst the worst offenders that might just lend some credence to the notion that their collective failure is determined by something outside their control. However hard they try, this band of clubs might be up against more than just the opposition on the pitch. Some may dismiss this as so much mystical poppycock and superstitious bunkum but there is such a strong seam running through the middle of this history of under-achievement that it has to be considered, at the very least, as a catastrophic coincidence.

When prying into the Play-Offs version of 'specialists in failure' there is a worrying factor that unites some of the worst offenders. There are four clubs banded together not only for their particularly dismal record of repeated disappointments but also by the fact they traditionally wear the same strip. This is the curse of the Red, White and Blacks. Step forward Brentford, Lincoln City, Sheffield United and Sunderland. Between this sorry bunch, who have traditionally shared the same kit of red- and white-striped shirts with black shorts, there have been umpteen attempts to achieve Play-Offs promotions yet none have actually done so. For these clubs they act as a modern version of the Sword of Damocles, hovering menacingly over their sorry heads. The only exception – somewhat proving the rule – was Sunderland's promotion in 1990, which, as has already been covered, saw them sneak in very much through the back door left ajar by Swindon's financial shenanigans.

This feeble quartet has somehow managed to amass well over twenty attempts to gain promotion through the Play-Offs and have failed every time. Not only this but they have found so many new ways of failing that at times these defy belief, and they have set numerous unwanted records along the way. This may lead some to suspect that a change of kit might be needed to bring about a change in fortune, exterior dark forces at work needing to be exorcised. Perhaps by lifting the strip, along with the monkey, off their backs they could approach their next brush with the Play-Offs with an emboldened, fresh attitude; otherwise they seem destined to come up short again and again. Let's face it, anything is worth a try after such a trail of endemic failure.

To make matters worse, if that were not quite bad enough already, Sunderland and Sheffield United share the misfortune of having amassed the most number of points in a league season and then failing to be promoted. In 1998, Sunderland, and then in 2012, Sheffield United, both reached the ninety points mark, but that was still not enough to get either of them up. That must hurt. A lot. Together these two have been failing and flailing ever since the Play-Offs began and will be twinned in angst and anxiety if they ever have the dishonour to qualify again. Naturally we begin the following detailed view of the victorious and the vanquished with an in-depth look at this less than fabulous four, starting with the sorry case of sad Sunderland, who were there at the very start and have suffered ever since.

THE CURSED

SUNDERLAND: THAT BLOODY PENALTY

Sunderland's quartet of appearances began with the dramatic, pulsating and ultimately agonising defeat to Gillingham in 1987. Gary Bennett, who scored late on in the second leg to take the tie into extra time, is in little doubt as to the poignancy of the Black Cats' bitter defeat on the away goals rule. "There's no question, that was the worst moment of my entire career," explains Gary. "In fact, everyone at the club was completely devastated and for weeks the whole place was in a state of total shock. Even Lawrie McMenemy, who'd left the club some weeks earlier, had been deeply upset that he was leaving the club on the brink of relegation." Welcome to the Play-Offs' house of pain.

Martyn McFadden has been running the Sunderland fanzine *A Love Supreme* for almost as long as the Play-Offs have been going. In that time McFadden has not had too much to celebrate, as the first issue came out in March 1989 just as Sunderland were beginning to rebuild in the old Division Two after their disastrous drop into the third tier courtesy of the initial Play-Offs in 1987. Connecting all four of their brushes with the Play-Offs were a series of penalty misses, like some sort of regular fault line that plagued them throughout, but all were slightly different in their character and significance and so they provide a handy guide to Sunderland's Play-Offs tale.

With the benefit of hindsight, McFadden considered that the relegation suffered in 1987 was a blessing in disguise "as they could clear out all the big-time charlies" who had arrived for their swansongs and a comfortable retirement. Under Lawrie McMenemy, who had done a similar thing at Southampton, they had assembled a cast of ageing international stars ready for their last hurrah.

Sunderland have the joint-highest points' total of 90 without gaining promotion, alongside perennial Play-Offs strugglers, Sheff United.

But the likes of "Alan Kennedy and George Burley couldn't be arsed and were completely lacking in motivation", so it was for the best that they were subsequently jettisoned as Division Three beckoned. Denis Smith was brought in by chairman David Murray because of Smith's thorough understanding and experience of this new environment after many years at York and he injected some new blood into the squad to cope with life at the lower level.

The semi-final against Gillingham had been a rude awakening for a team like Sunderland that was admittedly in decline but had never spent a season below the second tier before. The Gills' football style was rudimentary but also mightily effective. With the muscular presence of the back four and midfield running through the team all the way to the bustling Tony Cascarino upfront, there was not much room for subtlety or finesse. Such a powerful, physical approach was "a massive culture shock" according to McFadden but they had to get accustomed to this type of football as it was about to become their level and they had better get used to it. McFadden admits that they deserved to go down and could have no complaints with the Play-Offs as they would have been relegated under normal circumstances anyway. There had been an inevitability about Sunderland's slide, harshly illustrated by Mark Proctor's uncanny ability to miss penalties at crucial moments, including one on the last day of the regular season that could have saved Sunderland all this bother. Proctor repeated the trick in the second leg of the semi-final and the malaise that had gripped the club was in a way symbolised by Proctor's propensity for poor penalties. He was not to be the last Sunderland player who would have spot-kick failure forever associated as his trademark.

And so life in the third tier became a reality for the Black Cats in 1987 but they showed an impressive resilience to turn things around and spent just the one season there, bouncing straight back as champions in impressive style, amassing

93 points and tying up the Division Three title with games to spare. The happy knack of responding positively to Play-Offs disappointment was a pleasing trait that Sunderland managed to perfect over their subsequent failures, providing some comfort to the fans, and they also managed to somehow master the art of losing but still getting promoted, which is certainly a handy technique, although this was nearly scuppered by some old friends and rivals.

In the space of a few years, Sunderland had made sufficient progress to enter the Play-Offs for promotion to Division One in 1990 and as luck would have it they were pitched in with Newcastle in the semi-final. With the first leg at Roker Park drifting towards a goalless draw, Sunderland were awarded a penalty deep into injury time. Paul Hardyman, described in the commentary as "the penalty king", stepped up to take it but was foiled by veteran keeper John Burridge, who dived to his right and managed to gather in the ball before Hardyman could get to the rebound. To compound Hardyman's misery he kicked out in frustration as Burridge collected the ball and ended up being sent off in what proved to be the last meaningful action of the match. It would be difficult to imagine a more complete reversal of fortunes as Hardyman's in that fateful minute – from potential hero to being dismissed and suspended for the second leg and becoming an absolute zero. So the momentum of the tie seemed to have switched in that moment, with Newcastle fully expected to finish the job at St James's Park.

McFadden recalled the second leg being played in "the most bitter and hostile atmosphere" which spilled over into massed pitch invasions holding up play as Sunderland turned the tables, winning 2-0 through goals from Marco Gabbiadini and Eric Gates. It was to prove to be Sunderland's sweetest Play-Offs victory.

Wembley beckoned but after the joy of beating their fiercest rivals, Bennett was at the centre of the drama when Sunderland met Swindon in the Final. The only goal came from an Alan McLoughlin shot that took a wicked deflection off Bennett, leaving the goalkeeper, Tony Norman, stranded. Little did Bennett know that his misfortune on the pitch and the match itself was to be superseded by the legal action off it and Sunderland crept back to the top flight courtesy of a disciplinary committee ruling as opposed to anything achieved on the field of play. When the die was cast for Swindon and their promotion was blocked, Newcastle put forward their case for replacing them rather than Sunderland, having finished third in the league. That was rejected and finally after much prevarication and protracted discussion, Sunderland were promoted on the back of that loss. Understandably perhaps, following such a convoluted and underserved route, Sunderland were relegated the following season. So the only time Sunderland gained promotion through the Play-Offs, in that irregular manner, they were relegated, whereas the three times they failed they have gone up as clear champions the next year. The idea of the Play-Offs being a poisoned chalice certainly has some credence as far as Sunderland are concerned.

By the time of Sunderland's next tilt at the Play-Offs in 1998, Bennett had finished his career but he would have undoubtedly suffered along with all fellow Black Cats through the agony of their defeat to Charlton – another pulsating match that ended 4-4 after extra time. Who else but a lifelong Sunderland fan would break their hearts, as Clive Mendonca scored the first Wembley Play-Offs Final hat-trick for Charlton. To add fuel to an already raging fire of emotion, the match then developed into one of the most dramatic penalty shoot-outs. Michael Gray took the role of pantomime villain when he feebly stroked his penalty into the waiting arms of Saša Ilić. The weakness of the penalty was exacerbated by the fact that, unusually, the first thirteen had all been converted and that Mendonca, the man who grew up on the same council estate as Gray, had slotted the first penalty home with aplomb. It is something that still haunts Gray nearly twenty years on.

"There are Play-Offs and there is the one and only Play-Off," Gray tweeted during the Swansea–Reading Final of 2011. "Good game this, but no comparison to our game." Gray recollected in a *Guardian* interview his reluctance to take a penalty: "I really didn't want to take one, it was something I just didn't want to do." Gray also remembers that as he looked around at his colleagues gathered in the centre circle, wondering who would take a penalty, he looked hopefully at striker Danny Dichio, who had come on as a substitute. The fact, however, that Dichio had already taken his boots off was a pretty strong signal that he was not going to be stepping up to the plate.

"I was a Sunderland boy, living the dream playing for my local team, and I just didn't want to be the person responsible for us losing such an important match." Even now, this miss is still top of many agendas. "I do Q&As up around the North-East and obviously that penalty miss is the story they all want to hear about. Nobody's interested in my England caps, in me finishing seventh in the Premier League with Sunderland or Blackburn . . . none of the good stuff. All they want to hear about is that bloody penalty."

The Sunderland manager, Peter Reid, appreciated the torment Gray was going through as a result of "that bloody penalty" and decided to offer his own remedy. Reid told Gray to send his wife and children away on holiday whilst the two of them would spend a week together with the solitary purpose of obliterating that memory by getting as drunk as possible. This they achieved and some to the extent that when Gray's family returned he had to go on holiday himself to recover from the battering he had endured under the watchful eyes of his manager. A hellish experience was then partially overshadowed by the week from hell. As ever, Sunderland, and Michael Gray in particular, responded in the only way they know how and absolutely romped the division the following season with an impressive 105 points, eighteen clear of second-placed Bradford. Meanwhile, Mendonca's Charlton were relegated

But Sunderland were not quite finished with the pain or the character building that Gray alluded to as they contested the semi-finals against Palace in 2004. The first leg was a tight affair with Palace edging it 3-2. The second leg then swung decisively in Sunderland's favour as they took a 2-0 lead and Julian Gray was sent off. Surely even Sunderland would not throw away such an advantage, but with only a few minutes remaining they conceded an equaliser, ensuring extra time, and almost inevitably penalties. If Michael Gray is still being reminded of "that bloody penalty" one hates to think how Jeff Whitley's effort is described. Whitley's pathetic Panenka attempt must send shudders down every Sunderland fan's spine when they recall how it just looped into Nico Vaesen's grateful hands and gifted Palace a passage to the Final. It was the sort of thing you try in your back garden but then abandon as a particularly rotten idea. The reaction of Mick McCarthy needed no words to underline his dismay as he kicked everything within reach. If there had been a black cat nearby the poor puss would have copped it as well. As with their previous two failed attempts, Sunderland managed to pick themselves up and dust themselves down, winning the Championship the next season with ninety-four points. Palace were relegated and so completed the circle of failure and success that makes the Sunderland Play-Offs story such an encouraging one for any team that stumbles. Their record of recovery has always seen them come back stronger and end up the following season in the division above their conquerors without fail which shows true resilience and, dare we say it, a sense of 'bouncebackability'.

LINCOLN CITY: FIVE YEARS, ONE OPEN-TOP BUS

Alan Marriott may not be a household name across the country but he needs no introduction to Lincoln City fans, who regard him as a legend. Having played for The Imps for nine years he made over 350 appearances and kept a club record number of clean sheets. Marriott was an ever-present in the Lincoln team that qualified for five successive Play-Offs between 2002/03 and 2006/07. No other club has managed to make five Play-Offs on the trot, but any who look at Lincoln's record may not be in too much of a hurry to emulate them.

Lincoln's remarkable run will always be associated with the late, much-lamented Keith Alexander, who took over the club at the end of the 2001/02 season when they finished a lowly twenty-second and entered administration. As a result of the poor financial status of the club they lost nine first-team players in the close season and clearly had little money to replace them. This sorry state left Alexander with hardly any room for manoeuvre and he was forced into drafting in non-league players as replacements, "not from one league below but from one below that" according to his assistant at the time, Gary Simpson.

In his first season in charge of a professional club, Alexander not only ensured survival, but Lincoln reached the Play-Offs for the first time in the club's history. This was achieved through a resolute defence; they conceded just thirty-seven goals in the whole season, the least of any club by a clear ten goals. Marriott was the rock on which success was built and he racked up his nineteenth clean sheet of the season in the second leg of the semi-final against local rivals Scunthorpe United, when a 1-0 victory earned them an aggregate win after a manic first leg at Sincil Bank had ended 5-3 to Lincoln.

So with confidence high and facing a Bournemouth team that they had defeated 1-0 away only four weeks beforehand, Lincoln were well set for the perfect fairy-tale ending to an incredible season. But it was not to be as that steely defensive resolve that had served them so well all season dissipated in an uncharacteristic 5-2 defeat which still stands as the highest score in a Play-Off Final.

LINCOLN CITY
PLAY-OFF
Journeymen
Lincoln are the only team to appear in Play-Offs over five consecutive seasons, unfortunately all unsuccessful.

With seventeen clean sheets in 2003/04 and another nineteen in 2004/05, the familiar reliability of the defence was well established but was then betrayed by some high-scoring Play-Offs defeats, none more soul destroying than the last match in their five-year run. After four successive failures, Marriott sensed there would be a change of fortune in 2007 when they were drawn against Bristol Rovers in the semi-finals.

"It's heartbreaking whether you lose in the semis or in the final," he said at the time, "The one thing is that this season we've got a lot of new players who have not experienced the Play-Offs, so it's a new buzz for them." Typically, in the two league encounters that season, Lincoln had not conceded a goal against Rovers, winning 1-0 and drawing 0-0, but Lincoln's Play-Offs fallibility came back to haunt them

New buzz it may have been but it was the same old story. After a narrow defeat away to Bristol Rovers in the first leg of the semi-final, the wheels came off in the second leg at home as they lost 5-3. Lincoln's five-year Play-Offs adventure ended just as it had begun; conceding five goals in suitably apocalyptic fashion. The most telling statistic is that over those five seasons when they competed in the Play-Offs they never conceded five goals in any of their 230 league matches. For the Imps the Play-Offs were a pretty dismal debacle but as Alexander ruefully commented after the last of his four attempts to secure promotion for Lincoln, "four years of failure in the Play-Offs is better than finishing bottom of the league every year".

Following the first Final loss against Bournemouth in 2003 they did not return to Lincoln with heads bowed; indeed it was quite the reverse, the match being deemed a cause for celebration. "There was an open-top bus parade back in Lincoln, with fans turning out in their thousands and even the Mayor was involved," Marriott said. Even amidst the debris there is some light and despite the lack of promotion, the ultimate success, there was a sense of pride in turning things round and at least providing the club with something positive to reflect on. Such is the magic of the Play-Offs that even failure can sometimes be uplifting.

BRENTFORD: ONE KICK

For a club that boasted two former chairmen in Ron Noades and Martin Lange, who were amongst the main architects of the modern-day English Play-Off system, Brentford must consider themselves particularly blighted to have such a poor return from their many attempts. Like Sheffield United they have been to the well eight times but they have always returned dry. The Griffin Park club is unusual in its capacity to shoot itself in the foot and certainly does not do defeat in any straightforward fashion, but tends to pile on the agony through ever more convoluted ways and means.

For example, in 1995 having finished second in League Division Two, under any normal circumstances David Webb's team would have been celebrating automatic promotion. But because of the streamlining of the Premier League back to twenty clubs for the following season, 1994/95 was the one campaign in which one less side went up from each division. This means that Brentford hold the not-too-proud record of being the only team to have finished in the top two of this division and not been promoted (Reading share that dubious honour from the division above). This was all too cruel, but somehow inevitable for the West London outfit, whose relationship with the Play-Offs could be described, at best, as tempestuous.

Their semi-final defeat against Huddersfield Town in 1995 was all the more painful not only because Brentford had finished runners-up but also because of the manner of their loss, as two drawn matches led to penalties being used to decide a Play-Off semi-final for the very first time. So another unwanted record for Brentford was sealed when losing 4-3 to the penalty kings, Huddersfield, who have by contrast won all four of their shoot-outs in the Play-Offs. When history is stacked against you there is a feeling that there is little you can do to stop the tide and Brentford have been swimming against it pretty much for their entire Play-Offs history. Most Bees fans must rue the day that Lange and Noades teamed up to such good effect and this is reflected in the caustic reflections of Dave Lane, long-standing editor of the *Beesotted* fanzine.

With seven unsuccessful attempts from the same division they have the worst record from the third tier.

Lane explains that Brentford fans approach any involvement with the Play-Offs with a weary fatalism, pretty much safe in the knowledge that things are going to go awry. The sense of inevitability is overpowering but is still not so strong that it eliminates hope entirely, despite the overwhelming evidence stacked up over seven futile attempts. Added to this specific litany of failure, Lane was keen to add the three losses in the Freight Rover/LDV Finals as proof of Brentford's anathema to success on the big stage. One of their more recent brushes with the Play-Offs in 2013 was in some ways more painful than any of their other bitter experiences.

Entering the last day of the league season, Brentford were at home to Doncaster and automatic promotion was up for grabs. The game entered its final minute still goalless and here Lane's commentary takes over.

ONE KICK

So the season had come to this, all boiling down to a minute of mad, twisted, sick drama at Griffin Park. The referee, who had shown he was totally out of his depth all afternoon, stunned everyone inside the stadium by awarding the Bees a penalty deep, deep into injury time... The Bees HAD to win to achieve automatic promotion, and here it was on a plate, Championship football, just ONE KICK away... But it was all too much for some fans to take... Men, women, children, all tearful; the magnitude of the moment was palpable...

Dark clouds were gathering overhead, but surely this ONE KICK would send the stadium in to delirium... This ONE KICK would eradicate all those Bees' heartache moments and consign the club's previous failures to a dark corner of our memories that we'd not have to revisit again...

This ONE KICK would transform the history of our football club.

But the players were arguing about who should take it... never a good sign... Marcello Trotta, the Fulham loan player who had been on the pitch for less than ten minutes, had grabbed the ball and was clearly in no mood to hand responsibility to anyone else... He WANTED it... He'd scored a penalty at Sheffield United, when Sam Saunders had missed, so why shouldn't he? Sam clearly DIDN'T want it, or knew it had been tasked to another... But what about Kevin O'Connor... The Brentford legend? Kev is club captain, an experienced penalty taker, the man for who it had apparently been AGREED would take penalties against Doncaster... he wasn't happy... Words were exchanged... But Trotta was adamant, he looked confident. Bees fans looked sick with worry.

I looked to the heavens and asked a question... Okay, I am not a man of faith, but this seemed a moment where, if a God does exist, he might just be in the mood to grant me a little favour... after all, I'm not a bad fella at the end of the day. I asked him, "Please, just this once, for me and for my son, and for all my mates that are here, and for all the Bees fans everywhere..." One little prayer, ahead of one big kick. ONE KICK.

The Italian stepped up purposely and absolutely leathered the ball... It was not one of those nervy, half-hearted, poor excuses of a penalty kicks, this was a manly wallop... The thousands standing behind the Ealing Road end goal visibly recoiled as the ball was struck. In that moment Brentford were about to be promoted, Doncaster stripped of their automatic place by a last gasp, cruel twist... Nine months of achievement, a large proportion of which had seen Rovers lead the table, was to be snatched away. This was our fate, our destiny, all our dreams, and the fantasy finish to a fantastic season... This was OUR time.

ONE KICK.

But what happened next was plain sick... SICK. Trotta hit it hard alright, so hard that he helped set up a goal for Doncaster. As the ball cannoned off the crossbar, eleven thousand hearts broke... it was simply too much to take, for most to comprehend, let alone cope with... Especially the players, many of whom had started to drop to the ground... Like they'd been taken out by a Donny sniper.

A green flare was let off in the away end by a Rovers fan who obviously didn't care about a ban from Griffin Park, they were going up again... But they weren't JUST going up were they? No, they had scored... They had scored from OUR penalty... And now they were friggin' CHAMPIONS. I've never heard anything so perverse in my life..

That shit doesn't happen in the real world, in fact I'm not sure that twisted shit happens in the fantasy world either. Has any team ever won the title with the last kick of the season from a rebounded penalty kick AGAINST them? That's impossible, right?

And my last impression of the afternoon as I left the stadium, with my young son bawling his eyes out, was of a giant police horse taking a giant piss on the centre circle... the centre circle where I should have been standing with him, watching the Brentford players held shoulder high. An ironic and poignantly surreal image if ever there was one.

And so it was that Brentford were consigned so cruelly to yet more Play-Offs penury as Doncaster somehow snatched promotion, and the title, away in that extraordinary turnaround. The odd and slightly unnerving fact was that this outlandish climax that could surely never be repeated, was replicated to the tee a few weeks later in the Watford vs Leicester Play-Offs Championship semi-final. Having snatched defeat from the jaws of victory there could be no more painful torture inflicted than another date with Play-Offs destiny. Even Brentford's victories contain heartbreaking moments and having been pegged back to 3-3 in the very last minute of the second leg of the semi-final they did eventually overcome Swindon, ironically on penalties. The Final pitted them against Yeovil and that all too familiar feeling of dread was hanging over the club.

As hard as their manager, Uwe Rosler, tried to dispel the sense of impending doom by insisting that there was no sense of historic failure and that this was a different club now with new players, there was still a sense of something hanging over them. On the day itself, as Mark Clemmit observed, as soon as he saw the players arrive at Wembley he knew the game was up. "They looked wracked with tension and there was a palpable feeling of apprehension and fear, compared to the Yeovil squad who were relaxed and smiling. There was just something in their body language that suggested this was not going to be their day." And so it turned out to be as they never recovered from an early Paddy Madden goal and were 2-0 down by half time. They did get a goal back, their first goal in a Play-Offs Final, but that was as good as it got and the result that felt as if it was etched into the stars did indeed materialise.

It is difficult not to feel a great deal of sympathy for Brentford in this whole farrago. Though it will be scant consolation for the Bees, at least they do not have to share the dubious honour with Sheffield United of appearing in more than one Final and not even finding the consolation of celebrating a goal.

SHEFFIELD UNITED: UP STEPS STEVE SIMONSEN

Sheffield United's Play-Off traumas are so intense that even a neutral must feel a tinge of anguish when reflecting on their spectacular, singular lack of success. This is not just failure, but failure on an epic scale, and the film title has already been writ large: "The Bluntest Blades". United's dismal performance is generally reserved for the grand stage, the showpiece Finals are their *tour de force* such that when they fall they do so with an earth-shuddering crash that cannot be ignored. They manage to make Sunderland's efforts look half decent.

Sheffield United have qualified for four Finals out of eight appearances, which is a reasonable effort that does not hint at any disasters. Their four semi-final defeats were painful but do not really come close to the agonies experienced in their four Finals. Firstly in 1988 they slipped into Division Three, one of the handful of clubs relegated (along with Sunderland naturally) during the two seasons where it was possible to go down through the Play-Offs, and had to suffer the ignominy of life in the third tier for only the third time in nearly 100 years. Then, in one of their semi-final failures, some ten years later in 1998, they managed to lose 3-2 to Sunderland, of all teams, after surrendering the first-leg advantage gained at Bramall Lane. It does not get too much worse but they managed to sink even lower.

Whilst these semi-final defeats were disappointing they pale into insignificance compared to the four Finals they have had to endure and they remain the only club to have made it to four Play-Offs Finals and not make any of them count. The first taste of bitter failure came in 1997, the year before their second semi-final loss, when they lost to David Hopkin's outrageous last-minute curler which has already been referred to earlier from a Palace perspective. What struck me most about that match, apart from the exquisite and vengeful glory of the only goal of a generally drab game, was the reaction of the United players to conceding. It was as if they were utterly bamboozled by this twist of fate and so when they kicked off to restart the match they simply booted the ball into touch as if to say we are too shell-shocked to consider going

SHEFFIELD UNITED

BLADES NOT SHARP ENOUGH

4 Finals   **0** Goals

Reaching four finals has not paid dividends for Sheffield United, who lost them all without scoring a single goal.

on any further. In fact there was no need to worry, as the final whistle blew shortly afterwards and they were duly consigned to their fate.

In an eerie and slightly sinister way, there was a carbon copy of that Hopkin goal reproduced a dozen years later in 2009 by Wade Elliott of Burnley, who similarly, and just as expertly, curled the ball into the top corner of the net from just outside the penalty area after the ball had come back to him. As with Hopkin, Elliott's fine strike was the only goal of the match. Sheffield United fans can rue reflectively and may even be able to console themselves that at least they were at the wrong end of two wonderful goals. But with some sort of surreal symmetry, six years on from the Palace Final and six years before the Burnley one – so at the midpoint of those two stunning strikes – there lies the Final of 2003, which makes these two 1-0 reverses seem like a gentle cuffing. Leading up to the game against Wolves at the Millennium Stadium in Cardiff, United had shown that they were ready for the fight by overcoming fellow Play-Offs strugglers Forest in a thrilling second leg 4-3, after being two goals down, to win 5-4 on aggregate.

Surely the momentum would be with Sheffield United, the fans must have believed, but not a bit of it; in only the 6th minute Mark Kennedy arrowed a shot into the corner from the edge of the penalty area, just for a change, and they capitulated, heading into the interval 3-0 down. There was no way back, as even a penalty was missed early in the second half, and that was not the only thing that United missed, as their ever-irascible and controversial manager Neil Warnock was sent to the stands after half time. So even with their patchy record, this Final plumbed new depths of mediocrity.

But Sheffield United are nothing if not consistent and they managed to reach possibly an even lower level in 2012 when facing their Yorkshire rivals Huddersfield Town in the League One Final. Again this was not the most exciting game, even when it stretched into extra time, and the BBC report was not exactly glowing with praise, "as in normal time, the extra thirty minutes did not provide a feast of action in the goalmouth". As the game went to a penalty shoot-out there was at last to be some action but few could have anticipated quite how dramatic this denouement would be. The teams' inability to score in open play did not seem to change terribly much as six of the first eight penalties were missed. Then, having reached 1-1, both sides woke up to the idea that penalties should be scored more often than not and managed to reel off thirteen successful kicks, including Huddersfield's goalkeeper Alex Smithies. However, in perfect Sheffield United Play-Off fashion, the last of the twenty-two players to take a penalty was their goalkeeper Steve Simonsen, who, unsurprisingly and quite horribly, hoisted the ball way over the bar.

Simonsen's reflections on his experience in an interview with BBC Sheffield in the aftermath are brutally frank and illustrate that depth of emotion which typifies the format. "It's been horrendous. Obviously it's the lowest part of my career. I've replayed it a million times in my head and I just can't bear to watch it. I'm gutted for myself, the club, the fans and my family." This proved to be Simonsen's epitaph as a Sheffield United player as he was released by the club soon afterwards and ended up being relegated the following season with Dundee from the Scottish Premier League. Simonsen's comments are reminiscent of Gary Bennett's when he was recovering from the disappointment that Sunderland suffered during the first year of the Play-Offs. We have travelled full circle, from the first to one of the most recent, and the common factor is the intensity of anguish both Bennett and Simonsen display.

And so under four different managers – Howard Kendall, Neil Warnock, Kevin Blackwell and Danny Wilson – the sorry tale of Sheffield United reaches its bitter conclusion. But this run of Finals' sorrow is made even worse by the fact that they have not yet even managed to score a goal during those four matches. That equals over six and a half hours of fruitless football, and it goes without saying that this is the worst record of any finalist. But there is even worse to come. As if to rub salt into local wounds, bitter city rivals Wednesday have appeared just the once in the Play-Offs yet not only do they boast a 100 per cent success rate, but they rattled in four goals in overcoming Hartlepool in 2005, scoring in each of the four halves of normal and extra time to mock United's inability to notch even one in any of their four Finals. United also have the dubious privilege of being the first club to have had a player sent off in a Championship Final, when Jamie Ward was dismissed late in 2009 after two handballs. If there is an unwanted Play-Offs record to be had then Sheffield United are pretty much nailed on to be in contention.

If I have failed to convince you, here is Sheffield United fan and blogger Ian Rands:

DEFEATS, THE DAVE CLARK FIVE, DORITOS, MIKE DEAN & A PENALTY YET TO DESCEND

The Dave Clark Five rang out around Wembley, with 30,000 Crystal Palace fans informing the departing Blades fans how they all felt "Glad All Over". Ninety minutes of cagey, turgid football, with few chances for either side, had been settled just thirty seconds before the final whistle. A Palace corner was cleared to the edge of the box where David Hopkin met it with a deft first touch and turn, before a screaming right-footed strike that arrowed into the top corner. In an instant 30,000 Sheffield hearts sank and Blades fans slumped back into their seats before they skulked off towards their coaches with the call and response of the 60s' beat combo indelibly locked in their brains.

Six years later, a third place finish in the Championship and a phenomenal 4-3 extra time victory over Forest at Bramall Lane in the semi-final, meant Blades fans visited the Millennium Stadium in a buoyant mood. United had reached both domestic cup semi-finals, losing by a single goal to both Liverpool and Arsenal and success in the season finale was surely deserved. By half time all hope was extinguished; three goals down and manager Neil Warnock sat in the stands, a victim of his lack of self-control.

The faint hope provided by a penalty award just after half time dissipated as Matt Murray pushed away Michael Brown's penalty. Many Blades drifted out into the Cardiff streets, long before the final whistle. Feeling let down. Utterly deflated. A season of if, nearly and what might have been.

Stopping at a service station on the M5 on the way home, I stood at the shop counter, a packet of Hula Hoops in hand. Wolves' fans in the old gold were all around and their shirts that season had a nacho-like crisp brand as sponsor. A Black Country voice bellowed in my ear, "Ow, you don't want Oola Oops, you wanna have Durreeetoooows!" There was nothing less I wanted right then.

Another third place Championship finish in 2009 saw a first visit to new Wembley. Surely this time… but again, for a third time, under a third different manager, for the third time as favourites, the Blades failed to turn up. A non-descript display saw the Blades blunted in attack and undone by a single Wade Elliott goal for Burnley. The nearest United came were two fair penalty claims waved away by referee Mike Dean, the subject of criticism from manager Kevin Blackwell, in the lead-up to the match.

For many United fans, the League One Final against Huddersfield in 2012 was one too far. Without the excitement of a first visit to new Wembley and having seen a seemingly guaranteed return to the Championship slip away in the latter stages of the season, conceded to cross-city rivals Wednesday, fans were disenchanted. The guilty verdict against top scorer Ched Evans, injuries and suspension reducing back-up options hit United hard in the run-in and crucially an injury to talismanic midfielder Kevin McDonald ruled him out of the Wembley Final against Huddersfield. The match was dire. 120 minutes that would have cured the most severely affected narcolepsy sufferer. Then penalties. And more penalties. Watching through gaps in fingers as hands clutch to faces.

Early advantage in the shoot-out was lost and finally it came down to the goalkeepers. Alex Smithies scores for Huddersfield and up steps Steve Simonsen. He planted his foot to strike the ball, his body with the posture of a limbo dancer. Leaning back, the ball rising and rising, above the crossbar and high into the stand.

I walked out of the stadium. I didn't want to hear victory songs, I couldn't complain about the referee and the last thing I wanted was a bag of crisps. All I wanted was a Play-Offs Final win.

So for Sheffield United the 2015 Play-Offs followed the dismal pattern of the previous seven attempts to climb the Play-Offs summit. Another year, another failure. Unfortunately for them this eighth failure, combined with Preston finally breaking their duck, means that they are now the not so proud owners of the title of the club with the most Play-Offs failures without any success. But at least another of the red- and white-striped quartet, Brentford, are keeping them company on eight failures following their loss to Middlesbrough at the semi-final stage in 2015. That is now twenty-five attempts and counting for this sorry, cursed group.

At least United can point to the faintest trace of glory in their failure to get past Swindon in the semi-finals. Having narrowly lost the first leg at home to a goal in added time, the second leg started badly and just got worse so that by the 18th minute they were 3-0 down and four goals behind on aggregate. Cue a quite remarkable transformation, battling back to 3-2 down on the night within the next twenty minutes and by half time all involved got a well-deserved breather, and maybe even a lie-down. The second half was just as relentless, with both sides trading goals around the hour mark to leave the tie hanging in the balance. Jonathan Obika's goal in the 84th minute seemed to have settled matters only for Sheffield United to score twice in the space of two minutes, setting Swindon nerves jangling for a tortuous nine minutes of added time, which was not short of drama or chances.

When the dust had finally settled from this Wild West shoot-out, Sheffield United were left to lick their wounds yet again and Swindon's defensive vulnerability was to be sorely exposed by Preston in the Final. Summing up the craziness of the night the United manager Nigel Clough admitted to Sky Sports that he had lost count at one stage and had to ask his assistant Chris Morgan the aggregate score but he was none the wiser. Two weeks later reality bit and, during the Play-Offs Final weekend, it was announced that Clough had been dismissed, probably still dazed and a little confused after the frantic goings-on at The County Ground. Clough was one of five managers who left their jobs shortly after their involvement with the Play-Offs was over.

Perhaps it is just bad luck or maybe those red- and white-striped shirts with black shorts are truly fated to never succeed. This quartet's miserable records possibly do point to some sort of hex or evil witchcraft that is working against those wearing that strip. Some may point to the fact that in a few of these many failures, some of the doomed quartet have worn an alternative kit, but the Play-Offs gods cannot be so easily fooled and they impart their rough justice with impunity.

But that is enough of misery (for now) and it is high time to look at some more positive stories, which will provide an element of balance to proceedings. There are some clubs who relish the Play-Offs and make the most of their appearances, and we will now look at a few who have enjoyed themselves for the most part.

ACCRINGTON Stanley

MORE REDS THAN GOALS

Two players were sent off in their only Play-Offs game so they are the only club to have more red cards than goals.

ALDERSHOT Town

23 YEARS

LONGEST GAP
BETWEEN APPEARANCES

Their first appearance came in 1987 with their second coming in 2010.

BARNET

3 SEMI-FINAL LOSSES

TO EVENTUAL WINNERS

Blackpool, Colchester and Peterborough all beat Barnet in the semi-finals before going on to win the Play-Offs.

BARNSLEY

AWAY LEG LEGENDS

Their two performances in away legs are impressive, beating Birmingham 4-0 in 2000 and Huddersfield 3-1 in 2006.

BIRMINGHAM City

SHOOT-OUT DROP-OUTS

The only team from the second tier to have lost two semi-finals on penalties during a run of three successive semi-final defeats 1999-2001.

BLACKBURN Rovers

PLAY-OFF & PREMIER LEAGUE CHAMPIONS

The only Premier League Champions who were promoted via the Play-Offs.

BLACKPOOL
MOST PLAY-OFF FINALS

They are the only team to have been promoted from all three divisions and have contested more Finals than any other team.

BOLTON WANDERERS
LAST TO WIN ON AWAY GOALS

The win against Ipswich in 1999 was the last time a team won a semi-final on away goals as Ipswich chairman, David Sheepshanks, had the rule changed.

BRADFORD City
1996 WEMBLEY DEBUT

The 1996 Final was Bradford city's first-ever appearance at Wembley.

BOURNEMOUTH
5-2 HIGHEST SCORING FINAL

2003 ended in a 5-2 drubbing of Lincoln. This is the highest-scoring Play-Offs Final over 90 minutes.

BRENTFORD
UNLUCKY 7

With seven unsuccessful attempts from the same division they have the worst record from the third tier.

BRIGHTON
2013 YEAR OF THE NO-SCORING SEAGULLS

Having scored in all five of their previous Play-Offs matches and both since, they failed to score in either leg of the 2013 semi-finals.

BRISTOL City

BRISTOL Rovers

3 FINALS FINALS 3

ZERO PROMOTIONS : ONE PROMOTION

After Brentford and Sheffield United, Bristol City have played more Play-Offs Finals without securing promotion.

Like their city rivals, Rovers have appeared in three Finals, but hold the bragging rights over City with one promotion.

CLEAN SHEET *Kings*

BURNLEY

During their triumph in 2009, Burnley did not concede a goal throughout the Play-Offs, one of only seven clubs to achieve this feat.

BURTON ALBION

14,007
SMALLEST FINAL ATTENDANCE

The crowd for the Final with Fleetwood in 2014 is the smallest Play-Offs attendance at Wembley.

BURY

NO MORE THAN ①1 GOAL IN A GAME

In 13 matches Bury have never scored more than one goal in a game. Their total of 5 goals gives a measly average of 0.38 per game.

CAMBRIDGE United

FIRST-EVER WINNERS

Cambridge became the very first winners of a Play-Offs Wembley Final on 26th May 1990.

HOME·LEG
BLUES

CARDIFF City

In their five unsuccessful campaigns, Cardiff have not won any of their semi-final home legs.

CARLISLE UNITED

2 x 2-0

Carlisle are the only team to have lost both semi-final home legs 2-0.

CHARLTON ATHLETIC

TRAPDOOR DODGERS

The only team to avoid relegation in the first two years of the Play-Offs in 1987 and 1988.

CHELSEA

40,550
LARGEST ATTENDANCE
OUTSIDE OF WEMBLEY & MILLENNIUM

The crowd for the home leg of their Final is the largest for any Play-Offs match outside of Wembley and the Millennium.

CHELTENHAM TOWN

TWO BOTTOM TIER PROMOTIONS

Alongside Blackpool, Cheltenham and Southend United are the only teams to have achieved two promotions from the lowest tier.

CHESTER CITY

0 - 3
AGGREGATE AGGRO

Just like Accrington Stanley Chester's 0-3 aggregate is one of the worst in the Play-Offs.

CHESTERFIELD

MOST GOALS
IN
EXTRA TIME

Chesterfield's three extra-time goals in their 1995 semi-final is the most scored by a single team in extra time.

COLCHESTER UNITED

SUPER SIBLINGS

In 1998 David and Neil Gregory became the first pair of brothers to play in a Play-Offs Final. David scored the decisive goal with a penalty.

CREWE ALEXANDRA

9-3

Crewe secured the highest winning aggregate margin of six goals in a semi-final 9-3 (5-1, 4-2) over Walsall in 1993.

CRYSTAL PALACE

MOST PROMOTIONS
TO THE TOP FLIGHT

The only team to have gained promotion to the top division four times, each in different decades – 1989, 1997, 2004 and 2013 – and at different venues – Selhurst Park, Old Wembley, Millennium Stadium & New Wembley.

DAGENHAM & REDBRIDGE
SHARP SHOOTERS
3.33

The Daggers' 10 goals in just three games gives them the best average goal per game ratio: 3.33.

DARLINGTON

FINALS GET THEM QUAKING IN THEIR BOOTS

Darlington have scored in all six semi-final legs, but have not scored in either Final.

DERBY COUNTY

5 DIFFERENT MANAGERS

Derby's five appearances have all been under different managers – Arthur Cox, Roy McFarland, George Burley, Billy Davies and Steve McClaren.

DONCASTER ROVERS

5-1 Doncaster's win over Southend is the largest League One home win.

FLEETWOOD TOWN

POPULATION 25,000

≈ **THE** ≈ **SMALLEST TOWN TO WIN** ≈ **THE** ≈ **PLAY-OFFS**

FULHAM

0 WINS

WORST RECORD IN LONDON

The only London club to have never won a single Play-Offs match, their 4-0 loss in 1989 is the biggest home loss in League One and the aggregate of 5-0 is the largest in that division

GILLINGHAM

SEMI-FINAL SUPERMEN

Gillingham and Orient are the two clubs with the most number of appearances (four) to have never lost a semi-final.

GRIMSBY TOWN

THE FINE-MARGIN MARINERS

In all six of their matches there has never been a winning margin of more than one goal.

HARTLEPOOL UNITED

The MONKEY HANGERS ALWAYS SLIP UP

In 2005 at the fifth time of asking they won a semi, beating Tranmere. The Final was an inevitable disappointment, beaten by Sheffield Wednesday 4-2 after extra time.

HEREFORD UNITED

2-1 2-1
TWIN TORMENT

Hereford are the only team to have identical scores in their games, both 1-2 defeats.

HUDDERSFIELD TOWN

20 *from* 24

Huddersfield have been involved in four penalty shoot-outs notching an impressive 20 out of 24 spot kicks, and have won all of them.

TIGERS ATTRACT THE CROWDS

86,703

The Second-biggest crowd for a Play-Offs Final 2008 against Bristol City.

HULL CITY

7

IPSWICH TOWN
SEMI-FINAL SORROW

Ipswich have now lost seven semi-finals; which is more than any other team.

LEEDS UNITED
169,439
HIGHEST TOTAL HOME ATTENDANCE
In five matches at Elland Road

LEICESTER CITY
5-0

THE LARGEST HOME WIN IN THE SECOND TIER

The 5-0 hammering of Cambridge in 1992 is the biggest home win in the second tier.

LINCOLN CITY
PLAY-OFF *Journeymen*

Lincoln are the only team to appear in Play-Offs over five consecutive seasons, unfortunately all unsuccessful.

LUTON TOWN

1 Semi   **1 Hat-trick**   **1 Loss**

In the 1997 semi-final David Oldfield scored three at Crewe but they eventually lost 4-3 on aggregate.

MACCLESFIELD TOWN
THERE'S ONLY ONE
game for
BRIAN HORTON

Despite over 20 years in charge of lower-league clubs, a semi against Lincoln in 2005 was manager Brian Horton's only Play-Offs match.

MAIDSTONE UNITED

A SHORT STAY FOR THE STONES

Maidstone's short-lived status (1989–92) in the Football League is the shortest of any Play-Offs club.

MANCHESTER CITY
76,935

Very Noisy Neighbours

The gate for the Second Division Play-Offs Final against Gillingham in 1999 had nearly 7,000 more people than the First Division Final.

MANSFIELD TOWN

2 SHOOTOUTS FOR THE STAGS

Only team to have two penalty shoot-outs in both semi-final and Final, as well as having the lowest successful penalty tally of 1-4 in a Final.

MIDDLESBROUGH

BRAGGING RIGHTS FOR THE BORO!

Only club out of the five from the North East to win a Final. (Sunderland were promoted in 1990 but only down to Swindon's irregularities.)

LIONS COWARDLY AT THE DEN

MILLWALL

Millwall have lost all three semi-finals they have played in the second tier, whilst losing every home leg.

MK DONS

DONS FREEZE AT HOME

For three out of four home legs they have not scored a goal, the poorest return of any club with multiple appearances.

NEWCASTLE UNITED

0 GOALS FOR THE GEORDIES

★ ★ ★ ★ ★ ★ ★

One of only three clubs who have not scored a goal in the Play-Offs. (Accrington Stanley and Chester are the others.)

MORECAMBE

6-0

The Shrimps' 2010 loss against Dagenham & Redbridge is the worst single-leg defeat.

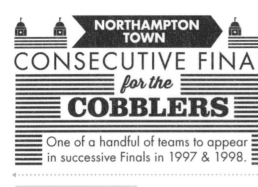

NORTHAMPTON TOWN

CONSECUTIVE FINALS
for the
COBBLERS

One of a handful of teams to appear in successive Finals in 1997 & 1998.

NOTTS COUNTY

BACK
TO BACK
PROMOTIONS

The only team to win back-to-back promotions via the Play-Offs in 1990 and 1991.

NORWICH CITY

EARLY BIRDS
CATCH THE WORM

In 2015 the Canaries became only the third team to score twice in the opening 15 minutes of a Final, alongside Preston in same year & Reading in 1995

NOTTINGHAM
FOREST

19
GOALS
CONCEDED

Forest have conceded 19 goals in their eight semi-final matches – at 2.4 goals per game this is the worst average of any side with more than one appearance.

SCUPPERED
BY A
Super
SUB

OLDHAM ATHLETIC

Both goals conceded in the 1987 semi-finals legs were scored by Keith Edwards, a substitute, in the 89th and 90th minutes.

ORIENT

4 *Semi-Final*
VICTORIES

Leyton Orient have never lost a semi-final and are the only team to have beaten Peterborough.

PETERBOROUGH UNITED

✳✳✳✳✳✳✳✳✳✳✳✳✳✳✳✳✳✳✳✳✳✳✳✳✳✳✳✳✳✳✳✳

The Posh 100%
ALWAYS GIVE

✳✳✳✳✳✳✳✳✳✳✳✳✳✳✳✳✳✳✳✳✳✳✳✳✳✳✳✳✳✳✳✳✳

Peterborough were the last club with multiple appearances to boast a 100% record before losing to Leyton Orient in 2014.

PLYMOUTH ARGYLE

THE PILGRIMS
ARE THE
BEST IN THE WEST

Plymouth are the most westerly team to win the Play-Offs.

PORTSMOUTH

88 pts
IS NOT ENOUGH

Portsmouth's 88 points in 1993 is the second-highest total without achieving promotion from the second tier.

VALIANT IN THE SEMIS

PORT VALE

The Valiants are one of only eight clubs to have multiple appearances but have never lost a semi-final.

PRESTON NORTH END

ATTEMPTS
10

PROMOTIONS
1

In 2015 Preston finally secured promotion via the Play-Offs at the tenth time of asking.

QUEENS PARK RANGERS

87,348
THE 2014 FINAL VERSUS DERBY IS THE LARGEST PLAY-OFFS CROWD EVER.

A ROYAL RETURN

BUT NO PROMOTIONS

Having scored seven goals in their three Finals, the Royals have scored the most Finals goals without being promoted.

READING

ROCHDALE

ONCE TWICE THREE

TIMES A LOSER

One of five clubs to have appeared three times just in the lowest tier but have never gained promotion.

ROTHERHAM UNITED

52 PTS

BUT STILL RELEGATED

Rotherham's 52 points in 1988 was the highest tally of all the teams involved in the relegation Play-Offs.

RUSHDEN & DIAMONDS

Diamonds AREN'T FOREVER

Rushden & Diamonds are the latest club involved in the Play-Offs to be dissolved.

SCARBOROUGH

ROCKETT MEN FAIL TO LAUNCH

Both goals against Torquay in the 1998 semi-final were scored by the appropriately-named Jason Rockett. They lost 7-2.

SCUNTHORPE UNITED

7 GAMES IN A ROW WITHOUT A WIN

The Iron racked up 3 draws and 4 losses in the Play-Offs between 1988 and 1992; this run of games is the longest winless streak.

SHEFFIELD UNITED

BLADES NOT SHARP ENOUGH

4 Finals 👍👍👍👍 **0** Goals 👎👎👎👎

Reaching four Finals has not paid dividends for Sheffield United, who lost them all without scoring a single goal.

SHEFFIELD WEDNESDAY

THE OWLS ARE HAVING A HOOT

1 Final 👍👍👍👍 **4** Goals 👍👍👍👍

Wednesday have won all three of their matches and scored four in the Final against Hartlepool in 2005.

SHREWSBURY TOWN

TAMING *of The* SHREWS

The Shrews have lost in both of their Final appearances. First against Bristol Rovers in 2007 and then against Gillingham in 2009.

NOT THE *Best Day* for the Saints

SOUTHAMPTON

Leon Best was unfortunate in the second leg of the 2007 Final; as well as scoring an own goal, he missed a penalty in the shoot-out.

SOUTHEND UNITED

3⏱⏱⏱ MINS WITHOUT CONCEDING

Southend did not concede a goal in their 2005 campaign, keeping a clean sheet over 300 minutes, equalling the record set by Cardiff in 2003.

STEVENAGE

DOUBLE PROMOTION PROMOTION FOR BORO

Stevenage are one of only two teams to win the Play-Offs the season after being promoted from the Conference.

5th TIME LUCKY

STOCKPORT COUNTY

Stockport finally won promotion at the fifth time of asking in 2008 when they beat Rochdale 3-2 and are one of six teams to have won promotion after four failures.

90 AND OUT

SUNDERLAND

Sunderland have the joint-highest points' total of 90 without gaining promotion, alongside perennial Play-Offs strugglers, Sheff United.

POTTERS
Produce The Points

STOKE CITY

82 pts

Stoke's 2000 tally of 82 points is the highest total achieved to qualify for last place in the Play-Offs.

23 YEARS LONGEST GAP ← BETWEEN → PROMOTIONS

SWANSEA CITY

The Swans' first win came in 1988 when they beat Torquay 5-4 over two legs. Their latest win was a 4-2 win over Reading in 2011.

THE ROBINS WUZ' ROBBED

SWINDON TOWN

The only club to win a Final and not be promoted. Promotion was snatched from their grasp because of previous misdemeanours.

TORQUAY United 3x

LOWER-TIER LOSERS

Torquay have lost more lower-tier Finals (three) than any other club.

TRANMERE Rovers 3

SEMI-FINAL DEFEATS
IN A ROW

The first team to lose three consecutive semi-finals, 1993-95.

WALSALL
4-0

HIGHEST VICTORY
IN A REPLAY

Their 4-0 win over Bristol City in 1988 was the highest victory of any Play-Offs replay.

WATFORD

The HORNETS have only been STUNG ONCE

Watford are the only team to have played in more than one Final and only conceded one goal, a penalty.

WEST HAM UNITED

CAPITAL PUNISHMENT
FOR THE
HAMMERS

The 2004 Final loss against Crystal Palace was one of only two times there has been an all-London Final out of 84 Finals.

WEST BROM

SUPER KEV BAGS THREE FOR THE BAGGIES

Kevin Phillips' three goals in 2007 make him West Brom's highest scorer in the Play-Offs.

WIGAN

FIRST PAST THE POSTS

Chris Thompson's goal in the semi-final against Swindon was the first-ever scored in the Play-Offs.

WOLVERHAMPTON WANDERERS

76 PTS

Wolves have qualified for the second-tier Play-Offs with 76 points four out of five times.

WREXHAM

THE DRAGONS DISAPPOINT

The only Welsh club out of three to have not gained promotion.

WYCOMBE WANDERERS

GARNER GOES A-WANDERING

Simon Garner scored in all three Play-Offs matches in 1994. It was his third successful campaign having won with Blackburn in 1992 and West Brom in 1993.

YEOVIL TOWN

The GLOVERS GIVE US FIVE

Yeovil's extraordinary performance at Forest in 2007 leaves them as the only team to score five goals in an away leg.

YORK CITY

YORK CITY ARE TRAGIC!

Gary Swann's two goals are the only ones York have scored in six matches of their Play-Offs history.

THE BLESSED

There are a handful of clubs that are the antithesis of the cursed four (let's call them the Fab Five) in that they have had one shot at the Play-Offs and have succeeded in gaining promotion the only time they have participated. Having only tasted success, Dagenham & Redbridge, Doncaster Rovers, Fleetwood, Manchester City and Sheffield Wednesday, must wonder what all the fuss is about. For all these clubs the Play-Offs represented a key staging post in their recent history, whether they were reaching new heights or climbing back up the ladder.

For both Dagenham and Fleetwood their singular success in the Play-Offs was the passport to their highest-ever league standing. As relative newcomers to league football, having gained league status for the first time in 2007 and 2013 respectively, their achievement of making it to League One should not be underestimated. For Fleetwood, it was particularly notable as in only their second season in the league they were promoted to League One, overcoming Burton in the Final to reach the third tier of English football for the first time. For Dagenham, promotion via the Play-Offs was secured in their third season as a league club. Although they lasted just one season and have spent the remaining period in League Two, the pinnacle of their history followed their stirring 3-2 victory over Rotherham in 2010.

Of the longer-established clubs, Doncaster Rovers' defeat of Leeds United in 2008 meant that not only had they claimed bragging rights over their more illustrious neighbours, but they were back in the second tier for the first time in over fifty years, thus providing a generation of supporters the chance to see them compete at this level for the first time. For another Yorkshire club, Sheffield Wednesday, the last fifteen years have not been blessed with success as they have bounced between the Championship and League One ever since they left the Premier League in 2000. So the defeat of Hartlepool in 2005 would certainly be one of the few highlights of a distinctly fallow period for the Owls. Ritchie Humphreys' presence in the Hartlepool team that day would have acted as a poignant reminder of how things used to be when they were an established top tier-club throughout the 1990s.

And then of course there is the exceptional case of Manchester City and how the seeds of their revival were sown in the last few minutes of that celebrated match against Gillingham in 1999. When people discuss defining moments, that Dickov goal could lay claim to being the ultimate. Although at the time the 95th-minute equaliser was hailed as rescuing them from oblivion, it became the platform for so much more over the next fifteen years, leading indirectly to their current pre-eminent position amongst the elite at the top of the Premier League. In fact all five of these 100 per cent clubs have, in their different ways, so much to thank the Play-Offs for and can be proud of their success in their only brush with them.

With these five as the only clubs to have achieved 100 per cent success it is telling that all of them have managed to achieve that feat as one-offs. Up to 2014 Peterborough were the only team to have a 100 per cent record having entered the Play-Offs more than once but that came to an end when Orient knocked them out in the League One semi-final. Still, Peterborough's three promotions out of four attempts places them firmly in the blessed category alongside the following clubs who can be said to have benefited overall from their experiences.

BLACKPOOL: THE KINGS

Blackpool have often been portrayed by the media as the kings of the Play-Offs. In addition to a positive record, winning just under 80 per cent of all their ties, which makes them part of the top dozen performing clubs, they can also boast of the unique distinction of being the only club to have been promoted on four separate occasions across all three divisions via the Play-Offs. However, there

are a few blemishes along the Golden Mile, which reflect a turbulent period in their history in the 1980s and 90s, as well as more recent troubles. For a club whose heritage included illustrious players such as Mortensen, Matthews, Ball and Armfield and the famous FA Cup victory of 1953, they had spiralled downwards badly and were in trouble at the end of the 1970s. Having spent their entire history in the top two divisions they suffered a ignominious slide, being relegated in quick succession in 1978 to the Third Division and then a few years later hitting rock bottom in the Fourth.

They are the only team to have been promoted from all three divisions and have contested more finals than any other team.

The next two decades were spent toing and froing between the bottom divisions with a worryingly rapid turnover of managers. Reaching the 1991 Play-Offs Final was a considerable achievement considering what had happened to the club recently, but their journey ended in disappointment after a 2-2 draw with Torquay United could not be settled in extra time and Blackpool became the first victims of a Play-Offs Final penalty shoot-out when they lost 5-4. Under

Billy Ayre they proved to be made of sterner stuff and the following season they qualified and again reached the Final where they met old adversaries Scunthorpe for the right to play in Football League Division Two. Yet again the match could not be settled over 120 minutes of open play, again going to penalties, and this time Blackpool emerged as winners, gaining swift revenge for the previous year's defeat, and a love affair began.

Four years later came the opportunity to reach the second tier after an absence of eighteen years spent in the bottom two divisions. This time under the guidance of Sam Allardyce, in his first full-time managerial spell in English football, Blackpool qualified for the semi-finals in third place. Armed with a 2-0 win from the first leg away at Bradford, Blackpool looked to be a shoo-in based on their traditional strength at home – they had conceded only twenty goals in twenty-three matches and lost just four of those throughout the season. But there was a shock in store as Bradford prevailed 3-0 in the second leg and Blackpool suffered their one and only defeat at the semi-final stage.

In all their other six Play-Offs semi-finals Blackpool have won their home legs, so this comprehensive defeat was completely out of character and galling for all concerned. Indeed so catastrophic and unexpected was this loss at home, which had been such a bastion of strength previously, that there was a widely held theory that the boardroom at Bloomfield Road was haunted. Furthermore, this was no common haunting but the work of the ghost of Lord Nelson no less. According to the *Independent*, Nelson's ire was roused when "his former flagship the *Foudroyant* had been beached off Blackpool in 1897 and the club used the wood from the ship to panel the boardroom walls". Hence the curse that did for Blackpool that night was a century-old nautical one, so the odds were stacked against them and they did not stand much chance, on reflection.

The chairman, however, felt that this Nelson theory was a little far-fetched and laid the blame fair and square on the head of the manager. But the relatively straightforward task of dismissing him had its own levels of intrigue and complications. Even the Lord Nelson theory did not compare to what happened to Allardyce after what he had described "as the worst night of my life". He did not anticipate being sacked, so that was a shock to the system in itself, but it was the manner in which his dismissal happened that made this one so distinctive, nay surreal. Blackpool's chairmen were not known for their patience or loyalty and Owen Oyston had ploughed a fair amount of money into the club. Desperate for success, Allardyce duly paid the price, as so many managers had done before and since, but what marked this sacking as so unusual was that he was dismissed whilst Oyston was languishing in a prison cell, awaiting trial for charges of rape and indecent assault. Some might have suggested that

Oyston could have waited for a more appropriate time to dismiss Allardyce, but as Oyston ultimately served three years of a six-year sentence, he would have had to wait until 1999. Chairmen such as Oyston like to act quickly, even if they are themselves not in the best position to do so, and Allardyce became the first English manager to be sacked by someone in prison, adding another extraordinary twist to the Play-Offs story.

After Blackpool had passed up this chance to get back to the upper reaches of the league, the yo-yoing between the bottom two divisions continued and relegation to the bottom tier in 1999/2000 was followed by a disastrous start to the season, epitomised by a 7-0 loss to Barnet, a team that ended up 92nd and rock bottom that season and relegated to the Conference. This shocking result left Blackpool in fifteenth place in mid-November and with little to play for but pride, it seemed. However, the galvanizing effect of being able to rescue a season through the Play-Offs worked wonders for Blackpool, who ultimately overtook Rochdale in the race for seventh spot, securing the last Play-Off place on the final day of the regular season, and the momentum of this heady rise up the table gave them self-belief.

They breezed through the semi-finals 5-1 on aggregate against fourth-placed Hartlepool and faced Leyton Orient in the Final. The Final was a microcosm of their season where a poor start was overcome by a strong finish. Despite conceding the fastest-ever goal scored in a Play-Offs Final after twenty-seven seconds following a howler from Phil Barnes, their keeper, and then going 2-1 down just before half time, Blackpool stormed back to win 4-2. This was their sixth straight victory at the business end of the season and secured promotion to the second flight under Steve McMahon. McMahon put it succinctly, "That game sums our season up. What a roller-coaster ride it was." This Big Dipper ended up in the right place and Blackpool were moving in the right direction, but could they keep that going and not fall backwards?

The next five years brought some stability as they established themselves in the third tier without too many dramas at either end of the table, finishing comfortably mid-table between thirteenth and nineteenth. In 2006/07 Blackpool celebrated their 100th year in the Football League and under Simon Grayson started to push for promotion. With impeccable timing and their customary late surge, Blackpool won their last seven league matches, culminating in a 6-3 win at Swansea, which confirmed third place.

In the semi-final they brushed aside Oldham 5-2 on aggregate, adding to their winning run, and approached the Final against Yeovil (who had turned the tables on Forest so spectacularly in the other semi-final) with the prospect of securing a record-breaking tenth consecutive win. Sure enough the Seasiders carried on their impressive form, running out 2-0 winners, and their inexorable rise continued, lifting them back into the Championship after twenty-nine years spent in the lower reaches.

Just as when they were promoted via the Play-Offs in 2001, they spent a couple of years establishing themselves in more elevated company with mid-table finishes. Then the mercurial Ian Holloway arrived for the 2009/10 season after the briefest of spells at Leicester, and the rise to the top division in the space of a decade was in sight. With Blackpool always on the fringes throughout the season, none of the late charges that had character-ised previous campaigns was required to make the Play-Offs this time around. Forest were dispatched with the obligatory home win in the first leg of the semi-finals, and, coupled with Forest's traditional generosity at the City Ground in the second leg, Blackpool sealed a 6-4 aggregate victory with a DJ Campbell hat-trick. This set up a Final with Cardiff, which proved to be a marvellously attack-ing match from the off, featuring one of the finest first halves seen at Wembley in recent years.

SHEFFIELD WEDNESDAY

THE OWLS ARE HAVING A HOOT

1 Final   4 Goals

Wednesday have won all three of their matches and scored four in the Final against Hartlepool in 2005.

The game began with Michael Chopra's early strike for Cardiff being can-celled out by Charlie Adam's fulminating free-kick. It was a Gascoigne-like strike in its purity and accuracy (if that is not an insult to a Scot). Joe Ledley continued the run of excellent goals with a slick finish after a neat one-two on the edge of the area, only for Blackpool to notch twice in the last five minutes of the first half to take the lead, and even then there was still time to squeeze in a disallowed goal by Darcy Blake. There was enough action in the opening forty-five minutes to satisfy the most demanding of fans and naturally the game petered out in the second half, especially in the searing heat – a temperature of over 106 degrees Fahrenheit was recorded at the pitch-side – but it was mission accomplished for Holloway and his team.

At long last Blackpool were back in the top division, having travelled up through the Football League the hard way via their series of three successive Play-Offs triumphs. It was all the more remarkable an ascent as it happened some ten years after looking as though they were never going to be able to rise again, seemingly mired in lower-league torpor. This was a truly amazing trans-formation achieved through the Play-Offs, and even the 2012 defeat to West Ham cannot take the shine off the fantastic achievement of gaining promotion through all three divisions in the space of a decade.

SHEFFIELD WEDNESDAY

As was pointed out a little earlier in this chapter, the joy for the Owls would have been accentuated by the trials and tribulations of their city rivals, United. This victory was sandwiched in between United failures, preceding the hammering by Wolves in 2003 and then being followed a few years later by their defeat to Burnley. United fans must have looked on in horror at the assurance with which Wednesday took to the whole affair. Where was the struggle, where was the torment? This was not how it was meant to be; it was supposed to be about anguish and disappointment rather than joy and fulfilment. Even Paul Sturrock's triple substitution on the day, the ultimate managerial gamble, worked like a dream, with two of the subs scoring; a sure sign that all is right in the world.

As rivals, the Sheffield clubs are generally evenly matched, with one team holding ascendancy for a while before the other comes back to challenge, and so forth. Over all the Steel City derbies that go back 125 years there is a small, marginal lead for United, with forty-five wins in all competitions against forty-two for Wednesday, but there is only one clear victor when it comes to the Play-Offs. Wednesday can lay claim to the bragging rights and to a whole lot more, as their perfect record mocks the repeatedly abject performances of United. Here, Wednesday fan and football writer Laura Jones talks us through her experience:

TWO SLICES OF THIN-CUT WHITE HOVIS
2005 LEAGUE 1 PLAY-OFF FINAL
SHEFFIELD WEDNESDAY V HARTLEPOOL

In May 2005 I nearly lost my friend Phil in a freak 'football descending to Earth' incident.

From within the densely packed crowd outside the Millennium Stadium in Cardiff, someone booted a Mitre football so hard and high in the air that when it came back down if it had hit him we'd have been taking him to hospital that afternoon and not to the League One Play-Off Final. It missed by a couple of centimetres. The higher the ball got the nearer you felt to impending doom. It's a fitting metaphor for the emotional turmoil Sheffield Wednesday put us through that day.

Wembley was being rebuilt so we travelled to Cardiff for the Final. We'd never been in a Play-Off before so we didn't know what to expect. Sheffield Wednesday fans have a lot of affection for the 2005 promotion team.

Not just because they gave us a much needed sense of joy after five years of relegation, financial problems and quite literally some of the worst managers ever to cross the Hillsborough threshold, but because they felt complete, more than just a collection of individuals. They weren't the greatest players in the world and only the likes of Chris Brunt and Glenn Whelan would go on to play top-level football but it's names like Lee Bullen, Lee Peacock, Jon-Paul McGovern and Steve MacLean who may not mean much to other supporters, but who bring a smile to any Wednesdayite's face. They were a team. They were our team.

Outside the Millennium Stadium there wasn't a square inch that wasn't covered in blue and white. Tightly packed together it was difficult to tell which fans were which. However, most of them were complaining about the city centre pubs only serving cans of Carling and having the nerve to charge £3 a pop for them. Inside the ground there were over 40,000 Owls fans, some of who had taken advantage of the tickets Hartlepool had returned. We were encroaching into their end of the stadium.

We dominated the first half but couldn't get the ball in the net. We left it until the stroke of half time when JP McGovern smacked it in off the under side of the crossbar. The relief among Sheffield hearts sent us sky-high over the break. But then Hartlepool scored within the first few minutes of the restart. Grumbles of 'typical Wednesday' came from all around us. From then on Hartlepool had the better of the game. The atmosphere completely changed in the 70th minute when they brought Jon Daly on and within a minute he'd put them in the lead. I remember saying over and over to my boyfriend, "I can't go home feeling like this!" The Owls couldn't go back to where we had been.

Wednesday's manager Paul Sturrock made a triple substitution in the 77th minute. In the depths of despair there was a shining light. Our leading goal scorer Steve MacLean, who had been out for three months with a stress fracture in his foot, hadn't expected to even make the bench that day but he was coming on. His mere presence on the pitch received one of the loudest ovations of the day. Within minutes, Hartlepool's Chris Westwood gifted us the chance to get back in the game. With the tamest of tackles and pushes on Talbot, he gave away a penalty and earned himself a red card.

Up stepped the talismanic substitute MacLean, who duly slotted the ball home to equalise. A young lad who was standing on his seat next to us, jumped up like the other 40,000 Wednesday-ites, but age and wisdom hadn't developed yet. The seat flipped up and when he came back down it was halfway to closing. He ended up in the row in front of us.

Isn't it funny how you can swing between pessimism and optimism within seconds? Going into extra time we just felt we could win it. When Glenn Whelan stayed on his feet to score from distance it was all over. Drew Talbot, rounding the keeper and scoring our fourth was just inevitable. I hadn't felt that kind of high since beating Sheffield United in the 1993 FA Cup Semi-Final at Wembley. My heart felt like it would burst. I was a loose woman with my hugging that day.

On the way back we stopped off at the services to get something to eat. The locusts had already reached Burger King by the time we got there. I asked for a Whopper and when it was handed to me, the flame-grilled burger was served between two slices of thin-cut white Hovis. The day had been so emotional that I almost cried eating this pathetic excuse for a burger. I'd been so high that I had to come crashing back down to earth like that Mitre football booted into the air. So close to impending doom but surviving it.

NOTTS COUNTY: WARNOCK'S RISE

As the oldest surviving professional football club in the world and one of the founding members of the Football League, Notts County have a pedigree that stretches back over 150 years. Having had some early involvement in the old Test Matches, the nineteenth-century predecessor of the modern Play-Offs *(as covered in Chapter One)*, County can lay claim to a Play-Offs ancestry spanning well over a century. Over a hundred years after their initial brush with the test matches they became the only team to have gained two successive promotions through the Play-Offs in 1990 and 1991 under the guidance of that wily young rascal, Neil Warnock. This remains a feat unrivalled over the twenty-eight years of Play-Offs history.

When Tranmere Rovers were beaten 2-0 in 1990 it was Notts County's first-ever appearance at Wembley and of course the first year the Play-Offs Finals had been held at the national stadium, so their timing was impeccable if a little delayed. It was deeply ironic that one of the original English football clubs had to wait such a long time to taste action at Wembley, and then they clearly enjoyed it so much that they returned there immediately in the following year when Brighton were dispatched 3-1 in the Second Division Final. So County returned to the First Division, with the Magpies reversing successive relegations of a few years beforehand. As the *Nottingham Post* put it, this was arguably "County's finest hour in all their 129 years". Warnock's reputation was being forged through these Play-Offs successes even to the extent that Chelsea expressed an interest in appointing him. Tommy Johnson was their hero, scoring three times in those two Finals, and is the only player to score in successive Finals in different divisions. Johnson also scored for Derby in 1994 and with four goals in total is the highest individual scorer in Play-Offs Finals.

NOTTS COUNTY

BACK TO BACK PROMOTIONS

The only team to win back-to-back promotions via the Play-Offs in 1990 and 1991.

County's heady rise to the top lasted just a single season in the top flight and soon they were relegated and on the way down to the bottom division within six years, including another stab at promotion through the Play-Offs which ended in a 2-0 Final defeat to Blackpool's conquerors, Bradford City, in 1996. That early 1990s Warnock double was as good as it got for County and they have now returned to flitting between the bottom two divisions.

THE UNFORTUNATES

There are always times when fans curse their luck as a coping mechanism for the continuing failure of their team. The view is that the players are performing satisfactorily and trying their hardest but fortune is not favouring their efforts and there is nothing else left but to put it down to the rub of the green. When fate has decided that your club is not going to succeed however hard they try or however much you want them to, resistance is futile. This is very much how supporters of the following clubs will try to rationalise their lack of success over many years, as the Play-Offs gods delivered their damning verdicts.

IPSWICH TOWN: SHEEPSHANKS'S RULE

Whilst Ipswich hold the record for the most appearances at the highest level, the club's most telling contribution to the history of the Play-Offs is actually derived from their erstwhile chairman, David Sheepshanks. Having racked up eight appearances but with only one success over those years, Ipswich had little to rejoice about at Portman Road *(see Heroes & Villains, Chapter Four)*. Indeed during this period they only made one Final, which they won, but it is in the detail of the semi-finals that the genuine interest was encapsulated.

After they had failed in 1987, the first year of the Play-Offs, against the eventual winners Charlton, Ipswich's series of three consecutive losses from 1997, which led to the intervention of Sheepshanks, was the foundation for creating their own mini soap opera. Ipswich reappeared ten years on from their debut loss, only to fail against perennial under-achievers Sheffield United in the semi-finals. After drawing the first leg 1-1 at Bramall Lane, Ipswich were strong favourites to progress. But in the home leg, Ipswich could only draw 2-2 and the away goals rule came into effect. A maddening way to lose and it was all too much for experienced Argentine Mauricio Taricco who left the field in tears, exasperated by the finest of margins and upset by some of the spikier characters in the Sheffield side.

If that was difficult to bear then worse was to follow. Yet again in 1998 they lost out to Charlton in the semi-finals, losing both legs 1-0. Back they came for another dose of their medicine the next year and this time they stumbled up against the prickly Bolton Wanderers. A narrow 1-0 defeat at Burnden Park made it all to play for in the second leg and cruelly, almost sadistically, a fluctuating tie ended 4-3 to Ipswich on the night, but with the scores level on aggregate there was more misery to be heaped on the Tractor Boys. For a second time in three years of trying, Ipswich were thwarted by the away goals rule.

The fans were at their wits' end, the players dumbstruck, coaching staff bereft of answers, so enter Sheepshanks, who decided enough was enough and was determined to take action. He put forward a motion to the League to remove the away goals rule and in future if aggregate scores were the same after extra time then penalties would decide the outcome. Sheepshanks's basic argument for changing the away goals rule was that it was unfair on the team that had finished higher in the league.

Previously, it had been perceived as an advantage to play the second leg at home in the full knowledge of what needed to be achieved but Sheepshanks argued that when it came to games that were level on aggregate, the advantage switched to the away team, who could be in a position to score a goal that was worth extra in the event of a draw and they had extra time in which to do it. Sheepshanks must have been very persuasive in his argument to the League as they passed the motion unanimously. It may also have helped their cause that he was chairman of the Football League between 1997 and 1999. Or maybe he cited the fact that on all six occasions Play-Offs semi-finals had been tied on aggregate the lower-placed team won through. Whether this was evidence that the playing field was slanted against the higher-placed team or not, Sheepshanks got his way. By comparison, European competitions such as the Champions League still operate an away goals rule but maybe no team has suffered in the same way as Ipswich had through the Play-Offs, so the Sheepshanks-inspired rules have stayed the same since 2000.

7 IPSWICH TOWN
SEMI-FINAL SORROW

Ipswich have now lost seven semi-finals; which is more than any other team.

Then, by a strange quirk of fate, or maybe provenance, Ipswich duly managed to qualify for the semi-finals the season after the change was made and it just happened to be against their nemesis from 1999, Bolton. There was a distinctly familiar pattern to the tie as Ipswich qualified in a higher position than their opponents, which meant hosting the second leg. A 2-2 draw in the first leg must have brought back bad memories for them, as their ability to carve out a decent result in previous away legs had not done them any good. When the second leg ended 3-3 after ninety minutes, at least the spectre of going out on away goals had been removed and in the end they triumphed 5-3 after extra time. So, ironically, away goals would not have counted anyway, but the thought lingered that maybe Bolton could have clung on, knowing that they would have gone through if there had been no more goals in extra time.

Sheepshanks had gained some sort of redemption and Ipswich went on to beat Barnsley 4-2 in a suitably thrilling fashion to reach the Premier League for the one and only time through the Play-Offs. The good people of Suffolk could in part thank their chairman for his fortitude and determination in the face of adversity.

As an unusual postscript to the day that Ipswich finally broke their Play-Offs duck, the referee, Terry Heilbron, was officiating his last-ever match. Having awarded Barnsley two penalties during the match, the Ipswich players were thirsting for some playful revenge. Their retribution was to dunk Heilbron into the team bath, meaning he then had to attend the medal ceremony dripping wet, quite an original way to bow out of his refereeing career.

To add to their trail of semi-final woes, even worse was to come in 2015, as they racked up their seventh loss and so, allied with Preston's success, Ipswich became the team with the most semi-final losses. However painful it would have been to carry this burden, it was the opposition who thwarted them this time round that provided them with the most acute angst. If the unfairness of the late 1990s was hard for them to take then the loss to East Anglian rivals Norwich City was perhaps the bitterest pill to swallow.

With Ipswich consigned to another year in the Championship it was particularly galling to see Norwich go on and win the Final for their first ever Play-Offs promotion and to gain another tilt at Premier League survival. Whilst Ipswich have been becalmed in the same division for over a dozen years, Norwich have been promoted four times and relegated three times with a spell in League One as well as the Premier League. So much for stability; most fans would exchange a period of stability for some excitement and a shot at the top table, however fleeting that might be.

The semi-final was billed as the biggest derby in their history because of the considerable prize that potentially lay ahead for the winners. In the end it turned out to be one of the less dramatic semi-finals. After the drawn match at Portman Road the second leg was pretty much decided early in the second half when Christophe Berra was sent off by the appositely named Roger East for handling the ball and Wes Hoolahan tucked away the resulting penalty. Despite Tommy Smith's rapid response Ipswich's defiance was broken by goals from Nathan Redmond and Cameron Jerome, who repeated the dose in the Final, and that was that for local bragging rights and the only meeting between these two rivals in the Play-Offs.

For Ipswich manager Mick McCarthy it was a fourth semi-final failure after previously losing with Millwall, Sunderland and Wolves. So for each English club he has managed he has suffered a semi-final defeat and he could be forgiven for not being too enamoured of the Play-Offs but he remains an advocate. "I'm a big fan of the play-off system. My record in them is not great, in fact I was the first to suffer disappointment when they were introduced. But I still think they're brilliant." McCarthy must view his counterpart Alex Neil's record of following up Hamilton's success last year in Scotland with Norwich's in England with an understandable envy.

Ipswich fans may not be quite so well disposed as their manager in their opinions of a system that has not been kind to them. But of all their semi-final flops this was undoubtedly the one that would have hurt them the most. Losing in the Play-Offs is bad enough but when it is to your bitterest rivals then that is as bad as it gets. Waiting at least another year before getting the chance to gain revenge adds to the frustration of being thwarted by your *bête noires*.

For Ipswich's latest brush with semi-final failure here's Gavin Barber of *Turnstile Blues* again and this time his pain is all the more acute because of the opponents.

IPSWICH SUFFER FROM FARMAGEDDON

There's no shame in admitting that Norwich beat Ipswich in the 2014/15 Play-Off semi-final because they had better players than us. No shame, but plenty of pain. The facts are: Norwich had a squad featuring several seven-figure signings (Cameron Jerome, Lewis Grabban, Nathan Redmond), and parachute money from their Premier League relegation meant that they could afford to retain the services of players with top-flight experience. By contrast, Ipswich had just about scraped together enough pennies to sign Freddie Sears from Colchester the previous January, to join a side otherwise comprised of free transfers, loanees and home-grown youngsters. Norwich had won both league fixtures during the preceding season without too much trouble.

Those are the facts, all of which were known before the semi-final, but this is football and this is the Play-Offs, where an intersection can sometimes be found in the Venn diagram of fantasy, hope and the occasional miracle. So, of course we thought we could win. "The pressure will be on them," we told ourselves and each other. "This is the Play-Offs: form counts for nothing." Etc. Just when you least expect it, just what you least expect, as the Pet Shop Boys once said.

But of course we were working so hard to convince ourselves that we could beat Norwich over two legs, that we actually did expect it. The first leg at Portman Road started at a frantic pace: Ipswich were refusing to be intimidated or bullied as they had been in most recent meetings with the Canaries. Paul Anderson came on as a first-half substitute for the injured Luke Varney: within minutes of being on the pitch he received an unceremonious welcome from Bradley Johnson's elbow (the same elbow which had made surreptitious but decisive contact with Luke Hyam's face in the league game between the two sides in August, which does seem extraordinarily coincidental). Far from being cowed, Anderson immediately got up to remonstrate with his considerably beefier opponent, and even after Town fell behind to Jonny Howson's goal on 40 minutes, it was Anderson who rifled home Town's equaliser in first-half injury-time. Finally, and for the first time in years, it seemed as though Town had the mettle to compete with their East Anglian rivals. So when the first leg ended 1-1, there was genuine hope that a similar performance in the second leg might just bring about some kind of dogged but heroic victory in the second leg.

(And whatever happened in the second leg, the first leg had given my eleven-year-old son, who has been coming with me to watch Ipswich since he was four, his first-ever taste of a properly packed and properly noisy and properly raucous Portman Road. And for that, I will always be grateful to Mick McCarthy and his team's achievement in reaching the Play-Offs at all.)

For the first half of the second leg Town matched Norwich and largely controlled the pace of the game. Then in the second half … well it all fell apart. Christophe Berra's handball was an act of pure instinct. Had it been the 90th minute, it would have been exactly the right thing to do. But in the 50th minute, conceding both a player and a penalty was always going to be a bit of a problem. Tommy Smith's equaliser gave us three minutes of frenzied hope-against-hope, but the one-man advantage was always going to allow Norwich's more skilful players the space and time that Town's dogged pressing had previously denied them.

And yes, it hurt. It hurt like hell. And the sad thing was that the cruelty of losing a Play-Off semi-final to our bitterest rivals overshadowed the continued progress made by Mick McCarthy and his team, culminating in a top-six finish which owed far more to organisation, discipline and determination than it did to free-flowing football. Norwich fans sneered at Town's perceived lack of style, but when you've sat through the mind-numbing, spineless apathy of the Roy Keane and Paul Jewell eras, a team that can summon up the collective will to perform as more than the sum of its parts is an extremely welcome improvement.

In *Fever Pitch*, Nick Hornby wrote about the dilemmas he wrestled with ahead of Arsenal's appearance in the 1979 FA Cup Final. "On the Thursday before the Cup Final, Mrs Thatcher was attempting to win her first General Election ... The Cup Final obviously concerned me most, although I was also perturbed, just as obviously, by the prospect of Mrs Thatcher becoming Prime Minister ... Yet the terrible truth is that I was willing to accept a Conservative government if it guaranteed an Arsenal Cup Final win." With the 2015 General Election falling just two days before the first leg of the Play-Off semi-final at Portman Road, some kind of record for the number of Faustian pacts being offered and debated across East Anglia and social media must have been reached. Whether Labour-supporting Norwich fans or Conservative-supporting Ipswich fans consider the outcomes to be a fair trade-off is something that only time will be able to tell them, but speaking as someone whose political heart beats red underneath a blue football shirt, it's safe to say that I've lost some degree of faith in the value of striking bargains with the metaphysical world when it comes to sport and politics.

READING: GOALS, GOALS, GOALS

If there is something noble about dramatic failure then Reading are surely the most splendid example in their ability to go down in a blaze of glory. Having qualified for three Finals out of five attempts they can point to a fair degree of success, but it is when they get to the Final that they really come to the fore in their ability to come up short so spectacularly at the last hurdle, and their Finals failures are beyond parallel. They are one of four teams to have buckled three times, but none have done so quite with the explosive aplomb of The Royals.

In three different stadia they have competed in high-scoring Finals, starting with a classic in 1995 when they met Bolton Wanderers as the second-best team in Division Two (just like Brentford's situation, this was the only time second did not guarantee promotion as there was a reorganisation of the league structure). Reading shot into a two-goal lead within the first dozen minutes and then were awarded a penalty just before half time. The game was there to be signed, sealed and delivered by Stuart Lovell, but he not only had his spot kick saved but also fluffed the rebound which came back to him in the six-yard box. Reading still held the two-goal advantage for most of the second half until a youngish Owen Coyle scored, followed by an equaliser five minutes from time by Fabian de Freitas to send the game into extra time. Bolton's charge could not be halted and they scored twice before Jimmy Quinn made for an interesting last few minutes. It ended 4-3 and Reading had blown it in spectacular fashion.

Having contributed massively to one of the most entertaining games to have been played at the old Wembley, within six years they were at it again but this time the

Having scored seven goals in their three Finals, the Royals have scored the most Finals goals without being promoted.

Millennium Stadium in Cardiff was the venue. Reading took the lead and were ahead at half time of the Football League Second Division Final against Walsall, only to let it slip early in the second half and give themselves another extra time stint. This time they took the lead early on but then in the second half of extra time a fluky own goal from Tony Rougier, swiftly followed by a Darren Byfield, strike meant that Reading were pipped at the post a second time. The familiar pattern of failure was emerging and The Royals were caught in its icy grip.

A decade on, the stage was the new Wembley for a showdown with Swansea City and their former manager Brendan Rodgers, who had been sacked from Reading after just twenty-three matches in charge back in December 2009. Having taken the lead and been victims of strong comebacks in both previous Finals, this was an altogether different match, as Swansea swept into a three-goal lead just before half time. Cue the comeback, with two Reading goals in the early part of the second half and a realistic opportunity emerged for them to become the team this time round to complete a remarkable revival. Such hope was finally extinguished by Scott Sinclair when he completed his hat-trick ten minutes from time, resigning Reading to another high-scoring, noble defeat.

So Reading can proudly point to the fact that they have scored seven times in their three Finals, which makes them one of the most prolific clubs at the Finals stage, but none of those have counted towards the ultimate success of promotion and so this excellent scoring record provides scant consolation to The Royals. Their fans will remember these days, even if not with any great affection, but certainly with a strength of emotion that will not be diminished by time.

BRISTOL CITY: HOPE GOES WEST

If Reading can consider themselves unfortunate in being high-scoring, gallant losers, less than a hundred miles down the road is a club with an identical record of two semi-finals and three losing Finals, but this club does not have the redeeming feature of a hatful of goals in a losing cause. Bristol City have already appeared on the radar a few times courtesy of Mark Watson's previous lament over their succession of failures. It all started with their wholesale and comprehensive capitulation to Walsall in the 1988 Division Three Final replay and since that 4-0 hammering they have not been able to make their presence felt when it matters most.

The major problem for The Robins is that whilst they are reasonably adept at overcoming opponents in the semi-finals, with a healthy 60 per cent success ratio, it is at the Finals that things start to fall apart at the seams and they are left centre stage stripped down to their less than natty undies. Their two failures at the semi-final stage in 1997, when they somehow succumbed to perennial losers Brentford, and in 2003 against Cardiff, when the Bluebirds recorded their only triumph out of six attempts, can be buried somewhat. When defeat is suffered in the limelight of high-profile Finals, however, there is no place to hide.

After the disappointment of 2003 City looked destined to achieve success the following year having secured their place in the Final with two late goals in the semi-final second leg against Hartlepool. Surely any team which scores the winning goals in the 88th and 90th minutes has their name etched into the winner's enclosure. However, their Final opponents Brighton, who had themselves only qualified through a 120th-minute equaliser from Adam Virgo and then on penalties against Swindon, proved to be made of even sterner stuff. Leon Knight's 84th-minute penalty was enough to seal their fate and consign them to their fourth failure.

For the third time in the space of six seasons City qualified in 2008, but for the first time they had a tilt at reaching the top division. Having disposed of Palace in the Championship semi-final with a couple of goals in extra time of the second leg at Ashton Gate they met Hull at Wembley. On this occasion they again lost 1-0 and were thwarted by Dean Windass's wonder strike. Deep down you probably know that when a thirty-nine-year-old journeyman in his second spell with the club unleashes an unstoppable volley from the edge of the penalty area and it flies in, fortune is probably conspiring against your own team ever winning.

BRISTOL City

3 FINALS ZERO PROMOTIONS

After Brentford and Sheffield United, Bristol City have played more Play-Offs Finals without securing promotion.

THE BLIGHTED

The final group of clubs merit attention neither through their misfortune nor because they are accursed. This rabble represent the bottom of the heap; there are no redeeming features, no mitigating circumstances; they are purely and simply the worst performers out of the nearly one hundred clubs. They have not so much been tainted as totally destroyed by the Play-Offs, with each successive appearance inflicting more pain and copious amounts of angst.

PRESTON NORTH END: TENTH TIME LUCKY

Unlike their North West neighbours and close rivals Blackpool, Preston North End do not hold too much affection for the Play-Offs and considering their unparalleled record of nine (this would be spelt out in bold if it was on *Football Focus* as if to underline the incredulousness of the number) attempts and no promotions before the 2015 success it is not hard to see why. No other club had such an undistinguished record of failure, which stretched over twenty-five years from the early days of 1989 all the way to 2014 and this catalogue of disappointment was strewn across all three divisions. The Lilywhites had managed to fail in such a variety of ways, ranging from abject failure to the tightest of margins, against familiar foes and some newer rivals, that one wondered what their next shortcoming might entail, or if they should change their kit to the red and white stripes most closely associated with failure. But 2015 changed all that and not before time.

Preston's first foray into the Play-Offs was unspectacular as they capitulated meekly to Port Vale in the semi-finals. Next up was a much more noble, but in many ways a more intense, excruciating exit. In 1994 Preston overcame a 2-0 first-leg deficit to overwhelm Torquay 4-1 at home and head off to a Final for John Beck's team against Wycombe Wanderers. Despite leading twice and being ahead at half time, Preston were beaten 4-2, and so a pattern of desperate flops in the Play-Offs was set in motion for Preston, which they have continued throughout their ensuing campaigns.

Perhaps the most painful of all their legion of defeats was in the 2000/01 Final. In 1998 David Moyes took up his first managerial position and having steadied a sinking ship, by staving off relegation from the Second Division Moyes steered them towards the Play-Offs in his first full season. Another semi-final defeat to Gillingham followed but at least Preston were moving in the right direction, and Moyes led them to automatic promotion in 1999/2000.

Reaching the Play-Offs the following season was a significant achievement. They were eyeing a second successive promotion and a return to the top division for the first time in forty-four years. However, that long absence from the top table was not about to end. To add to the hurt, they lost out to their most bitter rivals and fellow League founders, Bolton Wanderers. But this wasn't in the same vein as the Wycombe loss, in that they were hammered 3-0 by a clearly superior Bolton team that themselves had come up short in the Play-Offs in the previous two years. Moyes departed for Everton next year and whilst Preston hovered on the edge of promotion over the next ten years, their attempts to reach the Premier League, inevitably faltered and a Final loss to West Ham in 2005, followed by semi-final defeats in 2006, 2009 and 2014 seemed to have rounded off a thoroughly miserable record in suitably dismal fashion before they gained full and unmitigated redemption.

The most striking element of the 2015 Play-Offs was that Preston finally broke their hoodoo at the tenth time of asking, and how. As their manager, Simon Grayson, pointed out, they had already achieved a notable first by winning the away leg of their semi-final with Chesterfield so were primed to break the jinx. The League One Final was their twenty-fourth Play-Offs match and with their comprehensive 4-0 demolition of Swindon at Wembley, it was as if the frustration of those previous nine failures had been unleashed. Preston broke quite a few long-standing Play-Offs records in the process, including the highest winning margin in a Wembley Final (matching that of Walsall in the 1988 Division Three replay). Having been solid defensively throughout the season, conceding only forty goals over the forty-six regular matches (the second best defence in the division), they joined a small, elite band of clubs who have kept clean sheets throughout the semi-finals and Final. Additionally their overall aggregate of 8-0 over all three matches is by far and away the best of any of the handful of clubs to achieve that feat.

For Grayson, this was his third Play-Offs promotion with a different club, after he led both Huddersfield in 2012 and Blackpool in 2007 to success, all from the same division and so he has become the most successful manager for promotion from League One. He joins Neil Warnock as one of only two managers to oversee Play-Offs promotions with three different clubs. Added to which, he is also one of the select few to have

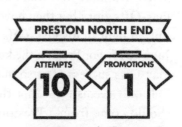

In 2015 Preston finally secured promotion via the Play-Offs at the tenth time of asking.

won multiple Play-Offs as both a player when with Leicester City in 1994 and 1996, which is something that Warnock never achieved, and as a manager. All in all, having achieved five Play-Offs promotions, he could be regarded as something of a talisman and specialist. Clearly he was the right man to lead Preston to their long-awaited triumph. After six previous managers, including David Moyes and John Beck, had tried and come up short, Grayson proved to be Preston's saviour.

Then there is the small matter of Jermaine Beckford's scoring feats as he added a hat-trick in the Final to his three goals in the semi-finals, including his outrageous chip from the halfway line in the second leg at Deepdale. With six goals overall, that is the highest tally for any player in a single year and his hat-trick is only the fourth in Play-Offs Finals history. Following on from Walsall's David Kelly in the Division Three Final replay in 1988, Clive Mendonca for Charlton in 1998 and Scott Sinclair for Swansea in 2011, Beckford's is the quickest Wembley Play-Off Final hat-trick by five minutes, having taken him just fifty-four minutes to complete. For Beckford it was a case of fourth time lucky, having suffered Play-Offs Final heartache with Leeds in 2006 and 2008 and ironically, with Grayson in charge, they also lost the semi-final to Millwall in 2009.

The pity was that Beckford's noble gesture of giving his shirt to a young fan after he was substituted was stained by the odious actions of the woman who ripped it away from him and then tried to sell it online. To their credit Preston and Beckford arranged for eight-year-old Ted Dockray to receive a signed shirt to replace the one snatched away from him. Thus 31-year-old Beckford's iconic status with long-suffering Preston fans is guaranteed, especially considering he almost gave up football entirely earlier in the year because of a persistent and severe ear infection. It is also worth noting that Beckford was only on loan to Preston from Bolton so he may not even have been at the club he helped to promote the following season. Just like loanee Kevin Phillips in 2013, the match winner could well have joined a long line of players who have secured Play-Offs glory but then have played little or no part in the future of that club. But, in light of his Play-Offs heroics, Beckford duly signed a two-year deal in June 2015. For Preston the key was that they had finally and decisively enjoyed Play-Offs success after so many bitter disappointments.

It only seems right that the last word on the end of this horrible sequence should come from a Preston fan, so here is Olly Dawes, writer/ founder of *Here Is The City*.

FINALLY

Nine Play-Off campaigns, no promotions. Many things have changed over the years at Preston; players and managers have come and gone, but one aspect has remained a constant – the club's woeful Play-Off record.

From the 1994 Third Division final defeat to Martin O'Neill's Wycombe Wanderers to missing out on the Premier League to West Ham United in 2005, no team does heartache on the biggest stage quite like Preston North End.

So, when the Lilywhites bottled automatic promotion on the final day of the League One season with a 1-0 defeat at Colchester United, many supporters – including myself – entered the Play-Offs with that familiar sinking feeling. Fans who had travelled the length and breadth of the country to watch us were now apathetic, scarred by the events in Essex just days earlier. Never have Preston supporters gone into a Play-Offs campaign so downbeat – and that's saying something.

However, the semi-finals largely went without a hitch; a 1-0 win away at Chesterfield was followed by a 3-0 victory at Deepdale, which saw Jermaine Beckford score from the halfway line before success-starved supporters launched a full-scale pitch invasion in a rare moment of Play-Offs joy. Momentum was gathering, and many believed that the Play-Offs hoodoo would be broken as North End hit form once again.

Optimism had started to creep back before the final against Swindon Town, but as fans made the long trip down to London, the dread and panic surrounding the lottery of the Play-Offs had become prevalent once again, and there was an overriding feeling that North End would set a new record of ten failed Play-Offs campaigns.

Supporters in pubs scattered around Wembley largely felt that, if Preston couldn't go up automatically, they certainly wouldn't be winning promotion through the Play-Offs. North End's comical inability to win the big games had left its mark on many, who were simply waiting for the next chapter of our brutal Play-Offs record.

Yet, all the fear and apprehension was virtually laid to rest inside the first two minutes at Wembley as Beckford opened the scoring, sparking pandemonium amongst supporters who had now started to firmly believe that this could, finally, be their moment in the spotlight having seen rivals Burnley and Blackpool recently win promotion to the Premier League at Wembley.

By the time Paul Huntington had tapped home the second goal just ten minutes later, Preston fans realised that the curse was finally about to be lifted, barring a characteristic North End collapse. As half time arrived just seconds after Beckford had put us 3-0 up, the atmosphere amongst supporters had already turned to celebration – though there were still underlying nerves as cries of 'we need one more goal' were audible, displaying just how nervous fans still were even at 3-0.

A hat-trick goal from Beckford followed shortly after the break to make it 4-0 as the game turned out to be a 90-minute-long party in Wembley's West Stand, with Preston efficiently dispatching Swindon to the point where the game was barely a contest.

Preston supporters went through the full range of emotions as the final whistle blew; disbelief, joy, relief, pride, even pain from celebration-induced injuries – whilst many even acknowledged that Swindon's anonymous display was exactly how North End had performed in the previous nine Play-Offs campaigns. It's a strange feeling to be on the other side of a Play-Offs Final.

As Tom Clarke and John Welsh raised the trophy aloft, some fans were still having to pinch themselves as the shock of winning promotion through the Play-Offs finally set in. All the heartache and tears accumulated over the years had been wiped away by one incredible evening at Wembley.

Preston not only conquered Swindon Town, but also the 26-year-long Play-Offs curse which had been hanging over the club, and the promotion was made all the sweeter with the knowledge that North End would be taking Blackpool's place in the Championship. Preston supporters couldn't have written the script better themselves in what, surprisingly, became the most perfect end to a season imaginable.

NOTTINGHAM FOREST: "UTTER MADNESS"

If near-neighbours County can lay claim to one of the more successful Play-Offs records, then their city rivals Forest are the polar opposite. Not only have they not achieved promotion in four attempts, they have not even made it to a

Final and are vying for the title of the worst Play-Offs team. For a team that had scaled the heights on both domestic and European fronts under Brian Clough in the late 1970s and early 1980s, this is a sad indictment of how far they have fallen in the last decade.

Nothing can encapsulate their woeful performances more than their 2007 encounter with Yeovil Town. Forest dominated the first leg away from home and cruised into a 2-0 lead, so the City Ground faithful expected little more than routine progression to the Final. Despite the setback of going 1-0 down in the second leg, order was restored with Stephen Dobbie's strike early in the second half. The game seemed to be meandering towards its inevitable conclusion when Yeovil scored twice in the last eight minutes, stalwart Marcus Stewart netting the third (his fourth Play-Offs goal for a different club) to force extra time. Yeovil then took the lead, only to be pegged back on aggregate, but finally Yeovil's fifth goal completed Forest's misery and sent them out 5-4. As the *Guardian* described it, Forest "suffered one of the most humiliating defeats in their history", whilst for Yeovil this was probably one of the highest points in their ten-year league record.

Capitulation in the home leg was calamitous but not out of the ordinary for a team that has managed to turn the traditional home advantage into a home handicap. Not once have Forest managed to win a home leg during their four attempts, which is sloppy and verges on the woeful. Even the most optimistic Forest fans must dread the very idea of qualifying for the Play-Offs as they know that heartache is not too far away, and here we turn to writer and *Football365* editor Daniel Storey for the insider's view.

INGLORIOUS FAILURE

Imagine the sickest feeling in your stomach imaginable. You're on the way to the biggest interview of your life and you realise that you've forgotten your CV. And all of your clothes. As you jump off the bus and run back home, you realise that your house keys have fallen out of your pocket in your dash to disembark. As you stand cold and naked in the street, a white van splashes through a puddle and showers you in freezing, dirty water.

That's how the Play-Offs feel to a Nottingham Forest supporter.

Despite the Play-Offs closing in on their 30th birthday, Forest have only been occasional sufferers at the cruel hand of their fate. We've crammed the heartache into four sorry campaigns. Each time we have failed to reach the Final. Each exit has seemed more complex than the last, a club displaying a farcical ability to kick itself in the face when it matters most.

For those who assume that my claims of preposterous incompetence are melodramatic, let me give you a list of our four semi-final first-leg scores: 1-1, 2-0, 1-2, 0-0. Tight and tense, exactly as the Play-Offs should be. Now let me present to you our four second-leg scores: 3-4, 2-5, 3-4, 1-3. Utter madness.

It is an almost award-winning tribute to choking on the biggest stage. Sixteen goals conceded at a rate of one every twenty-six minutes. If you can keep your head when all about you are losing theirs... you'll reach the Final at Forest's expense. Many fans of many clubs will darkly boast that theirs is the club most proficient at snatching despair from the jaws of triumph. This is my bid on behalf of Forest.

The defeat to Sheffield United in 2003 was terrible, 3-1 up on aggregate with half an hour to play in the second leg. Had away goals counted we would have gone through, but a wonder goal from Paul Peschisolido and a(nother) Des Walker own goal sealed our fate. I stood at Bramall Lane and nursed a pain that I thought would never end.

But nothing beats Yeovil in 2007 for sheer horror. It had been billed as David vs Goliath, two-time European champions against a club that had only been in the Football League for four years. In the first leg at Huish Park, we effectively ended the tie as a contest, winning 2-0. David can only win every so often.

And then the second leg, the epitome of Forest's inglorious failure. We performed atrociously throughout, but still led 3-1 on aggregate with eight minutes of normal time remaining. What followed was four goals conceded in twenty-seven minutes, a sending off and an injury after all three substitutes had been used. We were consigned to our fate and stuck in League One, former greats now disgraced and mocked for our ineptitude. Derby County were promoted to the Premier League that season, just for good measure.

It often feels as if Forest are paying for our European Cup success, a 35-year karmic rebalancing act. You had all that unexpected joy, so here is a deserved dose of extended misery.

There'll be hope, of course, but only as a prelude to pain. The Play-Offs provide that in spades. Triumph, sure, but mainly the worst kind of hope.

The only team that are seriously challenging Forest for the unwanted title of the Worst Play-Offs team are those kings of relocation, MK Dons. Only formed in 2004 from the ashes of the old Wimbledon FC, they have none of the proud history that Preston can claim or the European glories enjoyed by Forest. But their similarity with Forest is that they have made four futile attempts to win a semi-final. Although not quite as spectacularly bad as Forest at home, their record is certainly not one to shout from the rooftops. In their first outing in 2007, having secured a goalless draw away to Shrewsbury, they took a leaf out of Forest's book and lost the home leg. In 2009 they once again managed a draw away from home but then matched it with a draw at home, only then to lose out to Scunthorpe on penalties.

In their last two appearances in 2010 and 2011 they have made a reasonable fist of getting through to that elusive Final. Having won both their home legs the Dons have lost their away legs by larger margins and have been eliminated on aggregate by one goal on each occasion. One small crumb of comfort is that at least MK Dons can claim to be one of only two teams to have defeated Peterborough in a Play-Offs game. Admittedly that may seem little consolation but they can also assert superiority over feeble Forest at the foot of the Play-Offs table and avoid the ignominy of being considered rock bottom.

NOTTINGHAM FOREST

19 GOALS CONCEDED

Forest have conceded 19 goals in their eight semi-final matches – at 2.4 goals per game this is the worst average of any side with more than one appearance.

LEEDS UNITED: DAMN AND BLAST

Leeds United have been involved from the very start of the Play-Offs back in 1987 and from beginning to end they have also failed. After the heartbreak of losing out in the Final Replay of 1987 *(as covered in Chapter Five)* there was a considerable gap before their next appearance. It was as if they had been badly burned by their painful baptism and were not that keen to repeat the experience too soon. Perhaps they were also far too busy in this period turning themselves from a Champions League team into a League One outfit in the shortest space of time possible.

Second time around was almost twenty years later in 2006. Leeds qualified for the first Championship Final, and the last to be played at the Millennium Stadium, by defeating perennial Play-Offs failures Preston in the semi-finals after a drawn first leg at Elland Road and winning 2-0 at Deepdale.

Watford were the opponents, and having beaten the Hornets at home and drawn away in the league, the prospects looked good. But this was to be a pretty calamitous afternoon as Watford coasted home 3-0, including a freakish own goal courtesy of a looping deflection and a cruel bounce off the goalkeeper Neil Sullivan. This was not to be their day and the hangover lingered into the following season when they were relegated to League One, their first-ever taste of life in the third tier, partly propelled there by the bitter disappointment of their Cardiff failure.

The Elland Road club did not have to wait long for their next brush with the Play-Offs. Having suffered a deduction of fifteen points for entering administration the previous season, finishing fifth in League One was no mean achievement. After a squeaky win over Carlisle, having trailed 2-0 at home in the first-leg of the semi-final, they were rescued by an injury-time Dougie Freedman goal

LEEDS UNITED
169,439
HIGHEST TOTAL HOME ATTENDANCE
In five matches at Elland Road

in that match and then a 2-0 second-leg victory at Brunton Park. In the Final they were up against local rivals Doncaster Rovers, who were bidding to return to the second tier for the first time in fifty years. It was Doncaster surprisingly, given the relative strengths and pedigrees of their squads, who ended up as 1-0 winners. Remarkably the crowd for that Final was in excess of 75,000, so a third-tier game attracted appreciably more than the Euro 2008 Final between Spain and Germany in Vienna, which only drew in 51,000. This could not have happened in any other country but offers scant consolation to a team that would have been promoted automatically were it not for the points deduction. After their impressive efforts in reaching the Play-Offs, this was an extremely timid, limp end for Leeds.

Bouncing back the following season, they were now entering the Play-Offs for the third time in four seasons, but recent experience did not prove to be of any assistance. This time they did not even reach the Final as they had done on the previous occasions. A semi-final loss to Millwall (the second leg of which was played out in front of 38,000 fans at Elland Road, the highest attendance for a Play-Offs semi-final) scuppered their second attempt to make it back to the second tier of the league and left Leeds with a lamentable record of four attempts, three Finals and no success.

Leeds are one of four clubs to have appeared in three Finals but to have never gained promotion, alongside Bristol City, Reading and accursed Brentford. With a total of fourteen attempts and not one promotion between them the three clubs alongside Brentford are amongst the poorest performers and could challenge the cursed red-and-white foursome for the title of Play-Offs patsies. So if any of this blighted trio get within a sniff in the future one could forgive their fans for wanting to avoid the Play-Offs, given that they have only brought heartache and despair. The tantalising prospect of finally achieving some success has to be balanced with, and in all probability outweighed by, the far more likely continuation of further failure and frustration. As a fan, sometimes you have to accept that the Play-Offs dice are loaded against you, including such random forces as a naval curse, a hexed strip or just an inglorious, never-ending capacity to implode.

THE

RESULTS

1987

Division 2 Semi-finals

First Legs - Thursday 14th May
Ipswich Town 0
Charlton Athletic 0
Att: 18,465 Portman Road

Thursday 14th May
Leeds United 1 (Edwards)
Oldham Athletic 0
Att: 29,472 Elland Road

Second Legs - Sunday 17th May
Charlton Athletic 2 (Melrose 2)
Ipswich Town 1 (McCall)
Att: 11,234 Selhurst Park

Sunday 17th May
Oldham Athletic 2 (Williams, Cecere)
Leeds Utd. 1 (Edwards)
Att: 19,216 Boundary Park

Division 2 Final First leg

Saturday 23rd May

Charlton 1 (Melrose, 87')
Leeds United 0

Att: 16,680 Selhurst Park

Charlton: Bolder, Humphrey, Reid, Peake, Thompson, Miller, Gritt, Stuart (Milne), Melrose, Walsh, Crooks, Manager - Lennie Lawrence

Leeds United: Day, Aspin, McDonald, Aizlewood, Ashurst, Ormsby, Edwards, Sheridan, Pearson (Ritchie), Baird, Adams, Manager - Billy Bremner

Division 2 Final Second leg

Monday 25th May

Leeds United 1 (Ormsby, 52')
Charlton 0

Att: 31,395 Elland Road

Leeds: Day, Aspin, McDonald, Aizlewood, Ashurst, Ormsby, Ritchie (Edwards), Sheridan, Taylor, Baird, Adams, Manager - Billy Bremner

Charlton: Bolder, Humphrey, Reid, Peake, Shirtliff, Miller, Gritt, Lee, Melrose, Walsh, Crooks, Manager - Lennie lawrence

Division 2 Final Replay

Friday 29th May

Charlton Athletic 2 (Shirtliff, 113', 117')
Leeds Utd 1 (Sheridan, 99') AET

Att: 15,841 St. Andrews

Charlton: Bolder, Humphrey, Reid, Peake, Shirtliff, Miller, Gritt, Lee, Melrose (Stuart), Walsh, Crooks Manager - Lennie Lawrence

Leeds: Day, Aspin, McDonald, Aizlewood, Ashurst, Ormsby, Stiles (Edwards), Sheridan, Pearson, Baird, Adams, Manager - Billy Bremner

Division 3 semi-finals

First leg - Thursday 14th May
Gillingham 3 (Cascarino 3)
Sunderland 2 (Proctor 2)
Att: 13,804 Priestfield Stadium

Thursday 14th May
Wigan Athletic 2 (Thompson, Lowe)
Swindon Town 3 (Bamber, Quinn, Coyne)
Att: 6,718 Springfield Park

Second leg - Sunday 17th May
Sunderland 4 (Gates 2, Bennett, Bertschin)
Gillingham 3 (Pritchard, Cascarino 2)
Att: 25,470 Roker Park

Sunday 17th May
Swindon 0
Wigan 0
Att: 12,485 County Ground

Division 3 Final First leg

Friday 22nd May

Gillingham 1 (Smith, 81')
Swindon 0

Att: 16,775 Priestfield Stadium

Gillingham: Kite, Haylock, Pearce, Berry, Quow, Greenall, Pritchard, Shearer, Smith, Elsey, Cascarino, Manager - Keith Peacock

Swindon: Digby, Hockaday, King, Barnard, Parkin, Calderwood, Jones, Kamara, Quinn (Henry), Bamber, Berry, Manager - Lou Macari

1987

Division 3 Final Second leg

Monday 25th May

Swindon Town 2 (Coyne, 61', Henry, 80')
Gillingham 1 (Elsey, 17')

Att: 14,382 County Gound

*Swindon: Digby, Hockaday, King, Coyne, Parkin,
Calderwood, Bamber, Kamara (Henry), Berry, White,
Barnard, Manager - Lou Macari*

*Gillingham: Kite, Haylock, Pearce, Berry, Quow, Greenall,
Pritchard, Shearer, Lovell, Elsey (Smith), Cascarino,
Manager - Keith Peacock*

Division 3 Final Replay

Friday 29th May

Swindon Town 2 (White, 2', 65')
Gillingham 0

Att: 18,491 Selhurst Park

*Swindon: Digby, Hockaday, King, Coyne, Parkin,
Calderwood, Bamber, Berry, Henry, White, Barnard,
Manager - Lou Macari*

*Gillingham: Kite, Haylock, Pearce, Berry, Quow, Greenall,
Pritchard, Shearer, Robinson (Smith), Elsey, Cascarino,
Manager - Keith Peacock*

Division 4 semi-finals

First legs - Thursday 14th May

Aldershot 1 (Johnson)
Bolton Wanderers 0
Att: 4,164 Recreation Ground

Thursday 14th May
Colchester Utd 0
Wolverhampton Wanderers 2 (Kelly, Bull)
Att: 4,829 Layer Road

Second legs - Sunday 17th May

Bolton 2 (Caldwell 2)
Aldershot 2 (Anderson, Burvill) AET
Att: 7,445 Burnden Park

Sunday 17th May
Wolverhampton Wanderers 0
Colchester Utd 0
Att: 16,330 Molineux

Division 4 Final First leg

Friday 22th May

Aldershot 2 (McDonald, 4', Barnes, 47')
Wolverhampton Wanderers 0

Att: 5,069 Recreation Ground

*Aldershot: Lange, Blankley, Friar, King, Smith,
Wignall, Barnes B, Mazzon, Ring, McDonald,
Johnson, Manager - Len Walker*

*Wolves: Kendall, Stoutt, Barnes D, Streete, Kelly,
Clarke, Purdie, Thompson, Bull, Mutch, Holmes,
Manager - Graham Turner*

Division 4 Final Second leg

Monday 25th May

Wolverhampton Wanderers 0
Aldershot 1 (Barnes, 81')

Att: 19,962 Molineux

*Wolves: Kendall, Stoutt, Barnes D, Streete, Powell, Clarke,
Dennison (Purdie), Thompson, Bull, Mutch, Holmes,
Manager - Graham Turner*

*Aldershot: Lange, Blankley, Friar, King, Smith, Wignall,
Barnes B, Mazzon, Ring (Fielder), McDonald, Johnson,
Manager - Len Walker*

1988

Division 2 Semi-finals

First Legs - Sunday 15th May
Blackburn Rovers 0
Chelsea 2 (Durie, Nevin)
Att: 16,568 Ewood Park

Sunday 15th May
Bradford City 2 (Goddard, McCall)
Middlesbrough 1 (Senior)
Att: 16,017 Valley Parade

Second Legs- Wednesday 18th May
Chelsea 4 (K Wilson 2, Dixon, Durie)
Blackburn 1 (Sellars)
Att: 22,757 Stamford Bridge

Wednesday 18th May
Middlesbough 2 (Slaven, Hamilton)
Bradford City 0 AET
Att: 25,868 Ayresome Park

Division 2 Final First leg

Wednesday 25th May

Middlesbrough 2 (Senior, 30', Slaven, 81')
Chelsea 0

Att: 25,531 Ayresome Park

Middlesbrough: Pears, Parkinson, Cooper, Mowbray, Hamilton, Pallister, Slaven, Ripley, Senior, Kerr, Glover, Manager - Bruce Rioch

Chelsea: Hitchcock, Clarke, Dorigo, Pates, McLaughlin, Wicks, Nevin, Bumstead, Dixon, Durie, Wilson, Manager - Bobby Campbell

Division 2 Final Second leg

Saturday 28th May

Chelsea 1 (Durie, 18')
Middlesbrough 0

Att: 40,550 Stamford Bridge

Chelsea: Hitchcock, Clarke, Dorigo, Pates, McLaughlin, Wicks, Nevin, Bumstead, Dixon (Hall), Durie, Wilson, (McAllister), Manager - Bobby Campbell

Middlesbrough: Pears, Parkinson, Copper, Mowbray, Hamilton, Pallister, Slaven, Ripley, Senior, Kerr, Glover, Manager - Bruce Rioch

Division 3 semi-finals

First legs - Sunday 15th May
Bristol City 1 (Walsh)
Sheffield United 0
Att: 25,335 Ashton Gate

Sunday 15th May
Notts County 1 (Yates)
Walsall 3 (D Kelly 2, Shakespeare)
Att: 11,522 Meadow Lane

Second Legs - Wednesday 18th May
Rotherham Utd 1 (Johnson)
Swansea 1 (McCarthy)
Att: 5,568 Millmoor

Wednesday 18th May
Scunthorpe Utd 1 (Lister)
Torquay Utd 1 (Loram)
Att: 6,482 Old Show Ground

Division 3 Final First leg

Wednesday 25th May

Bristol City 1 (Walsh, 40')
Walsall 3 (Christie, 60', Kelly, 78', 90')

Att: 25,128 Ashton Gate

Bristol City: Waugh, Llewellyn, Newman, Humphries, Pender, McClaren, Milne, Galliers, Shutt, Walsh, Neville, Manager - Joe Jordan

Walsall: Barber, Taylor, O'Kelly, Shakespeare, Forbes, Goodwin, Hawker, Hart, Christie, Kelly, Naughton, Manager - Tommy Coakley

1988

Division 3 Final Second leg

Saturday 28th May

Walsall 0
Bristol City 2 (Newman, 31', Shutt, 64') AET

Att: 13,941 Fellows Park

Walsall: Barber, Taylor, Dornan, Shakespeare, Forbes, Goodwin, Hawker, Hart, Christie, Kelly, Naughton, Manager - Tommy Coakley

Bristol City: Waugh, Llewellyn, Newman, Humphries, Pender, McClaren, Milne, Galliers, Shutt (Caldwell), Walsh, Jordan, Manager - Joe Jordan

Division 4 semi-finals

First legs - Sunday 15th May
Swansea City 1 (McCarthy)
Rotherham Utd 0
Att: 9,148 Vetch Field

Sunday 15th May
Torquay United 2 (Caldwell, Dobson)
Scunthorpe Utd 1 (Flounders)
Att: 4,602 Plainmoor

Second legs - Wednesday 18th May
Sheffield Utd 1 (Morris)
Bristol City (Shutt)
Att: 19,066 Bramall Lane

Wednesday 18th May
Walsall 1 (Christie)
Notts County 1 (Yates)
Att: 8,901 Fellows Park

Division 3 Final Replay

Monday 30th May

Walsall 4 (Kelly, 12', 17', 63', Hawker, 19')
Bristol City 0

Att: 13,007 Fellows Park

Walsall: Barber, Taylor, Dornan (Sanderson), Shakespeare, Forbes, Goodwin (Jones), Hawker, Hart, Christie, Kelly, Naughton, Manager - Tommy Coakley

Bristol City: Waugh, Llewellyn, Newman, Humphries, Pender, McClaren, Milne, Galliers, Shutt, Walsh, Jordan, Manager - Joe Jordan

Division 4 Final First leg

Wednesday 25th May

Swansea City 2 (McCarthy, 73', Love, 86')
Torquay Utd 1 (McNichol, 88')

Att: 10,825 Vetch Field

Swansea: Guthrie, Harrison, Coleman, Melville, Knill, James, Davies, Bodak (Love), McCarthy, Raynor, Hutchison, Manager - Terry Yorath

Torquay: Allen, McNichol, Kelly, Haslegrave, Cole, Impey, Dawkins, Lloyd, Loram (Caldwell), Dobson, Gibbins (Gardiner), Manager - Cyril Knowles

Division 4 Final Second leg

Saturday 28th May

Torquay 3 (McNichol, 33', 39', Caldwell, 67')
Swansea 3 (Raynor, 23', McCarthy, 28', Davies, 45')

Att: 4,999 Plainmoor

Torquay: Allen, McNichol, Kelly, Dawkins, Cole, Impey (Sharpe), Caldwell, Lloyd, Loram, Dobson, Gibbins, Manager - Cyril Knowles

Swansea: Guthrie, Harrison, Coleman, Melville, Knill, James, Davies, Love, McCarthy, Raynor, Hutchison (Lewis), Manager - Terry Yorath

1989

Division 2 Semi-finals

First Legs - Sunday 21st May
Blackburn Rovers 0
Watford 0
Att: 14,008 Ewood Park

Sunday 21st May
Swindon Town 1 (Hopkins OG)
Crystal Palace 0
Att: 16,656 County Ground

Second legs - Wednesday 24th May
Watford 1 (Redfearn)
Blackburn Rovers 1 (Garner)
*Blackburn win on away goals
Att: 13,854 Vicarage Road

Wednesday 24th May
Crystal Palace 2 (Bright, Wright)
Swindon 0
Att: 23,677 Selhurst Park

Division 2 Final First leg

Wednesday 31st May

Blackburn Rovers 3 (Gayle, 20', 26', Garner, 89')
Crystal Palace 1 (McGoldrick, 86')

Att: 16,421 Ewood Park

*Blackburn: Gennoe, Atkins, Sulley, Reid, Hendry,
Mail, Gayle, Millar, Miller, Garner, Sellars,
Manager - Don Mackay*

*Palace: Suckling, Pemberton, Burke, Madden (Pennyfather),
Hopkins, Hedman, McGoldrick, Pardew, Bright, Wright,
Barber, Manager - Steve Coppell*

Division 2 Final Second leg

Sunday 3rd June

Crystal Palace 3 (Wright, 16', 117', Madden, 47')
Blackburn Rovers 0 AET

Att: 26,358 Selhurst Park

*Crystal Palace: Suckling, Pemberton, Burke, Madden,
Hokpins, O' Reilly, McGoldrick, Pardew, Bright, Wright,
Barber, Manager - Steve Coppell*

*Blackburn: Gennoe, Atkins, Sulley, Reid, Hendry, Mail,
Gayle (Ainscow), Millar, Miller (Curry), Garner, Sellars,
Manager - Don Mackay*

Division 3 Semi-finals

First Legs - Sunday 21st May
Bristol Rovers 1 (Penrice)
Fulham 0
Att: 9,029 Twerton Park

Monday 22nd May
Preston North End 1 (Jemson)
Port Vale (Earle)
Att: 14,280 Deepdale

Second legs - Thursday 25th May
Fulham 0
Bristol Rovers 4 (Clark, Holloway, Bailey, Reece)
Att: 10,668 Craven Cottage

Thursday 25th May
Port Vale 3 (Beckford 3)
Preston North End 1 (Patterson)
Att: 13,416 Vale Park

Division 3 Final First leg

Wednesday 31st May

Bristol Rovers 1 (Penrice, 30')
Port Vale 1 (Earle, 73')

Att: 9,042 Twerton Park

*Bristol Rovers: Martyn, Alexander, Clark, Yates, White,
Jones, Holloway (McClean), Mehew, Reece, Penrice,
Purnell, Manager - Gerry Francis*

*Port Vale: Grew, Mills, Hughes, Walker, West,
Glover, Jeffers, Earle, Futcher, Beckford, Porter,
Manager - John Rudge*

Division 3 Final Second leg

Sunday 3rd June

Port Vale 1 (Earle, 52')
Bristol Rovers 0

Att: 17,353 Vale Park

*Port Vale: Grew, Mills, Hughes, Walker, West, Glover,
Jeffers, Earle, Futcher, Beckford, Porter (Finney),
Manager - John Rudge*

*Bristol Rovers: Martyn, Alexander, Clark, Yates, White,
Jones, Holloway, Mehew, Reece, Penrice, Purnell,
Manager - Gerry Francis*

1989

Division 4 Semi-finals

First Legs - Sunday 21st May
Leyton Orient 2 (Cooper 2)
Scarborough 0
Att: 9,298 Brisbane Road

Sunday 21st May
Wrexham 3 (Wright, Kearns 2)
Scunthorpe Utd 1 (Cowling)
Att: 5,449 Racecourse Ground

Second Legs - Wednesday 24th May
Scarborough 1 (Russell)
Leyton Orient 0
Att: 4,377 McCain Stadium

Wednesday 24th May
Scunthorpe Utd 0
Wrexham 2 (Russell 2)
Att: 5,516 Glanford Park

Division 4 Final First leg

Tuesday 30th May

Wrexham 0
Leyton Orient 0

Att: 7,915 Racecourse Ground

Wrexham: Salmon, Salathiel, Wright, Hunter, Beaumont, Jones, Thackeray (Buxton), Flynn, Kearns, Russell, Bowden, Manager - Dixie McNeil

Leyton Orient: Heald, Howard, Dickenson, Hales, Day, Sitton, Baker (Ward), Castle, Harvey, Cooper, Comfort, Manager - Frank Clark

Division 4 Final Second leg

Sunday 3rd June

Leyton Orient 2 (Harvey, 44', Cooper, 81')
Wrexham 1 (Bowden, 47')

Att: 13,355 Brisbane Road

Leyton Orient: Heald, Howard, Dickenson (Ward), Hales, Day, Sitton, Baker, Castle, Harvey, Cooper M, Comfort, Manager - Frank Clark

Wrexham: Salmon, Salathiel, Wright, Hunter, Beaumont, Jones, Thackeray (Buxton), Flynn (Cooper G), Kearns, Russell, Bowden, Manager - Dixie McNeil

....

1990

Division 2 Semi-finals

First Legs - Sunday 13th May
Blackburn Rovers 1 (Kennedy)
Swindon Town 2 (White, Foley)
Att: 15,636 Ewood Park

Sunday 13th May
Sunderland 0
Newcastle 0
Att: 26,641 Roker Park

Second Legs - Wednesday 16th May
Swindon Town 2 (Shearer, White)
Blackburn Rovers 1 (Gayle)
Att: 12,416 County Ground

Wednesday 16th May
Newcastle United 0
Sunderland 2 (Gates, Gabbiadini)
Att: 32,216 St James' Park

Division 2 Final

Monday 28th May

Swindon Town 1 (McLoughlin, 27')
Sunderland 0

*Swindon denied promotion because of financial
irregularities, Sunderland promoted in their place

Att: 72,873 Wembley

*Swindon: Digby, Kerslake, Bodin, McLoughlin,
Calderwood, Gittens, Jones, Shearer, White, MacLaren,
Foley, Manager - Ossie Ardiles*

*Sunderland: Norman, Kay, Agboola, Bennett, MacPhail,
Owers, Bracewell, Armstrong, Gates (Hauser), Gabbiadini,
Pascoe (Atkinson), Manager - Denis Smith*

....

Division 3 Semi-finals

First Legs - Sunday 13th May
Bolton Wanderers 1 (Philliskirk)
Notts County 1 (Lund)
Att: 15,108 Burnden Park

Sunday 13th May
Bury 0
Tranmere Rovers 0
Att: 7,019 Gigg Lane

Second Legs - Wednesday 16th May
Notts County 2 (Johnson, Bartlett)
Bolton Wanderers 0
Att: 15,197 Meadow Lane

Wednesday 16th May
Tranmere Rovers 2 (Malkin, Muir)
Bury 0
Att: 10,343 Prenton Park

Division 3 Final

Sunday 27th May

Notts County 2 (Johnson, 31', Short, 62')
Tranmere Rovers 0

Att: 29,252 Wembley

*Notts County: Cherry, Palmer, Platnauer, Short, Yates,
Robinson, Thomas, Turner, Bartlett, Lund, Johnson,
Manager - Neil Warnock*

*Tranmere Rovers: Nixon, Garnett, Mungall (Fairclough),
McNab, Vickers, Malkin, Harvey (Bishop), Steel, Muir,
Thomas, Manager - Johnny King*

....

Division 4 Semi-finals

First Legs - Sunday 13th May
Cambridge United 1 (Cheetham)
Maidstone United 1 (Gall)
Att: 7,264 Abbey Stadium

Sunday 13th May
Chesterfield 4 (Plummer 3, Ryan)
Stockport County 0
Att: 8,277 Recreation Ground

Second Legs - Wednesday 16th May
Maidstone Utd 0
Cambridge Utd 2 (Dublin, Cheetham) AET
Att: 5,538 Watling Street, Dartford

Wednesday 16th May
Stockport County 0
Chesterfield 2 (Plummer, Chiedozie)
Att: 7,339 Edgeley Park

Division 4 Final

Saturday 26th May

Cambridge United 1 (Dublin, 77')
Chesterfield 0

Att: 26,404 Wembley

*Cambridge United: Vaughan, Fensome, Kimble, Bailie,
Chapple, O'Shea, Cheetham, Leadbitter (Cook), Dublin,
Taylor (Claridge), Philpott, Manager - John Beck*

*Chesterfield: Leonard, Francis, Ryan, Dyche, Brien, Gunn,
Plummer, Hewitt, Chiedozie (Waller), Rogers, Morris,
Manager - Paul Hart*

1991

Division 2 Semi-finals

First Legs - Sunday 19th May
Brighton & Hove Albion 4 (Barham, Small, Walker, Codner)
Millwall 1 (Stephenson)
Att: 15,390 Goldstone Ground

Sunday 19th May
Middlesbrough 1 (Phillips)
Notts County 1 (Turner)
Att: 22,343 Ayresome Park

Second Legs - Wednesday 22nd May
Millwall 1 (McGinlay)
Brighton & Hove Albion 2 (Codner, Robinson)
Att: 17,370 The Den

Wednesday 22nd May
Notts County 1 (Harding)
Middlesbrough 0
Att: 18,249 Meadow Lane

Division 2 Final

Sunday 2nd June

Notts County 3 (Johnson, 30', 59', Regis, 70')
Brighton & Hove Albion 1 (Wilkins, 89')

Att: 59,940 Wembley

Notts County: Cherry, Palmer, Paris, Short, Yates, O'Riordan, Thomas, Turner, Regis (Bartlett), Draper (Harding), Johnson, Manager - Neil Warnock

Brighton: Digweed, Chivers, Gatting (Chapman), Wilkins, Pates, Bissett, Barham, Iovan (Byrne), Small, Codner, Walker, Manager - Barry Lloyd

Division 3 Semi-finals

First Legs - Sunday 19th May
Brentford 2 (Evans, Godfrey)
Tranmere Rovers 2 (Cooper)
Att: 9,330 Griffin Park

Sunday 19th May
Bury 1 (Lee)
Bolton Wanderers 1 (Philliskirk)
Att: 8,000 Gigg Lane

Second Legs - Wednesday 22nd May
Tranmere Rovers 1 (Brannan)
Brentford 0
Att: 11,438 Prenton Park

Wednesday 22nd May
Bolton Wanderers 1 (Philliskirk)
Bury 0
Att: 19,198 Burnden Park

Division 3 Final

Saturday 1st June

Tranmere Rovers 1 (Malkin, 99)
Bolton Wanderers 0 AET

Att: 30,217 Wembley

Tranmere: Nixon, Higgins, Brannan, Irons, Hughes, Garnett, Morrissey, Martindale (Harvey), Steel (Malkin), Cooper, Thomas, Manager - Johnny King

Bolton Wanderers: Felgate, Brown, Cowdrill, Comstive, Seagraves, Stubbs, Storer (Green), Thompson, Cunningham (Reeves), Philliskirk, Darby, Manager - Phil Neal

Division 4 Semi-finals

First Legs - Sunday 19th May
Scunthorpe United 1 (Lillis)
Blackpool 1 (Rodwell)
Att: 6,536 Glanford Park

Sunday 19th May
Torquay United 2 (Elliott, Edwards)
Burnley 0
Att: 5,600 Plainmoor

Second Legs - Wednesday 22nd May
Blackpool 2 (Eyres)
Scunthorpe United (Hill)
Att: 7,596 Bloomfield Road

Wednesday 22nd May
Burnley 1 (Evans OG)
Torquay United 0
Att: 13,620 Turf Moor

Division 4 Final

Friday 31st May

Torquay United 2 (Saunders, 28', Edwards, 37')
Blackpool 2 (Groves, 7', Curran OG, 76') AET
Torquay won 5-4 on penalties

Att: 21,615 Wembley

Torquay United: Howells, Curran, Holmes, Saunders, Elliott, Joyce, Myers, Holmes, Evans (Rowland), Edwards (Hall), Loram, Manager - John Impey

Blackpool: McIlhargey, Davies (Sinclair), Wright, Groves, Horner, Gore, Rodwell, Taylor, Garner, Eyres, Manager - Billy Ayre

1992

Division 2 Semi-finals

First Legs - Sunday 10th May
Cambridge United 1 (O' Shea)
Leicester City 1 (Russell)
Att: 9,225 Abbey Stadium

Sunday 10th May
Blackburn Rovers 4 (Sellars, Newell, Speedie 2)
Derby County 2 (Gabbiadini, Johnson)
Att: 19,677 Ewood Park

Second Legs - Wednesday 13th May
Derby County 2 (Comyn, McMinn)
Blackburn Rovers 1 (Moran)
Att: 22,920 Baseball Ground

Wednesday 13th May
Leicester City 5 (Wright 2, Thompson, Russell, Ormondroyd)
Cambridge United 0
Att: 21,024 Filbert Street

Division 2 Final

Monday 25th May

Blackburn Rovers 1 (Newell, 27)
Leicester City 0

Att: 68,147 Wembley

Blackburn: Mimms, May, Wright, Cowans, Moran, Hendry, Price, Atkins, Speedie, Newell, Sellars (Richardson), Manager - Kenny Dalglish

Leicester: Muggleton, Mills, Whitlow, Walsh, James (Gee), Thompson, Grayson, Wright, Ormondroyd, Russell, Manager - Brian Little

Division 3 Semi-finals

First Legs - Sunday 10th May
Stockport County 1 (Ward)
Stoke City 0
Att: 7,537 Edgeley Park

Monday 11th May
Peterborough United 2 (Charley, Halsall)
Huddersfield Town 2 (Onuora, Robinson OG)
Att: 11,751 London Road

Second Legs - Wednesday 13th May
Stoke City 1 (Stein)
Stockport County 1 (Beaumont)
Att: 16,170 Victoria Ground

Thursday 14th May
Huddersfield Town 1 (Starbuck)
Peterborough Utd 2 (Sterling, Cooper)
Att: 16,167 Leeds Road

Division 3 Final

Sunday 24th May

Peterborough United 2 (Charley, 52', 89')
Stockport County 1 (Francis, 87')

Att: 35,087 Wembley

Peterborough: Barber, Luke, Robinson, Welsh (Howarth), Sterling, Ebdon, Adcock, Charley, Barnes, Manager - Chris Turner

Stockport: Edwards, Knowles, Todd, Frain, Barras, Williams, Gannon, Ward (Wheeler), Francis, Beaumont, Preece, Manager - Danny Bergara

Division 4 Semi-finals

First Legs - Sunday 10th May
Barnet 1 (Carter)
Blackpool 0
Att: 5,629 Underhill

Sunday 10th May
Crewe Alexandra 2 (Hignett, Naylor)
Scunthorpe Utd 2 (Heliwell 2)
Att: 6,083 Gresty Road

Second Legs - Wednesday 13th May
Blackpool 2 (Groves, Garner)
Barnet 0
Att: 7,588 Bloomfield Road

Wednesday 13th May
Scunthorpe United 2 (Martin, Hamilton)
Crewe Alexandra 0
Att: 7,938 Glanford Park

Division 4 Final

Saturday 23rd May

Blackpool 1 (Bamber, 40')
Scunthorpe United 1 (Daws, 52') AET
Blackpool won 4-3 on penalties

Att: 22,741 Wembley

Blackpool: McIlhargey, Burgess, Cook, Groves, Davies (Murphy), Gore, Rodwell, Horner (Sinclair), Bamber, Garner, Eyres, Manager - Billy Ayre

Scunthorpe: Samways, Joyce, Longden, Hill, Elliott, Humphries, Martin, Hamilton, Daws (White), Buckley (Alexander), Heliwell, Manager - Bill Green

1993

First Division Semi-finals

First Legs - Sunday 16th May
Leicester City 1 (Joachim)
Portsmouth 0
Att: 24,538 Filbert Street

Sunday 16th May
Swindon Town 3 (Mitchell, Vickers OG, Maskell)
Tranmere Rovers 1 (Morrissey)
Att: 14,230 County Ground

Second Legs - Wednesday 19th May
Portsmouth 2 (McLoughlin, Kristensen)
Leicester City 2 (Ormondroyd, Thompson)
Att: 25,438 Fratton Park

Wednesday 19th May
Tranmere Rovers 3 (Proctor, Nevin, Irons)
Swindon Town 2 (Moncur, Maskell)
Att: 16,083 Prenton Park

First Division Final

Monday 31st May

Swindon Town 4 (Hoddle, 42', Maskell, 47',
Taylor, 53', Bodin, 84')
Leicester City 3 (Joachim, 56', Walsh, 68', Thompson, 69')

Att: 73,802 Wembley

*Swindon: Digby, Summerbee, Bodin, Hoddle, Calderwood,
Taylor, Moncur (Hazard), MacLaren, Mitchell, Ling, Maskell
(White), Manager - Glenn Hoddle*

*Leicester: Poole, Mills, Whitlow, Smith, Walsh, Hill, Oldfield,
Thompson, Joachim, Agnew, Philpott, Manager - Brian Little*

Second Division Semi-finals

First Legs - Sunday 16th May
Stockport County 1 (Gannon)
Port Vale 1 (Glover)
Att: 7,856 Edgeley Park

Sunday 16th May
Swansea City 2 (McFarlane, Hayes)
West Bromwich Albion 1 (McFarlane OG)
Att: 13,917 Vetch Field

Second Legs - Wednesday 19th May
Port Vale 1 (Foyle)
Stockport County 0
Att: 12,689 Vale Park

Wednesday 19th May
West Bromwich Albion 2 (Hunt, Hamilton)
Swansea City 0
Att: 26,025 The Hawthorns

Second Division Final

Sunday 30th May

West Bromwich Albion 3 (Hunt, 66', Reid, 82', Donovan, 89')
Port Vale 0

Att: 53,471 Wembley

*West Brom: Lange, Reid, Lilwall, Bradley, Raven, Strodder,
Hunt (Garner), Hamilton, Taylor, McNally, Donovan,
Manager - Ossie Ardiles*

*Port Vale: Musselwhite, Aspin, Kent (Billing), Porter, Swan,
Glover, Slaven, Van der Laan (Cross), Foyle, Kerr, Taylor,
Manager - John Rudge*

Third Division Semi-finals

First Legs - Sunday 16th May
Bury 0
York City 0
Att: 6,620 Gigg Lane

Sunday 16th May
Crewe Alexandra 5 (Naylor 2, Clarkson, Edwards, Ward)
Walsall 1 (Cecere)
Att: 6,198 Gresty Road

Second Legs - Wednesday 19th May
York City 1 (Swann)
Bury 0
Att: 9,206 Bootham Crescent

Wednesday 19th May
Walsall 2 (Clarke, O'Connor)
Crewe 4 (Naylor 3, Ward)
Att: 7,398 Bescot Stadium

Third Division Final

Saturday 29th May

Crewe Alexandra 1 (McKearney, 119')
York City 1 (Swann, 104') AET
York won 5-3 on penalties

Att: 22,416 Wembley

*Crewe: Kiely, McMillan, Hall, Pepper, Stancliffe (Tutill),
Atkin, McCarthy, Canham, Barnes, Swann, Blackstone,
Manager - Dario Gradi*

*York: Smith, McKearney, Smith, Evans, Carr, Whalley,
Ward, Naylor, Lennon, Walters (Clarkson), Edwards
(Woodward), Manager - Alan Little*

1994

First Division Semi-finals

First Legs - Sunday 15th May
Tranmere Rovers 0
Leicester City 0
Att: 14,962 Prenton Park

Sunday 15th May
Derby County 2 (Cowans, Johnson)
Millwall 0
Att: 17,401 Baseball Ground

Second Legs - Wednesday 18th May
Leicester City 2 (Ormondroyd, Speedie)
Tranmere Rovers 1 (Nevin)
Att: 22,593 Filbert Street

Wednesday 18th May
Millwall 1 (Berry)
Derby County 3 (Gabbiadini, Johnson, Van der Hauwe OG)
Att: 16,470 The New Den

Second Division Semi-finals

First Legs - Sunday 15th May
Burnley 0
Plymouth Argyle 0
Att: 18,794 Turf Moor

Sunday 15th May
York City 0
Stockport County 0
Att: 8,744 Bootham Crescent

Second Legs - Wednesday 18th May
Plymouth 1 (Marshall)
Burnley 3 (Francis 2, Joyce)
Att: 17,515 Home Park

Wednesday 18th May
Stockport County 1 (Beaumont)
York City 0
Att: 6,743 Edgeley Park

Third Division Semi-finals

First Legs - Sunday 15th May
Torquay United 2 (Darby, Moore)
Preston North End 0
Att: 4,440 Plainmoor

Sunday 15th May
Carlisle United 0
Wycombe Wanderers 2 (Thompson, Garner)
Att: 10,862 Brunton Park

Second Legs - Wednesday 18th May
Preston North End 4 (Ellis, Moyes, Hicks, Raynor)
Torquay United 1 (Goodridge)
Att: 11,442 Deepdale

Wednesday 18th May
Wycombe Wanderers 2 (Carroll, Garner)
Carlisle Utd 1 (Davey)
Att: 6,265 Adams Park

First Division Final

Monday 30th May

Leicester City 2 (Walsh, 41', 86')
Derby County 1 (Johnson, 27')

Att: 73,671 Wembley

Leicester: Ward, Grayson, Whitlow, Willis, Coatsworth (Thompson), Carey, Gibson, Blake, Walsh, Roberts (Joachim), Ormondroyd, Manager - Brian Little

Derby: Taylor, Charles, Forsyth (Kitson), Harkes, Short, Williams, Cowans, Johnson, Gabbiadini, Pembridge, Simpson, Manager - Roy McFarland

Second Division Final

Sunday 29th May

Burnley 2 (Eyres, 29', Parkinson, 66')
Stockport County 1 (Beaumont, 2')

Att: 44,806 Wembley

Burnley: Beresford, Parkinson, Thompson, Davis, Pender, Joyce, McMinn, Deary, Heath, Francis (Farrell), Eyres, Manager - Jimmy Mullen

Stockport: Keeley, Todd, Wallace, Connelly, Flynn, Williams (Miller), Gannon (Preece), Ward, Francis, Beaumont, Frain, Manager - Danny Bergara

Third Division Final

Saturday 28th May

Wycombe Wanderers 4 (Thompson, 31', Garner, 47', Carroll, 55', 68')
Preston North End 2 (Bryson, 32', Raynor, 37')

Att: 40,109 Wembley

Wycombe: Hyde, Cousins, Titterton, Crossley, Creaser, Ryan, Carroll, Thompson, Reid, Garner, Guppy, Manager - Martin O'Neill

Preston: Woods, Fensome, Kidd, Cartwright, Squires, Moyes, Ainsworth, Whalley, Raynor, Ellis, Bryson, Manager - John Beck

1995

First Division Semi-finals

First Legs - Sunday 14th May
Tranmere Rovers 1 (Malkin)
Reading 3 (Lovell 2, Nogan)
Att: 12,207 Prenton Park

Sunday 14th May
Wolverhampton Wanderers 2 (Bull, Venus)
Bolton Wanderers 1 (McAteer)
Att: 26,153 Molineux

Second Legs - Wednesday 17th May
Reading 0
Tranmere Rovers 0
Att: 13,245 Elm Park

Wednesday 17th May
Bolton Wanderers 2 (McGinlay 2)
Wolverhampton Wanderers 0
Att: 20,041 Burnden Park

First Division Final

Monday 29th May

Bolton Wanderers 4 (Coyle, 76', De Freitas, 87', 119',
Paatelainen, 105')
Reading 3 (Nogan, 4', Williams, 12', Quinn, 119') AET

Att: 64,107 Wembley

*Bolton: Branagan, Green, Phillips, McAteer, Bergsson,
Stubbs, McDonald (De Freitas), Coyle, Paatelainen,
McGinlay, Thompson, Manager - Bruce Rioch*

*Reading: Hislop, Bernard (Hopkins), Osborn, Wdowczyk,
Williams, McPherson, Gilkes, Gooding, Nogan (Quinn),
Lovell, Taylor, Manager - Mick Gooding & Jimmy Quinn*

Second Division Semi-finals

First Legs - Sunday 14th May
Bristol Rovers 0
Crewe Alexandra 0
Att: 8,538 Twerton Park

Sunday 14th May
Huddersfield Town 1 (Billy)
Brentford 1 (Forster)
Att: 14,160 McAlpine Stadium

Second Legs - Wednesday 17th May
Crewe Alexandra 1 (Rowbotham)
Bristol Rovers 1 (Miller)
Bristol Rovers won on away goals
Att: 6,578 Gresty Road

Wednesday 17th May
Brentford 1 (Grainger)
Huddersfield Town 1 (Booth)
Huddersfield Town won 4-3 on penalties
Att: 11,161 Griffin Park

Second Division Final

Sunday 28th May

Huddersfield Town 2 (Booth, 45', Billy, 81')
Bristol Rovers 1 (Stewart, 45')

Att: 59,175 Wembley

*Huddersfield: Francis, Trevitt (Dyson), Cowan, Bullock,
Scully, Sinnott, Billy, Duxbury, Booth, Jepson, Crosby (Dunn),
Manager - Neil Warnock*

*Bristol Rovers: Parkin, Pritchard, Gurney, Stewart, Clark,
Tillson, Sterling, Miller, Taylor (Browning), Skinner,
Channing (Archer), Manager - John Ward*

Third Division Semi-finals

First Legs - Sunday 14th May
Mansfield Town 1 (Hadley)
Chesterfield 1 (Robinson)
Att: 6,582 Field Mill

Sunday 14th May
Preston North End 0
Bury 1 (Pugh)
Att: 13,297 Deepdale

Second Legs - Wednesday 17th May
Chesterfield 5 (Lormor, Robinson, Law 2. Howard)
Mansfield Town 2 (Holland, Wilkinson)
Att: 8,165 Saltergate

Wednesday 17th May
Bury 1 (Rigby)
Preston North End 0
Att: 9,094 Gigg Lane

Third Division Final

Saturday 27th May

Chesterfield 2 (Lormor, 23', Robinson, 41')
Bury 0

Att: 22,814 Wembley

*Chesterfield: Stewart, Hewitt, Rogers, Curtis, Carr, Law,
Robinson, Howard (Perkins), Lormor (Davies), Morris, Hazel,
Manager - John Duncan*

*Bury: Kelly, Woodward, Stanislaus, Daws, Lucketti, Jackson,
Mulligan (Hughes), Carter (Paskin), Stant, Rigby, Pugh,
Manager - Mike Walsh*

1996

First Division Semi-finals

First Legs - Sunday 12th May
Charlton Athletic 1 (Newton)
Crystal Palace 2 (Brown, Veart)
Att: 14,618 The Valley

Sunday 12th May
Leicester City 0
Stoke City 0
Att: 20,325 Filbert Street

Second Legs - Wednesday 15th May
Crystal Palace 1 (Houghton)
Charlton Athletic 0
Att: 22,880 Selhurst Park

Wednesday 15th May
Stoke City 0
Leicester City 1 (Parker)
Att: 21,037 Victoria Ground

First Division Final

Monday 27th May

Leicester City 2 (Parker, 76', Claridge, 120')
Crystal Palace 1 (Roberts, 13') AET

Att: 73,573 Wembley

Leicester City: Poole (Kalac), Grayson, Whitlow, Watts, Walsh (Hill), Izzet, Lennon, Taylor (Robins), Claridge, Parker, Heskey, Manager - Martin O'Neill

Crystal Palace: Martyn, Edworthy, Brown, Roberts, Quinn, Hopkin (Veart), Pitcher, Houghton, Freedman (Dyer), Ndah, Tuttle (Rodger), Manager - Dave Bassett

Second Division Semi-finals

First Legs - Sunday 12th May
Bradford City 0
Blackpool 2 (Bonner, Ellis)
Att: 14,273 Valley Parade

Sunday 12th May
Crewe Alexandra 2 (Little, Rivers)
Notts County 2 (Finnan, Martindale)
Att: 4,931 Gresty Road

Second Legs - Wednesday 15th May
Blackpool 0
Bradford City 3 (Shutt, Hamilton, Stallard)
Att: 9,593 Bloomfield Road

Wednesday 15th May
Notts County 1 (Martindale)
Crewe Alexandra 0
Att: 9,640 Meadow Lane

Second Division Final

Sunday 26th May

Bradford City 2 (Hamilton, 8', Stallard, 75')
Notts County 0

Att: 39,972 Wembley

Bradford City: Gould, Huxford, Jacobs, Mitchell, Mohan, Youds, Kiwomya (Wright), Duxbury, Shutt, Stallard, Hamilton (Ormondroyd), Manager - Chris Kamara

Notts County: Ward, Derry, Baraclough, Murphy, Strodder, Richardson, Finnan, Rogers, Martindale, Battersby (Jones), Agana, Manager - Steve Thompson & Colin Murphy

Third Division Semi-finals

First Legs - Sunday 12th May
Hereford United 1 (Smith)
Darlington 2 (Gregan, Blake)
Att: 6,622 Edgar Street

Sunday 12th May
Colchester United 1 (Kinsella)
Plymouth Argyle 0
Att: 6,511 Layer Road

Second Legs - Wednesday 15th May
Darlington 2 (Painter, Appleby)
Hereford United 1 (White)
Att: 6,584 Feethams

Wednesday 15th May
Plymouth Argyle 3 (Evans, Leadbitter, Williams)
Colchester United 1 (Kinsella)
Att: 14,525 Home Park

Third Division Final

Saturday 25th May

Plymouth Argyle 1 (Mauge, 65')
Darlington 0

Att: 43,431 Wembley

Plymouth: Cherry, Patterson, Williams, Mauge, Heathcote, Barlow, Leadbitter, Logan, Littlejohn, Evans, Curran, Manager - Neil Warnock

Darlington: Newell, Brumwell, Barnard, Appleby, Crosby, Gregan, Bannister, Gaughan (Carmichael), Painter, Blake, Carss, Manager - Jim Platt

1997

First Division Semi-finals

First Legs - Saturday 10th May
Crystal Palace 3 (Shipperley, Freedman 2)
Wolverhampton Wanderers 1 (Smith)
Att: 21,053 Selhurst Park

Saturday 10th May
Sheffield United 1 (Fjortoft)
Ipswich Town (Stockwell)
Att: 22,312 Bramall Lane

Second Legs - Wednesday 14th May
Wolverhampton Wanderers 2 (Atkins, Williams)
Crystal Palace 1 (Hopkin)
Att: 26,403 Molineux

Wednesday 14th May
Ipswich Town 2 (Scowcroft, Gudmundsson)
Sheffield United 2 (Kachura, Walker) AET
Sheffield United won on away goals
Att: 21,467 Portman Road

First Division Final

Monday 26th May

Crystal Palace 1 (Hopkin, 90')
Sheffield United 0

Att: 64,383 Wembley

Crystal Palace: Nash, Edworthy, Gordon, Roberts, Tuttle, Linighan, Muscat, Hopkin, Shipperley, Dyer, Rodger, Manager - Steve Coppell

Sheffield United: Tracey, Ward, Nilsen, Hutchison (Sandford), Tiler, Holdsworth, White, Spackman (Walker), Fjortoft, Katchouro (Taylor), Whitehouse, Manager - Howard Kendall

Second Division Semi-finals

First Legs - Sunday 11th May
Bristol City 1 (Owers)
Brentford 2 (Smith, Taylor)
Att: 15,581 Ashton Gate

Sunday 11th May
Crewe Alexandra 2 (Rivers, Little)
Luton Town 1 (Oldfield)
Att: 5,467 Gresty Road

Second Legs - Wednesday 14th May
Brentford 2 (Taylor, Bent)
Bristol City 1 (Barnard)
Att: 9,496 Griffin Park

Wednesday 14th May
Luton Town 2 (Oldfield 2)
Crewe Alexandra 2 (Little, Smith)
Att: 8,168 Kenilworth Road

Second Division Final

Sunday 25th May

Crewe Alexandra 1 (Smith, 34')
Brentford 0

Att: 34,149 Wembley

Crewe: Kearton, Unsworth, S Smith, Westwood, Macauley, Charnock (Lightfoot), Whalley, Little, Rivers (Garvey), Murphy (Johnson), Adebola, Manager - Dario Gradi

Brentford: Dearden, Hurdle (Ashby), Anderson, Hutchings, Bates, McGhee, Asaba, Smith, Bent (Canham), Statham, Taylor, Manager - Dave Webb

Third Division Semi-finals

First Legs - Sunday 11th May
Cardiff City 0
Northampton Town 1 (Parrish)
Att: 11,369 Ninian Park

Sunday 11th May
Chester City 0
Swansea City 0
Att: 5,104 Deva Stadium

Second Legs - Wednesday 14th May
Northampton Town 3 (Sampson, Warburton, Gayle)
Cardiff City 2 (Fowler, Haworth)
Att: 7,302 Sixfields

Wednesday 14th May
Swansea City 3 (Thomas, Torpey, Heggs)
Chester City 0
Att: 10,027 Vetch Field

Third Division Final

Saturday 24th May

Northampton Town 1 (Frain, 90')
Swansea City 0

Att: 46,804 Wembley

Northampton: Woodman, Clarkson, Frain, Sampson, Warburton, Rennie (Peer), Parrish, Grayson, Gayle (White), Lee, Hunter, Manager - Ian Atkins

Swansea: Freestone, Thomas (Brown), Moreira, Walker, Edwards, Ampadu, Heggs, Penney, Torpey, Molby, Coates, Manager - Jan Molby

1998

First Division Semi-finals

First Legs - Sunday 10th May
Ipswich Town 0
Charlton Athletic 1 (Clapham OG)
Att: 21,681 Portman Road

Sunday 10th May
Sheffield United 2 (Marcelo, Borbakis)
Sunderland 1 (Ball)
Att: 23,800 Bramall Lane

Second Legs - Wednesday 13th May
Charlton Athletic 1 (Newton)
Ipswich Town 0
Att: 15,585 The Valley

Wednesday 13th May
Sunderland 2 (Marker OG, Phillips)
Sheffield United 0
Att: 40,092 The Stadium of Light

First Division Final

Monday May 25th

Charlton Athletic 4 (Mendonca, 24', 72', 104', Rufus, 86')
Sunderland 4 (Quinn, 50', 74', Phillips, 58',
Summerbee, 99') AET
Charlton won 7-6 on penalties

Att: 77,739 Wembley

*Charlton: Ilic, Mills (Robinson), Bowen, Jones, Rufus, Youds,
Newton, Kinsella, Bright (Brown), Mendonca, Heaney
(Jones), Manager - Alan Curbishley*

*Sunderland: Perez, Holloway (Makin), Gray, Clark (Rae),
Craddock, Williams, Summerbee, Ball, Quinn, Phillips
(Dichio), Johnston, Manager - Peter Reid*

Second Division Semi-finals

First Legs - Saturday 9th May
Fulham 1 (Beardsley)
Grimsby Town 1 (D Smith)
Att: 13,954 Craven Cottage

Sunday 10th May
Bristol Rovers 3 (Beadle, Bennett, Hayles)
Northampton Town 1 (Gayle)
Att: 9,173 Memorial Stadium

Second Legs - Wednesday 13th May
Grimsby Town 1 (Donovan)
Fulham 0
Att: 8,689 Blundell Park

Wednesday 13th May
Northampton Town 3 (Heggs, Clarkson, Warburton)
Bristol Rovers 0
Att: 7,501 Sixfields

Second Division Final

Sunday May 24th

Grimsby Town 1 (Donovan, 19')
Northampton Town 0

Att: 62,988 Wembley

*Grimsby: Davison, McDermott, Gallimore, Handyside,
Lever, Burnett, Donovan, Smith (Black), Nogan (Livingstone),
Lester, Groves, Manager - Alan Buckley*

*Northampton: Woodman, Clarkson, Frain, Sampson,
Warburton, Hunt, Peer, Heggs, Freestone, Gayle (Seal),
Hill (Gibb), Manager - Ian Atkins*

Third Division Semi-finals

First Legs - Sunday 10th May
Barnet 1 (Heald)
Colchester United 0
Att: 3,858 Underhill

Sunday 10th May
Scarborough 1 (Rockett)
Torquay United 3 (Jack, Gittens, McFarlane)
Att: 5,246 McCain Stadium

Second Legs - Wednesday 13th May
Colchester United 3 (D Gregory 2, Greene)
Barnet 1 (Goodhind) AET
Att: 5,863 Layer Road

Wednesday 13th May
Torquay United 4 (Jack 2, McCall, Gibbs)
Scarborough 1 (Rockett)
Att: 5,386 Plainmoor

Third Division Final

Friday May 22nd

Colchester United 1 (D.Gregory, 22')
Torquay United 0

Att: 19,486 Wembley

*Colchester: Emberson, Dunne, Betts, Skelton (Duguid),
Greene, D Gregory, Wilkins, Buckle, Sale, N Gregory
(Lock), Forbes, Manager - Steve Wignall*

*Torquay: Gregg, Gurney, Gibbs, Roberts, Gittens, Watson,
Clayton, Leadbitter, Jack, McFarlane (Thomas), McCall
(Bedeau), Manager - Committee*

1999

First Division Semi-finals

First Legs - Sunday 16th May
Bolton Wanderers 1 (Johansen)
Ipswich Town 0
18,295 Burnden Park

Sunday 16th May
Watford 1 (Ngonge)
Birmingham City 0
Att: 18,535 Vicarage Road

Second Legs - Wednesday 19th May
Ipswich Town 4 (Holland 2, Dyer 2)
Bolton Wanderers 3 (Taylor 2, Frandsen) AET
Bolton won on away goals
Att: 21,788 Portman Road

Thursday 20th May
Birmingham City 1 (Adebola)
Watford 0 AET
Watford won 7-6 on penalties
Att: 29,100 St. Andrew's

First Division Final

Monday 31st May

Watford 2 (Wright, 38', Smart, 89')
Bolton Wanderers 0

Att: 70,343 Wembley

Watford: Chamberlain, Bazeley, Kennedy, Page, Palmer, Robinson, Ngonge (Smart), Hyde, Mooney, Johnson, Wright (Hazan), Manager - Graham Taylor

Bolton: Banks, Cox, Elliott, Frandsen, Toddm Fish, Johansen (Sellars), Jensen, Gudjohnsen, Taylor, Gardner (Hansen), Manager - Colin Todd

Second Division Semi-finals

First Legs - Saturday 15th May
Wigan Athletic 1 (Barlow)
Manchester City 1 (Dickov)
Att: 6,762 Springfield Park

Sunday 16th May
Preston North End 1 (Eyres)
Gillingham 1 (Taylor)
Att: 18,584 Deepdale

Second Legs - Wednesday 19th May
Gillingham 1 (Hessenthaler)
Preston North End 0
Att: 10,505 Priestfield Stadium

Wednesday 19th May
Manchester City 1 (Goater)
Wigan Athletic
Att: 31,305 Maine Road

Second Division Final

Sunday 30th May

Manchester City 2 (Horlock, 89', Dickov, 90')
Gillingham 2 (Asaba, 81', Taylor, 86') AET
Manchester City won 3-1 on penalties

Att: 76,935 Wembley

Manchester City: Weaver, Crooks (G Taylor), Edghill, Wiekens, Morrison (Vaughan), Horlock, Brown (Bishop), Whitley, Dickov, Goater, Cooke, Manager - Joe Royle

Gillingham: Bartram, Southall, Ashby, Smith, Butters, Pennock, Patterson (Hodge), Hessenthaler, Asaba (Carr), Galloway (Saunders), R Taylor, Manager - Tony Pulis

Third Division Semi-finals

First Legs - Sunday 16th May
Rotherham United 0
Leyton Orient 0 AET
Leyton Orient won 4-2 on penalties
Att: 9,529 Millmoor

Sunday 16th May
Swansea City 1 (Bound)
Scunthorpe United 0
Att: 7,828 Vetch Field

Second Legs - Wednesday 19th May
Northampton Town 3 (Sampson, Warburton, Gayle)
Cardiff City 2 (Fowler, Haworth)
Att: 7,302 Sixfields

Wednesday 19th May
Scunthorpe United 3 (Dawson, Sheldon 2)
Swansea City 1 (Bird)
Att: 7,098 Glanford Park

Third Division Final

Saturday 24th May

Scunthorpe United 1 (Calvo-Garcia, 6')
Leyton Orient 0

Att: 36,985 Wembley

Scunthorpe: Evans, Harsley, Dawson, Logan, Wilcox, Hope, Walker, Forrester (Bull), Sheldon, Gayle (Stamp), Calvo-Garcia (Housham), Manager - Brian Laws

Orient: Barrett, Joseph, Lockwood, Smith, Hicks (Maskell), Clark, Ling, Richards (Inglethorpe), Watts, Simba, Beall, Manager - Tommy Taylor

2000

First Division Semi-finals

First Legs - Saturday 13th May
Birmingham City 0
Barnsley 4 (Shipperley, Dyer 2, Hignett)
Att: 26,492 St. Andrew's

Sunday 14th May
Bolton Wanderers 2 (Holdsworth, Gudjohnsen)
Ipswich Town 2 (Stewart 2)
Att: 18,814 Reebok Stadium

Second Legs - Thursday 18th May
Barnsley 1 (Dyer)
Birmingham City 2 (Rowett, Marcelo)
Att: 19,050 Oakwell

Wednesday 17th May
Ipswich Town 5 (Magilton 3, Clapham, Reuser)
Bolton Wanderers 3 (Holdsworth2, Johnston)
Att: 21,543 Portman Road

Second Division Semi-finals

First Legs - Saturday 13th May
Millwall 0
Wigan Athletic 0
Att: 14,091 The New Den

Saturday 13th May
Stoke City 3 (Gunnlaugsson, Lightbourne, Thorne)
Gillingham 2 (Gooden, Hessenthaler)
Att: 22,124 Britannia Stadium

Second Legs - Wednesday 17th May
Wigan Athletic 1 (Sheridan)
Millwall 0
Att: 10,642 JJB Stadium

Wednesday 17th May
Gillingham 3 (Ashby, Onuora, Smith)
Stoke City 0 AET
Att: 10,386 Priestfield Stadium

Third Division Semi-finals

First Legs - Saturday 13th May
Barnet 1 (Arber)
Peterborough United 2 (Lee, Clarke)
Att: 4,535 Underhill

Saturday 13th May
Hartlepool United 0
Darlington 2 (Liddle, Gabbiadini)
Att: 6,995 Victoria Park

Second Legs - Wednesday 17th May
Peterborough United 3 (Farrell 3)
Barnet 0
Att: 10,515 London Road

Wednesday 17th May
Darlington 1 (Strodder OG)
Hartlepool United 0
Att: 8,238 Feethams

First Division Final

Monday 29th May

Ipswich Town 4 (Mowbray, 28', Naylor, 52',
Stewart, 58', Reuser, 90')
Barnsley 2 (R Wright OG, 6', Hignett, 78')

Att: 73,427 Wembley

*Ipswich: R Wright, Croft, Clapham, Mowbray, McGreal,
Venus, J Wright (Wilnis), Holland, Johnson (Naylor),
Stewart (Reuser), Magilton, Manager - George Burley*

*Barnsley: Miller, Curtis (Eaden), Barnard, Morgan, Chettle,
Brown, Appleby, Hignett, Shipperley, Dyer (Hristov), Tinkler
(Thomas), Manager - Dave Bassett*

Second Division Final

Sunday 28th May

Gillingham 3 (McGibbon OG, 35', Butler, 114',
Thomson, 118')
Wigan Athletic 2 (Haworth, 52', Barlow, 99') AET

Att: 53,764 Wembley

*Gillingham: Bartram, Ashby (Butler), Edge (Smith),
Southall, Butters, Pennock, Lewis, Hessenthaler, Onuora
(Thomson), Asaba, Gooden, Manager - Peter Taylor*

*Wigan: Stillie, Green, Sharp, McGibbon, Balmer,
De Zeeuw, Kilford, Sheridan, Haworth (Peron), Lidell
(Bradshaw), Redfearn (Barlow), Manager - John Benson*

Third Division Final

Friday 26th May

Peterborough United 1 (Clarke, 25')
Darlington 0

Att: 33,383 Wembley

*Peterborough: Tyler, Scott, Drury (Hanlon), Jelleyman, Rea,
Edwards, Cullen, Castle, Oldfield, Clarke (Green), Farrell,
Manager - Barry Fry*

*Darlington: Collett, Aspin, Heckingbottom (Naylor), Liddle,
Tutill, Atkinson (Holsgrove), Gray, Oliver, Duffield (Nogan),
Gabbiadini, Heaney, Manager - David Hodgson*

2001

First Division Semi-finals

First Legs - Sunday 13th May
West Bromwich Albion 2 (Roberts, Hughes)
Bolton Wanderers 2 (Bergsson, Frandsen)
Att: 18,167 The Hawthorns

Sunday 13th May
Birmingham City 1 (Eaden)
Preston North End 0
Att: 29,072 St. Andrew's

Second Legs - Thursday 17th May
Bolton Wanderers 3 (Bergsson, Gardner, Ricketts)
West Bromwich Albion 0
Att: 23,515 Reebok Stadium

Thursday 17th May
Preston North End 2 (Healy, Rankine)
Birmingham City 1 (Horsfield) AET
Preston NE won 4-2 on penalties
Att: 16,928 Deepdale

First Division Final

Monday 28th May

Bolton Wanderers 3 (Farrelly, 17', Ricketts, 89', Gardner, 90')
Preston North End 0

Att: 54,328 Millenium Stadium

*Bolton: Clarke, Barness, Charlton, Frandsen (Elliott), Hendry,
Bergsson, Farrelly, Nolan, Holdsworth (Whitlow), Hansen
(Ricketts), Gardner, Manager - Sam Allardyce*

*Preston: Lucas, Alexander, Edwards, Murdock, Kidd,
Gregan, Cartwright (Anderson), Rankine, Healy, Macken,
McKenna (Cresswell), Manager - David Moyes*

Second Division Semi-finals

First Legs - Sunday 13th May
Stoke City 0
Walsall 0
Att: 23,689 Britannia Stadium

Sunday 13th May
Wigan Athletic 0
Reading 0
Att: 12,638 JJB Stadium

Second Legs - Wednesday 16th May
Walsall 4 (Ward OG, Matias 2, Keates)
Stoke City 2 (Kavanagh, Thorne)
Att: 8,993 Bescot Stadium

Wednesday 16th May
Reading 2 (Butler, Forster)
Wigan Athletic 1 (Nicholls)
Att: 22,034 Madejski Stadium

Second Division Final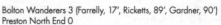

Sunday 27th May

Walsall 3 (Goodman, 48', Rougier OG, 108', Byfield, 109')
Reading 2 (Cureton, 31', Butler, 91') AET

Att: 50,496 Millennium Stadium

*Walsall: Walker, Brightwell, Aranalde, Bennett (Bukran),
Barras, Tillson, Hall (Gadsby), Keates, Leitao (Byfield),
Goodman, Matias, Manager - Ray Graydon*

*Reading: Whitehead, Murty, Robinson, Parkinson, Viveash,
Williams (Hunter), McIntyre (Rougier), Harper, Butler,
Cureton, Igoe (Forster), Manager - Alan Pardew*

Third Division Semi-finals

First Legs - Sunday 13th May
Blackpool 2 (Ormerod 2)
Hartlepool United 0
Att: 5,720 Bloomfield Road

Sunday 13th May
Hull City 1 (Eyre)
Leyton Orient 0
Att: 13,310 Boothferry Park

Second Legs - Wednesday 16th May
Hartlepool United 1 (Henderson)
Blackpool 3 (Ormerod 2, Hills)
Att: 5,836 Victoria Park

Wednesday 16th May
Leyton Orient 2 (Watts, Lockwood)
Hull City 0
Att: 9,419 Brisbane Road

Third Division Final

Saturday 26th May

Blackpool 4 (Hughes, 35', Reid, 45',
Simpson, 77', Ormerod, 88')
Leyton Orient 2 (Tate, 1', Houghton, 37')

Att: 23,600 Millennium Stadium

*Blackpool: Barnes, Parkinson, Hills, Wellens
(M Milligan), Reid, Hughes, Coid, Clarkson,
Murphy, Ormerod (Thompson), Simpson (J Milligan),
Manager - Steve McMahon*

*Leyton Orient: Bayes, Joseph, Lockwood, Smith, Downer,
Walschaerts (Castle), McGhee, Harris, Ibehre, Tate
(Brkovic), Houghton (Martin), Manager - Tommy Taylor*

2002

First Division Semi-finals

First Legs - Sunday 28th April
Bimingham City 1 (Hughes)
Millwall 1 (Dublin)
Att: 28,282 St Andrew's

Sunday 28th April
Norwich City 3 (Rivers, McVeigh, Mackay)
Wolverhampton Wanderers 1 (Sturridge)
Att: 20,127 Carrow Road

Second Legs - Wednesday 1st May
Wolverhampton Wanderers 1 (Cooper)
Norwich City 0
Att: 27,418 Molineux

Thursday 2nd May
Millwall 0
Bimingham City 1 (John)
Att: 16,391 The New Den

First Division Final

Sunday 12th May

Birmingham City 1 (Horsfield, 102')
Norwich City 1 (Roberts, 91') AET
Birmingham won 4-2 on Penalties

Att: 71,597 Millennium Stadium

*Birmingham: Vaesen, Kenna, Grainger, Hughes, Vickers
(Carter), M Johnson, Devlin, John, Horsfield (A Johnson),
Tebily, Mooney (Lazaridis), Manager - Steve Bruce*

*Norwich: Green, Kenton, Drury, Holt, Fleming, Mackay,
Rivers (Notman), McVeigh (Sutch), Nielsen (Roberts),
Mulryne, Easton, Manager - Nigel Worthington*

Second Division Semi-finals

First Legs - Sunday 28th April
Stoke City 1 (Burton)
Cardiff City 2 (Earnshaw, Fortune-West)
Att: 21,245 Britannia Stadium

Sunday 28th April
Huddersfield Town 0
Brentford 0
Att: 16,523 McAlpine Stadium

Second Legs - Wednesday 1st May
Cardiff City 0
Stoke City 2 (O' Connor, Oulare) AET
Att: 19,367 Ninian Park

Wednesday 1st May
Brentford 2 (Powell, Owusu)
Huddersfield Town 1 (Booth)
Att: 11,191 Griffin Park

Second Division Final

Saturday 11th May

Stoke City 2 (Burton, 16', Burgess OG, 45')
Brentford 0

Att: 42,523 Millennium Stadium

*Stoke: Cutler, Thomas, Clarke, Handyside, Shtaniuk,
J O'Connor, Gudjonsson, Dinning (Brightwell), Burton,
Gunnlaugsson (Vandeurzen), Iwelumo (Cooke),
Manager - Gudjon Thordarson*

*Brentford: Smith, Dobson, Anderson, Ingimarsson, Powell,
Rowlands (K O'Connor), Sidwell, Hunt, Owusu, Burgess
(McCammon), Evans, Manager - Steve Coppell*

Third Division Semi-finals

First Legs - Saturday 27th April
Hartlepool United 1 (E Williams)
Cheltenham Town 1 (Grayson)
Att: 7,135 Victoria Park

Saturday 27th April
Rushden & Diamonds 2 (Wardley, Butterworth)
Rochdale 2 (McEvilly, Simpson)
Att: 6,015 Nene Park

Second Legs - Tuesday 30th April
Cheltenham Town 1 (L Williams)
Hartlepool United 1 (Arnison)
Cheltenham Town won 5-4 on penalties
Att: 7,165 Whaddon Road

Tuesday 30th April
Rochdale 1 (Peters OG)
Rushden & Diamonds 2 (Lowe, Hall)
Att: 8,547 Spotland

Third Division Final

Monday 6th May

Cheltenham Town 3 (Devaney, 27', Alsop, 49', Finnigan, 80')
Rushden & Diamonds 1 (Hall, 28')

Att: 24,368 Millennium Stadium

*Cheltenham: Book, Griffin, Victory, Walker, Duff, Williams,
Finnigan, Devaney (Grayson), Alsop, Naylor, Yates,
Manager - Steve Cotterill*

*Rushden: Turley, Mustafa, Underwood, Wardley, Peters,
Tillson, Butterworth, Hall, Partridge (Angell), Lowe, Gray
(Brady), Manager - Brian Talbot*

2003

First Division Semi-finals

First Legs - Saturday 10th May
Nottingham Forest 1 (Johnson)
Sheffield United 1 (Brown)
Att: 29,064 City Ground

Saturday 10th May
Wolverhampton Wanderers 2 (Murty OG, Naylor)
Reading 1 (Forster)
Att: 27,678 Molineux

Second Legs - Thursday 15th May
Sheffield United 4 (Brown, Kabba, Peschisolido, Walker OG)
Nottingham Forest 3 (Johnson, Reid, Page OG) AET
Att: 30,212 Bramall Lane

Wednesday 14th May
Reading 0
Wolverhampton Wanderers 1 (Rae)
Att: 24,060 Madjeski Stadium

First Division Final

Monday 26th May

Wolverhampton Wanderers 3 (Kennedy, 5',
Blake, 21', Miller, 45')
Sheffield United 0

Att: 69,490 Millennium Stadium

*Wolves: Murray, Irwin, Naylor, Cameron, Lescott, Butler,
Newton, Ince, Blake (Proudlock), Miller (Sturridge),
Kennedy, Manager - Dave Jones*

*Sheffield United: Kenny, Curtis, Kozluk, Rankine (McCall),
Page, Jagielka, Tonge, Brown, Asaba (Allison), Kabba,
Ndlovu (Peschisolido), Manager - Neil Warnock*

Second Division Semi-finals

First Legs - Saturday 10th May
Cardiff City 1 (Thorne)
Bristol City 0
Att: 19,146 Ninian Park

Saturday 10th May
Oldham Athletic 1 (Eyres)
Queens Park Rangers 1 (Langley)
Att: 12,152 Boundary Park

Second Legs - Tuesday 13th May
Bristol City 0
Cardiff City 0
Att: 16,307 Ashton Gate

Wednesday 14th May
Queens Park Rangers 1 (Furlong)
Oldham Athletic 0
Att: 17,201 Loftus Road

Second Division Final

Sunday 25th May

Cardiff City 1 (Campbell, 114')
Queens Park Rangers 0 AET

Att: 66,096 Millennium Stadium

*Cardiff: Alexander, Weston (Croft), Barker, Gabbidon, Prior,
Boland, Whalley, Kavanagh, Thorne, Earnshaw (Campbell),
Legg (Bonner), Manager - Lennie Lawrence*

*QPR: Day, Kelly, Padula (Williams), Palmer, Carlisle, Shittu,
Bircham, Pacquette (Thomson), Furlong, Gallen, McLeod,
Manager - Ian Holloway*

Third Division Semi-finals

First Legs - Saturday 10th May
Bury 0
Bournemouth 0
Att: 5,782 Gigg Lane

Saturday 10th May
Lincoln City 5 (Weaver, Mayo, Smith, Yeo 2)
Scunthorpe United 3 (Calvo-Garcia 2, Stanton)
Att: 8,902 Sincil Bank

Second Legs - Tuesday 13th May
Bournemouth 3 (O' Connor, Hayter 2)
Bury 1 (Preece)
Att: 7,945 Fitness First Stadium

Wednesday 14th May
Scunthorpe United 0
Lincoln City 1 (Yeo)
Att: 8,295 Glanford Park

Third Division Final

Saturday 24th May

Bournemouth 5 (S Fletcher, 29', C Fletcher, 45', 77',
Purches, 56', O'Connor, 60')
Lincoln City 2 (Futcher, 35', Bailey, 75')

Att: 32,148 Millennium Stadium

*Bournemouth: Moss, Young, Purches, Browning, C Fletcher,
Gulliver, Elliott (Thomas), O'Connor (Stock), S Fletcher
(Holmes), Hayter, Cummings, Manager - Sean O'Driscoll*

*Lincoln: Marriott, Bailey, Bimson, Weaver (Cornelly),
Morgan, Futcher, Smith (Yeo), Butcher, Cropper (Willis),
Mayo, Gain, Manager - Keith Alexander*

2004

First Division Semi-finals

First Legs - Friday 14th May
Crystal Palace 3 (Shipperley, Butterfield, Johnson)
Sunderland 2 (Stewart, Kyle)
Att: 25,287 Selhurst Park

Saturday 15th May
Ipswich Town 1 (Bent)
West Ham United 0
Att: 28,435 Portman Road

Second Legs - Monday 17th May
Sunderland 2 (Kyle, Stewart)
Crystal Palace 1 (Powell) AET
Crystal Palace won 5-4 on penalties
Att: 34,536 Stadium of Light

Tuesday 18th May
West Ham United 2 (Etherington, Dailly)
Ipswich Town 0
Att: 34,002 Upton Park

First Division Final

Saturday 29th May

Crystal Palace 1 (Shipperley, 62')
West Ham United 0

Att: 72,523 Millennium Stadium

Crystal Palace: Vaesen, Butterfield (Powell), Granville, Popovic, Leigertwood, Derry, Routledge, Riihilahti, Johnson, Shipperley, Hughes, Manager - Iain Dowie

West Ham: Bywater, Repka, Mullins, Lomas, Melville, Dailly, harewood (Reo-Coker), Carrick, Connolly (Hutchison), Zamora (Deane), Etherington, Manager - Alan Pardew

Second Division Semi-finals

First Legs - Saturday 15th May
Hartlepool United 1 (Porter)
Bristol City (Rougier) 1
Att: 7,211 Victoria Park

Sunday 16th May
Swindon Town 0
Brighton & Hove Albion 1 (Carpenter)
Att: 14,034 County Ground

Second Legs - Wednesday 19th May
Cardiff City 0
Stoke City 2 (O' Connor, Oulare) AET
Att: 19,367 Ninian Park

Thursday 20th May
Brighton & Hove Albion 1
Swindon Town 2 (Parkin, Fallon) AET
Brighton won 4-3 on penalties
Att: 6,876 Withdean Stadium

Second Division Final

Sunday 30th May

Brighton & Hove Albion 1 (Knight, 84')
Bristol City 0

Att: 65,167 Millennium Stadium

Brighton: Roberts, Virgo, Harding, Carpenter (Reid), Butters, Cullip, Oatway, Hart, Iwelumo, Knight, Jones (Piercy), Manager - Mark McGhee

Bristol City: Phillips, Carey, Hill, Doherty, Coles, Butler (Goodfellow), Rougier, Woodman, Roberts, Miller (Murray), Tinnion (Wilkshire), Manager - Danny Wilson

Third Division Semi-finals

First Legs - Saturday 15th May
Lincoln City 1 (Taylor-Fletcher)
Huddersfield Town 2 (Onuora Mirfin)
Att: 9,202 Sincil Bank

Sunday 16th May
Northampton Town 0
Mansfield Town 2 (Day, Mendes)
Att: 6,960 Sixfields

Second Legs - Wednesday 19th May
Huddersfield Town 2 (Schofield, Edwards)
Lincoln City 2 (Butcher, Bailey)
Att: 19,467 McAlpine Stadium

Thursday 20th May
Mansfield Town 1 (Curtis)
Northampton Town 3 (Richards, Hargreaves, Smith) AET
Mansfield Town won 5-4 on penalties
Att: 9,243 Field Mill

Third Division Final

Monday 31st May

Huddersfield Town 0
Mansfield Town 0
Huddersfield won 4-1 on penalties

Att: 37,268 Millenniunm Stadium

Huddersfield: Rachubka, Yates, Lloyd (Edwards), Holdsworth, Mirfin, Sodje, Schofield, Worthington (Fowler), Booth, Abbott (McAliskey), Carss, Manager - Peter Jackson

Mansfield: Pilkington, Hassell, Eaton, Curtis, John-Baptiste, Day, Lawrence, Williamson (MacKenzie), Disley (Larkin), Mendes (D'Jaffo), Corden, Manager - Keith Curle

2005

Championship Semi-finals

First Legs - Saturday 14th May
West Ham United 2 (Harewood, Zamora)
Ipswich Town 2 (Walker OG, Kuqi)
Att: 33,723 Upton Park

Sunday 15th May
Preston North End 2 (Nugent, Cresswell)
Derby County 0
Att: 20,315 Deepdale

Second Legs - Wednesday 18th May
Ipswich Town 0
West Ham United 2 (Zamora 2)
Att: 30,010 Portman Road

Thursday 19th May
Derby County 0
Preston North End 0
Att: 31,310 Pride Park

Championship Final

Monday 30th May

West Ham United 1 (Zamora, 57')
Preston North End 0

Att: 70,275 Millennium Stadium

West Ham: Walker (Bywater), Repka, Powell, Mullins, Ferdinand, Ward, Newton (Noble), Reo-Coker, Harewood, Zamora (Dailly), Etherington, Manager - Alan Pardew

Preston: Nash, Mawene (Alexander), Hill, Davis, Lucketti, O'Neill (Etuhu), Sedgwick (Agyemang), Lewis, Cresswell, Nugent, McKenna, Manager - Billy Davies

League One Semi-finals

First Legs - Thursday 12th May
Sheffield Wednesday 1 (McGovern)
Brentford 0
Att: 28,625 Hillsborough

Friday 13th May
Hartlepool United 2 (Boyd 2)
Tranmere Rovers 0
Att: 6,604 Victoria Park

Second Legs - Monday 16th May
Brentford 1 (Frampton)
Sheffield Wednesday 2 (Peacock, Brunt)
Att: 10,823 Griffin Park

Thursday 1st May
Tranmere Rovers 2 (Taylor, Beresford)
Hartlepool United 0
Hartlepool won 6-5 on penalties
Att: 13,356 Prenton Park

League One Final

Sunday 29th May

Sheffield Wednesday 4 (McGovern, 45', MacLean, 82', Whelan, 94', Talbot, 120')
Hartlepool United 2 (Williams, 47', Daly, 71') AET

Att: 59,808 Millennium Stadium

Sheffield Wednesday: Lucas, Bruce (Collins), Heckingbottom, Rocastle, Bullen, Wood, McGovern, Whelan, Peacock (Talbot), Quinn (MacLean), Brunt, Manager - Paul Sturrock

Hartlepool: Konstantopoulos, Barron (Craddock), Robson, Strachan, Nelson, Westwood, Butler (Williams), Sweeney, Porter (Daly), Boyd, Humphreys, Manager - Martin Scott

League Two Semi-finals

First Legs - Saturday 14th May
Lincoln City 1 (McAuley)
Macclesfield Town 0
Att: 7,032 Sincil Bank

Sunday 15th May
Northampton Town 0
Southend United 0
Att: 6,601 Sixfields

Second Legs - Saturday 21st May
Macclesfield Town 1 (Harsley)
Lincoln City 1 (McAuley)
Att: 5,223 Moss Rose

Saturday 21st May
Southend United 1 (Eastwood)
Northampton Town 0
Att: 9,152 Roots Hall

League Two Final

Saturday 28th May

Southend United 2 (Eastwood, 105', Jupp, 110')
Lincoln City 0 AET

Att: 19,635 Millennium Stadium

Southend: Flahavan, Jupp, Wilson, Pettefer, Prior, Barrett, Maher, Nicolau (Gower), Eastwood (Edwards), Gray (Dudfield), Bentley, Manager - Steve Tilson

Lincoln: Marriott, McAuley, Sandwith, McCombe, Morgan, Futcher, Green (Beevers), Butcher, Yeo (Asamoah), Taylor-Fletcher (Bloomer), Gain, Manager - Keith Alexander

2006

Championship Semi-finals

First Legs - Friday 5th May
Leeds United 1 (Lewis)
Preston North End 1 (Nugent)
Att: 35,239 Elland Road

Saturday 6th May
Crystal Palace 0
Watford 3 (King, Young, Spring)
Att: 22,880 Selhurst Park

Second Legs - Monday 8th May
Preston North End 0
Leeds United 2 (Hulse, Richardson)
Att: 20,383 Deepdale

Tuesday 9th May
Watford 0 Crystal Palace 0
Att: 19,041 Vicarage Road

Championship Final

Sunday 21st May

Watford 3 (DeMerit, 25', Sullivan OG, 57', Henderson, 84')
Leeds United 0

Att: 64,736 Millennium Stadium

Watford: Foster, Doyley, Stewart, Spring, DeMerit, Mackay, Young, Mahon, Henderson, King, Chambers (Bangura), Manager - Adie Boothroyd

Leeds: Sullivan, Kelly, Kilgallon, Derry, Butler, Gregan (Bakke), Richardson (Blake), Miller (Healy), Hulse, Douglas, Lewis, Manager - Kevin Blackwell

League One Semi-finals

First Legs - Thursday 11th May
Barnsley 0
Huddersfield Town 1 (Taylor-Fletcher)
Att: 16,127 Oakwell

Thursday 11th May
Swansea City 1 (Ricketts)
Brentford 1 (Tabb)
Att: 19,060 Liberty Stadium

Second Legs - Monday 15th May
Huddersfield Town 1 (Worthington)
Barnsley 3 (Hayes, Reid, Nardiello)
Att: 19,223 Galpharm Stadium

Sunday 14th May
Brentford 0
Swansea City 2 (Knight 2)
Att: 10,652 Griffin Park

League One Final

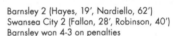

Saturday 27th May

Barnsley 2 (Hayes, 19', Nardiello, 62')
Swansea City 2 (Fallon, 28', Robinson, 40')
Barnsley won 4-3 on penalties

Att: 55,419 Millennium Stadium

Barnsley: Colgan, Hassell, Heckingbottom, Kay, Reid, McPhail, Nardiello (Shuker), Howard (Tonge), Hayes, Richards (Wright), Devaney, Manager - Andy Ritchie

Swansea: Gueret, Ricketts, Austin, O'Leary, Monk, Tate, Britton, Tudur Jones, Fallon (Akinfenwa), Knight (Trundle), Robinson (McLeod), Manager - Kenny Jackett

League Two Semi-finals

First Legs - Saturday 13th May
Lincoln City 0
Grimsby Town 1 (Jones)
Att: 8,037 Sincil Bank

Saturday 13th May
Wycombe Wanderers 1 (Mooney)
Cheltenham Town 2 (Finnigan, Guinan)
Att: 5,936 Adams Park

Second Legs - Tuesday 16th May
Grimsby Town 2 (Futcher, Jones)
Lincoln City 1 (Robinson)
Att: 8,062 Blundell Park

Thursday 18th May
Cheltenham Town 0
Wycombe Wanderers 0
Att: 6,813 Whaddon Road

League Two Final

Sunday 28th May

Cheltenham Town 1 (Guinan, 63')
Grimsby Town 0

Att: 29,196 Millennium Stadium

Cheltenham: Higgs, Gill, Armstrong (Bell), Caines, Duff, Wilson, Vincent (Spencer), Finnigan, Guinan, Gillespie (Odejayi), McCann, Manager - John Ward

Grimsby: Mildenhall, Croft (Futcher), Newey, Jones, Whittle, Woodhouse, Parkinson, Parkinson, Bolland, Jones, Reddy (Cohen), Mendes (Goodfellow), Manager - Russell Slade

2007

Championship Semi-finals

First Legs - Saturday 12th May
Southampton 1 (Surman)
Derby County 2 (Howard 2)
Att: 30,602 St. Mary's Stadium

Sunday 13th May
Wolverhampton Wanderers 2 (Craddock, Olofinjana)
West Bromwich Albion 3 (Phillips 2, Kamara)
Att: 27,750 Molineux

Second Legs - Tuesday 15th May
Derby County 2 (Moore, Best OG)
Southampton 3 (Viafara 2, Rasiak) AET
Derby won 4-3 on penalties
Att: 31,569 Pride Park

Wednesday 16th May
West Bromwich Albion 1 (Phillips)
Wolverhampton Wanderers 0
Att: 27,415 The Hawthorns

Championship Final

Monday 28th May

Derby County 1 (Pearson, 61')
West Bromwich Albion 0

Att: 74,993 Wembley

Derby: Bywater, Mears, McEveley, Oakley, Moore, Leacock, Fagan (Edworthy), Johnson (Jones), Howard, Peschisolido (Barnes), Pearson, Manager - Billy Davies

West Brom: Kiely, McShane (Ellington), Robinson, Koumas, Perry, Sodje (Clement), Greening, Koren, Kamara, Phillips, Gera (Carter), Manager - Tony Mowbray

League One Semi-finals

First Legs - Friday 11th May
Yeovil Town 0
Nottingham Forest 2 (Commons, Perch)
Att: 8,935 Huish Park

Sunday 13th May
Oldham Athletic 1 (Liddell)
Blackpool 2 (Barker, Hoolahan)
Att: 12,154 Boundary Parkrk

Second Legs - Friday 18th May
Nottingham Forest 2 (Dobie, Holt)
Yeovil Town 5 (Davies 2, Wright OG, Stewart, Morris)
Att: 27,819 City Ground

Saturday 19th May
Blackpool 3 (Southern, Morrell, Parker)
Oldham Athletic 1 (Wolfenden)
Att: 9,453 Bloomfield Road

League One Final

Sunday 27th May

Blackpool 2 (Williams, 43', Parker, 52')
Yeovil Town 0

Att: 59,313 Wembley

Blackpool: Rachubka, Barker, Williams, Southern, Jackson, Evatt, Forbes (Fox), Jorgensen, Morrell, Parker (Gillett), Hoolahan (Vernon), Manager - Simon Grayson

Yeovil: Mildenhall, Lindegaard (Lynch), Jones, Guyett, Forbes, Cohen (Kamudimba Kalala), Davies, Barry, Stewart, Gray, Morris (Knights), Manager - Russell Slade

League Two Semi-finals

First Legs - Saturday 12th May
Bristol Rovers 2 (Disley, Walker)
Lincoln City 1 (Hughes)
Att: 10,654 Memorial Ground

Monday 14th May
Shrewsbury Town 0
Milton Keynes Dons 0
Att: 7,126 Gay Meadow

Second Legs - Thursday 17th May
Lincoln City 3 (Hughes 2, Stallard)
Bristol Rovers 5 (Campbell, Lambert, Walker, Igoe, Rigg)
Att: 7,694 Sincil Bank

Friday 18th May
Milton Keynes Dons 1 (Andrews)
Shrewsbury Town 2 (Cooke 2)
Att: 8,212 National Hockey Stadium

League Two Final

Saturday 26th May

Bristol Rovers 3 (Walker, 21', 35', Igoe, 90')
Shrewsbury Town 1 (Drummond, 3')

Att: 61,589 Wembley

Bristol Rovers: Phillips, Green, Carruthers, Anthony, Elliott, Campbell, Igoe, Disley, Lambert, Walker, Haldane (Rigg), Manager - Paul Trollope

Shrewsbury: Mackenzie, Herd (Burton-Godwin), Tierney, Hall, Langmead, Hope, Asamoah, Drummond, Cooke (Humphrey), Symes (Fortune-West), Ashton, Manager - Gary Peters

2008

Championship Semi-Finals

First Legs - Saturday 10th May
Crystal Palace 1 (Watson)
Bristol City 2 (Carey, Noble)
Att: 22,869 Selhurst Park

Sunday 11th May
Watford 0
Hull City 2 (Barmby, Windass)
Att: 14,713 Vicarage Road

Second Legs - Tuesday 13th May
Bristol City 2 (Trundle, McIndoe)
Crystal Palace 1 (Watson) AET
Att: 18,842 Ashton Gate

Wednesday 14th May
Hull City 4 (Barmby, Folan, Garcia, Doyle)
Watford 1 (Henderson)
Att: 23,155 KC Stadium

Championship Final

Saturday 24th May

Bristol City 0
Hull City 1 (Windass, 38')

Att: 86,703 Wembley Stadium

Hull: Myhill, Ricketts, Dawson, Turner, Brown, Ashbee, Garcia, Hughes, Windass (Folan), Campbell (Marney), Barmby (Fagan), Manager - Phil Brown

Bristol City: Basso, Orr (Johnson), McAllister, Elliott, Fontaine, Carey, Carle (Byfield), Noble (Sproule), Adebola, Trundle, McIndoe, Manager - Gary Johnson

League One Semi-Finals

First Legs - Friday 9th May
Southend United 0
Doncaster Rovers 0
Att: 9,109 Roots Hall

Monday 12th May
Leeds United 1 (Freedman)
Carlisle United 2 (Graham, Bridge-Wilkinson)
Att: 36,297 Elland Road

Second Legs - Thursday 15th May
Carlisle United 0
Leeds United 2 (Howson 2)
Att: 12,873 Brunton Park

Friday 16th May
Doncaster Rovers 5 (Stock, Barrett OG, Coppinger 3)
Southend United 1 (Bailey)
Att: 13,081 Keepmoat Stadium

League One Final

Sunday 25th May

Doncaster Rovers 1 (Hayter, 48')
Leeds United 0

Att: 75,132 Wembley Stadium

Doncaster: Sullivan, O'Connor, Roberts, Hird, Mills, Green, Stock, Wellens (McCammon), Hayter, Price (Lockwood), Coppinger (Guy), Manager - Sean O'Driscoll

Leeds United: Ankergren, Richardson, Johnson, Kilkenny, Huntington, Michalik, Douglas, Howson, Freedman (Hughes), Beckford, Prutton (Kandol), Manager - Gary McAllister

League Two Semi-Finals

First Legs - Saturday 10th May
Darlington 2 (Kennedy, Miller)
Rochdale 1 (Dagnall)
Att: 8,057 Darlington Arena

Sunday 11th May
Wycombe Wanderers 1 (Facey)
Stockport County 1 (Gleeson)
Att: 6,371 Adams Park

Second Legs - Saturday 17th May
Saturday 17th May
Rochdale 2 (Dagnall, Perkins)
Darlington 1 (Keltie),
Rochdale won 5-4 on penalties
Att: 9,870 Spotland

Saturday 17th May
Stockport County 1 (Dickinson)
Wycombe Wanderers 0
Att: 9,245 Edgeley Park

League Two Final

Monday 26th May

Stockport County 3 (Stanton OG, 34', Pilkington 49', Dickinson 67')
Rochdale 2 (McArdle 24', Rundle 77')

Att: 35,715 Wembley Stadium

Stockport County: Logan, Smith, Rose, McNulty, Owen, Turnbull, Gleeson (McSweeney), Dicker, Rowe, Dickinson (McNeil), Pilkington, Manager - Jim Gannon

Rochdale: Lee, Ramsden, Kennedy, D'Laryea (Buckley), Stanton, McArdle, Higginbotham (Muirhead), Jones, Dagnall, Le Fondre (Howe), Rundle, Manager - Keith Hill

2009

Championship Semi-Finals

First Legs - Friday 8th May
Preston North End 1 (St Ledger)
Sheffield United 1 (Howard)
Att: 19,840 Deepdale

Saturday 9th May
Burnley 1 (Alexander)
Reading 0
Att: 18,853 Turf Moor

Second Legs - Monday 11th May
Sheffield United 1 (Halford)
Preston North End 0
Att: 26,354 Bramall Lane

Tuesday 12th May
Reading 0
Burnley 2 (Paterson, Thompson)
Att: 19,909 Madejski Stadium

Championship Final

Monday 25th May

Burnley 1 (Elliott, 13')
Sheffield United 0

Att: 80,518 Wembley Stadium

*Burnley: Jensen, Duff, Kalvenes, Alexander, Carlisle, Caldwell, Elliott, McCann (Gudjonsson), Thompson (Rodriguez), Paterson, Blake (Eagles)
Manager - Owen Coyle*

Sheffield United: Kenny, Walker, Naughton, Montgomery, Morgan, Kilgallon, Cotterill (Ward), Howard (Lupoli), Halford, Beattie, Quinn (Hendrie), Manager - Kevin Blackwell

League One Semi-Finals

First Legs - Friday 8th May
Scunthorpe United 1 (Woolford)
Milton Keynes Dons 1 (Wilbraham)
Att: 6,599 Glanford Park

Saturday 9th May
Millwall 1 (Harris)
Leeds United 0
Att: 13,228 The New Den

Second Legs - Thursday 14th May
Leeds United 1 (Becchio)
Millwall 1 (Abdou)
Att: 37,036 Elland Road

Friday 15th May
Milton Keynes Dons 0
Scunthorpe United 0 AET
Scunthorpe won 7-6 on penalties
Att: 14,479 Stadium:MK

League One Final

Sunday 24th May

Millwall 2 (Alexander 37', 39')
Scunthorpe United 3 (Sparrow 6', 70' Woolford 85')

Att: 59,661 Wembley Stadium

*Millwall: Forde, Dunne, Frampton (Robinson), Bolder, Whitbread, Craig, Grabban (Hackett), Abdou (Laird), Harris, Alexander, Martin
Manager - Kenny Jackett*

*Scunthorpe United: Murphy, Byrne, Morris, Crosby, Mirfin, McCann, Sparrow, Togwell (Trotter), Hayes, Hooper (Forte), Woolford
Manager - Nigel Adkins*

League Two Semi-Finals

First Legs - Thursday 7th May
Shrewsbury Town 0
Bury 1 (Ashton OG)
Att: 8,429 Prostar Stadium

Thursday 7th May
Rochdale 0
Gillingham 0
Att: 4,450 Spotland

Second Legs - Sunday 10th May
Bury 0
Shrewsbury Town 1 (McIntyre) AET
Shrewsbury won 4-3 on penalties
Att: 7,673 Gigg Lane

Sunday 10th May
Gillingham 2 (Jackson 2)
Rochdale 1 (Dagnall)
Att: 9,585 Priestfield Stadium

League Two Final

Saturday 23rd May

Gillingham 1 (Jackson 90')
Shrewsbury Town 0

Att: 53,706 Wembley Stadium

*Gillingham: Royce, Fuller, Nutter, Weston, King, Richards, Wright, Lewis, Jackson, Oli, Barcham,
Manager - Mark Stimson*

Shrewsbury Town: Daniels, Moss, Ashton, Murray (Worrall), Coughlan, Langmead, Humphrey (Ashikodi), Davies, Holt, Chadwick (Riza), McIntyre, Manager - Paul Simpson

2010

Championship Semi-Finals

First Legs - Saturday 8th May
Blackpool 2 (Southern, Adam)
Nottingham Forest 1 (Cohen)
Att: 11,805 Bloomfield Road

Sunday 9th May
Leicester City 0
Cardiff City 1 (Whittingham)
Att: 29,165 Walkers Stadium

Second Legs - Tuesday 11th May
Nottingham Forest 3 (Earnshaw 2, Adebola)
Blackpool 4 (Campbell 3, Dobbie)
Att: 28,358 City Ground

Wednesday 12th May
Cardiff City 2 (Chopra, Whittingham)
Leicester City 3 (Fryatt, Hudson OG, King) AET
Cardiff won 4-3 on penalties
Att: 26,033 City of Cardiff Stadium

Championship Final

Saturday 22nd May

Cardiff City 2 (Chopra 9', Ledley 37')
Blackpool 3 (Adam 13', Taylor-Fletcher 41', Ormerod 45')

Att: 82,224 Wembley Stadium

Cardiff City: Marshall, McNaughton (Gerrard), Kennedy, Hudson, Blake, McPhail, Burke (McCormack), Ledley, Chopra, Bothroyd (Etuhu), Whittingham, Manager - Dave Jones

Blackpool: Gilks, Coleman, Crainey, Southern, Evatt, John-Baptiste, Taylor-Fletcher (Burgess), Adam, Ormerod (Dobbie), Campbell, Vaughan (Bannan), Manager - Ian Holloway

League One Semi-Finals

First Legs - Friday 14th May
Swindon Town 2 (Austin, Ward)
Charlton Athletic 1 (Burton)
Att: 13,560 County Ground

Saturday 15th May
Huddersfield Town 0
Millwall 0
Att: 14,654 Galpharm Stadium

Second Legs - Monday 17th May
Charlton Athletic 2 (Ferry OG, Mooney)
Swindon Town 1 (Ward) AET
Swindon Town won 5-4 on penalties
Att: 21,521 The Valley

Tuesday 18th May
Millwall 2 (Morison, P Robinson)
Huddersfield Town 0
Att: 15,463 The New Den

League One Final

Saturday 29th May

Millwall 1 (Robinson)
Swindon Town 0

Att: 73,108 Wembley Stadium

Millwall: Forde, Barron, Craig (Frampton), Abdou, Robinson, Ward, Schofield, Batt (Hackett), Morison, Harris, Trotter, Manager - Kenny Jackett

Swindon: Lucas, Amankwaah, Sheehan (Darby), Ferry, Cuthbert, Jean-Francois, McGovern (O'Brien), Douglas, Austin, Paynter (Pericard), Ward, Manager - Danny Wilson

League Two Semi-Finals

First Legs - Saturday 15th May
Aldershot Town 0
Rotherham United 1 (Le Fondre)
Att: 5,470 Recreation Ground

Sunday 16th May
Dagenham & Redbridge 6 (Benson 2, Scott 4)
Morecambe 0
Att: 4,566 Victoria Road

Second Legs - Wednesday 19th May
Rotherham United 2 (Le Fondre, Ellison)
Aldershot Town 0
Att: 7,082 Don Valley Stadium, Sheffield

Thursday 20th May
Morecambe 2 (Duffy, Artell)
Dagenham & Redbridge 1 (Benson)
Att: 4,972 Christie Park

League Two Final

Sunday 30th May

Dagenham & Redbridge 3 (Benson 38', Green 56', Nurse 70')
Rotherham United 2 (Taylor 39', 61')

Att: 32,054 Wembley Stadium

Dagenham & Redbridge: Roberts, Doe, McCrory, Ogogo, Vincelot, Arber, Green, Nurse (Montgomery), Benson, Scott (Walsh), Gain, Manager - John Still

Rotherham United: Warrington, Lynch, Gunning, Mills (Marshall), Fenton, Sharps, Law, Harrison, Taylor, Le Fondre, Ellison (Bell-Baggie), Manager - Ronnie Moore

2011

Championship Semi-Finals

First Legs - Thursday 12th May
Nottingham Forest 0
Swansea City 0
Att: 27,881 City Ground

Friday 13th May
Reading 0
Cardiff City 0
Att: 21,485 Madejski Stadium

Second Legs - Monday 16th May
Swansea City 3 (Britton, Dobbie, Pratley)
Nottingham Forest 1 (Earnshaw)
Att: 19,816 Liberty Stadium

Tuesday 17th May
Cardiff City 0
Reading 3 (Long 2, McAnuff)
Att: 24,081 City of Cardiff Stadium

Championship Final

Monday 30th May

Reading 2 (Allen OG, 49', Mills 57')
Swansea City 4 (Sinclair 21', 22', 80' Dobbie 40')

Att: 86,581 Wembley Stadium

Reading: Federici, Griffin (Robson-Kanu), Harte, Leigertwood, Mills, Khizanishvili, McAnuff, Karacan, Long, Hunt (Church), Kebe, Manager - Brian McDermott

Swansea City: de Vries, Rangel, Tate, Britton (Gower), Monk, Williams, Sinclair, Dyer, Dobbie (Pratley), Borini, Allen (Moore), Manager - Brendan Rodgers

League One Semi-Finals

First Legs - Saturday 14th May
AFC Bournemouth 1 (McDermott)
Huddersfield Town 1 (Kilbane)
Att: 9,043 Dean Court

Sunday 15th May
Milton Keynes Dons 3 (Powell, Baldock, Balanta)
Peterborough United 2 (Mackail-Smith, McCann)
Att: 12,622 Stadium:MK

Second Legs - Wednesday 18th May
Huddersfield Town 3 (Peltier, Ward, Kay)
AFC Bournemouth 3 (Lovell 2, Ings) AET
Huddersfield Town won 4-2 on penalties
Att: 16,444 Galpharm Stadium

Thursday 19th May
Peterborough United 2 (McCann, Mackail-Smith)
Milton Keynes Dons 0
Att: 11,920 London Road

League One Final

Sunday 29th May

Huddersfield Town 0
Peterborough United 3 (Rowe 78', Mackail-Smith 80', McCann 85')

Att: 48,410 Old Trafford

Huddersfield Town: I. Bennett, Hunt, Naysmith, Peltier, Clarke, Kay, Roberts, Arfield (A. Lee), Afobe (Rhodes), Kilbane, Ward (Cadamarteri), Manager - Lee Clark

Peterborough United: Jones, Little, Basey (C. Lee), Wesolowski, R. Bennett, Zakuani, Rowe (Whelpdale), McCann, Tomlin (Ball), Mackail-Smith, Boyd, Manager - Darren Ferguson

League Two Semi-Finals

First Legs - Saturday 14th May
Torquay United 2 (Zebroski, O'Kane)
hrewsbury Town 0
Att: 4,130 Plainmoor

Sunday 15th May
Stevenage 2 (Long, Byrom)
Accrington Stanley 0
Att: 4,424 Broadhall Way

Second Legs - Friday 20th May
Shrewsbury Town 0 Torquay United 0
Att: 8,452 Greenhous Meadow

Friday 20th May
Accrington Stanley 0
Stevenage 1 (Beardsley)
Att: 4,185 Crown Ground

League Two Final

Saturday 28th May

Stevenage 1 (Mousinho 41') Torquay United 0
Att: 11,484 Old Trafford

Stevenage: Day, Henry, Laird, Roberts, Charles (Beardsley), Bostwick, Wilson, Mousinho, Reid (Harrison), Byrom (Murphy), Long, Manager - Graham Westley

Torquay United: Bevan, Mansell, Nicholson (Rowe-Turner), Robertson, Branston, Lathorpe (Oastler), O'Kane, Kee, Robinson (Stevens), Tomlin, Zebroski, Manager - Paul Buckle

2012

Championship Semi-Finals

First Legs - Thursday 3rd May
Cardiff City 0
West Ham United 2 (Collison 2)
Att: 23,029 City of Cardiff Stadium

Friday 4th May
Blackpool 1 (Davies OG)
Birmingham 0
Att: 13,832 Bloomfield Road

Second Legs - Monday 7th May
West Ham United 3 (Nolan, Vaz Te, Maynard)
Cardiff City 0
Att: 34,682 Upton Park

Wednesday 9th May
Birmingham City 2 (Zigic, Davies)
Blackpool 2 (Dobbie, M. Phillips)
Att: 28,483 St Andrews

Championship Final

Saturday 19th May

Blackpool 1 (Ince 48')
West Ham United 2 (Cole 35', Vaz Te 87')

Att: 78,523 Wembley Stadium

Blackpool : Gilks, Eardley, Crainey, Martinez (Dicko), Evatt, John-Baptiste, Ince, Ferguson, Dobbie (Bednar), Phillips (Sylvestre), Phillips, Manager: Ian Holloway

West Ham United: Green, Demel (Faubert), Taylor, Nolan, Tomkins, Reid, O'Neil (McCartney), Noble, Cole, Vaz Te, Collison, Manager: Sam Allardyce

League One Semi-Finals

First Legs - Friday 11th May
Stevenage 0
Sheffield United 0
Att: 5,802 The Lamex Stadium

Saturday 12th May
Milton Keynes Dons 0
Huddersfield Town 2 (Rhodes, Hunt)
Att: 11,893 Stadium:MK

Second Legs - Monday 14th May
Sheffield United 1 (Porter)
Stevenage 0
Att: 21,182 Bramall Lane

Tuesday 15th May
Huddersfield Town 1 (Rhodes)
Milton Keynes Dons 2 (Powell, Smith)
Att: 15,085 Galpharm Stadium

League One Final

Saturday 26th May

Huddersfield Town 0
Sheffield United 0 AET
Huddersfield Town won 8-7 on penalties

Att: 52,100 Wembley Stadium

Huddersfield Town: Smithies, Hunt, Woods, Miller, Clarke, Morrison, Higginbotham (Roberts), Johnson, Novak (Arfield), Rhodes, Ward (Lee), Manager - Simon Grayson

Sheffield United: Simonsen, Lowton, Magiure, Doyle, Collins, Hill, Flynn (O'Halloran), Williamson, Cresswell (Porter), Montgomery (Taylor), Quinn, Manager - Danny Wilson

League Two Semi-Finals

First Legs - Saturday 12th May
Crewe Alexandra 1 (Dugdale)
Southend United 0
Att: 7,221 Alexandra Stadium

Sunday 13th May
Cheltenham Town 2 (McGlashan, Burgess)
Torquay United 0
Att: 5,273 Whaddon Road

Second Legs - Wednesday 16th May
Southend United 2 (Harris, Barker)
Crewe Alexandra (Leitch-Smith, Clayton)
Att: 8,190 Roots Hall

Thursday 17th May
Torquay United 1 (Atieno)
Cheltenham Town 2 (McGlashan, Pack)
Att: 3,606 Plainmoor

League Two Final

Sunday 27th May

Cheltenham Town 0
Crewe Alexandra 2 (Powell 15', Moore 82')

Att: 24,029 Wembley Stadium

Cheltenham Town: Brown, Elliott, Jombati, Garbutt, Bennett, Pack (Penn), McGlashan, Mohamed, Goulding (Duffy), Burgess (Spencer), Summerfield, Manager - Mark Yates

Crewe Alexandra: Phillips, Tootle, Davis, Dugdale, Artell, Westwood, Mellor, Powell (Clayton), Leitch-Smith (Martin), Moore (Bell), Murphy, Manager - Steve Davis

2013

Championship Semi-Finals

First Legs - Thursday 9th May
Leicester City 1 (Nugent)
Watford 0
Att: 29,650 King Power Stadium

Friday 10th May
Crystal Palace 0
Brighton & Hove Albion 0
Att: 23,294 Selhurst Park

Second Legs - Sunday 12th May
Watford 3 (Vydra 2, Deeney)
Leicester City 1 (Nugent)
Att: 16,142 Vicarage Road

Monday 13th May
Brighton & Hove Albion 0
Crystal Palace 2 (Zaha 2)
Att: 29,515 AMEX Stadium

Championship Final

Monday 27th May

Crystal Palace 1 (Phillips 105')
Watford 0 AET

Att: 82,025 Wembley Stadium

Crystal Palace: Speroni, Ward, Moxey, Gabbidon, Delaney, Dikgacoi (O'Keefe), Williams (Phillips), Garvan (Moritz), Wilbraham, Zaha, Jedinak, Manager - Ian Holloway

Watford: Almunia, Cassetti, Pudil, Chalobah (Battocchio), Ekstrand, Doyley, Anya (Forestieri), Abdi, Deeney, Vydra (Geijo), Hogg, Manager - Gianfranco Zola

League One Semi-Finals

First Legs - Friday 3rd May
Sheffield United 1 (McFadzean)
Yeovil Town 0
Att: 15,262 Bramall Lane

Saturday 4th May
Swindon Town 1 (Luongo)
Brentford 1 (O'Connor) 1
Att: 10,595 County Ground

Second Legs - Monday 6th May
Yeovil Town 2 (Dawson, Upson)
Sheffield United 0
Att: 8,152 Huish Park

Monday 6th May
Brentford 3 (Rooney OG, Donaldson 2)
Swindon Town 3 (Rooney, Devera, Flint) AET
Brentford won 5-4 on penalties
Att: 9,109 Griffin Park

League One Final

Sunday 19th May

Brentford 1 (Dean 51')
Yeovil Town 2 (Madden 6', Burn 42')

Att: 41,955 Wembley Stadium

Brentford: Moore, Logan, Bidwell, Craig, Dean, Diagouraga (Hayes), Forrester (Saunders), Adeyemi, Donaldson, Trotta (Wright-Phillips), Forshaw, Manager - Uwe Rosler

Yeovil Town: Stech, Ayling, McAllister (Maksimenko), Burn, Webster, Dawson, Upson, Hayter (Dolan), Madden, Foley, Edwards, Manager - Gary Johnson

League Two Semi-Finals

First Legs - Thursday 2nd May
Bradford City 2 (Wells, Thompson)
Burton Albion 3 (Zola-Makongo 2, Weir)
Att: 14,657 Valley Parade

Thursday 2nd May
Northampton Town 1 (O'Donovan)
Cheltenham Town 0
Att: 6,563 Sixfields

Second Legs - Sunday 5th May
Burton Albion 1 (Maghoma)
Bradford City 3 (Wells 2, Hanson)
Att: 6,148 Pirelli Stadium

Sunday 5th May
Cheltenham Town 0
Northampton Town 1 (Guttridge)
Att: 5,955 Whaddon Road

League Two Final

Saturday 18th May

Bradford City 3 (Hanson 15', McArdle 19', Wells 28')
Northampton Town 0

Att: 47,127 Wembley Stadium

Bradford City: McLaughlin, Darby, Meredith, Jones, McArdle, Davies, Reid (Atkinson), Doyle (Ravenhill), Hanson, Wells (Connell), Thompson, Manager - Phil Parkinson

Northampton Town: Nicholls, Cameron, Collins (Widdowson), Carlisle, Tozer, Guttridge, Hackett, Harding, Platt (Akinfenwa), O'Donovan, Demontagnac (Hornby), Manager - Adie Boothroyd

2014

Championship Semi-Finals

First Legs - Thursday 8th May
Brighton & Hove Albion 1 (Lingard)
Derby County 2 (Martin, Kuszczak OG)
Att: 27,118 AMEX Stadium

Friday 9th May
Wigan Athletic 0
Queens Park Rangers 0
Att: 14,560 DW Stadium

Second Legs - Sunday 11th May
Derby County 4 (Hughes, Martin, Thorne, Hendrick)
Brighton & Hove Albion 1 (Lua Lua)
Att: 32,602 iPro Stadium

Monday 12th May
Queens Park Rangers 2 (Austin, 2)
Wigan Athletic 1 (Perch) AET
Att: 17,061 Loftus Road

Championship Final

Saturday 24th May

Derby County 0
Queens Park Rangers 1 (Zamora, 90')

Att: 87,348 Wembley Stadium

Derby County: Grant, Wisdom, Keogh, Buxton, Forsyth, Hendrick, Thorne, Hughes (Bryson), Russell (Dawkins), Ward (Bamford), Martin, Manager - Steve McClaren

Queens Park Rangers: Green, Simpson, Hill (Henry), Barton, Dunne, Onuoha, Hoilett, O'Neil, Austin, Doyle (Zamora), Kranjcar (Traore), Manager - Harry Redknapp

League One Semi-Finals

First Legs - Saturday 10th May
Peterborough United 1 (Assombalonga)
Leyton Orient 1 (Odubajo)
Att: 9,519 London Road

Saturday 10th May
Preston North End 1 (Garner)
Rotherham United 1 (Revell)
Att: 17,221 Deepdale

Second Legs - Tuesday 13th May
Leyton Orient 2 (Cox, Dagnall)
Peterborough United 1 (Washington)
Att: 8,545 Matchroom Stadium

Thursday 15th May
Rotherham United 3 (Thomas, Frecklington, Agard)
Preston North End 1 (Gallagher)
Att: 11,576 New York Stadium

League One Final

Sunday 25th May

Leyton Orient 2 (Odubajo, 34', Cox, 39')
Rotherham United 2 (Revell, 55', 60')
Rotherham United won 4-3 on penalties

Att: 43,401 Wembley Stadium

Leyton Orient: Jones, Omozusi, Baudry, Clarke, Cuthbert, Vincelot, Cox (Batt), James, Mooney (Lundstram), Lisbie (Dagnall), Odubajo, Manager - Russell Slade

Rotherham United: Collin, Tavernier, Skarz (Milsom), Frecklington, Morgan, Arnason, Smallwood, Pringle, Revell (Vuckic), Thomas (Brindley), Agard, Manager - Steve Evans

League Two Semi-Finals

First Legs - Sunday 11th May
Burton Albion 1 (McGurk)
Southend United 0
Att: 4,581 Pirelli Stadium

Monday 12th May
York City 0
Fleetwood Town 1 (Blair)
Att: 5,124 Bootham Crescent

Second Legs - Friday 16th May
Fleetwood Town 0
York City 0
Att: 5,194 Highbury Stadium

Saturday 17th May
Southend United 2 (Leonard, Straker)
Burton Albion 2 (Holness, McGurk)
Att: 9,696 Roots Hall

League Two Final

Monday 26th May

Fleetwood Town 1 (Sarcevic, 75')
Burton Albion 0

Att: 14,007 Wembley Stadium

Fleetwood Town: Maxwell, McLaughlin, Taylor, Goodall, Roberts, Pond, Blair (Parkin), Sarcevic, Ball, Hume (Murdoch), Morris, Manager - Graham Alexander

Burton Albion: Lyness, Edwards, Hussey, Cansdell-Sherriff, Holness (Diamond), Weir, Bell (Palmer), Kee, MacDonald (Ismail), McGurk, McFadzean, Manager - Gary Rowett

2015

Championship Semi-Finals

First Legs - Friday 8th May
Brentford 1 (Gray)
Middlesbrough 2 (Vossen, Amorebieta)
Att: 11,691 Griffin Park

Saturday 9th May
Ipswich Town 1 (Anderson)
Norwich City 1 (Howson)
Att: 29,166 Portman Road

Second Legs - Friday 15th May
Middlesbrough 3 (Tomlin, Kike, Adomah)
Brentford 0
Att: 33,266 Riverside Stadium

Saturday 16th May
Norwich City 3 (Hoolahan, Redmond, Jerome)
Ipswich Town 1 (Smith)
Att: 26,994 Carrow Road

Championship Final

Monday 25th May

Middlesbrough 0
Norwich City 2 (Jerome, 12', Redmond, 15')

Att: 85,656 Wembley Stadium

Middlesbrough: Konstantopoulos, Whitehead (Nsue), Ayala, Gibson, Friend, Adomah, Leadbitter, Clayton, Tomlin, Vossen (Kike), Bamford, Manager - Aitor Karanka

Norwich City: Ruddy, Whittaker, Martin, Bassong, Olsson, Tettey, Redmond (O'Neil), Howson, Hoolahan (Dorrans), Johnson, Jerome (Grabban), Manager - Alex Neil

League One Semi-Finals

First Legs - Thursday 7th May
Chesterfield 0
Preston North End 1 (Beckford)
Att: 8,409 Proact Stadium

Thursday 7th May
Sheffield United 1 (Freeman)
Swindon Town 2 (Ricketts, Byrne)
Att: 20,890 Bramall Lane

Second Legs - Sunday 10th May
Preston North End 3 (Beckford 2, Garner)
Chesterfield 0
Att: 15,641 Deepdale

Monday 11th May
Swindon Town 5 (Gladwin 2, Smith 2, Obika)
Sheffield United 5 (Thompson, Basham, Davies, Done, Adams)
Att: 13,065 County Ground

League One Final

Sunday 24th May

Preston North End 4 (Beckford, 3', 44', 57', Huntington, 13')
Swindon Town 0

Att: 48,236 Wembley Stadium

Preston North End: Johnstone, Clarke, Wright, Huntington, Woods, Welsh, Kilkenny, Johnson, Gallagher (Browne), Beckford (Davies), Garner, Manager - Simon Grayson

Swindon Town: Foderingham, Stephens, Thompson (Ricketts), Turnbull, Byrne, Luongo, Kasim, Gladwin (Thompson), Toffolo (Williams), Smith, Obika, Manager - Mark Cooper

League Two Semi-Finals

First Legs - Saturday 9th May
Plymouth Argyle 2 (Ansah, Banton)
Wycombe Wanderers 3 (Hayes, Holloway, Craig)
Att: 14,175 Home Park

Sunday 10th May
Stevenage 1 (Parrett)
Southend United 1 (Corr)
Att: 5,183 Lamex Stadium

Second Legs - Thursday 14th May
Wycombe Wanderers 2 (Hayes, Mawson)
Plymouth Argyle 1 (Brunt)
Att: 7,750 Adams Park

Thursday 14th May
Southend United 3 (Leonard, McLaughlin, Timlin)
Steveage 1 (Pett)
Att: 8,998 Roots Hall

League Two Final

Monday 26th May

Wycombe Wanderers 1 (Bentley OG, 95')
Southend United 1 (Pigott, 120')
Southend won 7-6 on penalties

Att: 38,252 Wembley Stadium

Wycombe Wanderers: Lynch, Bean, Mawson, Pierre, Jacobson, Yennaris (Murphy), Wood, Saunders (Bloomfield), Hayes, Ephraim (Craig), Holloway, Manager - Gareth Ainsworth

Southend United: Bentley, White, Bolger, Barrett, Coker, Worrall (Payne), Atkinson (Weston), Leonard, Timlin, McLaughlin (Pigott), Corr, Manager - Phil Brown

THE AGONY & THE ECSTASY

INDEX